OF DREAMS & THORNS

a novel

J.C. SALAZAR

JC Salazar Publisher

Designed by David Provolo

Produced in The United States of America

The Library of Congress has catalogued this edition under Salazar, JC

For information, e-mail csal55@aol.com

ISBN 9780999149621

CONTENTS

This book is dedicated to all fathers and mothers, and to every immigrant everywhere.

CHAPTER 1: *Chicago 1950*

I f a man is going to begin a journey in search of his dream, Chicago is as good a place as any to get started. Ramiro Ocañas had lost track of the number of dreams he had pursued in his brief adulthood. Maybe two? Four? One thing he was sure of: this time was going to be different. This was his most ambitious dream, *y al carajo quien se atravesara*—"And anyone gets in the way, he's going down."

In all his twenty-eight years, Ramiro had never experienced cold as intense as what he was feeling pacing outside the Greyhound bus station in downtown Chicago that bleak November night. He wondered again whether he should have made the trip, although a day before nothing could have dissuaded him. Hard as he tried to focus his mind on getting on with his mission to reach Nico, his good buddy, the wind chill freezing his body was turning that simple mission into a major ordeal. He knew he had to find the boarding house whose address he had written on a worn piece of wrapping paper from his father's general store back in Naranjales. Looking around this strange new environment, his village in Mexico seemed like a million miles away.

It was winter back home, too, but the northers in his village never cut this deep. His thoughts flew back home for refuge from the cold. The perpetually warm, fertile valley at the base of Saddle Hill of Monterrey: the endless rows of fruit trees of all sorts; oranges, tangerines, limes, and grapefruit; the pecan and avocado groves; the winding river of laughing waters on rocky beds within fragrant banks that traversed the dozen or so villages surrounding Naranjales. All these were in his heart. Suddenly they became a yearning as if he'd been away for years, not days.

The hunger pangs didn't help his situation either. He thought of his mother's or Eliza's home-cooked meals. They never failed to make him lap up every last morsel on his plate, sopping up the gravy with freshly made tortillas. Ramiro thought he had struck gold when he first tasted Eliza's cooking. She had a knack for turning even a scrambled egg into a delicacy.

"Was this a mistake?" he thought. "Should I have stayed home? I miss Eliza. I so miss the kids."

But there was no turning back. "Think pleasant thoughts, Ramiro." So he thought about his triumph of having finally arrived in Chicago; arriving to "the other side" and reaching the land of opportunity, where the lore said work was plentiful. He recalled fragments of childhood stories of people sweeping money off the streets in Gringoland. Now he was in the very place where he could finally grasp at a future for his family. He was determined to make it work.

He was lucky to have friends of the likes of Cesar, Santos, Martin, and Nicolas, who had paved the way for his journey. He wasn't particularly close to the others, especially Martin, whose personality clashed with his at times, but Nico was generous and trustworthy. It was *compadre* Nicolas, "Nico," who had sent him the fifty bucks for the bus fare from McAllen, Texas, to Chicago, and whose hospitality awaited him now somewhere in a small room in a boarding house on the West Side. And it was Nico who'd enabled him to apply for an immigration card. Nico obtained a letter from his boss at the railroad yards requesting Mexican workers thanks to a labor shortage the company was experiencing. It seemed half his peers had already left the farmlands of northern Mexico in search of better fortunes, so he took it as a rite of passage to do the same.

Ramiro's economic prospects in Naranjales had withered as the family's land vanished. The large Monterrey conglomerates had been gradually buying up the family farms, including his parents'. He had never been much good at the merchandising business his brothers and his parents ran. His parents started him off in life with a small grocery store, a wedding present. He had been too quick to give a poor woman —or a pretty one—credit, and every man in the village with a good sob story could soften his heart for promissory notes that were seldom paid. Even the rascals he disdained for all their treacheries somehow ended up on his long list of debtors. Only a handful ever managed to pay up.

So he gave up the grocery business soon after his first boy was born. Next he tried a meat market, but the story repeated itself. Once a week he would butcher a hog or a cow or two goats or ten chickens and made just enough for the family to eat well and keep going. The nice thing about having meat frequently was that the children ate heartily, and for a time even the frugal and modest Eliza wore more roses on her already naturally blooming cheeks. Then the butchering business, too, came to a halt, much to his and his mother's chagrin.

Doña Lupita was not a woman to indulge a son in any kind of experimentation with the rules of life. She had worked too hard all her life to allow weakness to seep into her character, and she expected all her children to know that that was what life was about. She taught them not to give in to the delusion of pity for undeserving squanderers, or idlers, or wastrels who were too quick to bring a man down if he wasn't careful. In her view, these vagabonds abounded.

No, Doña Lupita never missed a beat of each of her sons' doings, so she was quick to pronounce judgment on Ramiro for not making a better go of it. His mother's reprimands were a great source of shame, and there was nothing he wouldn't do to try to prove to her that he could amount to something she could be proud of. However, when Ramiro told her of his plans to leave Naranjales for the United States, there was a spontaneous overflow of tears followed by a profusion of affection. Doña Lupita was a demonstrative woman, as everyone knew. Her dainty frame was made of steel, and her furrowed brow was more a reflection of perseverance than the weakness of worry. She loved her children deeply, though, and she couldn't bear the thought of one of them trading the tough but genteel life of Naranjales for what she somehow knew to be that of a semislave. He might make perhaps four times his Mexican earnings, but at what sacrifice away from home and hearth? The news was enough to break her heart.

"What are you saying, son? You want to leave your family? Do you know what you're in for out there among strangers in that odd world," she asked, unable to control her tears. She reached for him and held him in a tight embrace.

"Mama, I will be fine. It's just for a time. I'll meet up with *paisanos*, buddies, from these parts: Cesar, Nico. I want to try my luck out there. I will visit when I can, and I will send for the family once I get settled there," he explained, his voice cracking a bit. He held her tenderly as his father watched the scene from behind the store counter. In the little house at the back of the compound, Eliza nursed her one month old, and the other three ate their stew unaware of the news they were about to receive.

Lupita's emotions did not surprise him because he had often been reminded that he mirrored her, not just in his earth-brown eyes but also in his profound capacity to feel. Nevertheless, it was inevitable that Ramiro seek better fortunes. It had taken a year since he submitted his documents to the U.S. consulate in Monterrey. Finally, months later, shortly after his fourth child, his second cherubic boy, was born the good news came. His paperwork had been approved, and his immigrant visa and green card were ready to be picked up. He kissed the letter that he had just collected from the post office in Valle Azul, after making a special trip for it, not waiting the additional two days it would have taken for it to arrive in Naranjales. He dashed home to share the good news.

He would soon embark for the "other side." All he needed was a clear destination and some bus money.

Nico, godfather to his firstborn, had been up north two years now. He had invited Ramiro to join him as soon as all his papers were ready. And just like Nico had experienced two years prior, Ramiro was himself torn to pieces at the prospect of leaving behind his glorious and beloved Eliza. He dreaded the thought of her, whose temperament prohibited even contradicting her elders, let alone raise her voice to one, left alone to fend for herself with Doña Lupita, who often ruled her clan with a tough-love philosophy that seemed to overflow where a daughter-in-law was concerned. Lupita never quite embraced any in-law, so her loving emotions were reserved for her own blood. It was like matching a dove to an eagle, and his heart broke for Eliza as much as hers broke for him.

Eliza's heart sank at the news. She feared for her status without him as a buffer to her mother-in-law, but her immediate plan was to support her husband, so she resolved to be compliant and hope for the best. She shifted her fears toward Ramiro's prospects. Eliza knew that Ramiro's strong, masculine build and his farm-fresh good health were in for a beating on what were, to her country wife's mind, undefined, mysterious factories in the North. She imagined dark, hot, cavernous places like she had once seen in a Pedro Infante movie in which the hero worked himself half to death for pitiful wages, sustained only by the love of a good woman.

The workplaces also reminded her of a picture of hell she had studied in a rare visit with the priest of the nearby city of Valle Azul. It depicted Satan as a horrid fiend suspended by powerful black wings over a multitude of sinners crashing down in free fall into a fiery abyss. Then her thoughts returned to the suffering Pedro Infante, for she thought of her Ramiro in just such a handsome portrait. The millions of Mexican women who swooned over the dashing crooner and movie star would certainly relate.

Ramiro was indeed handsome in a classic Spanish way, with dark bright eyes and natural ebony curls that sometimes had a life of their own. He was too refined in features, in fact, Eliza thought, to be sent to fry in a hellish American smelting plant. For a week she could hardly contain her tears, although she managed to keep her composure around Ramiro, the children, and especially around Doña Lupita, whose own deep pain had begun to be manifested in a misplaced, cruel blaming of Eliza and the children. Doña Lupita, steel dynamo that she was, could not--nor did she feel a need to--hide her tears and lamentations. But Eliza did, and it was thus that she mastered the art of stoicism, never again giving a loved one cause for alarm or pity, nor an avenue for manipulation. One day in the distant future, her, now-unimaginable, college-educated son would call her passive resistant. That was her only fortress in the face of her fate within a family of such authority over her. That was the society of her place and time.

The day of Ramiro's departure was a sad occasion, and it would not be an exaggeration to compare it to a local funeral. The entire village came out to say goodbye at Doña Lupita's general store. One by one the friends and neighbors shook hands, exchanged hugs, and bestowed their blessings to the young man who was about to depart to a far away land of unknown challenges.

Finally, it was just the son and his mother. He had just finished kissing his wife goodbye, and his cheeks were moist with tears. His mother's tight embrace and wailing kisses renewed the knot in his throat, and he forced himself to appear the stronger of the two as he kissed her a final goodbye. Then he boarded his brother Alberto's truck to go to the bus terminal in Valle Azul. It was a long and sullen trip from the valley of Monterrey to the relative bustle of McAllen, Texas, where he was to board a Greyhound bus. Destination: Chicago.

Chicago was cold that November, bone-chilling. Ramiro had felt it through the bus windows and at the stops along the way as they approached. It was cold even inside the Greyhound terminal where Ramiro retreated to steady his nerves and try to collect his wits. He was a stranger in a strange land, and, strangest of all, he was relegated to deaf-mute status. It wasn't that he couldn't hear, for he heard only too well the thousands of sounds that were now no different than a chorus of a million crickets in a dark forest for all the meaning he could gather from them. The normally lively and communicative fellow, who was used to the revelry and camaraderie only the son of the town's matriarch enjoys, had become a mere spectator. He who was used to the warmth and hospitality too often proffered to those individuals blessed with good looks for no other reason than they bring pleasure to the eye, now stood practically invisible and teetering in his nearly paper-thin Mexican cottons. Even layered as they were—three shirts under the gabardine jacket, three pairs of pants, triple socks— his clothes could barely blunt the knife-sharpness of the wintry gusts.

"Is this a mistake? Should I have stayed home? God, I miss Eliza, I miss the kids." He couldn't stop the echoes in his head.

Ramiro, again, tried to take refuge in the warm memories of his youth when, as majordomo, he was in charge of cultivating the family's orange groves and cornfields. He could fix his vivid imagination and immense memory on the warm, caressing breezes in the vast skies whose many azures and warm sunshine painted the brightest oranges, lemons, and tangerines. Despite his limited education, Ramiro had the heart and turn of phrase of a poet. He could make it all be real again. Those images brought enough pleasure to the robust young man that he could swear he knew God's very smile for a moment.

Suddenly his daydream was shattered. A shrill, panicky English sound like a cat's yowling startled him back to reality. It was a young woman with yellow hair that cascaded to her shoulders. She was wrapped in loose brown fur, and her face, that could have been that of a movie star, was painted in reds and blues. Her white-gloved hand was suddenly yanked by her giant companion. Ramiro stared at her hands instinctively. *Gloves.* How he wished he had packed a pair. He clenched his white knuckles grasping his valise.

The woman practically lost her balance but managed to steady herself despite the wobbling of her high-heeled pumps. The man seemed to be her husband, but Ramiro knew instinctively he was much less than that, and much more dangerous. The rugged character seemed a giant at 6'4" and weighing perhaps 250 pounds compared to

Ramiro's 5'8" and 160 pounds. But it was the mouth of the woman, whose beauty he found entrancing, which fixated his eyes, how her lips moved in loud sounds, meaning nothing to Ramiro except that she was not happy and was protesting. She shrieked in banshee-like bitter railings. Her mouth seemed an animated, bright red candy-apple, whose once-bitten condition revealed a set of splendid white teeth.

Ramiro was smitten for a moment. He was surely fond of female beauty despite having kept his sacred vows of faithfulness to Eliza. Where he came from, a woman who looked like this one was the prized asset of millionaires and other power brokers. Such a woman, if Mexican, however, would never stoop to such vulgar displays, nor would any man in his right mind even dream of mistreating her, especially in public. If either of those things happened, there would be hell to pay with her daddy and brothers. The rowdy couple soon disappeared behind the magically drawn glass doors, leaving him with the sensation of being more lost than ever, more a stranger than ever.

Ramiro looked at his watch. It was nearly midnight. He decided to venture into the howling chill darkness of the night to hail a cab.

As it was late on a Sunday, Ramiro could not spot a cab, and he was unable to determine a process by which to attract one. He waited outside, sometimes walking up the cold street then back down again. His eyes darting in all directions and he stretched his neck this way and that, but there were no taxis to be seen. His numb and frosted body became unaware of its great discomfort as his mind began to panic that he might not find a way to his friend's house.

He felt sure he could figure out how to use a pay phone he had spotted at the station, but he had no way of determining a phone number for a cab. He couldn't call his friend because Nico had not given him a number. He went inside and attempted to communicate with, first, a clerk behind a ticket window, then a fellow traveler, but to no avail. He explained to each of them in perfectly complete Spanish, though in elevated volume, exactly what he needed, but they only looked at him amusedly and shrugged.

Two taxis passed him by in the course of an hour, ignoring his frantic motions for reasons he could not fathom. He was in a dizzying free fall of physical and mental anguish that far surpassed any of the discomforts caused by his mother's discipline—his mother, whose embrace he could kill for. His mother's image warmed his heart enough to bring him strength.

It was at this point of renewed hope, though still shivering, that he felt a hand press firmly on his shoulder. His near frozen condition and the strange noises in his head thwarted any sensation for a moment, but he suddenly became aware of the intrusion and jerked back almost into the path of an approaching garbage truck. But the uniformed man grabbed him quick as lightning, and Ramiro found himself in the arms of a body that could have been his double but for the bluest eyes he had ever seen.

Ramiro was face to face with a man that for a moment he almost mistook for a beloved brother. Ramiro wondered if he was becoming delirious, for, of course, it was not a brother but a Chicago cop. The man in uniform proceeded to speak to him in what sounded like a helping tone. He thought he understood the officer whose badge and nametag were hidden under the heavy navy pea coat he wore. Ramiro later learned his name was Patrick O'Kane. The cop was asking him questions he couldn't comprehend. He could understand the interrogative inflections in the officer's speech, but all Ramiro could do was shrug his shoulders, and, pleadingly, repeat into the man's blue eyes, "Taxi? Taxi!"

Officer O'Kane escorted Ramiro into the lobby of a small hotel that was around the block. It was inside the warm lobby that Ramiro first saw the officer's name when the cop unbuttoned his coat. "O'Kane," he thought, without really grasping a pronunciation for it. He then simply made a mental note of his accustomed Spanish phonetic pronunciation for words, "Okahneh,… Ocane." In the next second he found himself smiling at what he perceived to be a related pronunciation to his own name, "Ocañas." The officer's strained English pronunciation of his name—"Rrahmeerrow Okaynass"—seemed to reassure him of a strange common bond. As Ramiro pondered the other and his possible names' association, the officer completed a call on the pay phone.

Officer O'Kane proceeded to extract by questions, signs, and gestures from the lost stranger a piece of paper, neatly folded in his thin wallet with the name of Nicolas Perales and an address on Laramie Street. About that time a cab pulled up outside. The officer continued speaking unintelligibly to Ramiro as he escorted him to the taxicab, opened the door, and motioned him to slide into the back seat, but Ramiro stood by the door as the officer spoke to the driver.

"Take this young man to 2750 Laramie Street. He doesn't speak English, so see if you can deliver him without incident."

"Sure thing, officer, No worries!" said the cabbie.

Ramiro's vacuum deafness somehow suddenly turned, and although the officer's words were strange, they were not so foreign anymore, and he thought he understood what the exchange meant. Officer O'Kane told the driver that he was to wait until he ascertained that Ramiro had reached his destination and met up with the Nicolas on the piece of paper. He instructed the cabbie and conveyed to Ramiro that if for some reason Nicolas could not be found at the given address, the cabbie was to bring Ramiro back to this same spot and Officer O'Kane would investigate about the location of Nicolas' correct address. The officer smiled wide at Ramiro, petted him on the shoulder, shook his hand, and muttered something that Ramiro gathered from the bright blue eyes to be "Good luck."

Ramiro shook the officer's hand profusely and used his best, most polite Spanish to convey, "Thank you so much. You are very kind and helpful. May you have the best of fortunes. Thank you, thank you." And with that he threw his valise onto the back seat and jumped in to escape the freezing cold.

It was almost 2:00 a.m. when the cab pulled up to the old house. Ramiro noticed its large, squatty size. The structure appeared to be painted white, but in the darkness, it could just as easily been a gray or some bleached pastel. The light was on in the front porch, but all the twelve windows in view were dark. Despite the house showing no sign of life, Ramiro felt a sense of relief and even a little excitement. He had spent the better part of the ride in complete awe at the kindness and compassion of the policeman. That kind of generosity gave him an inexplicable urge to embrace the man, as he would have any buddy or brother back home. He imagined that a lawman like O'Kane was the epitome of integrity and good character, and he attributed those traits to the uprightness of America. It felt good believing that at least the law here was more trustworthy than the corrupt, poorly trained cops of his country.

Ramiro could not prevent the flood of memories of his own brief stint as a lawman. He had been deputized on a number of occasions to assist in keeping order at the town's special events or large fiestas. There were the many instances of breaking up a fistfight between friends who'd drunk too much. He was particularly proud of defending a young lady's honor when a drunk or too-eager suitor got handsy with her. His prowess in a fistfight—always in self-defense, of course—was legendary. His love and expertise of guns were well known, and his high mindedness, compassion, and courage were well respected by the local authorities. Ramiro had toyed with the idea of a law enforcement job, but they were too poorly paid, and, besides, his parents would never have approved. He was also too independent to become the expected supplicant or sycophant of some egotistical commissioner. He dreamed of the day neither politician nor policeman could be blinded to justice by the glint of a silver piece. Yes, indeed, Officer O'Kane instantly became a hero in his eyes.

The voice of the cabbie startled him back to reality with instructions to look for his host. He understood the cab would wait there as the officer had instructed him to do. The cabbie didn't even demand his fare before letting Ramiro ring the doorbell.

After pressing the lighted button several times, alternating with decisive, back-home raps at the locked screen door, his fingers numbing again, his jaw locked and his teeth shattering, a fiftyish-looking woman opened the door a few inches. She seemed upset to be awakened in the middle of the night, but Ramiro was happy to recognize her Mexican features despite her tinted reddish hair and her English words. The woman wore a pink terrycloth, floor-length bathrobe over a white flannel nightshirt with tiny red roses on it, and she shivered as she shifted to an arrested, sixth-grade Spanish upon realizing Ramiro could not speak English. Her annoyance gave way to sympathy when she remembered that new tenants were sometimes referred to her at the oddest hours.

After verifying that Nico had room seven upstairs, Ramiro returned to the cab to pay the five-dollar fare, plus a one-dollar tip. Seeing he only had a five-dollar bill left, he reached in his pockets to count his change. One dollar and thirty-five cents, if all his coin studying had stuck.

As he approached the front porch, the door of the house swung open, and he thought he saw the most beautiful sight he had ever seen.

"Compadre Ramiro!" Nico stood there, arms outstretched.

"Compadre Nico! I'm here! Son of a gun, I've arrived!" and they both laughed in a giddy brotherly embrace.

"Compa, que gusto de verte. Ya me ansiaba oir esa risa contagiosa tuya," "So great to see you, buddy. I couldn't wait to hear that infectious laugh of yours again," gushed Nico.

"Pues ya llegué, compa! Aquí estamos, y no nos vamos, jaja-jaa!", "Well, I've arrived, buddy. Here we are, and here we'll stay," joked Ramiro.

The two men patted each other's back in a manly exchange of hugs then they disappeared into the house shutting out the cold, for the time being.

CHAPTER 2: *The Rail Yard*

Ramiro's body was enveloped in comfort as it entered the fourth stage of sleep progression. He was finally beginning to enjoy some rest after the grueling truck and bus trips he had endured in the previous four days. Then the trilling ruckus of an alarm clock yanked him out of his slumber. It felt as if he were being jolted by a crash of iced water. It took a full minute of the clock ringing before he realized he was awake. In fact, he had slept only two hours. In that one minute before he gained full awareness, he felt as if he'd had an eight-hour dream. It was about going home a rich man with pockets full of dollars. Everyone lauded and bowed to him as he drove a shiny new convertible down the one road that everyone used in Naranjales to enter or leave the village. He hated waking up before reaching his wife.

"Oh, man, what's that noise?" he yawned as he spoke to no one in particular.

Nico laughed, "That's the alarm clock. Get up, buddy. We have to go to work. I'm sorry, but it's time. Or, do you want to wait until tomorrow? I understand if you do," said Nico as he stood beside the radiator for warmth, buttoning his work shirt.

"No, no, *compa*, buddy, I am ready," he laughed. "I mean, I'll be ready in a minute. It's 5:00 a.m. What time do we have to be there?" said Ramiro.

Nico responded, "Punch-in time is 7:00, so we should be there by 6:45. You can take a hot shower and then come down to breakfast. At least you have the shower to yourself because all the guys wash up at night after they get home from work."

"Okay, great," Ramiro nodded as he wrapped the blanket around his shoulders. The radiation system was not enough to stave the cold completely.

"You met *Miss* Mary last night," Nico said and winked. "She likes to be called Miss, so don't call her Doña. Doña offends her," he laughed and made roguish eyes. "'Too old!' Anyway, you met Mary, that's what I call her. She makes a pretty good breakfast for all the guys. She has six of us tenants; well, seven now, with you, but she still has a couple of vacancies. You'll like her cooking"

Ramiro thought of Eliza's breakfasts, and he hoped Nico was right about the landlady's way in the kitchen.

§

The breakfast was indeed filling, if not the most delicious because it was Gringo-style cooking. But Ramiro wasn't here for the food, so he would just have to put out of his mind the idea of having *huevos rancheros* for breakfast every day. He was too tired and preoccupied with the upcoming events of the day to take much notice of anything else that morning.

At 6:00, a car horn blew outside the house. Nico got up from the table while stuffing his face with the last of his pancakes and gulping his coffee. Everyone grabbed a lunch pail that Mary had helped prepare, and they filed out of the house to board their ride to the rail yards.

"*Buenos dias,* Danny," Nico greeted the driver. "I want you to meet Ramiro, my *compadre* from back home. He arrived last night, and I'm taking him with me to fill out a work application at the yard," he said.

Danny shook hands with Ramiro, "Pleased to meet you, Ramiro. Welcome to Chicago. I've been working at the yard for five years. Nico is a good buddy. He told me you would be arriving soon, so I'm glad to see you made it in all right. The foreman is expecting you, too," said Danny.

Ramiro, extended his hand to Danny and gave him a warm, firm handshake. "Very pleased to meet you, Danny. Where are you from? Nah, let me guess. From you accent I take it you're from the capital."

"No denying that. I'm a *Chilango*, as you northern guys call us, but around here we are all the same to the gringos." He laughed.

All the guys laughed. Ramiro had already exchanged similar niceties with the others back at the breakfast table. They were from Guadalajara, Reynosa, and Veracruz, a real mix of Mexican regions. His affinity was, of course, for the *norteños* and the *Regios*. Although Monterrey was almost as foreign to him as Chicago, he knew that the entire state of Nuevo Leon was home, and the people mostly resembled each other in customs, values, and such. Still, he now felt special warmth for his compatriots from other states. Danny was right; after all, he said, "We are all the same to anyone not familiar with the Mexican regions."

They arrived at the yard at 6:50 a.m., ten minutes early. Just in time to grab one more cup of coffee and punch in before being late. The place was a dingy office within a tall, cavernous building of corrugated steel. Half a dozen or so rail lines ran through it. It was a cold, uninviting office, with just enough creature comforts to pass as civilized. The foreman's office overlooked the worker's rest area and punch clock. It was a neatly kept place and tidy, but something about the idea of their boss always looking down on them, made it austere.

Ramiro observed these things as new and monumental concepts because his previous life experiences had not included so much technology or mechanics. He was particularly pleased with the vending area, which included machines that dispensed coffee and soft drinks as well as all manner of snacks and even cold sandwiches that he would later learn were necessary because many of the workers did not pack their lunches for reasons he would never figure out. He made a mental note to himself to resist all the temptations in the machines or else he would have no money left to send home to the family.

As he looked around, half in a daze due to his exhaustion from lack of sleep, he felt Nico grab his arm and call out a name. "John! *Buenos Dias! Mira, aqui esta mi amigo del que te habia hablado,"* "Good morning! This is my friend, the one I told you about." Ramiro immediately tensed up into a formal posture and wide smile to greet his would-be new foreman.

"Good Morning, Nick. Oh yeah, so this is your friend," said John.

"Ramiro, *te presento* a Mister John Bailey, *mi jefe y ojala el tuyo tambien,"* "My boss and hopefully yours, too," Nico said smiling and gesturing toward John just as he had done for John when introducing Ramiro.

"*Mucho gusto*, Mister Bailey," said Ramiro extending his hand for a firm handshake with John.

"Call me John, Ramiro. And can I call you Ram?" John said, as he extended a warm handshake to Ramiro but directing his statement to Nico to translate. It was obvious Ramiro couldn't speak a word of English.

Nico's own English consisted of a small collection of memorized wholes of phrases and essential words that he uttered in fits and starts, sprinkled generously with hand gestures and a little spice of Spanish for filler, but not much English was required on this job, and John was kind and flexible with the men. John could muster a few Spanish words, and, between both men's limited phrases and generous gestures, everyone at the rail yard got along just fine. Nico proceeded to help Ramiro fill out the basic paperwork, and after a half hour or so, John looked over the application and stamped it, "Hired." John shook Ramiro's hand once again, and instructed him to follow Nico around for the next three days or so, so he would learn every aspect of his duties. He reminded Nico to pay particular attention to the safety rules and regulations because he didn't want Ramiro ending up losing a foot or an arm on his first week on the job.

Ramiro was ecstatic. The stinging wind that could be stopped by nothing seemed much less miserable with the happy news that he was now employed. He started making calculations in his head about how much he would be making and saving. He spent every free moment of the morning in a daydream state of seeing his family receiving his first remittance to them. His wages would start at seventy-five cents per hour, and Nico told him he'd probably be working 50 hours a week or more. In his mind, he was already sending Eliza and the kids a hundred dollars a month.

As Nico and Ramiro went about the duties of the day—throwing track switches to route the train cars to different sections of the yard, raising levers to couple and uncouple cars for the make-up and break-up of trains, and so on—the two men had a chance to catch up on news from back home, and laugh at some of the stories Ramiro had to tell. "… and that's how Beto got himself thrown off the horse and Rosita laughed so hard that Beto refused to take her home after the dance. She had to hitch a ride with the Gomez sisters," Ramiro finished, and Nico howled with laughter.

"So, tell me, compadre, how does it feel to be finally here?" Nico asked.

"Oh man, compadre, I tell you, it feels all kinds of ways. First, I'm sure it will feel different tomorrow or whenever I get a decent night's sleep," he laughed. "But, honestly, the thing I feel most is hope. Yessiree, Nico, this could be the start of my future. I am going to save every cent and peso I can. I can see already the work here is tough. I'll tell you one thing, this monster of a city is so big, I still don't believe it. But this work isn't my dream. It is just the way to my dream."

"Well, Ramiro, every man has to have a dream. Glad to see you so hopeful," Nico answered.

"Yes sir. I am going to bust my ass for a few years. I think maybe five. Then I will return to my family with enough dollars to start my little farm. I'm going to buy me some land in Naranjales, just outside the northern edge they have some pretty fertile acres that no one is farming. Don Cuco owns that land, but he has no plans for it, so I think I can make a good deal with him. I can raise corn, sorghum, plant a few dozen orange trees, limes, and tangerines. I can dig a deep well and build irrigation ditches. The river is just half a kilometer away. Maybe later on buy land close enough to graze some cattle and let them drink directly from the river. Yeah. That's my plan, starting today, *compadre,*" Ramiro sighed.

But his daydreams came to a sudden stop when lunchtime came around. A group of men gathered around several of the tables in the employee rest area to eat their lunches. Nico, Danny, and the others sat down and opened their lunch buckets of spicy chopped beef and bean tacos. They each had six to eight tacos wrapped in aluminum foil. They also had a thermos with hot coffee, and a banana or an apple, plus a supply of Mexican cookies called Marias.

At the adjacent table sat a group of men who looked a lot like them but whose language was mostly English and a little mixture of Spanish slang.

One of the men looked over at Ramiro and sneered as he gave him the up and down. Ramiro nodded back in a gesture of friendship although he felt uncomfortable by the man's stare. His name was Roger. Roger opened his sack lunch and proceeded to take out a couple of baloney sandwiches, potato chips, and a pack of donuts. "So you're the new guy, huh?" He spoke to Ramiro in English, and Danny quickly translated.

"Yeah, I'm the new guy. But why don't you speak Spanish to me?" Ramiro asked, assuming the other man was being disrespectful because he could clearly see that Ramiro only spoke Spanish.

Roger's table huddled in a little as Roger muttered something inaudible to them, and they burst out laughing. Ramiro didn't appreciate being the butt of their joke, whatever it might be. He tensed up, and his pride triggered his Spanish temper. Nico tapped his knee as if to say, "Ignore them."

"Yes, I'm the new guy. Ramiro Ocañas, at your service," he said with a forced smile in an effort to not cause any problems for Nico.

Another of the adjacent diners then spoke and asked Ramiro, "Ever seen a train before. Do they have these where you come from?"

and he laughed. The table mocked along with him as Ramiro's table made several remarks to the others, such as, "Don't be a jerk." Ramiro began to turn a couple of shades of red. He clenched his fist.

"Listen here, you sons of…, just because I can't speak English doesn't mean that you are better than me or that I haven't seen a freaking train. Maybe if you knew your own culture a little better you wouldn't ask such goddam ignorant questions," Ramiro blurted, his neck muscles expanding along with his nostrils.

To that, Roger got up from his seat and walked over to stand just inches from Ramiro, "Who you calling ignorant, you bastard wetback?" He was standing face to face with Ramiro, his black eyes piercing Ramiro's; his breath smelled of boloney and mustard as he blurted out his threat.

The entire room took notice of the tension. The tables where men of various other ethnicities—Black, Armenian, Irish, German, Italian, Russian—all turned around to look at what was about to happen. Some stood up and others strained their necks to see past their companions.

Ramiro's response to Roger's profanity was a swift punch in the nose that nearly knocked the guy out.

The guys rushed to restrain Ramiro from delivering any more punches. They yelled at Roger's friends to keep him away and avoid any further trouble. But it was too late. John had witnessed the blow that Ramiro had landed on Roger. Before Ramiro knew what happened, he was sacked.

From his picture window above the crew, John had seen it all. He stood looking out at the men. He had a puzzled and angry look on his face. He motioned for both Ramiro and Roger to step into his office. Ramiro looked over at Nico, and he felt deep shame because he thought he had let down his friend. No sooner did the men walk into John's office than the foremen lit into them. "What the hell happened out there? Guys, I will not have any of that nonsense in my crew," he said. Ramiro stood crestfallen and humbled, but Roger was defiant and accused Ramiro of assault. Ramiro was surprised to hear Nico beside him speak up and explain to John that Roger had provoked the incident.

John nodded and looked the men over, and he shook his head. "I have no alternative but to let you go, Ramiro. I just can't ignore what everyone else saw, that you landed a blow on Roger. I have to let you go." No amount of pleading by Nico and Ramiro would budge him.

Ramiro was allowed to hang out around the break room till the shift was over, however, so he could ride home with Nico and the guys. He took refuge in Danny's car where he proceeded to get some much-needed rest once he got past the shock and disappointment in himself. His body finally succumbed to all the stress of the morning and the exhaustion of several days of poor sleeping on a bus.

CHAPTER 3: *Miss Mary*

The next morning, Ramiro sat alone in the room he shared with Nico. He had lost his new job, and he was feeling a strange sense of fear and uncertainty. *"How could I have been so stupid? That pocho just wanted to make me screw up, and I let him. Stupid!"* he scolded himself. He couldn't help but see visions of Lupita, his mother, and Eliza: the one frowning at him for having messed up his first opportunity in America, the other sympathetic and encouraging. He quickly willed them both out of his thoughts before their memory could intensify his misery. Besides, he fully intended not to let any disappointment or mishap derail his plans to succeed in America.

Nico promised him that he would talk to John once more to plead for Ramiro's reinstatement. He would explain to John the situation and assure him that Ramiro was very contrite and promised never to let matters get out of hand again. So now Ramiro found himself silently praying even though he was not a religious man. "Please let it all go well today, God. Let John agree to take me back."

Then he laughed at himself as he recalled how often he had enjoyed riling up his Catholic friends and relatives by proclaiming his doubts about God and divine intervention. Deep down, he was truly more of an agnostic, "just in case." He instinctively crossed himself as his mind thought, *"I can't wait for Nico to come home and bring me good news tonight."*

Nico had not set the alarm—because he knew that Ramiro would not be going in to work the next morning—despite Ramiro's insistence on wanting to go and speak personally with John. Ramiro appreciated such consideration. Still, he awoke only about an hour after the fellows left for work. The morning cold prompted him to take a hot shower to warm up a little, but he was really just looking for any excuse to enjoy the amazing contraption that poured hot water over his entire body for as long as he wanted. It was a great device and a modern convenience that he had never enjoyed back home. He had showered last night after everyone else, but it was cold that morning and there was no one else around to inconvenience, so he jumped in again. "*Ah,*" he thought, "*how much better I feel after a good night's sleep and a long, hot shower.*"

He felt strong and rarin' to go. Only, there was no place to go. He started to reproach himself once again for losing the job, but he knew that course was counterproductive. He did not feel confident enough to venture out into the cold Chicago streets unaccompanied. He would wait to be shown around by someone who knew the city. He put his energy to good use by taking inventory of all his possessions and surveying his new quarters for where to accommodate his things. He prided himself on being organized and a bit of a neat freak, so he unpacked his valise and put away all his belongings in the small closet and the two drawers of the small dresser that Nico had indicated were for his use.

After tidying up the place, he was hungry for breakfast and a strong cup of coffee. He went down to see what he might find in the kitchen, and he found Mary making her own breakfast. He was about to give her a cheerful "Good Moring, Doña Maria," but he remembered Nico's warning, that Mary was very particular about being called "Miss." Ramiro's veneration for tradition and propriety made him wonder why a woman in her fifties would shun the title of Doña, seeing how it symbolized respect and dignity. "*What kind of person doesn't want to be respected?*" he wondered. He decided he liked the idea of having breakfast with her and maybe getting a little better acquainted. After all, he did enjoy meeting strangers, and he loved a good conversation.

"Good morning, Miss Mary!" he smiled.

"Oh, *muchacho*, you startled me! I forgot you were in the house," she snapped at him in her high pitched, melodious voice, turning around from the stove where she was scrambling eggs. She then looked him over and remembered to speak Spanish to him, so she repeated herself, this time smiling.

"Oh, well, a thousand apologies, Miss Mary. I didn't mean to scare you," he said. "May I join you for breakfast? Maybe you can give me some advice about how to get around and how to get along here in this city. It's all such a new world for me, you see."

"Yes, you can certainly join me for breakfast," she said. "I'll just scramble up some eggs here quickly for you. Take some of that bread over there and put it in the toaster, if you don't mind. There's butter and jam on the table, and bacon left over from the guys' breakfast earlier. Anything else you like?" She spoke as she moved swiftly about the business of making a new batch of eggs for her unexpected companion. "Ramiro, right?"

Ramiro smiled and gave a polite nod, "Yes, ma'am. Ramiro, at your orders; and, no, nothing else, thank you. I see you have bananas on the table also. Maybe I'll have one of those."

"Absolutely, Ramiro. Help yourself," she said as she scooped the eggs onto his plate and threw in some bacon. He remained standing by the toaster and proceeded to butter the toast. He passed on the jelly.

Ramiro observed Mary's every motion, the inflections and accents of her voice, and all details of her appearance. He traced that Mary had once been a beauty, but it appeared that life had been hard on her. Despite that, she could probably pass for someone in her mid-forties, though he was sure she was at least a decade older. Her satin nightgown and slippers exuded a kind of exotic allure even though she wore a heavy robe over her gown. Her graying hair, tinted red, was slightly permed and shoulder length, but she held its wilder strands back with a bright purple beret encrusted with rhinestones, which Ramiro found both bold and slightly comical.

They sat down to eat.

"Miss Mary, can I ask you a question?"

"Call me Mary, Ramiro. I like everything casual. Besides, something tells me we're going to be friends. Why not?" she smiled. "And, yes, of course, you can ask me anything. If I can, I'll give you answers; if not, I might just tell you a good story," she said, with a wink and a laugh.

"I kinda gathered. Nico mentioned something about your casual style," Ramiro nodded, pleased at her friendliness.

"And I have some questions for you, too, my new friend," she said. "Like what are you doing home today when you were supposed to get a job yesterday, huh?"

"Oh, that. I guess Nico or the guys didn't mention anything to you this morning. Well, I got the job right away. Man, that was so great. But then I had a problem with some jerk, and I had to punch him in the nose, and that got me fired," he confessed, reliving his shame over the incident.

She laughed a shrieky, hearty laugh. "What! Unbelievable. No one gets hired and fired on the same day. Most people wait a while before they go around picking fights on their coworkers. You're a feisty one, aren't you?" she said, mostly in her weak Spanish but interjecting English phrases when she felt like it. She reached over and held his wrist for a moment then withdrew it when she felt him shirk a little. "To tell you the truth, I did ask Nick why you didn't come down for breakfast, so he had to spill the beans."

"Ah, yes. Well, it was not quite that brazen. The guy provoked me to the point that I had to stand up for myself, that's all. After all, what man doesn't have his pride? The boss saw me strike the punch, so he just assumed the worst, and Nico couldn't convince him I wasn't at fault."

Mary shook her head as she got up to refill their coffee, walking past him, brushing her hip against his shoulder ever so slightly. As she bent over him to pour, again, she touched his arm. He noticed that her robe was open just enough to reveal some cleavage in her aquamarine satin gown that she wore underneath the robe. Ramiro looked away quickly, trying to ignore her perfume and pretending he felt nothing of her physical contact.

"I see. How unfair. So, what did you want to ask me?" she said.

"Well, Nico will plead my case today again. I am expecting good news tonight when he gets home. Anyway, I was wondering how a woman like you ended up in Chicago running a boarding house and all," he tells her. "Also, what are your rules for all your tenants? And maybe you can tell me how can I get around this neighborhood and the city as a whole, like how the buses work?"

"Oh, sure, honey. I can tell you all that," she said. "Ended up, huh?" she laughed.

Ramiro took notice of the word "honey." He liked it somehow. It gave him a sense of endearment although he also sensed that it was a catch-all word that women used to show friendliness.

Mary continued, "First I want to hear *your* story. Where do you come from, and why did you come all the way up here to this frozen world at this time of the year? Go ahead. Just tell me whatever you like. I won't interrupt you unless I don't understand something you say."

Ramiro looked at her, his head slightly bent and with a sideways, hesitant look. "Well, Miss Mary, I'm here for one reason only: to work. I come from Naranjales, Nuevo León. That's a small village in the fertile valley of Monterrey. I love that place, my land. I used to tend to my family's farm, but my parents and siblings dedicated more and more time to the merchandising business, and I wasn't too good at that. I love the outdoors and fresh air of the farms. Plowing, planting crops—corn mostly—the orange groves, and raising a small herd of cattle.

"I got married, so I had to strike out on my own because in my family no married man should depend on his parents. A married man has to support his wife and family by earning his own way in the world. My parents always said, 'If you're man enough to marry, you should be man enough to take care of a family without asking for help.' Anyway, the government is so corrupt, and the big landowners from Monterrey have taken over much of the land we used to work. That made it so we had to work for them for low wages or depend on smaller and smaller pieces of our own land.

"Finally, I tried the grocery and general merchandise business, but most people are poor and take too long to pay, so I was just not making it. Some of my buddies started to leave the villages, and get American work visas and green cards. I resisted, but eventually I saw it as my best option to make my dreams come true."

"Fascinating. And what exactly are those dreams of yours?" Mary asked, a bit amused yet respectful.

"Miss Mary, my dream is to own my own farm in Naranjales, with a beautiful little house of white cinderblock and hacienda-style gardens. I just want to have the land and crops and animals my family had when I was a boy. My plan is to earn enough dollars to make my dream come true one day, maybe in five years or so."

"So you're planning to work your tail off to earn enough dollars to buy yourself a Mexican farm in a few years?" She repeated his words as if they were too naïve to be taken seriously. "Sounds like a nice dream, but I think it's going to take you a lot longer than five years considering you speak no English and you'll be making minimum wage in most of your jobs." She said it almost shaking her head at the seeming impossibility of Ramiro's big dream ever coming true.

Her words deflated him for a few seconds but he would not be deterred. "Yes, ma'am. And I chose Chicago simply because this is where my best *compadre* is. He helped get me sponsored to come here," he replied.

"Whoa, there," Mary laughed, "no ma'am stuff, remember?"

"Oh, yeah. Sorry. Mary," he said sheepishly. "And now it's your turn."

"Well, Ramiro, my story is much more complicated, but I'll give you some idea of it. I have four grown daughters who live in Corpus

Christi, Texas. That's where I'm from. I was married to a nice man who was a longshoreman, Freddy. My husband died in an accident on oilrig about ten years ago. I have to confess, I was not the best of wives, but I was happy to have my daughters and a good man. I guess I didn't have the housewife-y, motherly instincts that most of my girlfriends had. I played my role, but I always wanted to be free and independent.

"When Freddy died, I took the insurance money he left me, and made my own opportunity to move up north, where I have a cousin. Cousin Julia. Married to a nice white lawyer; another long story. Anyway, I was able to start anew with the insurance money. I bought this place, and it's been almost ten years I've been making my living. Yes, it's a lot of work, but I like to work, and you guys always renew my energies with your company and your dreams.

"I am a fourth-generation American, not an immigrant. That's important, you know. Most people around here don't know enough history, so sometimes I have to remind them. I bet you don't know enough history yourself. You probably don't know that Mexican Americans like me are just as American as anybody. After all, I am a fourth-generation American," she repeated as if she had forgotten she'd said it already. "My people didn't cross any border. The border crossed us, not the other way around. Too much history behind what I'm telling you, young man."

He didn't like the "young man" stuff, but he let it go because he didn't want to sound like her by objecting to insignificant stuff.

Then she changed the subject, "And what about your wife and family? What did you say her name was?"

"Eliza. I married Eliza when she was seventeen years old. I was nineteen. I had to beg my father to give me permission to marry, then persuade him to go and ask for her hand. She was the most beautiful girl in the whole village." He told her the story as if in a dreamscape. "We got married on October 15, 1940. We now have four children. My youngest was born two months ago," he said, looking down and flexing his hands. "They're my reason for living, and I'll return for them as soon as possible."

"Why didn't you bring them along with you?"

"Well, it's not so easy to just pick up and move a bunch of people from one country to another. We'll survive a few years apart, and then we will be together. Eliza and the kids are not alone. Family is close back home," he told her.

Ramiro saw a noticeable expression of sympathy in her face, as if she were a loving aunt who was about to embrace him. "Was life really so bad back home that you had to sacrifice this separation?" she said.

"Oh, no. Not bad at all, just too uncertain. You see, Mary, creature comforts, fancy stuff, and modern conveniences are nice, but that's not what gives a man's life meaning. What really gives life meaning is the people you love and how well they love you back. I had my great family, both my own and my parents and siblings. We had most basic things but no luxuries. The village had no electricity or running water. So what? But a man has got to be a man and make a living and provide for his children, so here I am."

"What?" Mary exclaimed as if horrified, "No electricity or running water?" Of course, she was just trying to get a rise out of him. She had heard similar stories from other boarders before, so she was aware of the origins of her tenants.

"Nah. Minor stuff, but you know, Mary, when I arrived in McAllen I was so impressed with the power of electricity, all those neon signs and all the streets lighted. Then there were the other things, like so many new cars. But that was nothing, as I saw more and bigger cities along the bus route here, it just got more splendid. Then I saw the illuminated city of Chicago as the bus began to pull in. Wow. It was just spectacular.

"My eyes couldn't take it all in, but those lights! It was magical. And so many different kinds of people." He laughed. "Mary, you won't believe me but I had never seen black people before I got on that bus in McAllen. And you should have seen that blonde I saw at the station downtown. Man, what a sight," he laughed then blushed as he caught himself gushing like a child.

Mary laughed, too, "Ramiro you crack me up. So Chicago impressed you? No wonder! Your town didn't even have light bulbs," she teased.

He nodded, "Don't make fun, either, eh? No modern living, just outhouses, water wells, kerosene lamps. We did have stoves and butane gas tanks for them," he continued. "No luxuries or American comforts, but life was good. We expect the electricity lines will be up in a few years. The government keeps promising us. Yeah. Electricity, a paved road, and running water very soon," he said proudly. "Now, don't get me wrong. That is just the country villages. Monterrey looks just like Chicago, all modern and everything. Well, the buildings there are not so tall, but then again, Chicago doesn't have a mountain."

She expressed mock disbelief that his hometown did not have electricity. Mary was a city girl even if Corpus Christi was a small place, unlike Chicago. The surrounding countryside was mostly wired for electric service, and she had never seen firsthand anyone living in the almost primitive conditions that Ramiro was describing. She feigned sympathy, but Ramiro resented what he took for her condescending attitude. He brushed it off thinking to himself, "How ignorant *pochos* are, just as ignorant as gringos."

Mary went on to describe some of the house rules. "First, pay your rent on time. No drinking is allowed in the house, there's a curfew of 11:00 p.m. unless you have a good reason, rooms are to be kept clean and tidy—cleaning supplies are in the kitchen, you can cook anything you wish if you buy your own food, but always clean up after yourself."

Mary explained how to get around the city by bus. She told him that two blocks down the street there was a bus stop, and besides the stop was a mail collection box for his letters home. After a while she asked him if he would like another cup of coffee. Ramiro graciously declined. Mary got up to put the dishes in the sink, and he offered to help wash them. She thanked him with a touch of his cheek and a soft squeeze of his hand that caught him off guard again. "No, thank you, dear. I'll finish up in here, then I have much work to do. You go on and rest up if you like."

Ramiro thanked her for the breakfast and the conversation. He excused himself and returned to his room where he proceeded to write Eliza a letter. He took a notebook that Nico had placed on the dresser and his pen. "Dearest Eliza,..." As he tried to focus on what he wanted to say to his wife in this first letter, his mind wandered back to Mary. How she touched him more than once: "*Mary was making a pass at me.*" Then his thoughts flashed back to the blonde from the bus station again. She sure was pretty even in her strange condition.

He put away the paper and pen. He went to the door and latched it. He parted the curtains and looked out the window then closed them again and he took off his shirt. He turned back toward the bed as he began to unbuckle his belt.

CHAPTER 4: *Those Left Behind*

Doña Lupita spent the evening of Ramiro's departure in a somber mood, sighing and praying in silence for her boy's welfare. The next morning, she got out of bed and resumed her normal rituals and routines. "Good morning, Lola. Going out to milk the cow?" she greeted her daughter, then her husband. "Good morning, Timoteo. Don't get up yet. Breakfast will be ready soon. I'll call you."

Memories of Ramiro accompanied her throughout the day, but she contained her sadness. She was a woman of strong will. Lupita saw no contradiction in her expressing her pain, sometimes openly, and at the same time holding up steady as steel. It was the law of the land that her emotional and physical fortitude should withstand all. She was not uncommon in possessing those traits, for in such rural settings, barely disturbed by modernity, toughness was the order of the day. Lupita was all that any pioneer woman would have aspired to be. She was determined to tame the wild nature of her beautiful but demanding farm life. At only 4'10" and weighing a mere 90 pounds, anyone would have been fooled into thinking her fragile. They would have been wrong.

The village of Naranjales and its parameters was a man's world, and in those parts the men were as macho as they come. Lupita saw it as just one more challenge to overcome. Timoteo had suffered injuries from an old bullfight gone wrong. He was thirty-eight, she thirty-five, when Timoteo was gored in one arm at a regional amateur bullfighting event, some twenty years prior. Lupita spent weeks tending to his wounds and recovery. She was furious with him for his foolishness in insisting to get in the ring past his prime, but she nursed him till his arm healed. Timoteo had once been quite a dashing figure back in his bullfighting days, and he attracted many a *señorita*. Lupita had been drawn in by his bravado back then.

Timoteo was a traditional Mexican father of Spanish ancestry, quite expectant of the reverence of his family. But, physically weakened, he had become dependent on Lupita's strength. Lupita had asserted herself when she spent weeks mending him after the goring. They had children to bring up, a farm to run, and a store to tend to. Timoteo reluctantly accepted that his wife was going to play a non-traditional role going forward. When he was fully recovered, some of the men would tease him about being bossed around by a woman, but he only smiled and told them: "*Ustedes que saben? A mi ninguna vieja me manda. Lupita es la ponderosa porque asi me convine.*" "What do you guys know about it? No broad bosses me around. Lupita is a powerhouse because that's what suits me."

§

Weeks after Ramiro's departure, it was around noon when Lupita was busy in the kitchen preparing lunch. The winter breezes put a chill on everything, but food preparation remained as great a source of warmth as ever. She busily pressed the *masa* dough for the tortillas then expertly folded the flattened maize ball onto her hand and mechanically repeated the motion, laying the flat disc down onto the hot griddle. She paused every few minutes to slice the squash and shave fresh corn kernels off the husk.

Lola helped by cutting up a freshly plucked chicken. She had scooped it off the patio, where they often ran freely, about an hour prior. She swiftly spun its neck and then dunked it in boiling water to loosen the feathers for plucking. The large clay pot of boiled pinto beans stood ready for her mashing then frying in her homemade lard.

The entire house filled with mealtime smells of the chicken *guisado*, spiced with Lupita's usual combination of salt, pepper, cumin, garlic, onions, and tomatoes.

The entire patio, in fact, soon filled with appetizing aromas because Eliza's kitchen, just across the way, also provided its share of food smells. It was common that at noontime, every household in Naranjales emitted similar aromas as well as the sounds of clapping that every woman made as she shaped the *masa* dough into individual fist-sized balls that would be flattened by a tortilla press, an indispensable appliance. Every school kid rushing home for lunch could hear and smell these things, and their mouths watered anticipating a hot tortilla treat fresh off the griddle and smeared with homemade salted lard.

Life without Ramiro had swiftly returned to normal for Lupita. She willed herself not to think anymore about her pain. She would wait patiently for the first letter from Ramiro that she expected would arrive in a month or two.

Lupita was busy preparing lunch when Ramiro's kids rushed into her kitchen startling her with their squeals from a game of tag. She scolded and shooed them away, slapping the last one's behind as they rushed back onto the patio. "These darn kids, always traipsing around when one is busy. Oh, my son, your kids are going to drive me mad. That Eliza!" Lupita muttered out Eliza's name and talked to the sky about her burdens and her absent son. For just a few seconds, her maternal reflexes compelled her to pray that his journey was going well.

Outside, the children continued to play, excited to be home from school. They were completely oblivious to the business of the adults. Baldemar, eight, Esmeralda, six, and Alicia, three, could be heard squealing with joy as the girls ran from Baldemar's attempts to pull their pig tails or some other practical joke. Soon Eliza emerged to grab the girls and instructed them to help set the table. They also took turns looking in on baby Carlos as their mother prepared lunch. Eliza could hear the girls cooing with the baby and knew they were all right. She was coping with her loneliness and yet feeling a strange sense of freedom that she couldn't explain. Her husband had left her to be on her own for what would probably be most of a year. Still, she feared the unknown because her in-laws were bound to watch her more intently than ever.

For a while Eliza seemed like a new woman. She allowed the emptiness left by Ramiro to be filled with the joy of owning her own person. She went so far as to let the kids go naked on several occasions. When Lupita dropped in one afternoon and found her napping and the house unkempt, Eliza pretended not to wake up after hearing her *suegra's* reproachful mutterings at what a dump the house had become. Secretly, she was glad the old woman got a glimpse of her rebelliousness. It made her joyous for an instant, but not as happy as knowing that she no longer had to fear her lusty husband's demands every night for the next year. Although she loved Ramiro, she had come to detest his manner of taking her body for granted, to partake of it at will.

In the big house, Lupita and Lola could also hear the children from their kitchen, as could Timoteo. Their noises and horseplay reminded the family of their connection to Ramiro through them. The three relived their own memories of the farewell, each in his or her own way, but no one spoke of it. "Those poor kids. I wonder how the separation is affecting them," Lola finally spoke absentmindedly.

"They'll be just fine. We just have to watch they don't get spoiled. Eliza is not the spoiling kind, so that's a help," said Lupita. Everyone loved deeply, but children were never to be spoiled or indulged too much. That would risk making them soft and unsuitable for the rough duties of farm life in adulthood.

Beyond the immediate noises of the house could be heard the sounds of additional kids in garrulous exchanges. The sound of other children's play emanated from the street. The schoolhouse across the road had just let them out for their daily two-hour lunch siesta. A handful of them burst into the store, and Lola and Timoteo tended to those that dropped in to buy a piece of candy or sweetbread to munch on while on their way home.

"What'll it be, Reynaldo. How's your mother? And you, Jose Luis? Oh, a soda. Are we rich today, Braulito? How about you? What's that Maria del Pilar? Charge it to your mom's account? Does she know about this? Ok. Adalberto, tell your father his bill is past due, okay? Here you go. Here is your strawberry Barrilito. See you, kids. Don't forget, Adalberto. Okay. Adios. Adios."

There were not many affluent kids in those parts, as most families did not give children allowances or spending money of any kind. But there were always the few just a bit overindulged. Those kids, of course, tended to be the more popular ones in school, especially when they shared their sweets with their friends.

Within minutes all the kids scattered to their respective homes, their murmurs and squeals gradually subsiding. Their mothers awaited them with a freshly cooked meal consisting of tortillas, refried beans, and some other farm-fresh complement such as a scrambled egg or, when lucky, the ever-popular *arroz con pollo*, chicken and rice. Hearing no more chatter Lola could close the doors to the store and join her parents for lunch.

Lola was strong, wiry, and outspoken like her mother, but she was an obedient and dutiful daughter who respected parents above all, just as tradition required. She was pretty in a no-nonsense sort of way, but her overprotective brothers and her own fastidiousness had kept away the proper suitor, so she was now past marriage age. When Timoteo grabbed three Coca Colas from the store's icebox, the ice block was almost all melted. Lupita told him not to waste the sodas; Lola would make lemonade instead. He agreed to the lemonade. He was in tune with the women about not eating their profits. They sat down to eat.

§

No sooner had they begun their second tortilla than they heard the clopping of horse hooves on the rocky street out front, then the loud knocks on the store's tall wooden doors. Lola put down her glass and proceeded to see who it was. "I'm coming. Hold your horses."

She called out to the knocker. She unlatched the door and opened it. "Panchito, what's the matter?"

It was Panchito, her cousin's husband. "Lola, is Tia Lupita home? I need her help. Yolanda is having so much pain. I think she is about to have the baby." He spoke in a trembling voice about his wife's labor pains. "We need Tia Lupita's help," he pleaded.

"*Por Dios*, Panchito, calm down. It'll all be all right. Yolanda is not the first woman in the world to give birth. Yes, mother is here. I will tell her to get ready. I will go with her to help in the delivery," Lola reassured him.

The young couple were both twenty-one. This was their second child. They lived a few miles out, near the outskirts of the village, surrounded by wildlife and the unique vegetation that seemed to magically transform from a border of desert shrubs and rattlesnakes to the lushness of forest-like greenery and cultivated lands. They had been married three years, and their small adobe house consisted of two rooms. Yolanda was Lupita's brother's youngest daughter. Panchito's family was from the next village, some twenty kilometers out. Panchito, the term of endearment for Francisco, had relocated because the bride's father had given them the small house as a wedding gift, and he would be working with his in-laws in the family's sugar cane farm.

Panchito helped Lola hitch up a horse and buggy because it was not possible to fetch a motor vehicle at that time of the day. "It's ready, Mama, do you have what you need?" asked Lola as she saw her mother exit the house with Timoteo close behind, carrying a small canvas bag.

"Yes, I have everything. Did you hitch the wagon good and tight? Last thing we need is a loose buggy shaft and ending up flipped over," replied Lupita. Lola reassured her everything was a go on the carriage.

"Don't worry, Tia. It's all good and ready," reinforced Panchito. "Besides, I'll be right beside you on my horse the whole way."

The women arrived at the small adobe house within a half hour. They could hear moaning and crying even before they entered the hut. Lola quickly set about stoking the fire in the chimney and gathering clean linens while Lupita unpacked her midwife's tools. Lola gently guided the couple's two year old away from the bedside where he had been standing watching his mother in agony. The boy had a snotty nose, was barefoot and in diapers, and he was clearly hungry and irritable. Lola instructed the boy's father to take him and feed him something.

The older woman had set about lighting two votive candles and reciting a silent prayer, although she was not particularly religious. To her, Mother Nature was supreme because it seemed to her that whatever Mother Nature wanted, she got. It was Mother Nature that had toughened her to the realities of life and death during childbirth. She had delivered her share of stillborns and counted herself lucky that only once had she lost a mother. Her technique was simple patience. She knew Yolanda was as tough as they come for those parts, and she was relieved to know that the young woman had had a successful birth previously and no miscarriages.

After several hours of the young mother's agonizing labor, her water finally broke, and it was time to guide her through the contractions and eventual pushing of the baby through the birth canal. After much groaning, moaning, howling, and writhing by Yolanda, Lupita gently took hold of the baby's head, eased it out of its mother, snipped the umbilical cord, and, with Lola's help, wiped it and watched it wail to make its debut into the temporal world of Naranjales. It was a healthy boy.

The father was called into the house as Lupita cleaned up the infant and cleared out his nose and mouth by slapping his little bottom face down. She wrapped him up and placed him in the mother's arms. The time was approaching 9:00 p.m., and the two set for home well after dark, just after Yolanda's sister arrived and set about preparing dinner for Panchito and the women. Lupita left instructions with Yolanda and her caretakers for recovering from the pain and trauma she had just suffered.

§

On their way home Lupita and Lola stopped by Alberto's, the

oldest son's, house, which happened to be in the adjacent farmland to the new parents. There they ran into Julieta, the baby of Lupita's family, and her recent husband, Eduardo. The couple surprised the women with the announcement that they had both been approved for visas to immigrate to the United States. The news reopened the wounds left by Ramiro's departure, and Lupita spent the remainder of the buggy ride home in silence despite Lola's attempts at small talk. The bad "good news" was the first thing they shared with Timoteo when they arrived home at nearly midnight. He, too, had been missing his son and lamented that his baby daughter, his favorite child, was moving far away. But Timoteo's manly pride required that he maintain a stiff upper lip, and so he focused on the possibility of prosperity in a foreign land for both of his children.

In the absence of the women that night, Eliza had taken over their duties and fed Timoteo his supper. She had left her father-in-law unattended while she put the kids to bed, so she caught the tail end of the conversation when she walked back into the gathering room in the store area. "I am so sorry, Doña Lupita, but I'm sure Julieta is excited about starting a new life in Houston. And you will soon have a Gringuito grandchild," she teased uncharacteristically. "How did it go with the delivery of the baby?" The women gave Eliza a brief account of what had happened and assured everyone the new baby and mother were both fine.

§

As she walked back across the patio to her bungalow, Eliza couldn't help but recall the birth of her first baby nine years before. It was a stillbirth. Lupita had ordered it buried in the back yard without even so much as a headstone, although she did pray over the grave and asked God to take the baby into His bosom. Eliza had taken it all in stride as part and parcel of the harshness of life, but every time a new baby came into the world, she felt nostalgic for her lost child.

Such was the strength of Lupita's will and the acceptance of the inevitable laws of nature that no funeral or ceremony would be held for a stillborn. That would have been frivolous sentimentality and self-indulgent pitying. No one questioned it, and no one spoke about it ever again. It was understood that Doña Lupita was right.

Eliza returned to her little cottage where she had put the kids to bed. They were all sleeping soundly. It was getting cold. She looked over them to make sure they were warm then she undressed and put on a heavy flannel nightdress. She slipped under the woolen blanket that she had recently sewn together. She couldn't help a fleeting moment of pride as she felt her creation of combed wool and heavy cotton cloth of gold with prints of grape bunches and vines. She fell asleep almost instantly and began to dream of her handsome young husband on a horse, singing, "*Si Adelita quisiera ser mi novia, si Adelita fuera mi mujer, le compraria un vestido de seda para llevarla a bailar al cuartel*", "If Adelita were to be my girl, if Adelita were to be my wife…."

CHAPTER 5: *Inquietudes*

Dear Eliza,

I hope that the present letter finds you in good health in the company of the children as well as that of mother and father and Lola. As for me, I am well, thank God.

Chicago is an enormous city. It is very cold here. I arrived barely yesterday, Sunday, at midnight. I located Compadre Nico, and I am now installed in the house where he lives. When I have a chance to come home, I will tell you all the details of this city and the long bus ride to get here. There are so many new things that my eyes had never seen before. Everything is electric and there are lights everywhere. Like magic.

You probably know that I already miss you very much. I miss everyone. Say hello and tell them all that I love them. I know that your life will also change and it will be hard with me being gone, and you with so little money. I am doing all of this because it is necessary to make our dream come true. You will see that in three or four years I will return with many dollars, and we are going to buy us that little farm that we have talked about.

I don't know when it will be possible for me to visit you, but it is best not to raise our hopes for now. It could be six months, or maybe it could go into one or two years. I entrust the good care of the kids and mother and father to you, as I expect them to look after you.

Well, the only thing left to say is that I already found a job. Nico took me to the railroad yard where he works, and right away they

started me working. Of course, I can't understand when they speak
English, but Nico and others help me to get by and follow the rules.
Nico tells me that they pay every Friday, so soon I will start to save a
little money. First I have to pay rent and buy a few things for living,
then I will see how much is left to start saving.

I will now say goodbye, my dear Eliza. I know that you won't be
able to read much of this letter, so I expect Jacobo or Lola will read it
to you. Again, give my hello to everyone, and special hugs and kisses
for you and the kids.

With love and devotion, your husband,
Ramiro

He knew he had lied to her about the job, since he was hired
and fired on the same day. In his mind, he was just confident that he
would be working very soon. There was no sense worrying her about
something that minor when he was sure there was plenty of work in
that town. Ramiro proceeded to address an envelope that he borrowed
from Nico's dresser then he went downstairs to ask Mary about buying
postage stamps.

As he descended the stairs, he saw Mary sweeping the living room
rug with some kind of contraption. He was glad to see that the rugs
could be swept because he had an aversion to dust, and he imagined
that rugs trapped all sorts of dust in them, unlike the shiny concrete
floors in the houses of Naranjales. Those floors were constantly cared
for by the lady of the house, who made sure dust never survived past
a few hours. No self-respecting housewife ever let the glossy, glasslike
finish of her cinderblock house floors lose their luster.

Mary had changed into a pair of jeans and a flannel shirt. She
wore her red hair gathered under a multiflowered silk scarf of reds,
greens, and yellows that made up some kind of impressionistic bou-
quet. The scarf swept under the back of her head and tied in a knot
above her forehead.

"Pardon me, Miss, er, Mary. Can you tell me where is the best place to buy a postage stamp for this letter that I want to send my wife?" said Ramiro.

"Well, I think I can do that, all right," she said. "Seems you took a nap. I hope I wasn't too noisy down here," she said.

"Oh, no, not at all. I did catch up on my sleep a little, though." Ramiro replied.

"Good. Good. It's getting to be past lunchtime. Why don't you sit down in the kitchen, and I'll make us some tuna fish sandwiches. I can give you directions while we eat. There's a store down the street where they sell stamps. Can you do that, or are you in a hurry to mail off your love letter?" she teased and smiled a wide grin. "Would you like milk or Kool Aid to drink?"

"I guess I am getting hungry. Milk sounds good, thanks. I am not familiar with tuna fish sandwiches, but I am here to learn new things, so, sure, I'll have some lunch with you," he agreed, imagining the sandwich as some form of new delicacy he would enjoy.

"Fine, then, if you would just finish sweeping this hallway for me. Empty it out over there," and she pointed to a tall blue plastic wastebasket in the kitchen, "I'll get started on those sandwiches."

Ramiro nodded and proceeded to do as Mary asked. He was nothing if not swift in his ability to clean and making things tidy. He examined the thing she handed him and quickly figured out it was a mechanical broom with a rolling brush beneath and a dust trap.

Mary set down a plate of sandwiches in the center of the table and brought a tall glass of Borden's milk for Ramiro and a pitcher of cherry-flavored Kool Aid from the refrigerator for herself. Ramiro watched intently as she moved about the kitchen preparing their lunch. He was partly fascinated by Mary's assertiveness and partly by the new gadgets and the colorful prepackaged comestibles all around.

He took his first bite of the new fare. His taste buds approved mightily, and he chomped down on the rest. He made it a point to remember for future reference that Miracle Whip on tuna was a good thing. Mary had opened a pack of potato chips, and those, too, delighted him. Ramiro had not realized he was that hungry. His body seemed to be making up for the deprivation he suffered on his trip.

Mary poured him a second glass of milk and pointed to a package of chocolate chip cookies as if to say, "Have some dessert." All the while she told him about the layout of the neighborhood. She explained how to get to the convenience store where he could find most anything he might need but at higher prices than at the supermarket. Looking out the window, she added, "They say it might snow tomorrow."

Ramiro listened intently and made mental notes of all the directions. As he made pictures in his mind, he didn't notice when Mary moved closer after putting the dishes in the sink. Suddenly he smelled her perfume again and realized she was standing beside him, almost rubbing against him as he stood up to seek the mailbox. He excused himself smiling sheepishly and stepped around her.

"I've never seen snow. I'm looking forward to it. I just hope it doesn't make everything colder. It is already too cold," he smiled.

After Ramiro deposited his letter in the collection mailbox that was located a few blocks from the house, he strolled around the neighborhood and got familiar with the lay of the land. It was definitely not a fancy neighborhood. There was street after street of two- and three-story houses that might have once been beautiful, middle-class family homes. Now they seemed mostly converted to duplexes, triplexes, flop houses, boardinghouses, and just a smattering of single families still hanging on. The winter cold was intense even in the afternoon sun. There was no sign of green life anywhere. All trees had shed their leaves except for an occasional, bedraggled evergreen bush or pine.

He marveled at the scattered signs of Christmas all around. He remembered seeing a box of decorations at the boarding house. That must have been Mary's next project, he thought. Back home such decorations were never a part of his family's traditions. He never questioned why but accepted that it was probably due to the extra expense and work involved. His mother was not one to indulge in frivolous luxuries of that type.

The grocery store was a pleasant enough place. The clerk greeted Ramiro the instant he walked in the door and the jingle bells rang. "Welcome my friend! He shouted from across the room with a wide grin on his mustachioed mouth. He seemed to be the husband in the mom-and-pop operation. The wife swept the floor around a refrigerator near the back of the store. The couple looked physically as if they were Mexican, and from his region. But these people were Italian, as indicated by the sign outside that read Giuseppe's Market, plus the selection of cold cuts and Italian ices left no doubt about it.

Ramiro was fascinated by the large selection of colorful snacks and all the other items on the shelves and behind glass-door refrigerators. His funds were minimal, but he decided to indulge in a pink, spongy cake with coconut sprinkles. Turned out it was actually a mini chocolate cake hiding under the pink marsh-mellow cap. Two to a pack, and he sure enjoyed them. All told he spent sixteen cents—ten for the snack and six cents on two stamps because he wanted to have one handy for next week's letter.

On his way out of the store, he bumped into two young women, who seemed too involved in some gossip they were sharing and laughing about to notice him. The girls gave him a good looking over as he excused himself, "*Perdon, señoritas.*"

The girls were clearly Mexican American, but they mocked him with a "No problem-o, see-ñor," and they giggled again. They appeared to be around eighteen. Ramiro took their giggles in good humor, but he had his own brand of retort, which included pretending to flirt with them. In fact, he did find them attractive in a foreign sort of way, but he was quick to judge them as "loose."

One of them caught his eye, though, as a whiff of their cheap perfume invaded his nostrils. He felt an unwelcome stirring of sexual desire. As he proceeded toward Mary's place he wondered how he was going to deal with being far away from Eliza's touch. He was going to miss the lovemaking. Such memories and the encounter with the girls perturbed his thoughts once again.

Ramiro had never been unfaithful to Eliza. At least not in his heart and soul, he thought. His work in Naranjales had taken him on weekly road trips to faraway ranches and outposts where people had little access to supplies. He had met more than his share of aggressive housewives or randy maidens. His handsome face and jocular playfulness often attracted female admirers, but he spurned most advances graciously, content to simply accept the ego strokes.

Now here he was, confronted with a clear signal from Mary and thoughts he didn't want to have. Her allure was unmistakable, even at her age. The combination of her perfume, physicality, and skillful aura provoked him. He had never before considered older women desirable, much less approachable. Hard as he tried, He could not push such disturbing thoughts out of his head.

Ramiro's hormones had raged ever since adolescence. Like any normal boy he had dealt with such urges as best he could under the rules of his society that demanded respect for the opposite sex. Eliza had captivated him from the moment he saw her. Once smitten by her, he never really gave any other girl much thought. After their marriage, all his fantasies and desires were satisfied on a regular basis. No more deprivation in the raging hormone department.

His mother would have been appalled at the very idea of a woman her own age making a pass at her son, but somehow Mary seemed beyond the rules of his culture. The entire city of Chicago and its over three million inhabitants seemed a place of anonymity where he could do things he had never done before. He couldn't help but ponder the possibilities.

But Ramiro's culture was strong in him. He had sometimes given silent thanks that his parents had not indoctrinated him with Catholicism as was the norm in those parts. He sensed that he would have become insufferably judgmental if he had been taught the strict rules of the church. The culture itself had done enough, anyway, for he tended toward moralizing just a bit too strongly.

He was firm enough in macho sexism and general Catholic prudishness in all matters of sexuality. His erotic adventures before marriage had consisted strictly of daily self-pleasuring, though in remarkable frequency even for a young buck. Eliza had been his first actual experience in making love to a woman.

After marriage, Ramiro's rare encounter at the brothel in the city's red light district was not considered cheating. Such escapades were secret and beyond the realm of any actual relationship. But not enjoying his daily lovemaking with Eliza was something that he was now fearing could become a problem. How would he manage this aspect of his life that was already provoking such strong temptations?

When Ramiro approached the house, he made sure to avoid new contact with Mary. He went up to his room, and lay down, still thinking about the earlier brushes with desire. He closed his eyes and recalled his first kiss with Eliza. It was at the party to celebrate her fifteenth birthday that she finally conceded him a dance. Eliza was egged-on by her girlfriends to respond to the handsome suitor. They had swooned over Ramiro's serenade to Eliza with the "Adelita" song.

Ramiro was consumed in his memory of kissing Eliza's tender young lips when suddenly he saw a garish flash of red. The image of the blonde from the bus stop replaced Eliza's face. It panicked him and he bolted out of bed.

He shook his head. He felt a new chill in the air and pulled his jacket tighter. "What the hell am I thinking?" he told the image in the mirror.

It was dark outside. He looked at the clock. Five o'clock. The guys would soon be home. Maybe Nico would bring him good news about the job.

CHAPTER 6: *Eliza's Torment*

They were all laughing at her. The women especially. The chortling and cackling echoes reverberated in her head. They pointed and squealed in laughter. She saw their mouths, giant and wide open, fleshy lips of reds, oranges, pinks, and browns. Their teeth bared and multiplied in undulating sizes from normal to wall-sized. Some projected upward to the thatched ceiling of the hut. She covered her face with her hands, but she could see through her fingers. She tried to run away but her body was frozen in place against a cold, cinder-block wall. It was all so dark, so distorted. She only knew she was little. A girl. The men leered at her. Doña Lupita and the other women and girls glared at her with scorn. They told her she was forever stained. They turned a cold shoulder when she reached out for mercy. They turned and cackled louder.

"Noooooo!!!" she screamed, a long, silent wail.

§

Eliza jolted in bed, sweating, still in her silent scream. It must have been past midnight, but she had no sense of time. Still trembling, she scanned the room in swift, sweeping glances. Her father and siblings were fast asleep. Her mother was gone. Her mother's empty space in her father's bed reminded Eliza that it was her recurring nightmare. She buried her face in her hands and let her long, silky hair cascade forward as she crumbled in tears of shame. The emotion she felt was deep and painful.

§

Eliza was only twelve when her mother ran off with Don Meliton, the across-the-road neighbor, leaving the family motherless. The rumors ran like wildfire throughout the village of Naranjales and within a week, everyone up and down the countryside had heard some version of the brazenness of Carlota Benitez de Cervantes and the tragedy of her cuckolded husband and abandoned kids.

Eliza's two older brothers were fourteen and sixteen. They swore to hunt down the couple and kill Meliton, who himself had abandoned an ailing wife and three kids. But the couple was never found, and it took years before folks stopped making reference to the high drama of Carlota and Meliton's betrayal. Santos Cervantes, Eliza's cuckolded father, became a laughing stock for a while, but was soon enough simply pitied as a loser. The good people of Naranjales took to crossing the street when they passed him. It was their way of hiding their discomfort and embarrassment for him.

Santos was a forgiving man, gentle and compassionate. He had loved Carlota deeply despite her reputation for infidelity, which preceded their engagement. Had she chosen to return the next day or the next week, he would have taken her back no matter the ridicule. He actually waited and prayed for her return despite himself. But Carlota never returned.

Santos picked up the pieces of his broken life and raised his kids alone the best he could. He had six of them, and he had lands to till and animals to feed. He had become half useless since a tractor accident in the cornfields had mangled his right leg. That meant he had to work twice as hard to eke out a living for his wretched family.

Eliza instinctively took on the role of a surrogate mother to her three younger siblings. The two older boys could fend for themselves.

Eliza had abandoned school after the second grade to help out with the many chores around the house. Her literacy was arrested at that level. No one thought much about a girl's education in those parts, especially unhappy, adulterous mothers like Carlota. A woman's role was a predetermined one of dutiful wife and mother. That was the tradition of unambitious farm girls. Ambitious farm girls ended up in shady places with stained reputations, like Carlota.

Eliza's fortunes took on an unexpected turn, however, when she suddenly blossomed into an alluring specimen of young womanhood at the age of fourteen. Her perfect pearly skin, her symmetry in every curve, her golden-brown eyes, and flowing waist-length brunette waves of hair captivated every young male that crossed her path. Despite her ragdoll wardrobe, she had a light that shone strong and undeniable.

But the mother's sins were visited upon the innocent maiden. Punish the daughter because that was just how things went then. Not one day went by without someone using the word "harlot," or a variation of it, in regard to the young woman's heritage. Despite Eliza's impeccable behavior and extreme modesty, the gossip and innuendo persisted. Oh, it was never overt, for in those parts, discreetness was another rule, and these were people who respected rules. Instead, they did their snickering and pointing among select groups and settings only, but the effect took hold.

Her physical blossoming just made it that much more inevitable for the village gossips to attempt persecuting her. Allusions to Eliza's potential sexual exploits became rampant. And if there was one thing the village had, it was gossips.

The more audacious of the rumormongers were mocked by the less overt ones, as tends to be the wont among hypocrites of malicious intent. They even invented a special hand gesture to indicate when someone was a talker. It consisted of two fingers in the motion of scissors cutting cloth. That indicated that a given person was engaging in cutting others down, or at the very least talking about others behind their back. Everyone up and down the region knew that the women of Valle Azul/Naranjales could be mistresses of gossip. People joked about it by using the scissors sign with a wink and a nod whenever a conversation needed some spice.

The cutting scissors became almost as infamous as the tap on the bent elbow, signifying "cheapskate." That one had been developed for the Monterrey dwellers. Even as far away as Mexico City or Guadalajara people made the elbow tap when referring to the good citizens of Monterrey, either good-naturedly or in scorn. The Mexican people were famous for their regionalism, and ascribing such stereotypes gave them pleasure and a sense of superiority over a competing region.

Eliza had to put up with the scissors ladies. She did, however, possess a layer of protection. In those days social status was bestowed to the young women of the region based on their chastity and reputation. Categorizing unmarried girls that way somehow encouraged a culture of minimizing the competition through the rumor mill system. Every young woman past the age of puberty slowly developed an imaginary scorecard showing where she stood socially based on four major criteria. First on the list was chastity and virginity; second, her public behavior and modesty; third, her ability to display a family garden that was green, lush, and flowering; and fourth, how well she ironed the family's clothes. Eliza excelled in all of them except for the inherited stain from her adulteress mother, whom she had come to loathe.

Carlota's bad reputation left a deep scar on the young Eliza, and the village women were often unkind. But what she lost in social status, she more than made up in beauty. In time, her simple gracefulness and humility disarmed most of the girls who would have otherwise been bitterly envious of her. Her budding sexuality also had the boys lining up to win her favor, although the last thing on her mind was romance, let alone sexual contact of any sort.

It was with such weapons of beauty and propriety that Eliza Cervantes caught the eye of the handsome and hormone-laden Ramiro.

Eliza did not have much of a traditional feast on her fifteenth birthday, as might have been expected of a *quinceañera*, because of the family's destitute condition; nevertheless, her father, Santos, insisted on having a coffee social for her. He invited all the young people of the village and beyond, as was the custom. It was a simple affair, basically a *merienda* of coffee, hot chocolate, tamales, and cookies. All of it prepared by the birthday girl herself. There was music courtesy of her brother who could play the accordion, so the young people were able to dance to *norteño* tunes. Intermittently, there were songs from a transistor radio. Everyone's favorites were on the XEW station, and there were no *novelas* on a Sunday afternoon to interrupt the music.

Some of the more extroverted guests started sing-alongs, which were common at the time, as everyone enjoyed shared tastes in music. Before the evening was done, Ramiro dedicated Eliza a love song in a clumsy attempt to woo her. The song was "Adelita."—"*Si Adelita quisiera ser mi novia; si Adelita fuera mi mujer, le compraria un vestido de seda para llevarla a pasear al cuartel.*"

Eliza made the cookies herself as she was gifted in the kitchen. She had already earned a reputation as a great cook, and her humble sugar and cinnamon pastries were always a hit with whoever ate them. Far from playing the role of princess, however, the shy Eliza assumed an attitude of reluctant but gracious hostess to her friends. Deep down she secretly cherished the special day in celebration of her birthday. It was the only birthday party she had ever had.

On the day of the celebration, Ramiro was the first to arrive. He had groomed his best horse, and put on his Sunday best. His hair was slick with Brilliantine, and his shoes were shined especially for the occasion. He splashed orange blossom water on his face and sucked on cloves to freshen his breath. He brought with him a gift of a box of coconut cookies that he hoped would please this girl that had him so smitten. He had guessed they were Eliza's favorite cookies because his family's store was where everyone did their shopping. On rare occasions Eliza bought twenty cents worth of coconut cookies, and Ramiro had heard Doña Lupita say that she believed they were a special treat for Eliza herself.

§

All of these images traversed her brain in an instant, she thought, and yet it seemed her dream state was never ending for suddenly, she was swept into darkness once more, and Eliza found herself in a struggle to fight off an attacker. She scratched at his powerful arms and hands. The stranger gripped her wrists and attempted to tear off her clothes. He lunged his face into her neck, and his hot breath produced goose bumps of disgust all over her skin. Her attempts at screaming only choked her throat. All around her was complete blackness. She could not see his face no matter how she strained to look. She attempted to scream, to call out for help, but she was choking. Eliza was suffocating and writhing in fear when she got a strong whiff of orange blossom water.

It was Ramiro! She was horrified.

§

Eliza bolted up in bed for what she at first believed was a second time. She trembled and held her dizzying head in her palms. But it was only the first time she awakened. She had been dreaming the entire time. Her mouth was dry and still agape in silent shriek. Her face was sweaty, and ringlets of wet hair clung to her cheeks and neck. After a minute she regained her composure. She hated that recurring nightmare of childhood humiliation over her mother's horrid betrayal.

But this dream was different. She had never before seen Ramiro attempting to rape her in those dreams.

Ramiro was a passionate man. He partook of his husband's rights to her body freely and often, but he had never been violent in their lovemaking. Her thoughts raced, grasping for the present. She scanned the room and saw her children sleeping peacefully. The rooster crowed outside. Then she remembered Ramiro's recent departure. Their last embrace and kisses had been tender and teary. Why would she dream of him attacking her?

Eliza calmed herself by sitting in bed, hugging her knees and taking deep breaths. She looked at the pillow beside her and thought about the missing Ramiro. Her mind tried to imagine where about he might be in his journey north, but she had no concept of the geography or the distance he had traveled, much less what might be the sights and sounds of the foreign land that he now occupied. She tried to go back to sleep, but the early rooster began to crow. She thought it best to simply get an early start on that day. She got dressed and stoked the dying embers in the kitchen chimney.

CHAPTER 7: *Ravioli*

R amiro waited impatiently on the front porch of the old
boardinghouse that evening. He had visited that porch
repeatedly in stints of one to three minutes, ignoring the
40-degree temperatures, since five o'clock that afternoon.
Sometimes he sat down on the old wicker sofa or on the steps. Sometimes he paced till Mary shouted at him to step more lightly. Sometimes he walked down the sidewalk. All the time, he looked one way
then another, up and down the street.

He saw countless cars drive by and a number of pedestrians rushing home in bulky winter coats and mufflers. He made note of some
that he guessed were probably neighbors, and he scrutinized others
to gauge their styles or personalities. He tried greeting each, sometimes with a cheery "*Buenas tardes*," but found that what was a custom
of civility and politeness in his homeland was not exactly practiced
in Chicago.

He followed each car visually to try to detect what features he remembered from Daniel's car, which would be depositing Nico and the
guys any minute. He knew that Nico would not arrive till past 5:30,
yet he felt compelled to wait outside to greet him first thing. He had
to know right away if John had agreed to give him another chance in
the yard.

It was a quarter to six when the car with the white hood and
damaged grill pulled up. Ramiro grinned and waved with two out-

stretched arms. The sun had set almost an hour before, but it was still light enough to see Nico's poker face step out of the car. Ramiro's butterflies bumped his stomach as he studied Nico's demeanor and detected no spark of promise. The other guys exited the car and rushed into the house. Nico was last. He waved at Ramiro but seemed in no hurry to meet him, as the others had done. The man walked towards Ramiro, palms out and shoulders shrugged in a sign of "I did what I could," implying he had failed.

"Hello, *compadre*. I've been waiting for you," Ramiro said cheerfully but as matter-of-factly as he could so as not to betray his anxiousness. Having seen Nico's gestures, he braced for the bad news even as he feigned coolness.

"I see, *compadre*. I know why, too. Let me guess. You want to know what happened at the yard today. You want to know if John forgave you and is willing to give you another chance." He spoke in somber tones as if exhausted. Those words only intensified Ramiro's fears and anxiety. Finally, Nico couldn't hold back any longer, and he burst out laughing.

"The answer is yes!" he said, raising a victory fist in the air, and he laughed some more as he rushed Ramiro with a bear hug. "You're back on my shift, buddy!"

"Well, I'll be damned. You were screwing with me. Making me think you had bad news." Then he play-punched his buddy in the stomach and put him in a headlock. They both hugged and laughed some more.

"You should have seen your face. Playing it cool, huh? You're forgiven as far as John goes, but you have to prove yourself in the next couple of weeks. You start back tomorrow, so your vacation is up, eh?" Nico continued as they walked into the place, both friends beaming from the good news.

From behind the screen door, Mary had watched the whole scene, and she smiled at the guys' banter. She returned to the kitchen just as they started toward the door.

Ramiro promised Nico that he would be an exemplary employee, but Nico told him to not promise him anything. "Give all your thanks and promises to John tomorrow when you go in to work." As they stepped downstairs to dinner, promptly at 7:00, following the house rules, the guys continued their banter then switched to talk about the smells coming from the kitchen.

"Mmmmm, something sure smells good," said Ramiro. "I don't recognize that smell but I like it. I wonder what Mary has cooked up."

As if on cue, Mary announced to the troop, "It's ravioli tonight, boys."

The aroma of food that emanated from a large pot on the stove was something unusual to Ramiro. "Another new thing," he said to himself. Soon all the guys were lined up, plate in hand, to serve themselves from the big pot and a second, smaller one. At the end of the line was a loaf of Sunbeam bread split open so the boarders could help themselves with ease. Ramiro filled his plate with the ravioli in the first pot then scooped some sort of mixed vegetables from the second pot, spread them over the ravioli, and, finally, he grabbed two slices of bread. Some of the guys grabbed up to six slices of bread, and Ramiro thought, "fatsos," and laughed in silence.

As Ramiro served himself, Mary was milling about with various duties and pleasantries for the men. Ramiro reached out to replace the lid on the great pot when he felt Mary's hand over his own. "Here, give me that, hon," she said, and he felt her breast brush his arm as she took hold of the lid. "I will do that after I stir in a little more sauce."

Ramiro blushed a little and looked over to where his friend was sitting, hoping that Nico hadn't noticed Mary's boldness. But Nico was only too aware of the scene he had just witnessed. He gave Ramiro a look of raised eyebrows and cow eyes then winked as if to say, "I think she likes you." Ramiro shook his head and returned the look with an expression of "No way." Ramiro then sat beside Nico, and loudly praised the food in an attempt at normality.

"Well, *Compa* Ramiro, this sure isn't a Mexican dinner, but you better get used to it. Miss Mary is all-American, and she loves Italian food." Nico teased him knowing by his body language and facial expressions that Ramiro was having a cultural experience of more than one kind.

An hour or so later, they all had eaten their fill, and Nico and Ramiro retired to their room to hit the sheets early. The rules of working labor-intensive jobs required a good night's sleep and early risers, so they were fully in sync with following that rhythm. It was nine o'clock. Tomorrow would be a great new start, thought Ramiro.

"You know, that was not so bad, that ravioli stuff. Italian, huh? You guys sure eat a lot around here, though. Did you see how much bread even Mary was eating?"

Nico laughed, "Yup. Americans eat a lot. It's a good thing because we have to work hard, but you are right, some people just eat and eat. I guess it's because there is so much food all around. America is rich and fat. Wait till we go to the supermarket. You will be astonished by the selection of things. And cheap, too," he yawned. "In a couple of weeks, you will be really impressed when you see what they eat in a holiday they call Thanksgiving."

"By the way, *Compa*, looks like Miss Mary has taken a fancy to you. What happened today while the rest of us worked and the two of you were all alone in the house?" Nico teased.

Ramiro looked at him sideways. "Nah, *Compa*, nothing happened. Of course, not. I think Miss Mary is just a friendly person. She calls everybody 'honey.' Besides she's old enough to be my mother. Even if I wasn't married, there's no way." He shook his head and laughed.

"Well, okay, buddy, if you say so. Good night, *compadre*."

"Good night" said Ramiro, catching the contagion of yawning. He lay in bed a while longer before dozing off. He thought about Mary's perfume as she rubbed up against him by the ravioli that he had enjoyed so much. He thought about Eliza back home eating dinner with the kids. Eliza never wore perfume to dinner and certainly not to cook in. Eliza wore rose water, not fancy perfumes from Chicago department stores. He wondered if Eliza would like ravioli as he drifted into sleep.

CHAPTER 8: *The Provider*

Ramiro's return to the rail yard was a great relief to him. He now felt he hadn't really lied to Eliza in his letter. He arrived that morning eager to begin work, but first he had to face John. He approached John's office with steady steps but his heart was pounding. He was trying not to give himself away as nervous or to appear to be groveling, for, although he was contrite, Ramiro was a proud man. After putting away his lunch pail, he walked towards the supervisor's area.

He caught sight of John through the large plate glass window of his office. The man greeted him with a smile that immediately relieved his tension, and he felt grateful. Somehow he trusted that John understood why things had gotten out of hand. Ramiro stepped into John's office clutching his hard hat with both hands.

"*Buenos Dias*, John," he said, extending his hand. "I want to tell you how grateful I am for this second opportunity you are giving me." Ramiro expressed his remorse and promised that John would not regret the decision. Although John only understood the general gist of Ramiro's Spanish, he took it to mean pretty much what Ramiro intended to communicate.

"Good morning, Ramiro. Mhm, aha, yes. I think I understand. Yeah, bud, Nick explained it all to me. I know you're all right. Welcome back," replied John.

John motioned to Roger, who happened to be passing by the window, probably curious as to why Ramiro was on the premises. Roger understood that he was to come into the office as well. From the look on his face, he was not pleased to see Ramiro, but the boss was not to be refused. John made both men promise that there would be no more trouble. Ramiro was eager to let bygones be bygones, so he extended Roger a hand of friendship, and he meant it. Roger seemed less eager to make up, but he relented and extended his hand as well.

Finally, John shook both their hands, patted them on the back, and dismissed them. Ramiro zipped up his jacket, secured his hardhat and wool scarf, pulled up his gloves and set out to locate his friend. Soon he joined Nico out in the windy yard, where he was clearing debris from the less-used tracks in the outskirts.

"I think we got it all cleared up. John is a good man," he told Nico.

"Yes, he is, *compa*, but I'm not so sure about guys like Roger. Bring that trash can over there and fill it with the weeds I'm pulling," he said, pointing toward a large trashcan with wheels and a handle.

He continued, "Just be careful around them. Ignore any crap they give you." He paused for a second then added, "Ramiro, some of these Chicanos are mean as hell. They are not like the guys back home. Some of these guys think nothing about hurting you just to hurt you. Back home, when a man fights, he does it for good reason and he follows an honor code. A man has to be a man and fight fair and square with his hands. Whoever loses has to be a sport about it and move on. At least that is the general rule. But these guys don't respect the rule of *mano a mano*. Some of them gang up on you. Some use dirty tricks or weapons. Be careful for hidden knives, even chains," Nico admonished.

Ramiro was perplexed. "Well, son of a bitch. That is such a pity, *compadre*. Thanks for the warning. I still believe that a man deserves the benefit of the doubt, though. I'm willing to give him that chance. We all deserve a second chance to make up for a bad first impression. But I'll keep your words in mind. You know what my father always says, *'Hombre precavido vale por dos.'*"

And so it was that Ramiro reestablished himself in the rail yard.

It was a great load off his back, and he worked vigorously all day long.

§

Two weeks later Ramiro received his first paycheck. The Friday bell rang the end of the shift, and all the men lined up to punch out and collect their check from John, who was standing by the punch clock. Ramiro took the envelope, gave John a wide grin, and hurried to the parking lot. He stood by the car and clumsily tore open the envelope. He looked at the check. It was a beautiful sight. His first paycheck in America. He almost kissed it. Instead, he rubbed it with one hand then the other as if those gestures would bring him many more future paychecks.

Ramiro looked at his name printed on the check. It looked so official and important. He looked at the little box on the right side of the paper. It said $25.00. The wages represented less than a week's worth because of the time he missed for being fired briefly. The following week's check was much better, with $35.00 in the box, including a little overtime. The men told him that the government took out some of his wages for taxes, Social Security, and some other stuff they didn't quite understand. Even giving up some of his earnings made Ramiro happy. It felt to him as though he was somehow more official, more of a contributor to civilization.

§

His homesickness became more bearable with every new paycheck. He quickly became proficient at maneuvering the American system of work and rewards. He developed his own rhythm for routines and habits to enhance his performance. His supervisors took notice and praised him for his meticulous habits and for keeping his work areas tidy and clean at all times. Ramiro was learning things about himself as a worker. He was intimidated by the big city system of formal supervision and structures for acknowledging the worker, but that only made him try harder. His boss learned that Ramiro was his most punctual worker. Every evening he arrived home beaten down from the physical exertion of the job, but he wasn't about to complain. Not that it would have done any good.

Ramiro also developed a habit of arriving early enough at the yard to have a cup of coffee and focus on his day's assignments. That bit of leisure time in the morning gave him a sense of civility and class that he had learned back home were a sign of civilization and good breeding. Sometimes that insistence on arriving early to work annoyed the carpool because Ramiro pressured Daniel to pick them up as early as possible, and there was always someone running late.

Ramiro felt himself being transformed ever so slightly by the sights and expositions of his new environment. He marveled at the lifestyles of city dwellers. How different life was in the huge metropolis. Despite his routines and good management of his affairs, he was having trouble shaking a feeling of inadequacy. He imagined himself like a small ant in a giant anthill, indistinguishable from any other ant and insignificant. Only the memories of his family gave him strength and a sense of worth. His home and family were his universe, and they were the only realm in which he could be master.

One weekend in mid-December, Ramiro was feeling more nostalgic than usual. He had been working a month now, and he realized that Christmas was fast approaching. He set about writing a letter to Eliza. Just the simple act of writing gave him a feeling of closeness to her. In the minutes that his pen engaged the paper, he could feel her heartbeat and breath at his ear.

"I love you my darling. I miss you and the kids so much. Oh, how I wish you were in my arms right now, how I wish I could smell your scent and taste your lips." He was thinking all those thoughts and more. But he wrote the words then scratched them out. That style of expressing emotion was out of character for him and the people of his region. He subdued the message to a simple "I miss you and the kids and I hope to see you sometime next year."

Ramiro's devotion to his kids was paramount. He took his responsibilities as head of the household more seriously than most men. It was part of the legacy of his parents. He especially loved babies. Something about their vulnerability and how they depended on him. Oh, how he enjoyed a bouncing baby. When his first child was born, he was ecstatic. The boy was a blessing, especially after the catastrophe of Eliza's miscarriage of their first pregnancy. A man's pride and joy was always to have a son.

He played with the baby—whom he named Baldemar after his favorite uncle—every moment he could. Ramiro bounced the baby up and down, playfully pulled its ears and toes. He even pinched and bit the child's rosy cheeks pretending they were tomatoes. Then he'd tickle the boy crazy by kissing and sputtering his belly. When he dangled the baby by one foot, Eliza had to protest, but to no avail. Ramiro only laughed that much more.

The women of the family protested that he was too rough when he threw the baby in the air only to catch him and smother him with kisses on his belly. But he dismissed them as making too much fuss over nothing. "The baby is a man and can handle the rough play." Indeed, Baldemar laughed at most every risky game Ramiro put him in.

"Ramiro, you're too rough. You're going to hurt that baby. Ramiro, be careful. For God's sake! Please, Ramiro, don't do that to his belly," the women continued to protest, even knowing it would do no good.

"Dinner will be ready in five minutes, boys!" It was Mary calling from the bottom of the stairs.

Ramiro shook himself out of his daydream about the kids and missing home. He reminded himself that he was doing all this for them. He was determined to prove to his family what he was made of. Feeling lonely was a minor thing compared to true hardships that many people experienced, he told himself. Then he dashed downstairs for one of Mary's Italian dinners.

Despite his wanting to ignore Mary, dinners had gradually become a special time, with or without Italian food. Mary's flirtation had developed into almost a game, but it was a game Ramiro felt he was about to lose. Her voice calling out for dinner made his heart skip a beat. Ah, that voice. It was melodious, feminine, joyous. It was the kind of voice that keeps a woman eternally young. Ramiro no longer looked at Mary as a peer of his mother's but as a temptress with a heart of gold. His days often included reproaching himself for having feelings that felt more and more like betrayal of his Eliza. He forced himself not to contemplate any thoughts about Mary beyond that of landlady and tenant.

§

After dinner, Ramiro counted his savings. It had been a month of paychecks, and he had managed to save a few bills. He kept the money in a sock that he stuffed into one of the brass tubes that formed part of the headboard of his twin bed. The tubes had a cap that could be screwed on and off, so he used the space as his personal safe. He took out the stash of bills from the secret compartment. He carefully counted out some ones, four fives, four tens, and one twenty-dollar bill. He had just a little over $100.00.

Ramiro's mathematical training from years as a merchant and from helping his father keep the books kicked in. He quickly converted the dollar values to pesos. He figured that at $8.50 pesos per dollar that would put him at $850.00 pesos. He was disappointed it wasn't more, but, after all, it had only been a month. He sure wanted Eliza and the kids to have the money in time for the Christmas season and the Day of the Magi.

He went over the procedures and details of where the nearest Western Union was located. Mary and Nico had given him some idea of how to get the money transferred to his wife in Naranjales. He again regretted that he did not save enough. After all, $100.00 seemed like a lot in pesos, but he wished it could be more. He scolded himself for having indulged a little too much in American comforts. Ramiro was a disciplined man, but he promised himself he would become more frugal.

He stuffed the money in an envelope and returned to his unfin-
ished letter. He wrote Eliza about the money he was sending, when to
expect it, and how to collect it. She might need the assistance of Jacobo
to go to Valle Azul, the nearest place with a Western Union office in
the local bank. He told her to wish everyone a Merry Christmas and
to greet and hug everyone who remembered him, especially his mother
and father.

It was over a year later, on his first visit home, that Ramiro learned
that his second letter hadn't reached Eliza until mid-January. The present letter had taken an additional four weeks to arrive. Eliza received
the first remittance just in time for the January 6 all-important day of
gift giving, the Day of the Magi. She would have missed out on it had
not Jacobo, knowing that Eliza was expecting money, asked about it
casually when he was doing a routine business transaction in town. All
of Ramiro's concerns about giving her notice and instructions on collecting the money went for naught as they had arrived weeks past the
actual funds. Still, Eliza and the family enjoyed teasing over the crossed
communication, and they all laughed about it years later.

CHAPTER 9: *Ramiro's Seduction*

amiro's first big excursion into the city's major department stores came just a few days before Thanksgiving. He had never heard of such a holiday, and neither Nico nor others were able to explain it to him in a way that made a lot of sense. He finally gathered that it was a long holiday for the purpose of celebrating the good fortune of America. Mary told him about the actual history of it, with the typical details of the story of Indians offering food to the pilgrims. Mary had planned a feast for the men, and she invited Ramiro and Nico on her outing to the local A&P, a gigantic supermarket the likes of which Ramiro had never seen.

"Now, Ramiro, the main feature of the Thanksgiving feast is a roasted turkey," Mary explained as they got into her 1946 Packard Station Wagon. "All the other vegetables and desserts are supposed to complement the turkey." The three chatted the rest of the drive, mostly impressing Ramiro with stories of the great variety and quantities of food available in the supermarket. Ramiro had only shopped at the neighborhood grocers' thus far, so he was intrigued with what he was about to experience.

Ramiro thought it funny that Mary had invited the two *compadres* on her shopping spree. He had become suspicious that Mary was becoming a little too fond of him, but he took it in good humor that it was just a crush that would go nowhere, knowing himself as he did.

Indeed Mary had developed a greater and greater fondness for the young new immigrant in her house, and she naturally saw Nico as an extension of the young man with whom she wanted to spend more time. Thus, she thought it prudent to invite the pair rather than just Ramiro. She gave them the excuse that Thanksgiving shopping was heavier and she was going to need help. "Besides," she said, "I think it is a great way for Ramiro to learn more about his new country and our ways."

Ramiro laughed, "Now, wait just a minute, Miss Mary. This is not my new country. I'm just here to work for a few years."

Mary dismissed his protest with a wave of her bejeweled hand and said, "That's what they all say. If you say so. But my money is on your living in America the rest of your life." Then she leaned over and kissed him playfully on the cheek, a gesture that left him stupefied for a moment. He instinctively touched his cheek then rubbed the area in search of lipstick, which he made disappear by rubbing his hands together. He then pretended that it was nothing more than a teasing moment.

It was a Sunday evening and Thanksgiving dinner would be prepared on the coming Wednesday and finished on Thursday morning. "I almost went Christmas shopping today," Mary said, "but I decided to wait for the big sales next Friday, the day after Thanksgiving. Maybe you fellas will join me for some of that experience, too." The men looked at each other in wide-eyed astonishment.

"Mary, Christmas is a long way off," said Nico. "Why would anybody go Christmas shopping so early?"

"Young man, it's never too early to shop for Christmas," she laughed. "We have to enjoy the holiday season to the fullest, and what better way than to plan early and get everything done right. Right?"

"I guess that's a good point," said Ramiro.

They arrived at the store parking lot, and, sure enough, Ramiro was mightily impressed with the size of the parking lot and the number of cars. Dozens of people moved about like ants in and out of the sliding glass doors and a number of uniformed boys assisted customers with cartsful of bags of groceries. It was a dizzying frenzy of activity and movement of products. The former grocery man was duly impressed and he thought for a minute of how his parents could possibly grow their little general store into such a behemoth of a food emporium. "This is just amazing. Stupendous," said Ramiro unable to restrain his admiration. Mary smiled proudly as if she actually had anything to do with the success of such a marketplace.

Nico was less impressed as he had seen it all already, although he could still spend hours marveling at such sights.

Inside was one revelation after another as the three traversed the many aisles of tall shelves replete with every imaginable food product, each packaged for maximum attention. The tall ceiling covered with rows and rows of long tubes of phosphorescent lights in sets of four brightened the place beyond belief. But Ramiro's favorite section was in produce. It warmed his heart to see the great variety of fresh fruits and vegetables on display. As a former grower of some such produce, he was both nostalgic and excited by the beauty of it all.

The three canvassed the entire place whether an aisle had anything Mary needed or not. Mary had a written list of items that she asked Nico to check off as she placed item after item in the shopping cart. Ramiro pushed the cart while Mary wandered about comparing brands and prices and reading labels, a practice Ramiro thought unusual and funny for it was a far cry from the way people shopped in his parents' store. There, they simply asked for a thing and it was wrapped for them. Nothing more complex than that.

§

The trio completed their shopping, including a few treats for themselves. Ramiro sucked in the many new sights and symbols related to the holiday. There were turkey posters everywhere. He loved the images of cornucopias overflowing with delicacies and fruits. There were Indians and Pilgrims at outdoor dinner tables exchanging gifts and breaking bread. He learned that pumpkin pie was a tradition, and there were pictures of pumpkins all around. Finally, they arrived home and they helped Mary put away the haul. As the two men retired to their room, Mary reminded them that they would have to repeat the trip in a few weeks for the Christmas dinner preparations.

The Thanksgiving dinner was everything Ramiro had been promised and expected. He ate to his heart's content, and Mary even allowed a little wine drinking that evening. The guys succeeding in convincing her to let them have a couple of beers, as wine was not exactly a favorite of theirs. Mary excused herself early, explaining, "Tomorrow is a big day for Christmas shopping. Everyone will be at the big stores for great sales. I have to get some sleep, so I can get an early start and not miss out on the best bargains."

Seeing Ramiro headed to the bathroom, she hurried to catch up with him and whispered, "Don't forget you promised to accompany me to the stores tomorrow. Don't stay up too late." She then pecked him on the cheek and muttered, "6:00 a.m." as she hurried to her room, leaving behind the now familiar and provocative fragrance of Chanel No. 5.

Ramiro expected Nico to be included in the plan for Christmas shopping, but his friend said, "Nope. I wasn't invited. I think she wants to spend some time alone with you" and laughed. Ramiro gave his friend a stern look of disapproval at the teasing. Secretly, however, he was glad he would be spending the day alone with Mary.

That Friday, Mary introduced Ramiro to the biggest spectacle of conspicuous consumption. He experienced a form of anxiety seeing so many amazing products and so many shoppers in what seemed to Ramiro was a competition to see who could carry off the most. They visited Montgomery Ward, Marshall Fields, Sears, and Lord & Taylor. None of the names meant anything to Ramiro, but Mary narrated a list of qualities of each department store they visited. Ramiro couldn't believe the stamina Mary displayed on that day because he was exhausted after going through just a couple of the giant stores.

But the most memorable of things that Black Friday was how much fun he was having just being around Mary. She sometimes walked too close to him intoxicating him with her perfume. She held his hand or wrapped her arm around his when crossing streets or if a cold wind blew in a parking lot. She thanked him for small courtesies with a caress of his face or a peck on the cheek. When they paused for lunch, she insisted on treating him, and then they shared a strawberry milkshake by drinking out of the same glass with two straws. Ramiro alternated between thoughts of relating all the new sights to Eliza and his folks and forgetting about everything except Mary's attentions. His growing fantasies of Mary made him feel shame. He swore to himself that after today he would keep his distance.

The next day Mary was putting up the Christmas tree. Ramiro and Nico, stepping in from an errand outside, saw her lifting a box of ornaments and volunteered to help. She accepted gladly. Ramiro wondered if it wasn't too early for a tree, but Mary told him "Oh, no, not too early. I love the season so much. I can't wait to decorate the whole house now that Thanksgiving is over."

Ramiro told her, "Back home we didn't do much decorating. No one wants to spend precious resources on such frivolity." To which Mary arched her eyebrow and gave him a sideways glance to kill.

"What I mean, Mary," Ramiro quickly added, "is that I am enjoying decorating with you because I never had this growing up. It's a new experience for me. Just tell me what to do." Mary smiled and reached out to touch his shoulder.

"Here, hang this up over the archway," she told him, handing him a branch of mistletoe.

"And what the heck is this piece of weed?" he said laughing.

"Never mind," she said. "Just put it up. I'll tell you another day." She winked and shoved him playfully in the direction of the door.

§

The days flew by turning into weeks, and in no time Christmas Eve was upon them.

Several of the guys were able to leave town for the holiday, so the house was half empty. Ramiro being the new guy at the yard was nowhere close to having earned any vacation time, so he had to work long shifts and even double shifts. He didn't mind it because it meant more money for his savings although he came home dead tired every day. He spent little time at the house until Christmas Eve day, when everyone was given two days off. He went down for dinner that evening, and discovered that Mary had prepared a feast similar to her Thanksgiving meal. At the table were Mary, Nico, a couple of the other guys, and Ramiro.

Ramiro was taken by the elegance of the evening, starting with how stunning Mary looked. She wore a sparkly red gown, which showed off her ample cleavage and held up by two thin strings of red silk. Her creamy beige complexion shined healthy despite her years, and her face was made up to resemble a Hollywood star. She looked like a mature Rita Hayworth, with her shoulder length hair, newly colored a reddish auburn and in perfectly coifed waves. She greeted every new arrival with a hug and escorted him to the table. Ramiro took in all her radiance as she approached him, then he felt a brush of her hair in his face and the invasion of her fragrance. He thought he would swoon, but he looked up at the men to simulate coolness despite what he was feeling. He had not expected such a transformation, although he had come to expect allure from her.

After dinner everyone helped out with cleaning up the kitchen then moved into the living room, drinking wine or beer. Mary took pleasure in retelling the men about American Christmas traditions. As she was a little tipsy, she even sang some Christmas carols for them and translated their meaning. Her animation and fantastic appearance kept the men entranced.

"Hey, Mary," said Ramiro, "so when are you gonna tell us about that weed I put up atop the archway?"

"Oh, that. I did tell you I would explain what it was, didn't I? Well, it is a tradition that whoever stands under the mistletoe—that's what that weed is, mistletoe—whoever stands under it gets to be kissed by anyone who happens to be nearby," Mary explained with a twinkle in her eye and a sway in her body as she stood before the fireplace where several red stockings hung. "So boys," she said as she strode over to the doorway, "I'm standing under the mistletoe. No one's gonna kiss me?"

The guys looked at each other in amusement and a who's-gonna-go-first-face and they almost leaped out of their chairs. Nico fixed his eyes on Ramiro, who was standing nearest the door. Ramiro hesitated for a moment, then, helped along by the effects of the beer, he lunged at Mary and kissed her hard on the lips.

Mary fought him off, and slapped him. "Wait, wait just a minute, Mister. Not like that. That's for sweethearts only. We do it on the cheek." The other guys groaned in disappointment because they all had in mind to do exactly what Ramiro had just done.

Ramiro stood back, hurt at Mary's rejection, as he perceived it. He held his hand to his cheek where Mary had slapped him. He was confused because he had become convinced that she was dying for a kiss from him. *"What had all that flirting been about, anyway?"* he thought. He was so consumed in his rage at her overreaction that he hardly noticed the other men following through and kissing Mary's cheek then she kissing theirs.

The party ended shortly after that. Ramiro didn't say much the rest of the evening. Nico was the first to retire. The other two friends followed suit, but Ramiro stepped outside to the coldness of the front porch to watch the crisp night and the Christmas lights of the neighboring houses. His thoughts were about Mary at first, and he felt anger then relief that she had pushed him away so violently. It meant he could relax around her and see her simply as a natural tease. He would not be tempted anymore to be unfaithful to Eliza. Then he recalled the Christmas traditions of his hometown and good times with his family. He wondered if the money he'd sent had arrived and how his parents were treating his wife and kids.

After a while the cold began to sting, and he turned to reenter the house. It was then that the front door opened and Mary appeared.

She stepped outside to join him. She had changed into sleeping clothes with her usual heavy housecoat over her silk pajamas, no longer the stunning figure in red gown, high heels, and poster girl face. She gave him no time to say a word before she was upon him. She kissed him passionately, her breath sweet with wine. Her hands were tight around his neck then roaming all over his body.

Ramiro was startled for a second and started to protest but gave in before he knew what he was doing. He returned every kiss, every caress, and every passion. He had been starving to make love to Eliza, but now any woman would do. And Mary was not just any woman. She was better. Mary became the vessel to unload the repression of all the long, lonely weeks. He raged to possess her and he let himself be led by her into the house and into her bedroom.

The next day was a Monday. The whole city was home for Christmas. Everyone slept in at the boarding house on Laramie Street. Ramiro awoke at 10:00 a.m. to see Nico putting on his shirt to get ready for breakfast. "Buenos dias, *compa*," said Ramiro.

"Mas buenos para algunos que pa otros" ("Better for some than for others,") said Nico, finishing buttoning his shirt and looking at Ramiro with a combination of admiration and condemnation. "I don't think anyone is downstairs yet, but I'm going to make me some breakfast. Let Miss Mary sleep in this morning. Can I make you some, too?" he asked.

Ramiro looked sheepishly away from his friend. "Yeah, sure. Thanks, *compa*. Now, don't go getting any ideas. Nothing happened," he said in reference to the sarcasm in Nico's voice.

"*Compa*, I wasn't born yesterday. I'm your buddy. Who do you think you're fooling? I'm just saying, be careful, huh? I don't want any trouble for you, my friend," said Nico. "But if you go and try to play some game with me, play me for a sucker, I'm going to lose respect for you."

Ramiro turned three shades of red and looked down to the floor. "You're right, buddy. I messed up last night. I promise it won't happen again. I don't know how I lost control and let it happen. I feel awful about it. It won't happen again," he repeated as if trying to convince himself.

The days and weeks that followed were awkward.

Christmas night Mary motioned him to visit her room. When he got there, he blurted out, "Mary what happened last night was a mistake, I love my wife very much. I can't do this." He told her that he shouldn't have played with her emotions, that he took full responsibility, but it shouldn't happen again, ever.

Mary just looked at him and let him unload everything that was in his heart. She seemed defeated. She smiled wanly and promised him that she would be all right, not to worry. She assured him that she was fully aware of his love for his wife and that she would not allow him or herself to damage a good family bond. Ramiro thanked her, and he felt greatly relieved that she was so understanding. When she walked him to the door, however, he closed it almost violently and took her in his arms as his tongue searched for hers in a deep, hungry kiss. He carried her to the bed and both lovers tore off their clothes in a mad frenzy.

Only a week had gone by, and on New Year's Eve the scene repeated itself, what with the alcohol and all. The two unlikely lovers continued their affair sporadically because Ramiro's guilt became too unbearable and he feared slipping into complacency and a full-blown affair. After each encounter that occurred weekly or every other week, Ramiro would spend sleepless nights consumed with guilt and shame. Even his work began to suffer when John noticed that his reliable laborer was looking haggard and sometimes forgetful. Nico noticed it first, but he only repeated, "Be careful, buddy. End it as soon as you can."

A week before Valentine's Day, Ramiro made up his mind that his will power would have to be steeled. He spoke with Mary once again, and told her that this time it was definite. No more playing around. He would be faithful to his wife from now on and forever more. It was all he could do not to burst into tears and take refuge in Mary's perfumed bosom that he loved so much, but he managed to stay strong and firm.

This time when she walked him to the door, he walked through it and didn't look back.

When Valentine's Day came around, Ramiro made it a point to show his strength by not buying Mary any token of love, and he "respectfully" returned a gift she had left under his pillow. Much as he suffered temptation and wanted to give free rein to his passions, he kept his word and controlled himself. He remained polite and kind to Mary, but he avoided direct contact or alone time with her at all costs. On his days off he wandered off to walk the parks, admire the skyscrapers, or sun himself at the lake while writing letters to Eliza.

CHAPTER 10: *California Dreaming*

oon after Valentine's Day, a letter arrived for Ramiro from a cousin in Naranjales. Ramiro's cousin, Salomon Aguilar was a hard-working man. He had obtained green cards for his family in 1945, and they had been trekking to the California vineyards ever since. Their dedication and frugality had allowed Salomon to buy land, cattle, and equipment to run his little farm, just outside Naranjales. That winter of 1951 would mark the family's sixth journey to work in the fruited valley surrounding Fresno. It was time once again to head to the farmlands of California that would soon be ready for tending, then harvesting. Salomon gathered his clan of six: two boys, two girls, his wife, and himself, and loaded everyone into the station wagon.

This was a hearty, robust family. The boys were strapping, muscular young men, able to outrun most of their peers and able to out-pick most any migrant who challenged them. They were seventeen and sixteen. The girls were less athletic but just as sturdy and able to work the long hot days of California summers. They were fourteen and thirteen. All four of the Aguilar kids worked in the fields. They were close-knit and disciplined. The boys had no bad habits other than spending their spare time working out on weightlifting equipment. Their mother Elva stayed home, but her work never allowed for a moment of relaxation. She attended to all the preparations of making sure the five workers were well fed, wore clean clothes, and had a pleasant place to come home to. Some might say hers was the toughest job of all.

Ramiro respected them because they were a united family. Few others could equal their prowess in handling buckets of grapes, bushels of cucumbers, peach-pruning shears, wooden ladders, sacks of oranges, you name it. Basically, the Aguilar family was of the highest exemplar of migrant families. They could handle all the implements of the well-rounded farm worker, but, more important, they never squandered, never fought, and always shared in their goals and vision of procuring for their pastoral homestead. Salomon was a second cousin but family just the same, and thus a source of pride for Ramiro as much as role model.

Ramiro held the piece of paper tightly in his hands as a thousand thoughts crossed his mind. *"Dear Cousin Ramiro: I hope this letter reaches you in a timely fashion and finds you in good health. As for us, we are fine..."* Salomon wrote. He had spent the winter in Naranjales, and visited with Lupita, Timoteo, and the family. Lupita hinted to him that Ramiro might be better off in California than Chicago.

Salomon wrote Ramiro the letter a few days later, inviting him to join him and the family in Orange Cove, California. *"The sooner the better, but try not to wait past April or the crews could all fill up. There are more and more migrants every year eager to harvest,"* he said in the letter.

Ramiro finished reading the letter aloud. *"I hope you will consider joining me and my family down there in California. Sincerely, your cousin who wishes you well always, Salomon."* He sat at the edge of the bed for almost an hour mulling over all sorts of thoughts that Salomon had inspired in him. Sunshine, farm life, friendly faces, family, good money, warmth. He put the letter away and decided to wait till the weekend to reply while he weighed the pros and cons of the decision. Salomon's letter included a California phone number to call. He could be reached there after the first of March.

Ramiro spent the night in a restless state. The thought of moving to California just when he was getting used to Chicago and the rail yard was troubling his mind. He had to make a decision, but it was not an easy thing for him.

The next morning he had his breakfast—now hurried and quiet because of his discomfort around Mary—then he waited on the porch for the arrival of his ride. He got to work and was given extra hours, which he always welcomed for the time-and-a-half pay.

By sunset he found himself helping out on a late arrival along with his friend Tommy. Then tragedy struck.

Tommy should not have been there, as his shift had ended. But he wanted to give the fellows a hand due to a last-hour load of work. The train had arrived unexpectedly late. It would have to be left to the next crew, but then the new guys would have been backlogged. The current crew could at least get it started. Tommy was the first to volunteer.

Ramiro stood on a dock emptying out barrels of debris when he heard the incoming late train. He looked up to see Tommy and a couple of other guys rush the train, as was the norm. Tommy was attempting to hop on the arriving train. Ramiro watched in amusement and admiration at the hard-working young man.

The track was built on ground that had been elevated by some two feet. There was an embankment of loose, small, sharp rocks on both sides of the track. The train was moving at an unusually high speed. Tommy was one of a half dozen, or so, crew members, who were ready to pounce on the train and start checking off the list of things to inspect. Dusk was fast encroaching, so Ramiro strained his eyes to catch the flurry of activity. As the train approached, he saw Tommy flick off a cigarette butt to prepare to jump on. But the wind blew the still-burning tobacco almost into Tommy's face, and he had to dodge it. That threw off his precision, and he lost his footing just as he was about to jump onto the ladder of the last car of the train that was backing up.

That's when it happened: Tommy's slip on the loose rocks was enough to thwart a successful jump. His foot kicked out a small gush of gravel as he fell forward landing partially on the track. The train struck his head. Ramiro yelled a loud anguished cry of "Tooooooommmmyyyyy!" His heart pounded fiercely in his chest as if his whole torso would explode. But he stood frozen by the horror he had just witnessed.

Tommy was lucky to not have been decapitated, but the impact crushed his skull even as he was hurtled aside onto the rocky embankment. After a minute Ramiro caught his senses and rushed to his friend's side. He fought his way through the small crowd that had already gathered around Tommy. The rocks where he landed had torn up Tommy's body even further.

His death was almost instantaneous. At least everyone hoped so because no one could bear to imagine Tommy suffering the pain and agony of such a bloody accident.

An ambulance arrived quickly, and Ramiro stood stupefied for a long time before Nico approached him and guided him to the car. Ramiro was glad it had become dark enough that no one could see the sadness in his face or the welling up of tears in his eyes. He felt drained of all energy.

§

On the ride home, all Ramiro could say was "Poor Tommy," and his mind would drift away from everything. No one could change the subject or speak of anything pleasant for fear of appearing insensitive. Ramiro kept replaying the scene in his head. He wished he had never seen it and that he was far away from this cold and tragic city. Tommy's death left him shaken all week long, and as he pondered his cousin's invitation to California, it was Tommy's death that seemed to push him to leave.

The idea to leave Chicago and the rail yard somehow became easier after Tommy's accident. Ramiro started to feel excited about the prospect of going to work in the fields, which he loved, but in weighing the possibility of moving out west he also couldn't help but recognize that it wasn't just the allure of the sunny state and the open fields that mattered so much. It was also that he had never felt quite at ease in Chicago. The city was not really for him. The work at the rail yard had been grueling, and the city's harsh winter had not helped things.

Perhaps it was simply a matter of his associating the city with the loneliness he felt over his family.

One evening he sat on his bed reading once again Salomon's letter when Nico walked into the room. "Hey, buddy. Damn, you sure look like a man in another world. What's the matter?"

Ramiro reacted by springing out of bed and tucking the letter from Salomon into his back pocket. "Not much, *compadre*. I was just thinking about Tommy. What a damn shame."

"Oh, yeah. Damn shame about Tommy," said Nico. "Don't think about it too much, huh? It's not good for you," he added. "I'm starving. It's ravioli night. You coming down?"

"I'll be down in a few," Ramiro said. "Don't think about Tommy too much," he repeated Nico's words. But how could he not? Ramiro and Tommy had developed a unique friendship.

Actually, it was Tommy who had befriended Ramiro early on. Tommy had been sitting at what Ramiro's crew called the "gringo table" the day Ramiro and Roger got into the scuffle. Tommy had observed how Ramiro was provoked. He felt compassion for his novice coworker, as it was clear that Roger was bullying the new guy. Tommy was one of those souls possessed of a great sense of right and wrong, and he often was protective of underdogs and of victims of injustice.

Soon after Ramiro's return, Tommy approached him during a brief morning break and offered the immigrant a cigarette, "Hey buddy. How's it going?"

Ramiro smiled and waved his hand in decline of the proffered item, as he had never been a smoker. Tommy shrugged and offered a pack of Wrigley's spearmint gum, instead. With a gesture of salute to indicate "thank you," Ramiro felt an instant connection with the young man of red-hair, easy smile, and navy, wool peacoat. He extended a hand of friendship to Tommy then returned to his duties.

The unlikely friendship grew when the two continued to greet each other warmly whenever they crossed paths. Occasionally, one or the other initiated a playful exchange of humor communicated mainly by gestures and ending with a laugh and a slap on the shoulder. One time the two friends made everyone laugh when Ramiro tried to tell Tommy a joke about a donkey, a parrot, and a nun. First, Ramiro told the entire joke in Spanish, and he then doubled over in laughter, but Tommy stood looking at him smiling as if to say, "I have no idea what you are laughing about." So Ramiro tried retelling the joke in mime that Tommy responded to as if it were a game of charades. That part proved even more hilarious to all the workers watching.

It was a story about two jungle explorers who picked up a beautiful parrot as they traveled through the mountains by donkey. As the men went past a waterfall, one of them complained, "This damn drizzle. It doesn't wet you but it sure fucks with you." Then at some point one of the donkeys sat down and refused to go any further. The men tried pulling and yelling to no avail, until one of them says to the other, "I bet a good poke in the ass will get 'er up." And sure enough they were up and going again. When they returned to town, the men took the parrot to the church to get the parrot blessed in the tradition of good Catholics. When the priest sprinkled the holy water on the bird, the parrot squealed, "This damn drizzle. It doesn't wet you, but it sure fucks with you." At such vile language, a nun that stood near by gave a scream and fainted. Everyone gathered around her to try and bring her to. Then they hear the parrot say, "I bet a good poke in the ass will get her up."

It took an entire lunch break to tell the joke, and finally Ramiro had to give up and let someone translate it for Tommy. Tommy laughed heartily and shook his head even as he admired Ramiro's determination to finish his joke. Occasionally the two friends shared part of their lunches—a cookie, a bag of chips, a taco. And they exchanged awkward phrases and gestures to communicate about the weather or to cooperate on a given task.

One day the men broke for lunch and Ramiro noticed Tommy started to head over to sit with him. Ramiro was at his usual place where Nico and his other immigrant buddies gathered. When Tommy approached the table everyone fell silent and looked at him with suspicion. Tommy gave an awkward glance at his friend then looked around at the various tables as if to survey where he should go instead. He turned around and went to his usual place at a table filled with the Caucasian workers. Ramiro started to call him back, but a coworker gently held his arm as if to say, "Let it go." Ramiro looked around and for the first time saw a vivid picture of ethnic and racial division among the workers. He accepted that there were differences among the races, ethnicities, and cultures because even back home there were certain affinities of that nature. He simply shrugged his shoulders, but he felt uncomfortable about it and resented that his friend was turned away.

Chicago had been a magnet for workers of many cultural, ethnic, and foreign backgrounds back in those days. Ramiro took particular notice of the black men because he had never been around black people until arriving in Chicago. They were such a novelty to him simply because of their distinctive features. The blacks also seemed to hold a special place in American society, he thought, a place of inferiority that touched his heart.

The Caucasians were a different story. But for the profusion of blue eyes, they looked very similar to his people back home, especially the dark haired ones. His community of Naranjales was a northern Mexico community, primarily composed of descendants of European peasant stock, with perhaps less than half being of Mestizo heritage. In his region of Mexico, there had never been more than a few scattered families of indigenous looks or manner. Folks like his family tended to look down on the Indians as somehow less civilized. They sometimes mocked the Indian sing-song-y-ness of their speech or the native way of phrasing things. He intuitively transposed that phenomenon to the new society in his effort to comprehend the dynamics of the people around him.

Ramiro's limited education and exposure to the world prevented him from knowing about the history of slavery or Jim Crow in America. He also lacked understanding of the Chicano struggles over the century since the Guadalupe Hidalgo Treaty was signed, giving the

United States almost half of Mexico in what was now the western United States and Texas, although he did know that Texas and lots of other land had once belonged to Mexico. After all, such tidbits of history were common knowledge in Mexico.

Still, Tommy was special to him. Tommy was clearly in a category of his own. Although the other Caucasians were never particularly rude or troublesome to Ramiro, Tommy actually made overtures of friendship toward him. Tommy was a good guy, and Ramiro considered him a friend.

That's why Tommy's tragedy had him in a daze of confusion regarding his decision to stay or leave Chicago.

Ramiro began to recall the accident as he had done too often since it happened. The memory tended to affect him deeply. He behaved stoically on the outside but inside he felt a hollowing out. In his culture death was a serious thing. It required complete and deep respect. A friend, or even an acquaintance, was mourned almost as reverently as a blood relative. He considered Tommy such a friend, who might have been like a brother, just as Nico was, were it not for the language barriers. As he relived those moments, sitting there on the edge of his bed, Ramiro made his decision. He would leave Chicago and move to Orange Cove, California.

But if truth be told, Ramiro's decision was not only about Tommy. He had grown increasingly despondent at his temptation with Mary, and his guilt for having cheated on Eliza consumed him. Secretly, his decision to leave Chicago was as much or more due to Mary. Mary represented a constant reminder of his sin, but she also represented continued temptation. He had tried to convince himself that Mary was too old, that she wasn't attractive enough, that she didn't deserve him because she was too worldly, but no amount of Mary bashing could stop his burning for her touch. Leaving Chicago would put all his perturbations to rest.

He would leave the first of March.

CHAPTER 11: *Westward Ho!*

"Hey, Ramiro, look up there. Atop of the hill, that shiny light. I bet you anything it's a burger place. I'm starving. We gotta stop there," Martin pointed toward the horizon where the sun was setting behind a mountain.

"Sure thing, Martin. I'm hungry too, and so tired of driving. Let's eat and get a room somewhere. We can't drive through the night in this condition. We've been on the road fourteen hours straight. Besides, look at that scenery. Let's stretch our legs and take in all this beauty," said Ramiro.

They were crossing Colorado. The time was almost 7:00 p.m. The two men had been on the road since 5:00 a.m. It had been an ordeal for Ramiro because saying goodbye to his great friend Nico had been painful. Ramiro hated goodbyes. His *compadre* had tried to talk him out of moving, but Ramiro's mind was made up, and there was no changing it. Ramiro hoped that Nico would understand in time.

The goodbye to the guys at the rail yard was just as tough. Ramiro thanked John and apologized for leaving. He hugged all his new friends and told them he hoped to see them again. Finally, there was Mary. Saying goodbye to Mary was the hardest. Even without the layers of emotion of estranged lovers it would have been tough to say goodbye to her. There was just something more tender about a woman's sad face and trembling hug that touched Ramiro. Miss Mary the landlady and Ramiro the immigrant had grown beyond fond of each other, and he would remember her all his life.

"I'm going to miss you, Ramiro. Good luck out there, and be careful on the long roads. Tell your wife that a lady in Chicago thinks she is very lucky to have you," Mary told him as she held his hands and looked into his eyes trying to hold back tears.

"I sure will, Mary. I will never forget you. I hope your life is long and this house makes you happy always." He hugged her one more time, not wanting to ever let go, but he mustered all his will to release her after a few seconds. He pecked her on the cheek and rushed away.

Martin had announced to everyone at the boarding house a month earlier that California was calling him, too, and he needed to escape the Northern winters that he detested so much. It was a lucky break for Ramiro. Martin just happened to be one of the few migrants who had plunked down some money to buy a used car. The car was a five-year-old jalopy, a 1946 Plymouth Deluxe coupe. Martin had a passion for mechanics, so he kept it up well. The men agreed that the jalopy could handle the long trip. The thing was big and roomy inside, too, so it would be a comfortable ride.

Ramiro was not so sure he had much in common with Martin because the two had had only minor interaction with each other, but out there in the cold winds of Chicago any paisano quickly formed alliances with his fellow migrants. Martin had been a casual acquaintance of Ramiro's even back in Naranjales, but they had never gotten close. Ramiro had always been critical of Martin's somewhat flashy style, so he tended to avoid intimacies.

Martin had been one of the early leavers. He beat out most others by some four years, so he was better acclimated to the lifestyle of the United States. It bothered Ramiro that Martin acted as if his seniority in the country somehow gave him authority over the newcomers. It also bothered Ramiro that Martin openly flirted with Mary. He pretended that it was not about jealousy. After all, Mary had assured him that he was the only one. Martin had a wife and four boys back home, and Ramiro had a hunch the guy was not faithful to his wife nor devoted enough to his boys. Never mind that he had his own minor slip on record, but Ramiro justified his mistake as brief and over forever. All of these things made Ramiro uneasy in this new partnership, but he hoped it would all work out in the end.

The two men committed to the trip, and each agreed to pay for half the gas and other unexpected expenses they might incur on such a long sojourn. They shook hands on it. First order of business: learn to read a road map of this vast country.

"Mmmm. I was just getting used to the hotdogs of Chicago, but this hamburger is even better. I'm glad they have these burger stands just about everywhere," Martin mumbled as he wolfed down a Beltbuster.

"Save room for that beauty," Ramiro replied as he pointed to a magnificent picture of a banana split. "Although to be honest, I much prefer tacos to all this white bread stuff. Good ole tortillas made of fresh corn and just the right seasoning on the chopped beef. Now that's flavor."

Martin laughed. "I love me a hamburger anytime. No more tacos. You're right about that banana dessert, though."

Soon both friends were indulging in "the works," with a fresh banana sliced down the middle, and on top, whipped cream, pecan pieces, and three cherries. This was something they'd never find in Naranjales.

Next door to the Dairy Queen was a small motel with a large neon sign in blues and reds. The sign read, "Mountain View Motel, vacancy." They split the cost of a room for the night, and got much needed rest. Before dawn, they were on their way again.

§

Ramiro and Martin arrived on the outskirts of Fresno at three o'clock in the morning. They had been traveling cross-country on Route 66 then onto Highway 15. At Barstow, California, they took 58 up to Bakersfield where they switched to Highway 99 to get to Fresno.

At every turn, they argued about what exactly the map said, and they made wrong turns that sometimes took them half an hour to correct. From Fresno it would be a matter of a half hour before arriving at Orange Cove.

It was late, and they were exhausted, but they had decided to plow through no matter what. They couldn't wait to begin their new adventure. When they arrived at Salomon's house, they parked on the street and slept in the car so as not to wake everyone up. The loud engine of a Ford Deluxe woke them up. It was the station wagon the Aguilar men were warming up to go to work. It was five o'clock in the morning. They must have slept no more than an hour.

Ramiro got out of the car and greeted Salomon and the boys. It was a warm embrace with much backslapping and welcome gestures. Martin followed Ramiro and the men greeted him warmly, too. Salomon invited the men in for breakfast but told them that he and the kids were about to leave for the peach orchards. Ramiro and Martin accepted the breakfast offer, and Salomon delayed his departure for a little while, as he was usually half an hour early in getting to the fields. He gave the men an address just two blocks over where they could find lodging for Martin. Salomon offered Ramiro a place in one of the boys' rooms, but Ramiro thought it more prudent to get a room of his own in the rooming house, too.

In the back of his mind, Ramiro was thinking that he wouldn't want a man alone housed under the same roof with Eliza, so why should Salomon be any different. Where they came from, men never trusted other men around their wives alone, so it was customary to play it safe to avoid temptation. Salomon told him he understood and for the two men to get plenty of rest so tomorrow they could start to work if they wished.

California made Ramiro's heart glad. Everywhere he looked there were reminders of home. There were the open roads, never congested, and the smallness of the town gave him comfort. It felt welcoming and healthy, yet it was much better than home if only because it sported all the utilities for modern living. The houses were simple dwellings but each complete and comfortable unlike back home, where every other house seemed less than finished or certainly lacked the comforts of running water, indoor toilets, and electricity.

It was a beautiful California morning of bright, expansive skies, sunshine, and cool breezes. Ramiro and Martin took their respective rooms in the back of a large, square house of beige stucco exterior. The rooms included a kitchenette, which would come in handy to prepare their own meals rather than eating out. The windows were large and had elaborate ironwork although it was all plain and cheaply made. All in all, the accommodations were satisfactory, and, compared to the freezing temperatures of Chicago, this sunshine and open spaces were almost like back home. "I'm going to like it here," Ramiro said as he flopped onto his new bed. And so it was that Ramiro established his new residence in California.

The next day the two men accompanied Salomon to the fields and were hired on the spot. They began to work immediately. Their supervisor was an older gentleman from back home, from the nearby village of Water's Eye. His name was Francisco Salinas, but everyone called him Don Paquito.

The cool early spring mornings in California's central valley were amazing, but spending 12-hour days out in the fields was not exactly a day at the beach. By noon the sun quickly became unbearable. Rather than taking layers of clothes off like Americans in the outdoors, they covered up as much skin as possible to prevent sun damage. On Sunday, the men went shopping for proper field clothing to protect from the sun.

"I thought I'd start fresh here in every way." Ramiro was like that. He liked to be equipped for the situation with all the proper accoutrements. "Have we got everything? Let's see. I have the khaki pants, the long sleeve denim shirts, the wide rimmed hat, the supply of neckerchiefs for sun protection and to cover the nose so as not to breathe all that dust and pesticides, more bandanas for the sweat, and canvas gloves. The farmers will provide the pruning tools and such." He was mostly talking to himself because Martin wasn't much into the details of such things. "Oh, and the lunch box, of course. I think that's it."

Monday morning Ramiro joined Martin, Salomon, and another twenty or so men, women, boys, and girls at the designated farm where they were to work on thinning the budding nectarines. It was a colorful crowd of happy faces eager to work. Each person there, with the exception of one or two, was physically conditioned, like an athlete, for maximum exertion that would withstand the sun beginning at 6:00 a.m. and ending at 6:00 p.m. They each sized up their companions every time the crew changed in composition to measure the competition.

No one was going to be awarded any ribbons or trophies or recognized for breaking any kind of record, but each one had his or her honor on the line. The competitive spirit is built in into the character of man, and a similar version of it is practiced by women as well. Every man, woman, or youth in that motley caravan was as fiercely proud of his or her reputation as to never let up on their daily goals. Even the frailer ones were respected if they strove to do their best. Mental conditioning was as important as physical prowess. Not one person in the group was overweight or out of shape.

And so, the otherwise ragtag group of twenty-five, under the direction and supervision of Don Paquito, greeted each other. The newcomers were introduced. Explanations were given as to the regulars who had dropped by the wayside. The workers limbered up their bodies, hiked up their bandanas over their noses, secured and adjusted their hats to wide rims, collected their tools, and set about their business in speedy but measured strides. Two-person teams on a tree, 10-foot ladders set, everyone poised at the first tree of the row, then off like runners at the starting block. If there was one area where the farm boy Ramiro could compete, it was in farm work. He was proud and competitive, and he intended to be the best pruner or picker in the crew once he got used to the ebb and flow of the work.

The month of March was all about spring thinning of the peaches, nectarines, plums, and apricots. The orchards had all lost their blossoms and each tree was heavy with small green fruit that required thinning in order to insure full development of the remaining fruit desired by the wholesalers. Once the fruit began to mature, the trees were pruned to allow maximum sunlight for the fruit to ripen to its sweetest level. Finally the harvesting happened around June and July when all the crews climbed on the ladders that they hauled and leaned against the trees. They removed the fruit, placing it into large wooden bushels they hoist on their shoulders.

The workers compete amongst themselves to see who could pick fastest, who could pick the most baskets or sacks, and who ultimately would earn the most money. Every job was measured by some standard, whether it was by the tree, the row, the bushel, the weight, or some similar measure. The average worker made a dollar an hour, but the super pickers could earn as much as twice that.

Ramiro's crew included Don Paquito's daughter, son-in-law, and fourteen-year-old granddaughter. Don Paquito was a small man, about 5'6", but his size could fool you. In his day he was a super picker. Now he had been working as a crew leader for almost a decade. He was one of the old timers who left home in the village of Water's Eye some fifteen years before. His family had since accumulated a small farm by sheer discipline and several family members' contributions to it. They had built a handsome house of many rooms in Water's Eye that was the envy of most of his neighbors. The family spent the winters there in relative luxury. The rest of the year, from late February to early November, they spent in Orange Cove. They always arrived a week or two before the season as Don Paquito's supervisory responsibilities demanded.

Ramiro was indeed a good worker. He seemed to thrive in the open fields under blue skies that reminded him of home. He did not become the best only because some of the veteran hands were more skilled and less meticulous than he, but he gave them a run for their money. He was working six days a week and was making over a hundred dollars each week. His expenses hovered around $20 per week, so he was pleased at the prospect of taking home a good sum when he returned to his family.

He had already written Eliza three letters to express his happiness about the farm work. He told her how he was making money and to be patient until he went home. Ramiro was truly inspired by Don Paquito's story of saving enough to buy a small farm and a showcase home. He imagined Don Paquito living like a king during those winters that he spent at home and in his imminent retirement. He wanted that for himself, and now he believed more than ever that it could be achieved. He wondered if he might have his children join him in California to double and triple the earnings and arrive at that dream farm sooner rather than later. Of course, the kids were still too young for such work.

What he hadn't shared, because it was hard to admit even to himself, was how grueling the work was. He couldn't spoil the feelings of hope by talking about the Monday through Saturday, 4:00 a.m. to 6:00 p.m. endurance tests of work that mauled every muscle of his body. He was young and strong, but it took a heavy discipline of laser focus on work alone to attend to the needs of the body that it might withstand the pounding. Ramiro made it through every week by virtue of his hope and regiment. Above it all was his love and commitment to his family, and that mantra renewed his strength every Sunday of rest. The grueling routines had become bearable by the good nature and humor of his compatriots in the fields. He had even become proficient at preparing his large breakfasts and packing nutritious lunches and snacks every day.

As the summer went on and one crop harvest led to another, Ramiro had his fill of whatever fresh fruits or vegetables he gathered on any given week. There were luscious grapes, heavy, sweet tomatoes, crisp, juicy cucumbers, juicy oranges, and now succulent peaches, and glistening nectarines. It was July, and for the past month the workers had engaged in plenty of topics of conversation that they shared across the trees as they stood on their ladders ten and twelve feet above the ground.

But no topic had been as energetic or persistent as that of Isabel's upcoming birthday. She would be turning fifteen. She was the granddaughter of the supervisor, and, as such, the family was compelled to spare no expense on the girl's introduction to society. Don Paquito and his daughter Florinda were planning the event of the summer—a formal *quinceañera* feast. Ramiro, Salomon, and most of the others were invited, of course. Ramiro was even asked to be a *chambelan*, or escort, in the honor court of the young "princess." That request put him on the spot. How was he going to decline that solicitation without offending his boss?

CHAPTER 12: *Migrant Princess*

Every member of the Orange Cove migrant community was invited to the party. The anticipation of everyone who had been a member of the crew of pickers working in the fruit farms had been building all summer. Ramiro and Martin found themselves just as caught up in the excitement as everyone else. Maybe it was not going to be a Naranjales-style gathering of familiar faces and friends, but it sure looked like a couple of steps up from the countrified *pachangas* back home.

Ramiro struggled with how to tell the girl's family that he was not able to be an escort. Finally, he politely declined, citing his age and intimating that his wife would not approve of his escorting a young girl whom she did not know. The truth was that Ramiro had no intention of spending money on renting a tuxedo and whatever other expenses might be involved in such a commitment. Salomon was not so lucky. One of his boys and his eldest daughter would be part of the court of Isabel's.

Ramiro felt a little guilty not participating in Don Paquito's granddaughter's special day, not so much for the girl but for the grandfather. He had grown fond of the older man rather quickly, and he was sure the feeling was mutual. Ramiro thought of Don Paquito as a kind of surrogate father. His own father was not so outdoorsy in the farm-loving kind of way that Ramiro himself was. So when he looked at this ruddy-faced, energetic man, he felt a natural affinity with him.

He enjoyed hearing him speak and how he described with such enthusiasm the fruit laden trees with the oft-repeated phrase: "those limbs were sooooo heeeeaaavyy with fruuuuuuitt," and gesturing with both arms and hands as if holding giant bunches of grapes or long branches of peaches. Ramiro laughed affectionately every time he recalled such scenes or when he retold the story to others.

Day after day, the women in the fields initiated the talk about the party as soon as the work got started. They numbered about twelve, including five girls from ages thirteen to twenty, out of the twenty-five-member crew. The conversations flourished whenever they happened to work close enough to hear each other without straining to shout across the trees.

"Well, Isabel is not so keen on red, but I so wish she would listen to me and get a red gown. She wants pink. So does her father. Imagine, she tells me that red is gaudy and tacky for such an occasion. I say, 'Not if it's done in good taste, like a queen or something,'" Florinda, the girl's mother, would start.

The other women would laugh, and pick up the conversation with their own tidbit about so-and-so's daughter's party or the neighbor who sewed her dress. Or Isabel herself would shout out in her own defense that, "Pink is the proper color because it is a princess color, and a fifteen is supposed to be pure and simple like pink," and so on and on it went.

To Ramiro it was all like a soap opera that made the day go by a little smoother. He rather enjoyed hearing feminine voices as they reminded him of the many ladies he had left back home.

When such dialogue happened, the men mostly kept silent awhile until one would interject: "How about the beer supply, Don Paquito?" And everyone would laugh, at which point some of the men started a parallel thread of back and forth surrounding topics related to the grand festivity that was to happen the first Saturday of August. Of course, the topics veered to the parties back home and retelling of stories of courtships born and died on dance floors. There was always the drunken father story or the stories of jealous boyfriend fistfights.

And so it went that the day's hours passed faster with stories. One day it was all about the mariachis and what band would play the best polkas for the dance. One day it was all about *padrinos*, or sponsors, for the various elements of such an occasion: whether it was about the special last doll, or the multitiered cake and if it would have a champagne fountain or a miniature grand staircase leading up to the princess doll on top, and so on.

On the morning of the big event Ramiro and Martin were getting ready. All around Orange Cove people were also getting their best threads out and polishing their one pair of good shoes, which served them for all occasions not related to work. The same primping was happening in several of the surrounding towns from Fresno down to Bakersfield. Don Paquito and Florinda expected up to 300 guests, including many friends and friends of friends, most of them from back home in the Valle Azul region of Monterrey.

Back home, no party ever happened that did not have open invitations to all the residents, whether friend or not. That friendly tradition continued in the migrant, gipsy-like community in semi-exile. The hosts ended up not recognizing half the guests, and often the crowd exceeded the amount of food and drink that had been purchased on a guesstimate. Most late arrivals knew not to expect to be fed, but beer and soft drinks had a way of magically getting replenished.

Ramiro was feeling a tinge of excitement. Like most of his com patriots and the Monterrey crowd, he had always loved a good party, and he looked forward to dancing with any unattached lady who would accept his invitation. He put on his best gabardine slacks that he had bought up in Chicago one Saturday that he and Nico went shopping at an amazing place that they told him was called The Magnificent Mile. Many of the shops were too expensive for his budget, but he managed to find a fine little store of men's clothing and essentials. He selected two pairs of slacks, a brown one and a navy blue. That day he also bought himself what would become his lifelong accessory, a gray wool Stetson fedora. The hats were all the rage in those days, and all fashionable men wore them.

Ramiro shunned flashiness, but he certainly took pride in looking dapper and well groomed. He liked being just fashionable enough to relate to movie heroes and TV gentlemen. His going-out short boots were shined, and the final touch was a splash of Aqua Velva after-shave after his usual weekend moustache trimming, a source of pride. Vanity is the universal trait that simple country boys share equally with city dandies.

The reception hall had been rented in Fresno because the Salinas family wanted "only the best." That meant it would be a bit of a drive for most guests. They didn't mind. They all were used to the long commutes in pursuit of the latest crop in need of harvest. The usual carpools formed, and, from all points, the guests got on their way. Florinda had made sure every detail was to her specifications. Somehow she managed to corral a court of honor consisting of fourteen young couples. She was adamant that tradition required fourteen, so that the fifteenth was the *quinceañera*. Most of the young people were friends or acquaintances of Isabel's, but a handful were perfect strangers, recruited by a friend of a friend.

Florinda lost her battle for the red chiffon gown, "Oh, okay. You win. I don't know when you got so stubborn. The pink it will be," she succumbed. Isabel would appear in a splendid pink silk and tulle antebellum-style dress that also included pink velvet roses pinned all about the giant hoop skirt. The top consisted of a fitted silk and lace strapless bodice, also in pale pink.

Ramiro and Martin awaited in the reception hall along with some hundred other guests while the church ceremony took place. Meanwhile they took in the atmosphere. The banquet room had been elaborately decorated in various shades of pink ribbons, balloons, drapes, table dressings, and centerpieces. The sizable dance floor was freshly waxed, and the band was finishing their setup. Caterers were busy setting up a traditional feast of tamales, wedding-style rice, herb-spiced beans in cilantro and bacon, tortillas, and, of course, grilled beef and chicken, or "*carne asada and pechugas*." The head table was set for the princess and her escort in the center, throne-like chairs, with seven couples on either side. On the side of the hall opposite the serving line was a towering cake in multiple shapes of hearts, circles, and squares. Behind that table was another, in the corner, on which gifts in fancy pastel wrapping were piled up. Additional mementos were set up so that the *quinceañera* would never forget what it was like to be a princess for a day.

Ramiro couldn't help but shake his head at the extravagance of the event. He liked a good party, but he was too practical to ever indulge in such an ostentatious affair. What he lamented most was that he knew of families who could barely pay the rent but who saved up small fortunes to make happen such a special celebration. He realized this family was much more showy than his, and they could afford it, so he eased up on his normal criticism.

No one in the half-filled hall was allowed to begin eating or dancing until the celebrated girl arrived. Isabel and her court were still at the religious ceremony, which would be over by 5:00 p.m. The guests who skipped the church proceedings were the less formal types or ones not too keen on religious services. It was totally understood that most of the acquaintances only attended such formal Catholic masses out of obligation, and they were never resented if they skipped them altogether. What mattered most was the party.

The crowd kept a watch on the time. Most were eager to see the normally dust-covered tomboy from the fields transformed by the finery that had been discussed ad nauseam all summer long. Isabel was not particularly beautiful, but she was attractive in a sweet and flirty sort of way. She sported shoulder length hair of a sort of dishwater blonde color. She had a few freckles on her golden white skin, which she protected from the California sun with bandanas while working, just like most of the women and men who worked in the brutal sun. Isabel was playful and had a wide impish grin that revealed a gap in her front teeth. Her wide hazel eyes seemed to always sparkle with some unknown mischief or joy. She stood 5'2" and weighed all of 110 pounds.

"Here they come!" A little boy shouted into the hall. Everyone stood and instinctively formed two lines so as to allow for the honor court and the princess to walk into the dance floor. They all wanted to get a close-up look at the young girl in all her finery. And they were not disappointed. After the Maricahis strolled in playing "*Cielito Lindo*," in came the fourteen couples, splendidly dressed and fresh-faced. The bandleader formally announced from the microphone each couple by name. The maids wore rainbow gowns of pastels, and the escorts wore gray tuxedos with shirts to color-match their partner. Finally, Isabel and her escort were announced, and they emerged through the front door. No one was disappointed. She was a sight to behold. Florinda had spared no expense at the local beauty salon, and her gown and crown only completed the apparition that walked into the room. Everyone ooh-ed and aah-ed at the sight of the radiant young woman that appeared before them, seemingly for the first time. There was no trace of the peasant tomboy from the brutal California fields.

Following Isabel and her escort, strolled a procession that included her parents, the sponsors, or godparents, and all other family members. Then the rest of the church crowd followed, and everyone quickly found a place to sit at the various tables. The reception hall was filled to capacity by 7:00 p.m. and late arrivals had to finagle a place to sit and eat or stand on the sides of the hall.

The mariachis continued to play their traditional repertoire. The honoree was escorted to the dance floor for the traditional father-daughter dance to an emotional song about little girls who grow up and their daddies letting them go. Isabel then danced with her honor escort. For the crowd, it was part of the theater they came to see. The court of honor took to the floor next. A professional photographer snapped pictures of every detail. Finally, the dance floor was opened to all guests.

"Let the dance begin," pronounced Don Paquito from the microphone at the musician's stand. At that, the band loudly banged on the cymbals and began playing popular *norteña* dancing music. Meanwhile, the guests had been silently encouraged to line up and begin their dinner. Ramiro and Martin sat with Salomon and his family. They were halfway through their meal when the band began to play. The unattached men had been eyeing all the single ladies to try to gauge which ones might be amenable to dancing with strangers.

§

It was nearly midnight, and Martin had had his fill of beer and some tequila shots. Ramiro had only had four beers, but that was enough for him to fully let loose on the dance floor to his favorite polkas and *corridos*. As most of these events went, this was a family affair, so most men were in their best behavior.

Ramiro and the men of his village were always mindful of propriety around women, especially in family settings. While most adults indulged a little and danced with abandon to the music of their roots, the dance floor always included a stream of kids running around in play or trying to imitate the dance moves of the adults. All in all, it was a festive night without incident to mar the occasion. Until Martin disappeared.

CHAPTER 13: *Losing a Friend*

I sabel's *quinceañera* was nearing its final stage. Many families were ambling toward the parking lot. The birthday girl watched as her mother and friends hauled the many presents out to the car. Don Paquito was tipsy but proud that the day and the party had seeded many beautiful memories. Still, there were a few stalwart couples left on the dance floor, loathe to call it a night.

Salomon ushered his family out, so Ramiro began to look around for Martin to do the same. He became alarmed when he couldn't find his friend anywhere. Finally, Ramiro spotted him emerging from a far corner of the dance floor. Martin was getting a little too frisky with a young woman with whom he was dancing.

Just as he stood up from his chair to retrieve his friend, Ramiro was grabbed by the arm. It was Don Paquito, "Ramiro, you haven't danced with Isabel yet. She just mentioned it to me. You have to dance with my granddaughter on her special day," he said. At that point Isabel approached the men, and Ramiro instinctively reached for her hand.

"Don Paquito, may I have your permission to dance with your beautiful granddaughter?" he asked.

Ramiro guided the girl over to where Martin was dancing, where the lights were dimmer than on the rest of the floor. Ramiro leaned over and elbowed Martin on the side to convey the message that he was on display. Martin reacted by waving him off and sashaying away with his partner. The woman in Martin's arms noticed the exchange, and she turned to Ramiro as if tossing her long teased hair back, making sure he caught her smile and wink in a split second. Ramiro stared at the back of her beetle green dress as the couple strutted out of sight.

Before long, Martin was again out of sight. It was now past midnight, and Ramiro wanted to call it a night. He began to look throughout the place, but no luck spotting his friend. Finally, Ramiro decided he needed fresh air, so he stepped outside to walk off a little of the beer effects. That's when he saw something odd.

He looked toward Martin's car in search of his ride home, unconsciously thinking Martin might have left him stranded to take the woman somewhere. Ramiro noticed the car seemed to be swaying slightly, so he walked over to see if anyone was inside. When he looked through the back window, he saw the back of Martin's head and, beyond it, partial sight of Beatriz, a woman who occasionally worked with their crew. Ramiro was appalled. *"Estos desgraciados estan puteando en el carro. Mira nada mas, casi encuerados."* "These two lowlifes are whoring in the car. Look at them, practically naked." They were both married. Ramiro's mind flashed images of Martin's wife back in Naranjales. Maria was sweet and loyal. "She doesn't deserve this," he thought.

Ramiro banged on the window angrily. The startled couple looked up at him. Beatriz had a horrified look in her face. Martin was angry, "What the hell are you doing here, Ramiro?" he slurred.

"What the hell are you doing in there?" Ramiro demanded. "I'm ready to go home, and you are in no condition to drive. Beatriz, get the hell out of here. I didn't see a thing, don't worry."

The woman quickly composed herself and her clothes, pulling up her skirt and buttoning her blouse. "I'm sorry, Ramiro. Please don't say anything," she pleaded as she scurried away.

Martin looked at Ramiro with scorn, but he knew better than to protest. He was well aware of Ramiro's temper and of his right hook. "We're getting the hell out of here," Ramiro told him. "Hand me the keys. I'll drive."

A deep sadness came over Ramiro as he pondered the situation that he had just witnessed with Martin. He had just verified that his instincts. There was a reason he had always mistrusted Martin. He was unfaithful. If a man could betray his own family, he would betray anybody. Ramiro wasn't so naïve as to pretend that the men of his region were always faithful, but he somehow always believed the ones close to him were different.

When they got home Ramiro helped Martin into his bed, his friend too drunk to even take off his shoes. Just having to touch him made Ramiro almost sick to his stomach, feeling vile. His mind played the movie of the couple in the act over and over. He stepped into the shower but not even the scalding water could wash away the images he was seeing. Would things be the same—the cheating—if they were back home?

Ramiro's wrath seemed magnified by disgust at himself. He secretly felt jealous of the shameless couple because his loneliness often provoked similar temptations. Memories of Mary and his infidelity returned as well. How could he sit here in judgment when he himself was guilty of straying? He fell asleep writhing in guilty feelings, and his fitful sleep was heavy with dreams of his shame.

Ramiro dreamed about his own daughters, Esmeralda and Alicia, back home, who were now six and three years old. He saw them run away and scream at him uncontrollably, having learned that their father betrayed their mother and the children with a loose woman far from home. His dreams switched to Isabel's party merging into the *quinceañeras* of his daughters, that would one day arrive. How beautiful his girls looked.

§

After that night things changed between the two men. Ramiro felt instinctively cut off from Martin. He tried not to judge because, after all, men are men, but he couldn't hide his disdain for Martin's betrayal of his family. His own trespass seemed insignificant, he told himself, because he had never intended to let it last, but he could see that Martin's case was different. He had abandoned his family. Martin, for his part, avoided Ramiro's reproachful stare whenever he could. That awkwardness lasted all of a week.

When Ramiro knocked on Martin's door Monday morning to go to work as usual, there was no answer. Ramiro tried the door, and it was unlocked. He stepped inside, and noticed immediately that Martin had vacated the premises. The room was empty of any personal belongings. There was only a note on the bedside table. "Ramiro, I know you won't like this. I have moved away with Beatriz, the woman I love. You will probably be mad at me for a long time. I'm sorry I won't be around to share the car with you. I know you will manage. I love her, Ramiro. We have to give ourselves this chance at happiness." Martin and Beatriz had eloped, and would be starting a new life together.

Ramiro could only sigh. "Love!" Ramiro muttered to himself. "Any man who can leave his sons for a whore knows nothing about love. Love? Don't talk to me about love, you coward."

CHAPTER 14: *Homecoming*

I t was September 10, and the day was uneventful in Naranjales. The fact that it was Baby Carlos' birthday didn't mean very much in the little adobe house that sat behind Doña Lupita's. Eliza got up that morning as she did every morning, promptly at 6:30. She breast-fed her baby, who had a tendency to wake up with the rooster's crow. Then she set about her morning routine of fixing breakfast for the kids. The two older ones, Baldemar and Esmeralda would be heading to school by 8:00, so their milk with coffee and sweet cakes was her next priority. Alicia was not there because she spent nights with her grandmother across the patio, in the big house.

"Get up, you lazy bums. Baldemar! Esmeralda! Get up. It's morning and you have to go to school." Eliza spoke gruffly in contrast to her sweet Madonna look. The kids got up and ran outside to the water tank by the well where they filled a big bowl with water and washed their faces. Baldemar was not much of a student, but his younger sister loved almost every aspect of learning. The weather was cool and the low humidity in the region was perfect to invigorate any young and curious soul. The children ran back into the house and sat at the small kitchen table to eat their breakfast.

"Mama, can I go to the river after school with Beto and Toño?" asked Baldemar. "We're going to the river and we're going to hunt pigeons on the way back, with our slingshots. Will you cook my pigeons, mama?"

"I don't know about that, *muchacho*. Ask your grandfather. I don't want to be blamed if something happens to you out there in the wild," replied Eliza in her usual manner of avoiding the risk of a possible Ocañas reprimand. "Yes, I'll grill the pigeons if you kill any. I hope you bring enough for the girls, too," she said.

"Mama, my teacher, Miss Elena, told me that I was the best reader in first grade," piped in Esmeralda.

"That's good, Esmeralda. Maybe one day you can teach me how to read. I never had the chance to go to school. Always obey your teachers and listen to what they say. I don't know much, so learn it from the teachers. Now hurry, Esmeralda." Esmeralda. Eliza always called the children by their full names. The family generally would call Baldemar Balde and Esmeralda, Meri, but not Eliza. Ramiro had told her he didn't think much about parents who spoiled their kids with diminutive nicknames. He never would use the -ito suffix on relatives' names. He did, however, use shortened versions of names, such as Balde or Licha for Alicia. It was Eliza's timidity that equated the two concepts as a prohibition. His mother was fond of calling him Milo, short for Ramiro.

When the kids had left to school, Eliza sat down to eat her own breakfast. Afterwards, she began the typical chores that she took on as a way of showing Lupita her worthiness. She started by drawing plenty of water from the well for the many plants that grew in Doña Lupita's garden. Like most tasks to be performed, it was tough work. Pulling buckets of water from the well could rough up a girl's hands fast. Not that that was ever a concern of hers because things were just what they were, and rough hands on a farm girl were simply the norm. The rope was rough and course, and the weight of the water buckets required strength and stamina. Some of the girls in the village had arms strong as any man. After watering, she milked the cow, fed the chickens and hogs, and then tended to her own house sweeping and mopping the floors.

"Good morning, *suegra*. I hope your night's sleep was restful. ... Good morning, Lola. I hope your night's sleep was restful. ... Good morning, Don Timoteo, *suegro*. I hope you had a restful sleep." Eliza greeted everyone around with the same polite expression. Everyone replied in a similar fashion. It was expected and appreciated.

"Good morning, Eliza. Today is Carlos's birthday," said Lupita as her daughter-in-law watered the rose bushes absentmindedly. "I remember well his birth. It was only a few weeks later that his father went away to the other side. That poor creature hasn't seen his father in a whole year, but just a few more weeks, and he will be coming home."

"Yes, *Suegra*. His letter said he would arrive before the end of November, God willing," replied Eliza. She had been thinking about Ramiro's return for almost a week. Jacobo had delivered Ramiro's letter after one of his runs to Valle Azul when he had driven out to deliver some meats. As usual, Jacobo read the letter to Eliza. He enjoyed teasing her about anything that sounded in any way romantic because of how she would flush and squirm upon hearing the words. Jacobo would even make up stuff just to see her blush.

"I can't wait to take you in my arms and kiss you for hours," Jacobo would pretend to read then break out laughing when Eliza recoiled in horror at such intimacy being seen by her brother-in-law.

Because Ramiro left his return date inexact, she was wondering when to start preparations for his homecoming. She would like to have all the kids bathed and nicely dressed. The house was always clean, so that would not take much to tidy up. Lupita had told her not to worry about making a big to do because Ramiro would understand that the Christmas season was just around the corner. The family would simply plan an extra opulent Christmas feast in celebration of having Ramiro home. For the day of his return, just a nice chicken and rice dish would suffice. Eliza could make her special anise-spiced pumpkin empanadas if she liked, as they were a favorite of Ramiro's. Everything else could be taken from the store. Thus, everyone simply continued their routines while growing more anxious every day they awaited Ramiro's return.

§

Ramiro had not sent money home since arriving in California. He chose instead to save it all, and carry the cash with him when he traveled. He had managed to spend March through October working steadily. In late September, he wrote Eliza the last letter from California. He told her to expect him home sometime in late November. Salomon had told him that they would be making the trip around the fifteenth, so Ramiro figured it would take several days to arrive. He thought it better to add a couple of days in case there were delays; that way his family wouldn't worry if he didn't arrive when expected.

As he calculated in his head by simple addition, Ramiro felt pleased with his haul of eight months. He roughly calculated that he had saved around $80.00 per week, and he had been saving for eight months. That came to a grand total of $2,560.00. His passage home by way of gas contributions and a donation to Salomon or his wife, plus meals and a few more trinkets, would shave off some $50.00 of that total.

He safely calculated that $2,500.00 was what he had to show for all the hard work he had done over the long year he had been away from his family. He did a little more math in his head and multiplied his savings by 9 to get the amount of pesos he would have at his disposal. He thought to himself, 25 x 10 — rounding out the 9 to make the math easier — equals 250, and with the zeros, three of them, that makes it $25,000 pesos. He smiled widely. That didn't count the money he had sent home from Chicago, which was some $200.00, although that was surely all gone by now.

He lay on his bed, hands clasped behind his head and feet crossed, feeling pleased with himself. Images of his dream farm whirled in his head. He needed a nice long rest for his weary body, but he was eager to repeat the process come next March. There was something special about a man surveying the fruits of his labor, and Ramiro was no exception in feeling pride in his accomplishment.

§

It was now finally the day. Ramiro found himself nervous and excited beyond his expectations. He so yearned to see his family again. He couldn't wait to hold Eliza in his arms and make love to her every day and night. He longed to hug and squeeze the kids and wondered how big Carlos must have gotten in the year he'd been gone. He imagined everyone would be expecting gifts, so he made it a point to go shopping for special American foodstuffs that would be appreciated because of their rarity in Naranjales. He bought a box of Hershey chocolates and some M&M's and Wrigley's chewing gum, all three colors: green, white, and yellow.

Ramiro wasn't always the most considerate of others when acting on his wants, but he decided to keep his gifts to a minimum so as not to take up any more room than necessary on the station wagon. After all, Salomon's family would be inconvenienced enough with having an extra passenger and his luggage aboard. He would play it by ear and buy additional things on the other side once they were in Reynosa. Even the border town of Reynosa was big and exotic to the folks back home.

The return to the homeland was an event in Orange Cove and throughout the towns in the Central Valley. Suddenly the towns would be left half empty, so that was one economic blow to the local businessmen whose establishments depended on the migrants. But the families and groups of single men organizing their departures and loading up their vehicles, some boarding buses, was its own whirlwind. There was a flurry of activity and excitement in the air. Some also felt melancholy at saying goodbye to the many coworkers, whom they had grown to call friends over the season of spending long days side-by-side with them.

The station wagon, a 1948 Ford Deluxe, was packed full of all the belongings of four men and three women. They would ride three in the front seat, four in the back. The front passengers were Salomon, his oldest boy, and Ramiro. The three would also take turns at the wheel. The luggage and all other personal items were packed tightly into every inch of available space. Luggage and some other large items were neatly stacked and tied down atop the wagon.

The trip by car would have been a rough one in any year, but this was 1951. It was long and everyone was packed tightly into the car. Good thing it was November, and the weather was cool and pleasant. If it had been after the construction of modern highways, they could have anticipated a total travel time of 36 hours, longer if they stopped for a night to rest. Back then the roads made it much tougher and slower to make such a trip because the highways were not always completed or fully paved.

Ramiro had helped the boys plan the route home. They followed a plan that in present day would be: from Orange Cove, they took Highway 63 southward to Visalia where they switched to 99. They stayed on 99 until reaching Bakersfield. There, they changed roads to I-5 and stayed on it until reaching Los Angeles where they briefly stayed on CA-210. From 210 they exited to I-10 East. In 1951, I-10 was not yet built, but the Dixie Overland Highway traversed from Los Angeles to Georgia. Highway 80 took them all the way to Dallas. Then they took local roads onto San Antonio. From there, they drove south on I-37 then on 281 until they reached McAllen.

By 10 of that first night of their journey, the Aguilar family and Ramiro reached the outskirts of El Paso. The long trip had gone mostly without incident, other than the normal quick stops for restroom breaks or to grab a quick bite to eat, sometimes just to let everyone stretch their legs. The group decided to spend the night at a motel and sleep a few hours before continuing on to Dallas. They stopped at a gas station to fill up.

As they pulled in, the girls immediately noticed a pair of motorcycles. "Oh, look at those!" they cooed in admiration as they had romantic images from television of handsome road rebels on bikes.

It was dark, and there was a definite November chill in the air. Some of the passengers were sleepy and stayed in the car while some in the party went into the store for snacks. Ramiro stepped out back to where the sign pointed to the men's room. He splashed water on his face, then relieved himself and washed his hands.

There were some overgrown bushes on the back of the property, beside the restroom. When Ramiro exited the room, he suddenly felt his arms pulled back by a grip of great strength. The giant proceeded to put him in an arm twist that rendered him motionless. A big greasy hand pressed against his mouth to keep him quiet. "Don't you dare resist, you goddam greaser," the attacker spat into his ear.

At the very same instant a second man broke two beer bottles on each other and held the jagged glass to Ramiro's throat. His entire life flashed before his eyes. He thought these thugs would surely kill him. He saw flashes of his body lying slashed and bloodied on the ground. He saw Salomon finding him. He saw police flashing lights. He saw Eliza crying. His children. He saw Lupita in screams of agony. Ramiro simply had to survive this. He wasn't ready to die. His second thoughts were of how to stop them from robbing him and his family of the money he was carrying in the inside pocket of his jacket.

No sooner had Ramiro thought about the money than the guy with the broken glass to his neck reached inside his jacket and snatched the envelope with the $2,500.00. The bad guy then reached into Ramiro's back pocket and took his wallet, too. Then the watch. He tried to struggle, but it was clear he was overpowered. His mind went black with fury and he saw garish images of his lost fortune. The thought of losing an entire year's worth of wages was killing him. He managed to get in a swift kick to the groin of the one with the broken bottle, risking his life in a moment of sheer hatred toward his attackers. His fight only earned him a blow to the head that left him almost unconscious. He was lucky the biker didn't slash his throat.

Sobering up, he thought, *These guys mean business, so I better save my life.* They were big, heavy gangster types. They reeked of alcohol, so there was no predicting what they might do should Ramiro have continued to fight.

The robbers' entire heist took place in whispered tones nearly in his ear so as not to attract attention. The bushes and dim light had protected them and prevented Ramiro from noticing their loitering when he entered the restroom. They knew somehow that Ramiro spoke little English, so they used their best efforts to convey their obvious intentions in their broken Spanish. "Don't you dare move or make a sound, you dirty spic," said the giant holding his arms in a twist behind his back.

"You make a sound and you're dead, you dirty beaner," said the second man. The whole thing lasted less than a minute. The criminals kicked Ramiro in the groin and intended to shove him into the john then make a quick getaway. Suddenly the Aguilar men appeared just as swiftly as had the bandits. Immediately they were swinging at the two drunks. Caught off guard, the tough guys were a lot less big, and their drunken state didn't help them.

The Aguilar boys were body builders in their spare time, and the farm work added to their conditioning. The bad guys were knocked unconscious. Ramiro, still clutching his stomach, quickly swooped down and took back his small treasure, which Salomon and his boys had not even been aware of. The men quickly boarded the car and mentioned nothing of the incident to Elva and the girls. The mother and daughters noticed the men's heavy breathing. The ladies looked at each other with puzzled looks, but they did not ask what had happened. The party proceeded to the motel and entered the diner. They were ravenous for a steak dinner.

§

It had been a fifteen-hour drive just to get to El Paso. It was another eighteen hours from there to Dallas, and roughly five more hours to reach San Antonio after that. From San Antonio it was another eight hours, and they would be in McAllen. All of it exhausting, all of it scenic, most of it beautiful. Perhaps the most beautiful of all the drives was the one from Reynosa to Valle Azul. Every new stop along the highways brought renewed anguish to Ramiro. His mind kept replaying the scene of the attack. In the safety of the car and the company of the family he was able to reflect on the great loss that he would have suffered had the bandits gotten away with his year's worth of savings. The others laughed and told stories, but Ramiro could only smile robotically when he was gripped by unexplained fears and thoughts of what could have been.

They traversed mountains with magnificent views of rock cliffs and steep precipices; vast deserts where occasional rabbits hopped, eagles soared, and vultures circled some unknown carcass. There were small, picturesque Mexican towns of the northern variety. Each of them had a plaza with a kiosk for the locals' Sunday promenades. Ramiro breathed in deeply the distinct smells of such places, with their fragrant cooking at certain hours, or cow and horse manure here or there, or local merchants' burlap sacks filled with peanuts in the shell or with flour.

That last leg was the shortest, about three and one half hours, but it seemed a breeze compared to the two hours of hassle it took to get through the Mexican border inspection.

The travelers were told to park their vehicle in a designated slot. They were directed inside the customs building to have all their documents inspected and to validate their tourist sticker for the car. Outside, their trunk and roof of the station wagon were emptied of all their contents. Every package or suitcase was laid open on a concrete slab table that sat beside each of the car slots. The inspectors used every trick to arrive at a deal with the travelers that would procure a small donation. "Tipping" the officer would guarantee a quick inspection and a blind eye to any questionable items being transported into the country. Salomon resisted the blatant bribe seeking, but he did not want to hold up the long line of travelers behind them, either. Ramiro and Salomon finally relented and slyly handed an offering to the sweaty guy in the green uniform. The officer flashed a smile somewhere between sheepish and cavalier and waved them through as if they were VIPs.

§

It was four days since Ramiro had begun his homecoming trip. Eliza, Lupita, Lola, and Timoteo were consumed in their daily chores and routines, which never ceased to drain attention and physical commitment. The hour was 6:00, so dinner preparations were underway. The customary dinner hour was 8:00, and dinner in Naranjales was always made from scratch, for there was not a single restaurant in a fifty-mile radius. Even Valle Azul only had two or three places that provided meals, but only on weekends. Saturday night was a sure time for the special tacos that Don Benito sold across the street from the plaza, next door to the cinema. That was when all the young people promenaded in the plaza and congregated with friends for conversation and sing-alongs.

Eliza prepared her table in the little house while Lupita and Lola labored away in the big house. All the women were about the business of dinner preparations. The kids could be heard outside as usual. The girls were engaged in playing tag, hopscotch, pick-up-sticks, rope-jumping, Hula Hoop, jacks, or with rag dolls. Baldemar played with marbles, spinning tops, toy guns, target shooting with his slingshot, *balero*, or building a bow and arrow. The baby was only 1, but already he could walk, so the girls had to take turns watching him and keeping him out of trouble.

Carlos could easily wander off and do as he used to when he was a crawler. He would put anything he saw in his mouth. Eliza was horrified when she saw him once crawl toward a chicken dropping that looked like chocolate syrup. Carlos immediately dipped his hand in the stuff and put his fingers in his mouth. Eliza shrieked so loud that the boy began to cry, startled by her reaction. The girls laughed about it for days and repeated the story to their grandmother and Aunt Lola many times. "Carlos grabbed the chicken shit and put it in his mouth," they'd say and giggle for minutes. At first the women humored them and laughed along, but finally they told the girls that enough was enough with the story, "Alright, girls. Enough. We know the story. You can tell it tomorrow."

For days the family had been going about their duties with a growing sense of anticipation, knowing that Ramiro would be home any day. They did not know the exact day or time, but they felt it would be soon. They tried to put it out of their heads so as not to lose focus of their daily responsibilities. They also were too practical to simply stop what they were doing and daydream or even plan a homecoming. It was just a feeling of great joy to be able to hold their beloved again. Each of the women, the father, and even the children held their emotions to themselves. "He will get here when he gets here," said each of them in his or her own way. They were a model of patience.

§

Timoteo saw the station wagon first. He was behind the counter of the store, facing directly out the double doors that led to the front patio and the street beyond it. At first he was puzzled as to who it could be. A car like that was a rarity in the village, although he expected a few now that the migrants would be returning for the winter. He had seen Salomon's station wagon before, but he didn't make the connection at first. Most vehicles in those parts were large trucks for hauling fruits and vegetables or animals. This type of vehicle was considered a city thing, fancy and out of place in unpaved roads like the ones in Naranjales. Maybe it was someone passing through from Monterrey, he thought.

There was still enough sunlight out that he could clearly distinguish the scene. Timoteo paused briefly from his task at hand of wrapping a kilo of rice for Doña Elena, the village seamstress. When Timoteo returned to his work, Ramiro exited the station wagon with his valise, a new duffel bag, and a large paper bag, which he had reinforced by placing it in a large colorful Mexican plastic mesh bag he had bought in Reynosa. Salomon did not get out of the car so as not to distract from Ramiro's homecoming. He had already dropped off his own family in their home, now he would rejoin them for their own celebration with relatives.

Timoteo took the customer's bills and gave her change. When the woman turned to go, Timoteo followed past her with his eyes to see the station wagon gone and his son walking past Doña Elena towards the door. He quickly called out for his wife and daughter and rushed out to greet his son. "Lupita, Lola, He's arrived!"

There were tears in Timoteo's gray-blue eyes, and his hands shook from his Parkinson's more than normal from the excitement of seeing his son again. The men held each other tightly only for a second because the two women hurried out of the kitchen and were soon upon them as well. Doña Lupita was in silent happy tears herself, holding and hugging her son. Lola was no exception, despite her usual brusqueness and no nonsense personality. She took her turn in welcoming her brother home and hugged him tightly for a long time. Ramiro was ecstatic.

By the time Ramiro entered the house, Baldemar and Esmeralda came round the back door into the kitchen and heard the excitement. The kids looked at each other and their eyes went wide with happiness. But they did not rush toward their father as might be expected. Instead, they ran back to Eliza's cottage fast as lightning. "Mama, Mama, Papa is home! Papa is home!" they yelled.

"Did he arrive?" was all Eliza could say. She quickly took the food out of the fire, and rushed to the mirror on the armoire. She took off her apron and dabbed a little rose water on her neck. It all happened in less than a minute, as she instructed the kids to tidy themselves up because their father was home. The kids obeyed, of course, and they were all out the door.

The formality of the tough country life relegated children to be mostly seen and not heard, and Ramiro's kids had excelled at following that expectation. They did not rush to their father. They followed their mother or walked beside her, but they knew to let her be first in receiving their father home. As soon as she embraced Ramiro, so did they all. In seconds, Ramiro greeted each one in turn with hugs and kisses. Everyone was very glad to have Ramiro in their midst again. Although the custom and personalities maintained everyone orderly and controlled, the kids and Eliza rejoiced in Ramiro's embraces.

"Well, hey, how are you, Baldemar, Esmeralda, Alicia? Have you kids been good while I was gone? Did you help your mother with all the chores?" Ramiro asked of the kids, as he embraced them. The kids shyly replied that, yes, they had. And Ramiro picked each of them up and held the girls up in the air as they giggled in delight of having their papa back.

"Eliza. My Eliza. How I have missed you," he whispered in her ear as he hugged his wife, careful not to display too much passion because his parents and sister were watching the homecoming. All Eliza could say was, "Ramiro." And she put her arms around him briefly.

"And where is the baby? Where is Carlos? Is he sleeping or just hiding?" Ramiro asked, looking around as if the child might be crawling on the floor somewhere.

"I left him in the bed. I will go fetch him for you. But he's not a baby anymore. He walks now. You all go inside and sit down," Eliza asked the family, as she hurried back to her cottage for the baby.

"We didn't know when you'd arrive, so you have caught us unprepared to welcome you. You and your father go and sit in the store and talk. We women will finish dinner. We'll just have to make a few small modifications. It's not too late to kill a chicken to make you your favorite dish. Dinner will be just a little later than usual," Lupita said. "Let me get started. Baldemar, go and catch one of the chickens in the back patio. Pick a nice plump one. I think the white one with red head is a good one. Lola, put a pot of water to boil to defeather it." She then proceeded to inspect her meat cleaver.

Eliza walked in with Carlos in her arms, the boy unaware of what all the excitement was about. He looked at the man his mother was handing him to, and he recoiled a little, his face contorting as if in panic. His chubby face started to make mouth tremblings.

"It's your father, silly boy. Your papa. Go on, give daddy a kiss," urged Eliza.

Ramiro was grinning ear to ear as he snatched the boy before he could begin crying. The father smothered the little one with kisses and playful noises. Carlos stopped resisting and began to laugh. He looked at this man who was being so loving to him. Indeed, Ramiro's love was true and pure, and especially expressive with babies. Carlos was soon happy to respond to Ramiro's typical rough play.

Lola lit the kitchen kerosene lamp as Doña Lupita browned the chicken and spiced the rice. She then lit another lamp in the store waiting room where Ramiro and Timoteo chatted with the kids sitting beside them, clinging to their every word. The sun had set, so dinnertime was a little delayed. Lamps had to be lighted. The family usually used only one tall lamp in the store and another that was moved around the house as needed. It was to conserve kerosene and wicks. Tonight was a special occasion, so there would be light.

By eight o'clock, Lupita called everyone to the table. Her mood was such that she got a little generous and invited everyone to a bottle of pop. Even the kids could have a whole one each. She didn't even bother to compute the loss of profit from those lost sales as was her wont. Eliza brought over the tortillas, guacamole, and fresh cheese. There would be no empanadas this time, but she would make plenty tomorrow. Everyone enjoyed a delightful dinner and listened intently to Ramiro's stories about the other side and the gringos. The adults were as enthralled as the kids, and in everyone's eyes Ramiro took on an air of greatness he had not experienced before.

Lupita declared that he must be very tired, so they would call it a night by 10:00. That was music to Ramiro's ears. All through dinner his mind had been on the moment he and Eliza could put the kids to bed and retire to their own love nest. He could not wait to get some rest, but not before he ravished his wife in passionate love making. Sadly, Eliza was not feeling the same excitement as her husband. She was bracing herself for submission to her sexually aggressive husband after a year of respite in that department. She loved her husband, but sex always reminded her of her mother's betrayal, and his voracious appetite simply made it worse.

Ramiro excused Eliza from her expected role in helping clean up and wash the dishes. Lupita understood immediately, and shooed them away toward the little house. In no time, the kids fell sweetly to sleep. Finally, Ramiro thought. He quietly took his wife in his arms and kissed her lips and neck. Soon he was releasing all the pent-up emotion that had been bottled up inside him for so long. Between kisses and caresses, he found himself wiping an occasional tear of joy and Eliza's tears as well. His usual frantic passion was interrupted by moments of tenderness that were the product—as if an apology—of his remorse over his affair with Mary. It was 3:00 in the morning when he finally gave in to exhaustion and fell into a deep, sweet slumber.

CHAPTER 15: *Holiday Bliss*

"Ramiroooo! Ramiroooo!" Eliza was calling from the patio. He looked up and turned toward her voice from his work in the family's orange grove. He smiled and leaned the hoe against the tree he was banking to protect from the winter. It was a cold December day, but the work of insulating the trees from a possible harsh norther had Ramiro working up a sweat. He looked up at the sun, and realized it was about noontime.

"What am I good for?" he said, as she appeared from behind one of the trees just a few feet from him.

"Lunch is ready. Have you worked up an appetite? Come and eat."

"I could use a little something," he grinned, "or something else, too," he nodded in a teasing leer.

"Oh you. Wash up and come in when you are ready. Just don't let the tortillas get cold." She turned and walked back briskly, pulling up her coat collar tight over her chin.

The school kids were not yet home for lunch. Alicia and Carlos were huddled by the chimney trying to keep warm. Each of the kids was eating a freshly made maize tortilla, smeared with salted lard and tightly rolled into a flute-like taco. Eliza wanted to get Ramiro fed before the kids came home so he could get back to his work on Don Timoteo's orange trees.

It had been two weeks since his return, and Ramiro had quickly gotten into the swing of helping around the small orchard and a variety of other fruit trees that Lupita cared for around the property. The family's small compound was no more than 3 hectares, about 8 acres, but there was constant work to do. Ramiro was more than happy to feel productive around his parents. Besides, he was grateful for their help with his family while he had been away. It was the least he could do, he thought. Of course, there was also the family edict that no one was to ever sit around idle while there was work to do, and his pride compelled him to seek approval of his every move around his parents.

In addition to the family chores, he was also spending some time working with his brothers. They paid him what they could for his work in their farming and retail businesses, although he usually rejected their money, reminding them that he had just opened a nice savings account in Valle Azul. His brother, Jacobo was successfully operating an alfalfa field and raising a few cattle for market. He and his wife Chavela had two young children. Alberto, the oldest of his brothers, and his wife, Sofia, ran a grocery store and small orange grove at the northern end of the village. The couple had five kids. Both brothers owned their own trucks, so Ramiro was able to hitch rides with them for his business in town whenever he could coordinate with their schedules.

§

His sister, Maria Estela, lived in the next village with her husband, Saul. She and their four kids also followed in their parents' footsteps and ran a profitable grocery business as well as a small chicken ranch. Ramiro had plenty of family and friends he had been catching up with since his return. Everyone was happy to see him. Each home he visited, whether alone or with Eliza and the kids, the hosts insisted on celebrating his homecoming with a special meal. Usually a chicken would be killed, but on occasion the family might have some pork or goat from a recent slaughter that was occasioned by some other event. Ramiro took special pride in repaying every debt he owed. It lifted a heavy load off his mind, and it gave him peace and comfort to know he was getting ahead in life.

Everyone congratulated him on his courageous travels and for working hard to save money. Just as amusing, or perhaps complimentary, was how everyone wanted to hear stories of where he had been as if he'd been a movie star on a world tour and not a man down on his luck on a burdensome trek. He would always start with, "Well, one thing I can tell you for sure, what they say about sweeping money off the streets up there is not true." And everyone would moan in mock disappointment then laugh heartily. Every conversation he had with friends or relatives included a little teasing about how soon he was going to buy that farm he talked about so much. Ramiro would humor them, but insisted confidently. "Give me a little time. About three more years."

One thing was for sure, no one looked at him like the failed middle son of one of the village's prominent families any longer. No one looked at Lupita and Timoteo and say to themselves, "There go the Ocañases. Those poor parents of Ramiro, who has so much trouble making a go at business, unlike his hard-working parents and siblings." Now everyone looked at Ramiro and they saw a man of means, a future landowner whose simple but beautiful wife was the most loyal and whose kids were handsome and well behaved.

But as much as he was enjoying spending time with family and friends, Ramiro soon became troubled with the thought that he wanted to return to the States and earn more money. He was impatient about saving enough for his purchase. It would be some three months until his next departure.

§

"Mmmm, where is that boy named Carlos. I'm so hungry, I want to eat him. Where is he. MMMMgrr mm, grr mm." Ramiro walked into the little adobe house teasing the boy. Carlos squealed with delight and ran to hide under the bed. "I know he's around here. I can smell his stinky feet." And he laughed a silent laugh as he held a finger to his lips indicating to Alicia, who was hovering around her daddy, not to say a word as he was about to snatch the boy's foot from under the bed where it was clearly visible from the dining area where Alicia now clung to her papa's leg. Alicia was laughing, too, and covered her mouth with both her hands to indicate to her daddy that she would not say a word.

"You want to give him another haircut, Papa?" Alicia teased, remembering how Carlos had cried during his first haircut the day before.

Ramiro loved teasing the kids. He did it with a poker face that made the kids believe he was dead serious about intending to punish them for some unknown misdeed or another. His sense of humor went beyond the kids, though. It must have been an Ocañas family trait because every sibling gave as much as he took. Ramiro always found humor in every person he met, and even in those he didn't meet. He could laugh at every circumstance except truly grave ones. Like posing for a picture.

No one owned a camera in Naranjales. Traveling photographers came around every few months. The few pictures of Ramiro, or any of the family for that matter, never showed a smiling face. But in real life, there was always laughter and merriment. Ramiro laughed at the world, but he also laughed at himself. He never took anybody too seriously because he applied the same criteria to himself.

Eliza looked at Alicia and rolled her eyes smiling and shaking her head. "Leave the boy alone, and come and eat. Did you wash your hands? Ramiro, I warmed up some water for you to wash. Over there." She had returned to scrambling eggs into the shredded dried beef that would be his lunch. She had a *molcajete* with mashed tomatoes and spices that hissed and sizzled as she poured them onto the hot. "Ramiro, your *machacado* is ready. Some refried beans?" After washing and drying his hands, Ramiro scooped up some of the eggs and meat with the tortilla just as Eliza set down his hot cup of coffee, his favorite beverage.

"Mmm, I wasn't so hungry until I tasted this. Good." It wasn't exactly a direct compliment, but Eliza knew he was pleased, and that pleased her.

"Did you see the hog mama wants me to butcher for the twenty fourth?" Ramiro asked, in the vernacular for the Christmas feast, which was fast approaching. "It's a beaut. The big white one that has black patches on its back and eyes. He must weigh 150 kilos. A real beaut. That will give us plenty of *chicharrones*, all you can eat pork rinds. You women will be able to make a ton of tamales."

"The big, pinto one? That will be nice," she said. "Did your mother say if Julieta and Eduardo can be here in time for the twenty-fourth? Will they come down from Houston?"

"I think they arrive next week. Mother tells me that everyone will be here. This twenty-fourth is partly in my honor and partly to see Julieta. They have a new baby. Two months old. Did I tell you that Mom wants me to move to Houston? Wants me to be close to Julieta?"

"To Houston? What did you tell her? I think it's a good idea. A two-month old? Close to Carlos' birthday."

"I don't know about that move. Eduardo can be a son of a bitch sometimes. I think California is a sure thing for now. Cousin Salomon stopped by yesterday and we talked about a departure day. March first."

"Oh. That's in two months almost," said Eliza, images flashing in her head for a second round of goodbyes and loneliness.

"Two and a half months," Ramiro said.

As Ramiro finished his meal the two older kids came rushing in. Their school lunch break was two hours. Eliza moved quickly to serve them their lunch. They would have eggs and beans with a glass of milk. Ramiro carried the baby out to the front of the store to look at the kids rushing out of the school grounds on their way to their respective houses for lunch. The little boy giggled at the feel of Ramiro's whiskers on his cheeks and neck when he kissed him. He waved at the school kids and held on tightly to his father. The child instinctively kicked his little legs and planted a kiss on his father's cheek.

That was the new rhythm and pace of Don Ramiro Ocañas during his first visit home. Yes, "Don" Ramiro, for a man of means, as he now thought of himself, deserved respect. He had been away for a year, and

his three-and-a half-month visit was reenergizing him. The days flew
by. Before he knew it, Christmas had arrived.

§

On the twenty-second, Ramiro and his brothers gathered bright
and early on the side of the pigpen. They cleared a place for the killing
of the hog. There were some seven hogs of various sizes in the pen. Four
of them were large enough for the kill. The pigs were particularly noisy
that morning as if sensing their doom. Ramiro jumped into the pen
and chased the black and white pig until he succeeded in hogtying it.
The animal squealed loudly and continued to thrash about even after
the brothers held it down. When she saw a moment of stillness of the
hog, Lupita used a long, sharp, dagger-like knife and swiftly stabbed it
in the heart. The animal died instantly.

The children watched at a safe distance so as not to interfere or
be in the way of the adults who were working frantically on the operation. The girls shuddered a little, but Baldemar, at 8, had become
accustomed to such dramatic farm scenes. He took it all in as naturally
as if it were the felling of a tree. It was simply nature to him as to most
every man, woman, and child in those parts. The only death not taken
so matter-of-factly was that of a human being.

The hog carcass was prepared for dismemberment as they had
done many times before. The brothers scalded its hide to remove the
hairs with razor-sharp knives. They removed the entrails being careful not to accidentally puncture anything that might contaminate the
meat. They washed it out completely. They cut its head off at just the
precise location. They were finally ready to make every cut of meat
designated for various aspects of consumption. All of it was expertly
done from years of performing similar operations at the highest standards that their parents had imposed on them and carefully taught
them over time.

The brothers set up a large copper kettle the size of a small bath-
tub under a proportional-sized bonfire. There they placed the entirety

of the pork skin that had been removed and cut into pieces of roughly two square inches, ensuring that its thickness measured almost two inches of fat beneath the skin. The process was tedious and took most of what was left of the day.

The air was filled with the delicious aroma of bacon cooking. In the kitchens of both households the women prepared holiday delicacies of their own to correspond with the pork meats or some other foods. Eliza was busy baking empanadas. Lupita and Lola seasoned and salted various meat cuts for preservation or for the beginning of stuffing for tamales.

The children, for their part, played with their cousins, not minding the cold. They inhaled the aromas and delighted in the preview of what was to come. Already there were all sorts of sweets and other goodies to eat: hot chocolate, *buñuelos*, sugar glazed fruit, the candy-stuffed piñata they would break in two days. It was all they could do to hold in their excitement. The holiday was one time they could indulge without anyone reminding them to limit their portions because "money doesn't grow on trees."

Throughout the day additional relatives dropped by or arrived to stay. The highlight of the day was the glamour couple from Houston. Julieta and Eduardo were a young, vivacious couple. In Houston, they were at the center of a social circle that was made up of immigrants like themselves, who hailed from various surrounding villages such as theirs. Despite their status as a shadow community in black and white, the immigrants in Houston were all living-color among themselves, and they aspired to hold onto traditions and social status as if they lived back home. It being the fifties, conservatism and judgment were the order of the day in their community as it was in the general mainstream American society.

Now at the grandparents' house, each arriving sibling or cousin joined right in on the preparations for the festivities of the twenty-fourth. After pausing for profuse embraces and welcoming of Julieta and cooing over her first baby, it was all hands on deck again. The house filled with guests, and Lola instructed everyone what the sleeping arrangements would be for the duration of their stay. All children would sleep on the floor on foam mats. Some of the adults would share beds, but some would also sleep on blankets on the floor or on small cots. It was expected that all family members would accept the accommodations and be gracious and considerate of one another while in holiday mode in such close quarters.

"So when will you come live in Houston?" Julieta asked Ramiro, slipping her arm around his, as she came upon him while he stirred the *chicharrones*.

Ramiro leaned his face on her head. "Oh, sister, I assure you I am considering it. It won't be this year. I have already planned my return to California with Salomon and his family."

"Houston is a good place. Eduardo found a good job in a cement company, or something like that. They make walls out of concrete and rocks and things. He can get you in. If not, we have met some friends. They all work steadily. When you are ready, we will be there for you. Help you settle in," she hugged him and smiled. "Brrrr. It's getting too cold out here, and that fire is going to singe me if I get closer," She laughed and kissed his cheek to return to her mother's kitchen.

Three more years would pass before Ramiro took his sister up on her offer.

CHAPTER 16: *Touching the Dream*

n 1955, Ramiro moved to Houston, Texas, and so ended his migrant worker journeys. That was also the year Eliza got her first real home. In the fall of 1954, after his final stint in the California fields, Ramiro returned home determined to find a place to buy and begin developing his very own homestead. He had not counted on the search being so easy, but when he arrived, Doña Lupita gave him some unexpected but most welcome news. His brother's place was for sale.

"Mother tells me you are going to sell your place and expand your business in Valle Azul. Is that true?" said Ramiro.

"It is brother," said Alberto. I expect by the summer I will have my new place in Valle Azul ready to move in. My beloved little farm and home are on the market."

"I'd like to buy it from you. How much are you asking for it?" asked Ramiro.

"Well, I know you always wanted a place of your own, Ramiro. Are you sure you want to do this? Have you saved enough?" Alberto asked his younger brother. "It's a big responsibility. You will be away so much. Can Eliza live here alone?"

"She'll have the kids to help out, and we'll start out slow," replied Ramiro, "Yes, I can afford it. I've saved. I want to do this. You need a buyer. You want to move to Valle Azul as soon as possible. We'll both benefit. I've been saving. I'm ready."

"Well, Ramiro, if you are serious about this, the price for you, as my brother, is $15,000.00 Pesos," said Alberto.

Ramiro thought he was dreaming. He had been so focused on his mission of working and saving every cent he could that he hadn't considered that he could have bought a place the previous year. Maybe it was fated that he wait for the perfect place and time. Ramiro had been saving an average of $10,000.00 pesos yearly for four years. His dream was coming true.

He could afford to pay cash for the place and even have enough left over to furnish it modestly and to buy a few animals to supply milk, eggs, and pork for Eliza and the kids. The children now numbered almost six, one having been born since Ramiro's first migration north and another one expected in the spring.

The purchase of his brother's place was a major milestone for Ramiro. The property was a great place to start because it had a comfortable house, with space for a little grocery store should he wish to give that business another try. It had a storage room to keep plenty of inventory or general utility tools. Most important, the property had a small orchard of orange and lemon trees, a small corral, and access to irrigation ditches for planting corn or other crops.

His brother, Alberto, had run a successful grocery store there, but Alberto was ambitious and it had become apparent that he would have to move to a bigger town to truly make the profits he wanted. Alberto was the firstborn to Lupita and Timoteo. He also had the sharpest head for business out of all the siblings. He and Sofia had become a power couple in their cluster of villages. Alberto and Sofia had three boys and two girls. The elder children helped their parents run the store while their father was on the road delivering merchandise and selling groceries to folks in isolated places.

But the couple wanted better schools for the children and they insisted on all the kids finishing secondary school one day and going further if they chose to do so. Alberto fully expected to pay for room and board in Monterrey if one day the boys decided to attend the prestigious University of Nuevo Leon. Although Alberto had gained a reputation for being a tough creditor and negotiator, most everyone respected his business acumen and his generally ethical and humanistic approach to buying, selling, and moneylending.

The house Ramiro would soon occupy had been designed and built as a large cinderblock home with the typical simplicity of the country but with spacious, high-ceilinged rooms and shiny polished cement floors. The Spanish facade was a simplified baroque style that included a faux cupola center structure on the frontage wall of the structure above the entry door. Under that protrusion of wall were reliefs of Alberto's initials and the year the house was built. The kitchen had a great cooking chimney as well as a gas stove for flexibility in preparing all necessary meals.

§

"What do you, think, Eliza? Do you like it?" Ramiro asked her as the two couples sat down for *merienda* the following day before closing the deal. Eliza was unaware of the two brothers' negotiations.

"Like what?" Eliza said.

"This house, the land, the garden, the kitchen?" he said.

"Well, of course, I like it. I have told Sofia many times her home is beautiful. What a question to ask, Ramiro," she said and looked at him as if to scold him for his indiscretion. Alberto and Sofia looked on in amusement. Ramiro winked at them when Eliza took her eyes off him to proffer Sofia a silent apology for him.

"Then it is yours," Ramiro said.

Eliza looked at him, then she looked at Sofia, then she looked at Alberto. She wanted to see if they would start laughing at her naïveté, if they might show signs of being in on one of her husband's jokes. But they looked back with smiling faces and raised eyebrows, nodding as if to say, "Isn't it great?" She was beginning to believe her husband. No one gave any sign of jesting. She looked at Ramiro again. "What do you mean?" But she turned to Sofia as if she could only trust another woman for an answer, not someone of the Ocañas brood.

"It's true, Eliza. Alberto and I have decided to move to Valle Azul. We have sold the house to Ramiro. This is now your house," said Sofia with the biggest grin and walking over to where Eliza was seated, arms outstretched to embrace her. "Congratulations. You are the new lady of this house. Well, as soon as the papers are all final, you will be."

Eliza was almost in shock. She looked at Ramiro as if expecting him to break out in laughter for making her believe the joke. But Ramiro only stood up and hugged her. "You are the new lady of this house, *Mujer*."

He used the term "woman" as a substitute for "My love." Ramiro, like most of the folks in those parts was hesitant to profess love publicly, especially after marriage. To go around calling your wife "sweetheart" or "darling," let alone "baby," was considered too mushy, and mushiness was bad for the serious business of raising a large family in the country.

"This is your new home, *Mujer*," Ramiro repeated, and they all laughed. Eliza could hardly believe her ears, that she would be moving into that house that had, up to that point, symbolized affluence and success. She decided to simulate joy, and enjoy the moment with just a bit of her cautious I'll-believe-it-when-I-move-in attitude.

"Well, you're full of surprises this year," she said.

At that moment, the toddler in the bed began to cry. Eliza left the grownups and went to her little girl. She sat on the bed and took Sylvia in her arms despite her five-month pregnancy. She carefully helped the child out of bed and instructed her to sit quietly or go outside and play. As the girl quieted down, in response her mother's embrace, Eliza scanned the room trying to imagine herself the lady of such a great house. Through the large, Spanish-ironed window she could see the open space between the house and the corral. Beyond it, she looked at the green trees specked in bright orange dots and the immense blue sky above.

The house stood out as a glimmering white object amid a sea of green citrus trees between the ones that belonged to them and those that spread beyond, belonging to Monterrey corporations. It had a spacious patio, lined with mesquite trees and other varieties native to those parts, like *anacuas* and *pitas*, Joshua trees. The front of the house was unique, with an elevation of some four feet from the street. The slope from the street to the house included a four-sectioned tiered garden with a variety of flowers and a solitary *anacua* tree occupying one entire quadrant.

§

Within two months of the negotiation and shaking hands on the purchase of the homestead, Ramiro left home again, U.S. bound, only this time he wasn't going to California. The trip was also among the hardest Ramiro made because all he wanted to do was get to work on his newly acquired farm. Alas, he could not yet afford to sustain the place without more investment, so he accepted his fate and set out to patiently amass the remaining funds with American dollars. His new destination: Houston. Alberto assured him that all the paperwork would be done and the house ready for Eliza and the kids by Easter, which was when Ramiro had been told that everyone was given time off in the Houston factories. He figured he would be able to travel at that time to finalize the deal. Houston, after all, was a much closer drive than California. Only eight hours, give or take.

Getting settled in Houston reminded Ramiro a little of Chicago. Even Houston's January weather made him recall the chills he felt the first time he got off the Greyhound bus in the Windy City in what now seemed like ages ago. And Houston felt big and bustling, although in actuality it was one-third the size of Chicago. Still, compared to the country village of Naranjales, Houston was amazing. A city bright with lights, downtown skyscrapers, and fast cars on freeways was simply another world.

Ramiro took temporary residence with Julieta and Eduardo, and within a week he had gotten on with a construction company that was building a subdivision in the southwest part of the city. His work was menial and hard. He was digging ditches for house foundations. He soon found a boarding house in a Mexican American neighborhood near downtown. Some evenings he spent time strolling down Navigation Boulevard admiring the horizon of an emerging skyline that rose just a couple of miles west.

§

"*Ay*, Ramiro, it's wonderful that you're going to own Alberto's house. I bet Eliza is overjoyed, no?" Julieta asked from the front passenger seat of the '53 Chevy Eduardo was driving. Ramiro rode in the back seat as they made their way to Naranjales that Easter in 1955.

"She sure is. You should have seen her face when we first told her the news." Ramiro laughed. Then changing his tone, he said, "This is going to be a very busy four days. I have to get the family installed in the new place."

"But, really, Ramiro. Haven't you thought about just moving the family to Houston? Wouldn't that be the best plan since you will be working here so much anyway? You can have a man look after your place until you and the family are ready to return for good," Julieta said. "I know how much you miss them. It's not good for the kids to grow up without their father present every day. You are all missing so much of each other's lives."

"No, Julieta. Houston is not for my family. I will only be gone a couple more years. Save enough to buy another plot of land and a few head of cattle. Then I will join them. I will make up for lost time then, and we will all make our little farm prosper together. The U.S. is just not for us. Nothing like our own land and people to make a man happy," Ramiro replied.

Julieta's husband, Eduardo, mostly listened to the brother and sister in amusement. He was not one to intervene in those conversations. Truth be told, he simply didn't care much about their issues.

That Easter weekend, Ramiro arrived at his mother's house with the usual warm welcome, but those encounters had become less novel, more routine. He recruited his brother, Jacobo, and a few neighbors to assist him and Eliza with the move and settling in.

After finalizing the purchase by signing all the necessary papers and acquiring the title and deed, Ramiro surveyed his land once more: the white house and small grove of 3 hectares, or 7 acres. One morning he and Jacobo walked over just about every inch of the property as if counting the centimeters and feeling the texture of every piece of it. He had a thousand plans going through his head as to the projects to undertake in the small farm and the house proper. It would all have to wait until he had longer time to spend in his new castle. That was okay with him. He had time. Eliza and the kids moved in that Saturday.

That night was the first time Ramiro made love to his wife in a home that was all their own. They had no concern for anyone else but to make sure the kids were all asleep and their one-month-old baby Antonio was in his cradle. The next morning Ramiro returned to Houston just as reluctantly as he had left a few months earlier.

CHAPTER 17: *Campfire Horror*

Ramiro's ride to Houston on that beautiful Easter Sunday was bittersweet. He was ecstatic about having bought his first home with his own sacrifice of hard work and savings, yet leaving it was a struggle.

In Naranjales, it was Eliza who celebrated her new home the most, albeit in subdued ways. She had never quite shaken the feeling of being watched by her in-laws even when she wasn't. Now, she was out from under their shadow, and she felt free to be more herself. She would not be on constant guard to perform the role of model daughter-in-law. She relished being on her own, away from the vigilance of Lupita and Lola. The location of the house on the far northern edge of the village gave her not only space but distance from the hustle and bustle of the business and personalities of the Ocañases.

"Three years, tops, and I'll be here for good," Ramiro promised Eliza as he departed that Easter season. "That should allow me to save enough to return and get the business going."

Ramiro's toil continued as a laborer and general handyman in the construction site, and the days passed by slowly, becoming weeks and months. By Christmas time he was able to visit once again. It was a rather rushed trip, as he no longer had the extended time of a season off as when he was in California. Still, the traditional Christmas feast went on, with family and all the special foods of the season. Much of it was spent in his parents' house, but the evenings were for his family and, of course, he found time to resurvey the property that captivated most of his waking moments. On January first, he again tore himself away from all he loved, hitched a ride with a couple of other *paisanos* from the area, and back to Houston it was. But his inner joy at feeling his dream in the palm of his hand would not last too long, for soon he would be yanked back home under trying circumstances when one of the children suffered an accident.

It was mid-January, and the temperatures were near freezing in Naranjales. The Ramiro and Eliza estate was now all their own. It was one of the typical winter mornings in a house without any of the conveniences of the modern American home. Only the kitchen chimney warmed the house just enough to stave the cold. The family had not yet been in the house a year, so every day in it was still a celebration, especially for the kids. Baldemar in particular was enjoying the wide-open spaces and the pride of ownership that their father had contagiously spread to everyone. With Ramiro out of the country, and his being twelve years old, Baldemar also presumed he had the role of man of the house at times.

One wintry morning, Baldemar got up early and went outside to take in the beauty of the rising sun and listen to the howling of coyotes that could be heard coming from somewhere in the distance. Being twelve, he was already quite adept at managing his natural surroundings. Baldemar and his *cuates* often went into the surrounding desert or woods and hunted every sort of creature. They made their own traps, slingshots, bows and arrows, and sometimes borrowed a BB gun. One delicacy they captured was wild honey from the paper honeycombs that such bees made in the semiarid woods. And there was always a good rabbit or hare that the boys shot then roasted, along with some pigeons. He expertly built a small bonfire to keep warm as he stood out there defying the cold.

Eliza awoke soon after and went to the kitchen to start breakfast before getting the girls up to help with setting the table. The younger kids were still asleep but Carlos got up when he heard the coffee pot clang on the stove. At five years of age, Carlos greatly admired his big brother, although Baldemar had little time for the timid kid. Baldemar was too independent and, now, in puberty, too self-absorbed. He simply was too freewheeling and adventurous to take the time to bring a small boy along. Still, Carlos noticed that his big brother wasn't in bed like the rest, so he went outside to join him.

What happened next was the unthinkable for Eliza and a doom for Ramiro.

Carlos screamed. "I'm burning! I'm burning!"

"What the hell. Oh—Get on the ground. Roll on the ground!" Baldemar shouted as he realized what was happening and he desperately tried to put out the fire that was spreading up the boy's pajamas.

"I'm burning. Oh. Oh. My leg!" The boy kept crying as his big brother rolled him on the rough, upturned sod that surrounded them. The fire had been built at the edge of the patio, just a foot away from the field that would soon be planted with corn.

Eliza bolted out of the kitchen by the screams, and yelled out, waking up the girls. "*Dios mio*. What the heck are these *huercos* getting into now? Carlooooosssss!! Baldemaaaarrr!! What is happening? Oh, Jesus, Mary, and Joseph. What's happening?" And she ran out of the house toward the boys. All the children ran behind her as bundled up as they could get.

By the time Eliza reached the boys, Baldemar had succeeded in putting out the fire on his brother's clothes. Carlos was writhing in pain and crying uncontrollably. He was in agony and could not be calmed down, much as Eliza tried. The mother scooped the boy up in her arms and ran into the house to lay him on her bed. All the children were anxious and agitated at seeing their brother's burned leg and witnessing the chaotic scene. Eliza dispatched Baldemar to his uncle's house to fetch him and his truck to rush the boy to Valle Azul for treatment. Baldemar hopped on his bicycle and pedaled faster than he ever had.

The way Baldemar told it to Eliza, and Carlos confirmed, Carlos crept up on him. Baldemar had been keeping warm by straddling the small fire he had built, and he was listening to the call of the coyotes. When he stepped away from the fire to collect wood scraps to keep it going, Carlos decided he, too, would straddle the fire as he had seen his brother do. But Carlos being much smaller, his little legs could not clear all the fire. He was wearing a long flannel pajama. The hem of his baggy pajama bottoms made contact with a burning ember. In an instant, the bottoms were in flames. The result was that Carlos was severely burned in one leg, with some of the damage third-degree burns. His left leg suffered minor first-degree damage.

Eliza was devastated by the tragedy. Back from the town doctor in Valle Azul, she laid Carlos in the bed in the large room. She guided Baldemar out of the room, worried that the older boy, guilt ridden, was spending too much time trying to please Carlos, as if turning over his prized marble cache could take away the child's pain. The doctor had given Eliza a large supply of medicine. The child was in a fitful sleep, and Eliza knew from his furrowed brow that he was not resting. Although it was a freak accident, it was of greater severity than was normal to withstand, even for someone as tough as she. But her emotional fragility lay in her fear of the presumably ruthless judgment she might receive. She could imagine Ramiro shouting at her or blaming her for the incident. Not only would the medical bills eat up their savings, but his precious son's leg would be scarred for life. Guilt consumed her even though she had done nothing wrong, and she grasped the boy's hand and prayed that her body could absorb his pain.

When Ramiro was notified of the tragedy, his heart sank. It was an ordeal for a simple laborer to be given time off, not to mention the loss of wages that he would incur. Every blue-collar worker knows too well that workplace flexibility is not easily afforded them, especially if they are low on the totem pole, as Ramiro invariably was. He feared he might be fired, but he wasn't taking into consideration his greatest asset and one that every employer cherishes in a worker: he was always early to work and always dependable in performing his duties without complaint. His supervisor was disappointed that he would be shorthanded a few days, but he showed compassion for a father in desperation. He even surprised Ramiro by telling him to take all the time he might need to get his boy well again.

Ramiro silently thanked America for the little miracle of making him feel worthy of such dignity. He had heard stories of workers getting fired for requesting time off at peak periods. He booked the first bus available to reach his injure boy and the devastated wife. He was tortured imagining what kind of trip this would have been if the tragedy had been worse and his boy, or any of the other children, had died.

CHAPTER 18: *Chavela's Melodrama*

After the incident in which Carlos was burned, Eliza experienced great anxiety. Her normal duties seemed to have multiplied by adding the nursing detail to her plate. That forced her to open up to the offers of help from others. She became a little more sociable. It went against her nature to seek out company or ask for help from others, but her suffering child compelled her to reach out. One of her natural allies was Chavela, Jacobo's wife, as she was an outsider like herself. Because both women married into the family, they became temporary kindred spirits. They had both practically forsaken their own families to take up residence with their husbands in the social and physical domain of the Ocañases.

Chavela took to visiting Eliza after the fire incident, offering to help with the care of the boy, who had to undergo several weeks of recovery. His treatment consisted mostly of applying ointments and antibiotic creams to the affected areas. Eliza had to clean and dress the wounds to stave bacteria. Chavela had enough work of her own, but she managed to spend a few hours once or twice a week relieving Eliza of some of her burdens.

By the second visit, both women felt they each had a confidant in the other. When Chavela blurted her dislike of her domineering mother-in-law, Eliza felt they shared a common enemy. "Eliza, you probably guessed it by now, but the old lady doesn't like me. Well, I can't stand her either, I'll tell you."

"Ay, Chavela," said Eliza with a twinkle in her eye, putting her fingers to her lips as if to stop her mouth from saying anything more by pushing it back. "She is not so easy to get along with, I know. I wish I didn't have to see her so much, either," she added and giggled.

That secret they shared gave them an instant bond in spite of the fact that the two had almost opposite personalities. Where Eliza was petite and demure, Chavela was big boned and free spoken. Where Eliza was quiet and unassuming, Chavela was boisterous and flamboyant. Where Eliza was compliant and submissive to her husband, Chavela was prone to bouts of stubbornness and backtalk to hers. It seemed like it was those differences that drove the two women to form their sisterhood. But their bond was necessarily tepid because both women knew that their first loyalties were always with their husbands. They each appreciated the other's qualities and even attempted to borrow traits from each other, albeit with little success.

One afternoon Chavela was visiting with Eliza. She had only brought along her baby because Jacobo had taken the other children with him on a delivery he was making. She seemed particularly agitated.

"Eliza, I have to tell you about that filthy woman, my neighbor," she said.

"You're talking about Pancha, the cousin?" asked Eliza.

"Yes, her," said Chavela. "For a cousin, she sure acts like a dog."

"Well, what about her? I heard you two don't get along too well. Is that true? What's going on?" Eliza asked.

Chavela told her about the ongoing feud she had been having with Pancha for some time. The discord began when Pancha and her kids ventured onto Chavela's property and took some watermelons that were growing along the line that divided the two homesteads. There was no fence between them, only an irrigation ditch and a 300-meter row of pecan trees that Jacobo had planted. Chavela had been keeping an eye on the watermelons and cantaloupes in that section of the property as she loved those particular fruits and was looking forward to their ripening on the vine. One day, Chavela sent her oldest to check on the fruits. The girl came back and told her there were some plants with only one or two melons, and they weren't ready to be picked.

"How can that be? I have been checking on those plants. They had many melons," said Chavela. "I think someone's been stealing our melons, and I think I know who that is," she said, her face getting flushed with anger.

Of course, it could only be one person: Pancha.

It turned out Chavela was correct. Chavela set out to catch the thief red handed. The following week Chavela kept a close eye on the area. It didn't take long before she spotted the neighbor sneaking onto her land to take her precious melons. Chavela confronted the woman.

"And just what do you think you're doing? Is this the kind of neighbor I have, a thief? said Chavela, surprising Pancha to the point that the woman dropped her cache of fruit and stood pale and motionless for a moment.

Pancha didn't deny she was taking a few melons, but she felt that it was only neighborly to share. "Oh, Cousin. I wasn't stealing. You have so many. I know you can't possibly miss these few. What are a few more or less melons to you?"

"Don't you 'cousin' me, Pancha Varela! Why couldn't you just ask me for a melon or two? No, you just took what you wanted. It's not the first time, either, is it? You are just the lowest of the low. Stealing from your own family. I know we are nothing to each other, you and me, but our husbands are first cousins. That means nothing to you? For shame, Pancha, for shame! Now, you hand over those melons, and don't you ever steal from me again."

By that point both women's children had gathered at a distance, within hearing range, with Pancha's brood just on the other side of the irrigation ditch. The kids were excited and angry themselves. They sided with their respective mother, of course, and leered at the others in contempt.

"I won't, Chavela, I promise. But I can't believe you are making such a big deal of something like this. You have so many melons. Here, take your damn melons. And don't choke on them," said Pancha, hurt and defiant. "There is a God, Chavela, and God knows I was only taking a few, but you are a selfish woman, and God will record that about you."

And with that she turned heel and retreated to her house, her four children at her skirt.

That might have been the end of that except the fall brought with it a new incident. Pancha and her kids raised Chavela's ire once again by traipsing over the irrigation ditch and collecting a basketful of pecans from Chavela's trees.

"Now, Eliza, you know that pecans are a precious thing around here. Everyone wants pralines and I can sell them at good prices," Chavela explained to Eliza. Of course, Eliza knew that folks made all sorts of simple pecan and sugar confections for after-dinner enjoyment or more elaborate delicacies with condensed milk, caramelized varieties, as Doña Lupita had taught Eliza to make.

Chavela became incensed, and vowed to call the authorities if Pancha did it again. After all, Chavela made her extra household money from the sale of her pecans. Plus, it helped her win rare favor with her mother-in-law, who made the best caramel pralines around and sold them in her store.

The two women had a second confrontation, but Jacobo caught wind of it and intervened. He instructed Chavela to drop it and let Pancha get by this time. But Chavela wasn't the type to simply drop things when she felt wronged. She retaliated by going over to Pancha's garden one evening after dark and filling a flour sack with her neighbor's pumpkins. In the process of committing the act, she knocked over a tin bucket, which set the dogs to barking. When Pancha confronted her, the two women almost came to blows. It took Pancha's mother's intervention to stop them from pulling each other's hair out.

"I tell you, Eliza, that woman is going to make me do ugly things. And her husband is not much better. Do you know he barely speaks to Jacobo anymore? It's horrible. It's all that hag's fault," said Chavela.

Eliza could not believe her ears. She herself could not imagine engaging in such behavior even if it meant losing out on some of her belongings.

"No. I just can't believe how bad it has gotten. The two cousins are barely speaking? Oh, no, Chavela. You have to do something to make things better. Try to make peace with Pancha," pleaded Eliza.

"I know you're right. I am trying to let it go, but I can't promise anything. Jacobo is just as fed up, but he has always had issues with that slick cousin of his. I don't know what's going to happen," said Chavela.

"Well, Chavela, I worry about you. You know the old woman does not speak well of you. If she finds out this conflict is growing, she will blame you. Those people are her brother's family," Eliza warned.

"The old woman doesn't scare me. Jacobo knows she is unfair to me, and he is not happy about it. I can't wait to leave this miserable place and get away from her," Chavela continued. "I am trying to convince Jacobo to relocate. He's not budging. I don't know how to persuade him."

Eliza tried to give her hope by focusing on Lupita's better qualities.

"You know, last November was the closest I have ever felt to her. When she helped me give light to Sylvia," said Eliza, recalling the time when Lupita midwifed her last baby. "She acted almost loving. She was even gentle in her commands to me to breathe, or when to push, or how hard. She was almost tender in reassuring me everything was going to be all right. I almost felt her like a mother."

"I have to admit she does have her good qualities. She is just too nitpicky. Besides, you are her favorite. She loves it that you obey quietly and that you have lived by her side so long," Chavela said.

"But I hate it when she makes indirect jokes about my mother. You know my mother made mistakes. If you didn't before, I'm sure Jacobo has told you based on how his mother relishes laughing at others' expense. She loves telling all her intimates about it. It's true, my mother has never really been there for me. Not once has she come to care for me after the birth of one of my children. I know she lives far, but," Eliza said softly. "I'm ashamed to say it, but I can tell you."

"Sister, don't you pay her any mind. You are not your mother, just like I am not mine. Your mother made mistakes, I know. Yes, Jacobo told me something about it. She fell in love with another man. It happens. What can a woman do when the heart is the boss? Don't let anybody shame you, my sister," said Chavela.

Chavela looked out the window. A truck was pulling up in front of the house. It was Jacobo and the kids. Seeing the hour, and feeling grateful for Chavela's visit, Eliza invited the family to stay for dinner. At first they declined, not wishing to put Eliza through any trouble, but with a little nudging, they relented. The two women retreated to the kitchen to begin dinner preparations.

§

In Houston, Ramiro had been daydreaming as the time neared to clock-out for the day. He must have received Eliza's thoughts telepathically because he was recalling the time he left Naranjales and his pregnant wife. They had just moved into their new home. When he went through the night's rituals that signaled he wanted to make love, Eliza acted hesitant. He was disturbed by her reaction considering that they were in celebration mode. Finally, she confessed that she didn't like the physical contact in her condition.

At first, Ramiro took her words as a rejection and became indignant. He tried to focus on the new baby. It would be their sixth child. Images of previous births and the great joy he experienced helped ease his resentment.

Ramiro caressed her and massaged her until she relaxed enough to relent and pleased him as he was used to. Eliza never learned to say no to Ramiro, and his personality was too dominant and passionate to allow him to back off on his own. The next day was Easter Sunday, April 10, but he would spend much of it on the road back to Houston and his new job. How his heart ached for leaving. How he wished he could simply unpack his suitcase and go back in the house and look after his wife. How he wished he could be present for his new baby's birth.

Instead, he had to recoil to the status of the invisible menial worker. His head had never been much for school discipline, so he felt hopeless in learning the English language, and he knew that without that key skill, he would have to endure his lowly status. He finally snapped out of his funk, and his mind wondered toward finding positive things in his new world of work, like his new work pal Juan Luis. At least he was meeting new, quality people.

CHAPTER 19: *The Shooting of Jacobo*

I t wasn't exactly a gunfight. It wasn't exactly the old West. But it was a death, or rather two deaths, and guns were involved.

It was August 1956 when tragedy befell the Ocañas clan.

Jacobo was the apple of his parents' eyes. He was rambunctious, good natured, a prankster, and a big-hearted man. He was the baby of the boys and he was married to a woman detested by Lupita. Jacobo and Chavela had four children and a small farm on a cliff overlooking the river. Chavela was just as spirited as Jacobo but she was also prone to garrulous exchanges whenever she thought herself disrespected. Her unwillingness to ignore a slight or to share of her gifts had developed into a feud between her and Cousin Fernando's wife, Pancha.

When the entire village attended the wedding of the milliner's daughter, the usual merriment of such an event led to lots of dancing and drinking. The event was a sprawling outdoor gathering, at the bride's family's compound. Their large patio was on a natural rocky area that gave the guests plenty of smooth ground for their dancing. There was the usual, specially prepared wedding rice, wedding cookies made of fine sugar and cinnamon, tamales, and grilled beef. And, of course, there was plenty of beer, mescal, and tequila. The rotund, friendly milliner was proud, and the bride was radiant. As was to be expected, however, all the men became intoxicated to varying degrees by the time night fell. It was then that the party really got started.

Neither Chavela nor Pancha were present when the incident occurred, as they had both left at sunset because of the small children's restlessness. If truth be told, however, they left early because it was all they could not stand being near each other. Lupita and Lola did not attend, as they were not fond of large public gatherings. The cousins, Jacobo and Fernando, both remained at the celebration after their wives left. The men continued to dance with the few unspoken for women at the party.

One such woman was not well known in Naranjales because she was from a neighboring hacienda. Mireya, they called her. She was there with a male cousin and his girlfriend, and acquaintance of the groom. Mireya was not one to follow the normal rules of modesty and demureness that were customary of all single girls in the region. Something else no one knew was that she was Fernando's sometime paramour on the sly. After the band got in full swing and the spirits took effect, Fernando became a little bolder in both his polka moves and in frisking Mireya.

After Chavela left the scene, Jacobo, too, set his sights on the beautiful Mireya not knowing she was his cousin's gal. He told himself that he was going to spend the rest of the evening with her and have a good time dancing. He saw his chance when Fernando took a restroom break. Jacobo approached the girl, who must have been no older than twenty to his thirty-two. The woman looked him over with an expression of "are you kidding me?" on her face as he extended his hand and invited her to dance. Then her eyes widened a little as she caught sight of Fernando approaching fast. Before anyone knew what happened, Fernando had slapped Jacobo's hand away from Mireya. Both quite drunk, the two men stared at each other.

"I asked her for this dance," said Jacobo.

"Her card is full with only my name. You keep away," said Fernando.

The liquor didn't help matters when Fernando protested that Jacobo had no business cutting in on his girl. The crowd gave an audible gasp when Jacobo shoved his cousin and Fernando fell to the ground.

"Aren't you a brazen son of a bitch to openly admit to having a girl," said Jacobo.

What followed next can only be described as a volley of insults and curse words between the men. A struggle ensued and punches were thrown. The crowd moved back as the two men fiercely wrestled in the middle of the dance area. The bride was demanding someone stop them. A couple of young men tried to intervene, but stepped back when they saw the gun.

Fernando was carrying a gun because he had been deputized by the authorities to help out in maintaining order in the rural areas when celebrations were held. As the two men struggled, Jacobo attempted to take the gun from his opponent with the intention of disarming him and thus eliminating his opponent's upper hand in the fight. But the gun was not properly secured and went off in the struggle. At first no one knew who pulled the trigger or who was hit, but the answer was revealed soon enough. Fernando fell to the floor holding his stomach, blood staining his white *guayabera*.

Women yelled, children screamed, grown men hollered. Jacobo looked up like a raccoon caught in the headlights of a speeding truck. He quickly dropped the gun beside his fallen cousin. He fled before anyone could say a word to him or attempt to apprehend him. He ran wildly through the semidesert hill. His adrenaline kicked in and he sobered up quickly. He kept running. He ran for more than an hour, not sure where to run to, until he reached his parents' house.

Meanwhile Fernando lay on the ground, a puddle of blood slowly spreading around his body. His brothers had started to run after Jacobo but returned to attend to their brother when Fernando proved too fast a runner. The brothers had been on the verge of intervening in the fight and breaking up the two men, but they believed their brother would emerge the winner, and they wanted to see Jacobo get his just desserts after all the stories they had heard of the two men's growing feud. They looked up at the crowd and demanded someone give them a blanket and towels to stop the bleeding.

The brothers loaded Fernando onto a truck, and transported him home where their hysterical mother tended to his wound. Their mother was wailing the moment she caught sight of her boys carrying her favorite as if he were dead. The guys didn't say much more than necessary, and ordered the women to nurse their brother. They rushed out of the house guns in waistbands. The old woman looked at them in horror and pleaded with them not to do anything foolish.

"Above all, don't go and get yourself killed. Stay home, my sons. We'll have the authorities find Jacobo tomorrow," she begged.

All her wailing and pleading fell on deaf ears. The men's rage was enhanced by alcohol. They were out for revenge; nothing else would do. The night was black, but they grabbed a flashlight and hoped the half moon would guide them.

Meanwhile Jacobo had entered his parents' home in a whirlwind of passion and shaken by fright. He was as much in shock at the knowledge that he had taken the life of not just a man, but that of his own blood, his cousin. But he was in survival mode, and his mind was filled with horror at the thought of being sent to prison for life.

"Ma, I shot a man. I shot Fernando. I don't know what to do. I have to go away."

"Jacobo, look at you. My son, what happened? You killed Fernando? No, no, no. Your cousin. *Que barbaridad!* Tell me you didn't kill anybody. Oh, my son. Oh, Jesus, Mary, and Joseph! *Ay Dios mio*," said Lupita, and her words were echoed by Timoteo and Lola, who took turns holding the staggering man and looking in horror at his condition.

Jacobo could not fathom life without freedom. He would rather become a fugitive than be locked up like an animal. "He started the fight. He had a gun. It was not secured. It went off, I didn't mean it. They think I did it. They're coming after me. I have to run. I don't want to go to prison. I won't do it. I have to go," he said. "I will die if I have to be locked up and lose my wife and children. I'll be dead."

No one could reason with him, not even Lupita. Shortly after his arrival, Chavela burst in, having been notified by the children of the women next door. Jacobo ignored even his beloved's pleading not to flee. He held her tight and shed tears in her bosom, but he was crazed. His mind was made up. He demanded that Lupita give him a gun that he knew she kept in the armoire under lock and key. At first the mother refused. Within minutes she relented, upon Timoteo's urging, and she gave him the gun along with her blessings. "Here it is, son. Here's the gun. Please, son, don't go," she insisted.

The scene in the household was utter chaos. Chavela and the kids begged Jacobo, again, not to do anything foolish, but he remained adamant. His plan was to cut through the vast orange groves until he reached the next village to the north. There he would hitch a ride to Monterrey somehow. He would go incognito until he got word of a better solution. When he heard the sound of an engine outside, he knew it must be the cousins coming for him, and he grabbed the gun and ran through the back patio and the family grove to the corporate orange groves beyond.

He was right. It was his angry cousins looking for him, and they were mad, alright. One of the men stormed into the house and demanded to know where Jacobo was hiding. No answers satisfied them. Lupita and Timoteo ordered him out of the house. The men grumbled with grudging respect to their aunt and uncle and exited the house vowing Jacobo would be caught. They drove around to a side dirt road that ran through the farms, then they set out on foot to find Jacobo among the orange trees.

§

Eliza and the kids had gone to bed shortly after sunset as usual. That night Eliza remained awake, tossing and turning in her bed. From a distance, she thought she heard a gunshot. She sat up in bed, feeling nauseous. She looked around at the kids' beds. They were all asleep, she thought, but the two eldest were just as awake as she. Within a few minutes, she heard the gallop of a horse outside her window. Then it stopped. She shook in fear of who it might be in the middle of the night. Soon there was frantic knocking on the door.

"Who is it?" she said, no longer caring who it was in particular but anxious to know what could bring a lone rider out that late at night.

It was Paco, the carpenter's son, who lived some hundred yards from Lupita. He had terrible news. He told Eliza that Jacobo had been shot and killed. That he had been crouching under an orange tree in the corporate farm when the Gonzalez brothers had come upon him and shot him in the head. He told her to please come to Lupita's house. Her help would be needed. He had been sent by Chavela, who was very distraught and wanted Eliza there.

Eliza nearly fainted from the shock. She crossed herself and prayed to God that everything would be all right. Immediately her thoughts turned to Ramiro far away in Houston. How would he take the news? He would be crushed. The brothers were very close. She couldn't bear to think about the pain her husband would feel when he learned of the terrible news. She turned to Esmeralda and Baldemar, seeing that they were awake and had heard everything. She told Esmeralda to take care of the kids until she came back. Baldemar would accompany her by foot to her in-laws' house. It would take thirty minutes to get there, but she could not ride on a horse with Paco, so she would get there as she always had, by foot.

Lupita was inconsolable. Even before she arrived at the house, Eliza could hear the wails loud and clear. It was Lupita. She kept repeating, "They shot him like a dog. They shot him like a dog," and she would go into a tirade of curse words and name calling of her brother's entire family. She lay listless and prostrate with grief on the sofa in the living area of the house, the very place where the open casket would stand in the next days. Around the grieving mother were several neighbor women. Lola, of course, was devastated as well, but she kept calm in the face of her parents' grief. Timoteo was alone in a chair in the waiting area of the store. Lola would sit beside him for moments and hug him and console him when she noticed the tears roll down in silence from his gunmetal-blue eyes.

Eliza approached Chavela who was sitting surrounded by her

children, apart from her mother-in-law, in a darkened corner of the living room. Upon seeing Eliza before her, Chavella expelled a loud wail and began sobbing uncontrollably in her friend's arms. Eliza held her tightly as she herself joined in the public crying. Eliza held one of Chavela's younger daughters. The girl sniffled, not quite knowing what was going on. The older children stared across the room as people entered, paying their respects to them, crying and weeping as they showed their condolences. Eliza held the young girl tighter. Did she know? Did this little girl know she would never have a father to protect her or walk her down the aisle? Eliza couldn't help thinking about Ramiro. So much in fact, she thought she might suffocate. What was she thinking allowing her husband to leave her?

It was almost expected that every female who entered the house cried out loud as she paid her condolences to the various grieving family members. The mournful hubbub created a surreal atmosphere with dozens of people milling about in semi-dark quarters, pacing from one to another of the relatives in mourning, then settling into a sitting position of bowed heads and prayer. Each encounter raised a fresh flurry of crying, weeping, yelping, agonizing, howling, and every variation of condolence. The hour neared midnight and only a solitary kerosene lamp struggled to illuminate each cavernous room.

The entire family was devastated indeed. Death was to be respected. No amount of chest beating and despairing cries was too much to show the world how well loved and respected the departed had been. Eliza's thoughts wandered over the spectacle of death. On the sad occasions of a human passing, everyone mourned openly and conspicuously. Women dressed completely in black for a minimum of a year. Afterward, truly pious women wore variations of black and white for another six months. But by no means would any grieving woman be caught dressed in red even five years after the loss of a loved one, especially a husband or a son. Eliza would see about sewing a black dress tomorrow.

The few children who happened to be in the midst of all the

spectacle of grief would have to be strong not to be affected by it all. Weaker souls might develop nightmares or other psychosis years later from such sights as witnessed that night in the Ocañas home. Indeed, for many years poor Alicia was haunted by the days and nights that followed. No loved one should ever die without receiving such adoration and demonstrations of eternal sorrow over their loss.

§

When the news reached Houston, it was not a pretty sight, either. Julieta did not have a phone yet, as many homes in the barrios still lacked such a luxury. Whenever there was a need to receive or make a call, Julieta walked over to her next-door neighbor's house, where she was always welcomed. Iliana came calling that Monday afternoon. She told Julieta that there was a long distance call for her from Valle Azul. Julieta thought it odd, but she decided not to jump to conclusions about anything unpleasant. She picked up the receiver. It was Alberto.

"Sister, I'm afraid I have some bad news. Maybe you better sit down," he said.

Julieta lost all color from her pretty face and went completely cold. Suddenly she knew she was about to hear something terrible. She looked over at Iliana who was standing at the door of the dining room watching, curious about the long-distance call from home. Iliana noticed the anguish and paleness that swept over her friend.

"Alberto, what is it?" Julieta said as she extended her unsteady arm toward a sofa cushion to steady herself and break the fall as she flopped onto the sofa.

"There is no easy way to say it, so I will just say it. We have lost our brother. Jacobo has died. He was shot," he said.

"No," Julieta yelled into the receiver. "No. It can't be. *Mi hermano. Mi hermanito. Manito lindo. Lo hemos perdido*," she cried to the sky, she cried to Ileana. My brother. My beloved brother. Jacobo is dead? No. Alberto, tell me it is not true. This is a nightmare. Tell me, Alberto." She began sobbing uncontrollably. "How did it happen?"

Alberto continued, "It was the Gonzalezes at Jovita's wedding, Don Trino's daughter. He got into a fight with Francisco. Jacobo shot him accidentally, then the brothers killed him." He paused. "I'm sorry. How soon can you come home so we can have the funeral?" Alberto blurted it out machine gun style.

Julieta could not speak. Her brain went blank and her vision blurred as she gasped for air. Iliana rushed to her side desperate to help but not knowing what to do. She ran to the kitchen for a glass of water. She splashed some water on Julieta's face and put the glass in Julieta's trembling hands, helping her to sip from it.

Iliana was helpless to comfort her friend. She simply held her as tight as she could.

"Why? Why? What happened? Why did they shoot him?" Julieta spoke into the receiver. It was almost a whisper.

"That's basically it. We will know more details soon. You will learn everything when you come. I am very sorry, *Hermana*. Please, don't fall apart. We have too much work to do. You will tell Ramiro, won't you? Please try and get here no later than Thursday. The body will be iced down, but it is summer and it is hot as you know," said Alberto, always practical and conscious of expenses.

"Yes. Yes, *Manito*. We will be there as soon as Eduardo and Ramiro can arrange their leave. I expect we can be there Wednesday. Oh, God. My brother. My beloved Jacobo," Julieta kept repeating.

Ramiro swore he would kill the bastards who shot his brother.

When Eduardo went by the boarding house where he was living, Ramiro thought it was odd that his brother-in-law was visiting on a workday. He soon learned that it was more than just a visit. It was an invitation to come and have dinner with the family, with his sister.

"Something's happened. I think you should hear it from Julieta rather than me," Eduardo said.

Ramiro became a little alarmed, but he agreed to go with Eduardo. The brother-in-law made small talk in the short ride from the edge of the neighborhood to his house on Eastwood Street. Ramiro began to feel a gnawing at his stomach in a premonition of bad news. Sure enough, no sooner had he entered the house than he knew it was bad. Julieta came rushing toward him, and as soon as she put her arms around him she broke down in tears. Ramiro held on to her trembling body, absorbing all the pain and emotion she was feeling.

"It's Jacobo," she wailed.

Ramiro's heart sank.

"We've lost him," she said.

He felt a punch in the gut.

"He was killed."

Ramiro saw red and lost his balance for a split second.

"The Gonzalezes killed him," she cried as she continued to hold Ramiro's hands tightly.

She had blurted it out in rapid fire, but every word burned his soul. Ramiro guided her to the sofa and helped her sit. He had to do it or he would have collapsed himself. He needed to sit down as he continued to process the terrible news. In his manly world, men didn't cry in front of women, not even a sister. A man could cry with his mother silently, or shed a tear or two and then compose himself, but he was supposed to stay strong for his sister to have the comfort she needed. He remained stoic despite the moistening of his eyes and the knot in his throat. He held his sister warmly, trying to reassure her it would be alright.

Ramiro clenched his teeth. "I will kill the bastards who did this."

The following day, Ramiro went to work as usual. During the morning break, he went in to speak to his supervisor, a rangy leather-faced man of about forty-five by the name of Kyle. Ramiro was accompanied by his new friend, Juan Luis, the Catholic from Monterrey, who spoke enough English to translate his request for time off. Kyle was not too happy, but he seemed to feel compassion once again. He told Ramiro that he could take off that Thursday, and up to a week if he needed, but to come back as soon as possible. By Wednesday evening, the family was on the road to their brother's funeral some nine hours away. They arrived exhausted at 2:00 a.m. to meet the equally exhausted mourners who anxiously awaited their arrival.

Eliza was beside herself when she saw the pain in Ramiro's face. The swell of cries, wails, and lamentations, which had subsided since that fateful Sunday night, went up all over again at the arrival of the "American" relatives. For their part the kids were experiencing various levels of emotions. Baldemar stood silently outside where the men gathered. He was a sentinel, assuming a manly pose. Esmeralda stayed by her mother's side and emulated showing the proper respects and salutations. Sometimes she cried along with one woman or another, but she was confused about what she was feeling. Alicia flitted about from cousin to cousin as if she didn't understand the gravity of the situation but fascinated by so much mourning. The younger ones were too young to comprehend much. They were kept in the little house, where local women volunteered to look after them, along with several other young cousins. They were processing the events as best they could, but none of them had ever seen a funeral up close like that, and it was disturbing and exciting all at once.

No funeral had been so dramatic in the history of Naranjales or since. The casket was dark grey and sat in the middle of the large family room that served as both living room and sleeping area as was the norm. By the corners of the casket stood tall pedestals holding long fat candles of whitish wax. All the mirrors on the armoires were covered in white bed sheets. Visitors came and went at all hours of the day and night to view the body or pay their respects. The body lay in the box unembalmed, as such things didn't get done in the country in those days. Jacobo's face still bore cotton plugs where the bullet had penetrated. The corpse also had cotton or gauze stuffed in his mouth and every other orifice, for sanitary purposes.

The out-of-towners hardly rested that day. The burial took place at 3 that Thursday afternoon. A long procession of mourners walked to the cemetery from Naranjales to the village of San Jose, next door, about three miles away. There were two sets of pallbearers to take turns carrying the casket on their shoulders through the streets. Several of the men in the family carried large wreaths of waxed paper flowers in bright reds, yellows, pinks, and whites. All the women of the family rode on the back of Alberto's pickup truck.

After the burial, with its renewed torrents of tears and wails, the out-of-towners stayed the weekend to comfort their parents and each other. They also helped Chavela with a number of business issues she would have to attend to in the following months before she returned to the village of her father to start her life anew. Some made donations of money and supplies for the orphaned children whose futures now looked gloomy and more uncertain than ever.

Ramiro returned to Houston a torn man. He had barely exchanged words with his wife or his other siblings, nor had he said much to his grieving parents. Everyone was stunned by the tragedy of losing a brother in such traumatic circumstances, so no one noticed the social deficiencies. But it was almost as disturbing that they had lost an entire branch of the family. All the Ocañas brothers, as well as the Gonzalez clan, began to harbor ideas of revenge.

Naranjales was a small place. Valle Azul, although a city, was still small enough that it was hard for visitors not to frequent the same places. There was only one church, one doctor, one bank, one government office. On the evening after the funeral, Ramiro took Jacobo's truck and went into town. Along the way, he spotted a man herding a cow back from pasture. It was one of the, now enemy, cousins. Ramiro fought an urge to stop the truck and attack his cousin. Likewise, the other man looked intently into the cab of the truck as if he wanted to jump on it and attack the driver. The incident passed, and Ramiro went on to Alberto's place, but a black cloud came over him that seemed to foretell misfortune, and he shuddered at the thought of more killings in the family.

The Ocañas men couldn't help but wonder about protracted future paybacks. It seemed that Mother Nature gave greater force to hate than to the bonds of blood when it came to tragedies of this scope.

Those thoughts of revenge weighed heavily on Ramiro as his mourning wore on. But his was a compounded mourning. He also mourned, in a different yet perhaps in a more profound manner, the death of his dream. How could he keep his little piece of paradise? How could he ever return to that environment where his brother's killers roamed and not be compelled to avenge his death? His dream was dying before his eyes.

§

In the days that followed, back in Houston, Ramiro spent more time than usual with his sister. They comforted each other with reminiscences of Jacobo's legendary practical jokes and tales of his adventurous lifestyle.

A week later they received the news that Fernando had died of his wounds. The Gonzalezes naturally leveled murder charges against the already dead and buried Jacobo. Their claim to equal pain did not quell Lupita's condemnation. For months she yelled curses and lamentations whenever a Gonzalez passed on the street outside her store.

"My son was killed like a dog on the street," she'd yell, and the men would lower their heads and pick up their pace. As Lupita's property was located precisely in the center of the village, and there was only one road of access, no one could avoid walking or riding past her doors sooner or later.

In the process of healing that brought the siblings closer, Julieta recognized Ramiro's agony and profound sadness at letting go of his plans to return home and make his farm the envy of the region. She nudged him gently toward what she considered the only answer, the idea that if he truly felt the atmosphere so hostile in Naranjales, he should not risk being around any of the Gonzalez men. The surest way to do that was to bring his family to Houston and not return to Naranjales. Julieta knew, however, that if she didn't use finesse, Ramiro would recoil and not accede. She had to coax the idea out of Ramiro's own lips.

Finally, he spoke the words. "I will bring the family here for a few years. We can live here until the air is cleared down there. I will request a letter of sponsorship from my bosses at Texas Homes. I have no other choice. I will start the process of obtaining residency for Eliza and the kids. I'll do it tomorrow."

CHAPTER 20: *The Roughest Road*

J une 1957. The kids had never been as excited as they were that warm, sunny morning in Reynosa. Ramiro, Eliza, and their six kids had spent the night at the home of a second cousin. The lady served everyone hot Nescafé with milk and the customary sweet breads that Carlos recalled as a special treat to the kids, but that morning even the sweetbreads could not compete with their anticipated adventure. They were about to cross the international bridge, and their lives would be taking a drastic turn toward a future no one could imagine. All they knew was that their city-life fantasies were about to come true.

The family boarded the Continental Trailways bus in McAllen, Texas. The Mexican bus ride through the mountainside and then the tawdry and fantastical kaleidoscope that was the border city of Reynosa had been just the start. The younger ones—Alicia, ten, Carlos, seven, Sylvia, five, and Antonio, two—could have jumped up and down with joy the entire trip had it not been for Eliza's constant placating them. The two older ones—Baldemar, fifteen, and Esmeralda, thirteen—also took in every new sight and smell in awe and wonderment, but their emotions were more complicated. The teenagers regretted leaving behind their social life where they had started to taste the sweetness of popularity and camaraderie. Not the least of their sadness involved the separation from a special girl or boy with whom puppy-love romance was beginning to bloom.

§

Ramiro had joined his family in Naranjales for that fateful weekend of final packing and travel. After Alberto's truck ride to the city
of Valle Azul, they rode a bus to Reynosa. But before departing from
Naranjales emotions were high and so were tensions. It was the first
time that Carlos and his siblings had witnessed discord between their
parents. It happened as the family was boarding the back of the pickup
truck that was to deliver them to Valle Azul. Ramiro was calling out a
checklist of items that he considered essential. "Envelope with cash?"
The question was directed at Eliza.

Eliza searched her purse for the envelope but she could not locate
it. She looked at Alberto standing beside the truck, and at the kids, as
if hoping no one was watching. She became flustered and lost her composure. She could not recall where she had placed the envelope with
the money that was supposed to get them through the trip.

"Where is the envelope?" Ramiro said, his voice becoming testy.

Eliza looked startled and her eyebrows raised, her forehead furrowed. Her eyes contracted then expanded as she said, "It's not here. I
don't have it. I'm sure I put it on the table for you. I took it from the
armoire. I had it there, hidden. I took it. I think. I took it, and put it
on the table."

"I saw nothing on the table. Go back and find it," Ramiro said,
raising his voice, his neck turning red.

Then he looked over to where the kids were standing, and he
saw them mesmerized by what they had just witnessed. The kids all
watched in puzzlement, resentment creeping into their hearts at the
tone their father was using, as if they wanted to aid their mother in
locating the envelope but thought it better not to interfere, sensing
unfamiliar emotional territory. Noticing his children's confusion, the
red anger in the proud man's face turned for a moment into a variant
shade, the red of shame.

Their father paced briskly around the truck sometimes shaking
his head, looking up toward the house, looking at his watch. None
of the children dared speak. They had never bonded sufficiently with

their father to understand his outburst. They had always seen him as a bigger than life figure who showed up like a glamorous benefactor on special trips. He only stayed a short time then left again in a flurry of emotional goodbyes. The children had developed a habit of taking their countrified, functionally illiterate mother for granted. But this felt different.

This time their hearts leapt in sympathy for their berated mother. This time Ramiro was a hostile outsider breaking into their intimate world and threatening something previously unrecognized as precious in their lives. The children closed ranks in an unspoken spiritual agreement to protect Eliza, only they did it as if telepathically. No one could see them move any differently or speak up in protest in unison, but sure as the sun was shining, the kids hurt for her. Despite their confused rancor, they dared not speak up against the man they had admired for so long. Carlos, like the rest of them, processed what he could for his seven years and then tried to pretend that it wasn't so bad.

After five minutes that seemed an eternity, Eliza appeared on the front door. She held a piece of white paper in her trembling hand. It was the envelope. "It must've fallen. I looked all over and found it between the armoire's skirt and the wall," said their mother. The children rejoiced in silence and soon returned to their daydreams.

§

Eliza had been a nervous wreck for weeks. The entire ordeal of uprooting herself from the placid surroundings where she had become accustomed to enjoying her privacy and relative independence was overwhelming. Having a home full of young children who depended on her, even worshipped her, as young children are wont to do with a parent, had given her a sense of ownership and power these past seven years of her life. But the hustle and bustle of extreme packing and organizing the move of her entire clan was almost too much for her coping skills.

Eliza and the kids had had to endure several trips to Monterrey to secure their travel documents and passport at the American consulate. A photographer came to the house and took a family picture for the group passport of the mother and her kids, as they were all minors. All that trotting around in a huge scary city like Monterrey wore hard enough on her. But having to impose seven people on distant cousins for hospitality for two nights while in the big city was almost worse for the socially inept Eliza.

Then there was Houston. Simply imagining a vast and possibly inhospitable land in which she would become totally dependent on Ramiro beyond what she already was, gave her shudders. Somehow, she mustered the strength and stamina for most of the work at hand as it was her custom not to let her essential duties go unattended. Maybe it was something about her early training to do what must be done, to obey the orders of her superiors, of her husband, to show as little emotion as possible, to never complain about her station in life or her duties. She belonged, rightly or wrongly, to a time and place whose harshness was neither intentional nor spiteful. It simply was, and while some women, by dint of character and desperation, evolved to strengths beyond compare, as was the case with her mother-in-law, Eliza simply did not have that in her. Her only strength was her ability to cope.

§

Carlos observed his mother flustered and confused by her mistake, and he wished he could hold her in his small arms. But even at receiving affection Eliza put up a wall. She was not affectionate that way, not like his father used to be, and still was with the little ones. Eliza was a strict disciplinarian, and the kids had become accustomed to her gruffness and lack of the usual fussiness of other mothers.

The boy looked away, up at the cloudless blue sky. He saw a similar melancholy in his siblings. He looked at his surroundings as a way of saying goodbye to his sometimes-enchanted world. The butterflies fluttered and swept from flower to flower, oblivious to the drama be-

fore them, in the family's garden that his sisters had kept always flowering or lush. There was the back patio that the boys had always kept
clean and in which they all played constantly. The anacua tree up front,
just beside the truck, was heavy with the marble sized fruit he loved so
much and whose pits had once constipated him for days from eating
so many and not chewing the seeds properly, or was that from the delicious prickly pears? He recalled his grandmother's efforts at what she
called "unplugging" him, embarrassing even for a boy of 4 because she
probed his bottom with her fingers, out on the veranda, open to everyone's view. Across the way were the citrus trees in the grove, their limbs
bowed by the weight of green oranges that would soon be turning into
sweet balls of sunshine. He looked across the road in the distance at
the white boxes under mesquite trees in the neighbor's farm. They were
lined in rows, some three dozen of them, and he recalled the many
times he had eaten of the honey that was produced there and processed
into many products. He especially liked sucking the honey directly
from the honeycomb and chewing the waxy casings till the flavor was
all gone.

"Carlos, get in the truck. What are you dreaming about?" said
Esmeralda, his oldest sister. All the kids were already in the back of the
truck and his uncle Alberto was in the driver's seat. Ramiro was locking
up the gates to the property and would soon be boarding the cab of the
truck as well. Eliza looked on at her husband as she waited by the open
door of the vehicle for his return.

"I'm not dreaming," said Carlos, and he hopped onto the bumper
of the truck as Baldemar and Esmeralda reached for his hands to help
him up.

§

The family made one final stop in Naranjales. It was to say goodbye to their grandparents. The old folks were waiting anxiously by the
front gate to the patio in front of their store. There were several other relatives and neighbors who had gathered there to say goodbye to

the family as well. The grandmother was still deep in mourning for her Jacobo. She wore her usual black cotton dress, her head was covered by a black lace scarf. Since their uncle's death nearly a year ago, Mamagrande Lupita had experienced additional losses. Chavela had taken her children and moved away to live near her folks in the village of Las Jaras. This farewell of her most loyal son and his family felt strangely deeper to Grandmother Lupita. Her feelings were almost as intense as the pain of losing Jacobo. Ramiro's family was the closest thing she had that resembled normality, and now they, too, were leaving. The hugs were tight, prolonged and filled with sighs and gentle kisses. That's how Carlos remembered it. All the other kids held variations of the same memories of their grandma weeping and their father's silent sobs and somber motions as they finally reboarded the truck and the doors slammed shut. From the back of the work truck that felt more like a mini bullpen, with its high rails and straw-covered deck floor, the kids waved in silence at their teary grandparents, aunt, and the friends and the curious from the village.

§

On the bus to Reynosa, Carlos tuned out the rest of the world as his youthful imagination drifted toward the expanse of the unknown. He saw a kind of world ahead where everything would be as exciting as when the circus came to Naranjales once a year, or the monthly movies that were projected onto the school's back wall and which he occasionally got to attend after begging his mother for the peso that was the price of admission. Normally, her response was, "What do you want to give those people your money for? You're just making them rich, and they already have plenty."

But this experience of moving to a foreign country, to a big city, was going to be new, something beyond his imagination. He couldn't wait to get started.

§

The Continental Trailways Bus Station in McAllen was a cool, sleek place after what, at least for Carlos, seemed to be the carnival atmosphere of Reynosa. The street sounds were restrained, serene, and the smells were different, less aromatic, less organic, more neutral, more hygienic. The glass on the buildings gave the "other side" an immediate identity different from back home, shiny, antiseptic. The bus itself was quite a sight, long and silver with a plush red interior. And then there were the people and their sounds.

The boy had never heard an English word in his young life. He had once heard his grandfather describe "gringos" talking like cats, but the words he was hearing sounded like people's language, not cats' language. He sat quietly observing various passengers move about at the different stops along the way. He wanted to tell his mother about the man sitting in front of him, because he was black and his woolly hair fascinated the boy. Eliza quickly shushed him and whispered a scolding in his ear, "Don't stare at people. And don't talk about them. Just sit still and try to sleep."

Along the way, Carlos could not simply close his eyes and fall asleep. He tried to read every billboard along the road although none of the words made sense to him, but many of the pictures pleased him. He looked intently at so many automobiles. He was amazed to see so many cars being driven by women with red or blonde teased hair and pretty dresses. Already, at his young age, he had developed his culture's mores, supposing that women were meant to stay home or be driven places, not go out alone behind the wheel of a car. He could not imagine his mother driving a car out in the world all by herself.

When night began to fall, his focus became the neon signs and all manner of chaser lights advertising motels, grocery stores, gas stations. He had no idea what the various businesses the bright and exciting signs beckoned him to, but he sure wished the bus would stop longer at red lights so he could get a better look at the neon signs and enjoy the lights. Some places had decorations of plastic stringed triangles flying in many colors as well as strings of lights. Behind such strings were rows and rows of cars. Carlos thought, "Wow, there are so many cars over here."

At last, the family reached the downtown Houston bus station. The kids had been straining and stretching their necks in every direction trying to take in all of the downtown skyscrapers and so many other new sights. A discussion ensued about what such buildings were called, and Baldemar told them they were skyscrapers. They all laughed, imagining a building like a claw scratching the sky, as the Spanish word for "scrape" literally means "scratch." Eliza, in her usual self-conscious manner, pulled them back from giving full rein to their admiration and awe of the new sights. "Don't act like you've never seen a city before. People will think things."

Soon, the group of eight squeezed into a taxicab, and was on their way to Tia Julieta's house. Once again, Ramiro had to impose on his sister as the family arrived at the small frame house on the outskirts of the city, just at the foot of the ship channel, the Port Houston neighborhood. They were to stay as long as it took to find a rental house they could afford. Julieta's hospitality was beyond generous, and no one ever detected a hint of resentment or regret at helping out her brother. That was just what families did.

Carlos was too young to fully grasp that how painful it was for Ramiro to hoist such great inconvenience on Julieta and her fussy husband, but family devotion prevented any objections. The family arrived at nearly midnight. Everyone was exhausted. Julieta, Eduardo, and their two kids got out of bed to welcome the clan. They had been expecting them, but had no idea of the time of their arrival, so they had kept their normal schedule except to lay out sleeping arrangements for eight additional people. The arriving couple would take the two kids' beds. Julieta's two switched to sleeping in their parents' bedroom, on a crammed pair of cots. Ramiro's six children would all sleep in the small living room on pallets or blankets on the floor. The smaller ones could sleep on the sofa.

The kids were too sleepy that night to notice much of anything except the decorations on two lamp tables that framed the sofa. Each table consisted of a two-tier design in which the top level held a lamp and on the lower level sat a splendidly dressed doll fixture that looked like a Barbie doll inside a colorful sofa cushion made to look like a princess dress. His aunt had a fancy living room, they thought. The following days and weeks were a hardship for everyone, having to share such intimate spaces in the two-bedroom bungalow. Twelve people to one bathroom, twelve people to feed three times a day, twelve people to keep from turning on each other for all the peculiarities that human beings hold against each other on a daily basis, twelve people opening and closing doors from sunup to sundown.

§

Sometimes Carlos whiled away his time by wandering the streets that were in sight of his aunt's house as daytime traffic was sparse. He was taken by the pungent smell of black tar on the hot street pavement. Some of the tar was soft enough to stick to the soles of his shoes. He played with small balls of tar that he pinched off the sides of the pavement, rolling it with his fingers. It had the consistency of chewing gum, and he wondered if he could use it as a substitute. Chewing gum was one of many things that back home he could enjoy only occasionally because of the rationing that the frugal Eliza fiercely enforced.

Back home the kids had sometimes chewed whole grains of wheat with mint leaves to simulate a kind of chewing gum even though the flavor didn't last very long. One brief taste of the black goo, and he spat it out. He quickly gave up on that idea. Of course, he could play with his cousins and the neighborhood kids, some of them the children of *paisanos* from back home. Carlos got along fine with all of them, but one day didn't go so well.

Someone challenged him to read a book that was among the toys the American kids played with. They teased Carlos that he could not read, assuming that someone who could not speak English, naturally, couldn't read, either. Carlos was very proud of his ability to read. His big sister, Alicia, had taught him how to read when he was five. He defiantly told them, "Yes, I can read. I can probably read better than you." At which point all the kids laughed and told him to prove it.

The book was a Dr. Seuss story, and it had a bright green cover with a picture of a lion, a tiger, and a dog, balancing different numbers of apples on their heads. Carlos picked up the book and held it with both hands in front of his face. The other kids looked on with mocking smiles. He began to read the title, "Den up-less oop on tohp." And just at the precise moment that Carlos was about to give them a smug look of "See, I can read," they all burst out in laughter. They said, "No, no, no, that's not how you say it." Then they read the title "correctly" to him, "Ten Apples Up on Top." He'd been tricked. He turned a bright shade of red, and told them that yes, he could, too, read. It was just that he could not speak English yet. A part of him was so embarrassed he wanted to cry, a part of him wanted to punch something, one of them, a part of him blamed his Cousin Sergio for setting him up. He threw the book at their feet and walked away.

§

It was by sheer force of will and courtesies that the two families survived the experience of living in such close quarters. They remained friendly even as Ramiro and Eliza prepared to move into a place of their own almost a month to the day after their arrival. In August, the family of eight settled into a barely furnished house on the northern end of Port Houston, in the shadow of a giant levee.

Soon Eliza was practicing what she had learned from Julieta and her friends about the ins and outs of being a housekeeper in Houston, particularly regarding food preparation. She had quickly learned from Julieta the art of making fried chicken, tuna fish sandwiches, fried baloney, and grilled wieners. The month with Julieta, had already proved instrumental in giving Eliza the fundamentals of managing a modern household that now involved the use of modern technology and conveniences like toasters, blenders, flushing, in-door toilets, automatic washing machines, garbage collection days, and supermarket visits on Fridays after cashing the patriarch's paycheck at the Weingarten's courtesy booth.

The next big project for Eliza was to prepare the kids for school enrollment. The kids' vaccinations and visits to the St. Joseph Clinic downtown would require learning to navigate the bus system. And that was just the beginning of the many domestic hurdles the poor country wife was about to endure. Like it or not.

CHAPTER 21: *See Jane Run*

After settling into the house in the ship channel neighborhood, the family began to learn how to navigate the city and how to go about the basic functions of everyday life in Houston. Ramiro's stress level had never been higher as he began to fully assimilate the weight of being the sole supporter of a family of eight. The house rent, utilities, groceries, and the ongoing acquisition of furnishings for the house depleted their savings considerably. Eliza had never been one to take ownership of their treasury, so Ramiro seldom consulted with her about his money management, but he was quick to unload on her his frustrations over money. He was never one to rely on credit, and he hated debt. He was only comfortable when he had a small nest egg in the bank back home. "Oye, Mujer," he'd start. "Did you take any money from the box? We have only $50.00 for the next week. We're not going to make it." His plan was to build up a cushion to cover two month's worth of expenses. After that, he planned to start a little nest egg for emergencies, but that seemed a long way off.

"No, Ramiro, I haven't taken any money. The kids have been asking for extra nickels for school snacks, but I told them we can't afford it," she'd reply.

"You know, at this rate of saving, I am going to have to hitch rides too long. I have to save enough for a good used car. After that, we can build up a little cushion. "In this city a car is not a luxury. It is a necessity. Everyone must have one."

Ramiro paused to contemplate his precious kids asleep on lumpy used mattresses. Eliza watched him from afar as she prepared to turn off the kitchen light for the night. The man was still quite a presence in her eyes, and he brought her comfort despite his flaws. He stood at the door to the boys' room, his mind on a silent promise to himself and his kids that everything was going to work out fine. He imagined them becoming educated and speaking English with the best of them. His father's heart softened at the thought of the kids' struggles in a new country, but he was heartened at his absolute belief that they would be successful one day. That night he told himself a line the kids would be hearing for a long time: "Go to school so you don't have to work like a beast of burden or do back-breaking work like me. But if you're not going to study in earnest, then quit school and get a job. Everyone has to contribute in this family." He wasn't sure what exactly it meant to be "educated," but he figured that as long as it didn't require making payments, the younger kids, at least, should stay in school as long as required. Ramiro's country ways kept him from dreaming beyond "a good job" for his kids. He also knew that he was going to put the older kids to work as soon as they were able. That had always been the way of his people, and all children were expected to work for the family.

§

The biggest challenge for Eliza in the weeks that followed was getting the kids vaccinated for school. She had been told that in America every child had to have proof of vaccination. Eliza's former life was surely over now. She had never studied past the second grade, as her mother used her to help around the house so much. Now she was in the embarrassing position of depending on the generosity of Iliana's eldest, Debbie, a girl barely fourteen. Debbie had taken a liking to the family when they lived temporarily with Julieta. Being the next-door neighbor, she quickly made friends with Esmeralda and Alicia. She also developed a fancy for the handsome Baldemar. When her mother asked her to help guide Eliza in the procedures of getting the kids enrolled in school, she was happy to assist. As the child of immigrants, she was used to the job of translator, both in person and in deciphering written documents.

Eliza's simple life in the country had never presented such challenges as these. She could hear Debbie read a long list of required immunizations, but all the words went in one ear and out the other, much as she tried to retain them. She discovered that all immunizations were mandatory and had to be recorded in an official document of some sort. These records had to show the day, month, and year the shots were given. Debbie read on about how no child could start school before being immunized to some level, and she said something about exceptions and conditional something or other. It was all the same to Eliza. She just wanted to take the kids somewhere and get it done, whatever it was. The ladies in Julieta's circle all recommended the Clinica San José. It was a Catholic-run free clinic that would require taking two city buses to get there.

Their working-class neighborhood in the outskirts of East Houston was a swampy enclave located between the ship channel and the city's Magnolia and Second Ward neighborhoods. The bus service was less than efficient, and it would take transferring to a second bus to reach the clinic. Eliza, Debbie, and the five school-age kids boarded that bus, with Baldemar carrying the two-year-old in his arms, a stroller being a luxury they couldn't afford. The bus stop was on McCarty Street, the dusty thoroughfare that was a reasonable three-blocks walk from their new address. The ordeal of securing the fare in coins for every child was quite a task, but after some negotiating by Debbie with a local ice-house merchant, they were all set. As usual, Eliza had made sure every child was in his or her Sunday best and in his or her best public behavior. If there was one thing no mother from Naranjales ever tolerated it was any childish nonsense in a public place.

At the clinic the receptionist and others took immediate notice of the mother and her kids as they made their way through the double-door entrance. The faces of the clinic employees successfully con-

cealed a sense of panic at having to serve yet another immigrant mother with too many kids for her own good. But the staff's discomfort
quickly turned to compassion, then to joy, when the group was before
them, for they were a handsome group indeed, despite their immigrant
clothing, and they were all minding their best manners, lest Eliza quietly administer a dose of her usual discipline, a pinch above the elbow.
It was also a relief that they brought their own translator with them.

The nurse that attended them began to talk about diphtheria,
tetanus, and pertussis. She said something about doses, primary series, and boosters. She mentioned grades K to sixth, and K to twelve,
and so on. She talked about polio, measles, mumps, and rubella. How
many doses for hepatitis, varicella, or meningococcal? It was all a whirl
of more gibberish to Eliza, although she did recognize a number of
the terms. After all, she had just been through a series of vaccinations
that were required for the issuing of the green cards the family had
received recently.

As she found herself in the midst of too much information, Eliza somehow tuned her brain to a memory of the visiting clinic that
came to Naranjales once a year to immunize the children. She almost
laughed out loud remembering how Victor Cruz went about raving
that the vaccines were a government plot to control the people. He refused to have any of his ten children vaccinated despite repeated plead-
ings from the schoolteachers. Most of the other folks laughed at him
behind his back and called him an ignorant peasant.

Finally, each child was given a number of shots with exceptions
made for the ones Eliza could recall from the immigration process. She
did not have the proof of having taken them, but the nurses decided
to approve them. The federal government required a prescribed list of
certain vaccines to enter the country, so they must have been given,
they correctly reasoned.

Back at home, one of Eliza's new preoccupations was the safe-
keeping of documents and household cash. It was no longer a simple
matter of keeping birth certificates in a safe place as she was used to

back home. Now it was birth certificates, green cards, passports, vaccination records, and school registration papers, among other important documents. Ramiro even asked her to keep rent receipts. It was all a bit much for the functionally illiterate woman, but she managed to secure a shoebox for all those papers, including an envelope with whatever cash Ramiro put in it.

§

Ramiro determined that his kids must learn the English language at all costs. He told them all that he expected them to be speaking English in no time, so they better pay attention to everything the teachers told them to do. A father's encouragement is a great motivator for children, and the school kids pledged to not let him down. The kids had always been impressed with their father's various challenges to them during his visits from the other side. Sometimes, he would line up whatever kids were around when he was sitting with his father and other visitors. He would stand up and show the kids that he could bend down and touch the floor without bending his knees. "Now you do it." The kids attempted to please him, and sometimes failed, but they kept trying until they could touch the floor with flat hands although pained by their stretched hamstrings.

Ramiro issued the same kind of challenge with addition and subtraction problems. The little games made every kid study harder in math class, and they each wished they could spend more time with their father and show off when they memorized a multiplication table.

But now Ramiro was faced with a dilemma. He had to encourage the kids to learn the English language, but he himself had no ability to test them. He couldn't even model for them, not even a little. He feared going into unknown territory where he would lose control, but he gave the edict anyway, "I want everyone speaking English by next year."

Esmeralda jumped up and told him that she surely would. At almost fourteen she was to go to the junior high school in a neighborhood far from home. She would have to ride the bus every morning, but it was a comfort to know Baldemar would be with her. She was placed in the seventh grade while Baldemar was placed in the ninth. Upon her father's decree, she quickly began to memorize a few words and phrases she heard at school. But the school was not a friendly environment for her.

§

The junior high school girls were hostile to the pretty, green-eyed foreigner. The school culture she encountered was vastly different from where she came. Girls wore garish makeup and talked tough even at their young age of twelve and thirteen. The boys wore baggy pants and shiny shoes. Some of them wore bandanas on their heads, and after school they altered themselves even more to appear menacing and fierce. The kids also got into fights almost every day. Where Esmeralda came from girls were expected to act ladylike and never engage in physical confrontations with each other. The fights were mostly verbal protestations. Whenever two girls found their way into an actual physical attack, it was expected that the other girls or boys separated them immediately. Even the boy fights were held to rules of honor that included not attacking to cause undue harm, and the spectators were to intervene to prevent their hurting each other.

Esmeralda was soon fending off an aggressive Mexican American girl whose boyfriend flirted with her one day when she dropped a book at her locker. The boy helped her pick it up. Esmeralda tried to explain to the girl that she wanted no problems with her and that she had no interest in the girl's boyfriend. That only seemed to enrage the *chola* even more. Esmeralda had learned that Mexican American barrio girls were called *cholas* and the boys were called *pachucos*. The girl only twisted Esmeralda's words, and said, "Oh, you think you're too good for him? You think your doo doo don't' stink?" Only she used ugly language, the kind Esmeralda had been taught a young lady doesn't use. She became terribly confused and began to see the school as a hellish place.

After only a month, and after having been confronted by the

same aggressive girl and three of her friends during gym class, she had had enough. If it hadn't been for the sudden appearance of a teacher, which in itself was a rarity, Esmeralda might have ended up bloodied or worse. She went home and told her parents that she would like to quit school and go to work somewhere. Ramiro heard her out and agreed she was not safe at such a barbaric place. Secretly he shuddered at the thought that he could not defend her before the school officials or demand the other girls be disciplined. His lack of English would always be an impediment to protecting his children, plus he couldn't take off work.

They dressed her up to look older than her fourteen years and sent her to apply for work at a local bakery. "Tell them you're sixteen," her Aunt Julieta advised her. The following week she was working in the assembly line of the Texas Pecan Company, making fruitcakes and cupcakes.

§

The same story had been unfolding with Baldemar. But he didn't tell anyone about the fights he was dodging or the ones in which he beat up a kid or vice versa. When Esmeralda shared her story and was allowed to leave school, he had already stopped attending, spending his days walking the streets and soaking in the strange culture that surrounded him. He came forward and confessed to Ramiro that he, too, would not be returning to school. Ramiro's reaction was almost a sigh of relief. He expected to ask Baldemar to get a job and help out the family as soon as he turned sixteen. He worried that the boy might put up some resistance even though he had never cared much for school. This would avoid any conflicts had the boy taken a liking to the American school system. The rest of the kids adapted to their new schools much better.

Halloween had been quite an experience for the children. Then there came Thanksgiving. The Ocañas siblings who remained in school were amazed every day by the many ways in which American school was different from their little three-room school back home, but the size difference was the least of their marvels. For one thing, there were free art supplies of all kinds, unlike back home where they had only a small box of wooden colored pencils. Carlos, Sylvia, and Antonio would come home and tell their mother stories about an amazing thing called glitter that all the kids were allowed to use as if it didn't cost anything. The stuff was so beautiful. It made every picture sparkle and look magical, they said. How they loved using Elmer's Glue on the outline of an American flag then sprinkling the red, silver, and blue glitter on it. The flag itself was beautiful to them. Carlos stared at the fifty stars on it and the broad stripes of red and white. It was a unique design, and he wanted to draw it in every manner of waves and folds.

The kids also expounded on what their teachers were called. There was Mrs. Ammons, Miss Page, Miss Reynolds, Miss Powell. All the teachers were female, and none was Hispanic. Back home there were three teachers and each taught two grades in the same classroom. They were called "Señorita Elida" or "Profesor Polo." Alicia looked for a counterpart for Profesor Polo, but there were no male teachers in the new school. Still, she was in awe of Mrs. Ammons, her teacher, who must have been in her sixties. She was colorful not only in her manner of dress, but in her face makeup and her powdery perfume that always arrived a few seconds before she did and lingered minutes after she left. She was kind to her even though Alicia could not understand a word she spoke. Mrs. Ammons asked for a volunteer Mexican American student to assist her in communicating the assignments to Alicia. A friendly, dark-skinned Mexican American girl named Rebecca volunteered. All the kids seemed to mind Mrs. Ammons well enough.

Ramiro's edict to learn English stayed with them even as the two eldest dropped out of school. One day Esmeralda gathered all her siblings when they got home from school and declared that from this day forward everyone was to come home and use a new English word each day. She felt bad about not staying in school but hoped she could still learn English with help from the little ones. She proudly declared,

"Today I learned the word 'cotton'" and then told them what it was in Spanish. All the kids repeated the word, "cotton." To that they added a mix of gibberish intended to simulate a sentence in which the word cotton was used. They giggled. None of it made any sense, but they were all happy to have learned a new word.

Of course, the younger kids had been soaking up words like sponges already, although Alicia was shy about making mistakes. Carlos also held back because he did not want to be embarrassed as had happened at Oscar's house. Still, they all laughed at each other's nonsense sentences and proceeded to share a word of their own to contribute to the game. Alicia said, "I learned the word 'classroom.'" And everyone repeated it. Carlos said, "I learned the word 'cafeteria.'" Tony, the five year old said, "Crayon." And they all giggled again.

Eliza was in her usual place in the kitchen overhearing the banter, trying to think of a word of her own, but try as she could, not one word came to her. She then scanned the cupboard where she kept packaged foods. She read the word to herself: "Cheerios." She had no idea how to pronounce it. She looked at other packages. All her eyes could distinguish were the shapes, colors, pictures and lettering that, for the most part, meant nothing to her. She shook her head as she pulled down the corn flour for the tortillas. "Esmeralda. Alicia. Come and help me get dinner ready. Your father will be home soon."

CHAPTER 22: *Baldemar Gets a Job*

As the firstborn and a male baby, Baldemar was the apple of his father's eye. The child was the very picture of what in America was called a "Gerber baby." He was chunky, bouncy, and rosy-cheeked. His eyes were a gun-metal blue like his grandfather's. This was in contrast to Ramiro's deep brown eyes, which he inherited from his mother, Lupita. The boy possessed all the qualities that made Ramiro proud, for Ramiro was a great admirer of physical beauty, and his baby was beautiful. As the boy grew, he continued to hold his father's esteem and approbation on most ventures he attempted. The boy was adventurous, to be sure. Even when he proved to be less than scholarly and was caught hunting rabbits instead of attending classes, Ramiro tended to forgive him. Baldemar was also spared the customary whippings—the norm for all children in those parts—at least for minor offenses.

When Ramiro was away in California, and later in Houston, he sometimes thought he missed Baldemar the most out of all his children. Ramiro had a special place in his heart for the girls, but it was his happy-go-lucky boy he most enjoyed. By the time the family arrived in Houston, Baldemar was fifteen and he had grown distant over the long absences of his father's. Ramiro began to treat him more like a man, and, indeed, the boy preferred to feel independent of his old man. As such, at sixteen Baldemar was expected to find a job and help carry the load of supporting the family. Baldemar had swagger and a James Dean look, although he had no inkling as to who the American heartthrob was. He was now embarking in a lifestyle far from Hollywood glamor, a way of life remote from mainstream middle-class America. He was about to take the road of the unskilled, uneducated American laborer.

Ramiro was quietly proud and happy that his eldest son would be working and contributing to the family budget. He was ashamed to admit, also, that he was, as much as anything, excited about accelerating his savings to buy that car he'd been hoping for. Of course, the family's dire straits budget was a heavy burden on his mind, and that, at least would surely benefit from a second paycheck. He decided there was no sense in considering further that Baldemar might be better off in school.

Ramiro and Eliza never even considered that the boy should have been in school or what it meant that he would go through life without a diploma. They did not understand the value of a high school education. They especially had no concept of a university, although back home Alberto's boys had been making plans to move to Monterrey and study for professional careers. The couple's immediate reality dictated that everyone live in survival mode, but it all seemed only natural considering that their rural life had been a harsh one, free of talk of school credentials. That meant work to secure a roof over one's head and food on the table for eight people. Where they came from in the 1950s rural Mexican village far from the big city of Monterrey, it was normal for kids to finish the sixth grade and go directly to work in the family farm, no matter how small. Some who aspired to more went to Valle Azul for secondary study, and if their parents were enlightened and forward thinking—and, most importantly, willing to sacrifice—the kids went on to earn the full high school diploma, or *bachillerato*.

Baldemar was as rambunctious and outdoorsy as they come, prone to horseplay and practical jokes. He was an excellent hunter of rabbits and foul, which were plentiful in Naranjales. He was also a ladies' man. Though barely an adolescent, the boy already knew the rules of his society regarding the strict roles of males and females. Those rules dictated that life was first and foremost about finding your life's mate, the sooner the better. He was kissing girls as early as the age of six when he developed a crush on Conchita in first grade. The good girls of Naranjales being what they were, he never got past second base, but he sure had fun trying and the girls enjoyed being chased but never caught.

By the time he left for Houston, he had promised to go steady with the lovely Rosalinda whose long ponytail and gingham dresses on Sunday afternoons made him swoon. He had every intention of maintaining a long-distance relationship with her through letters, but somehow knew that he was going to play the field in the big city, and Rosalinda would forget him soon enough—or, rather, he would forget her.

Baldemar figured that if he was going to have a chance to get around in Houston as he had done back home, he was going to need cash in his pocket. That is why he couldn't wait to start working and earning dollars. He knew he would have to turn in practically his entire earnings to the family, but he would keep enough for his own needs to do with as he pleased. When Ramiro agreed to let him leave school and go to work instead, the boy was ecstatic. He accompanied Ramiro to the smelting plant that Monday, and applied for a job sweeping and tidying up the work areas.

He told them he was eighteen and was hired on the spot and told he could start the next day. The shop manager told Baldemar he had one month to get a Social Security card and should bring it in as soon as he had been issued a number. Baldemar could not contain his excitement. His first impulse was to run out and celebrate, but with not even a penny in his pocket, he chose instead to hang around the shop until Ramiro punched out for the day. During Ramiro's lunch break they shared the lunch that Eliza had packed for them in Ramiro's pail. Father and son talked about how now that there would be two incomes—plus the little Esmeralda could pitch in—Ramiro would soon be able to buy a car to get around in.

Driving his own car was a dream of Ramiro's, and he told Baldemar he had the same dream for him as well, but first the family had to get some stability, and they both had to save all the money they could. They would go out and look for a good used car that very weekend, they agreed.

That evening, the family celebrated Baldemar's good luck in obtaining his first job. Their usual dinner gathering was a happy hour of sharing Baldemar's experience, hearing about one or another of the kids' school tales if they could get a word in, and listening to Ramiro extol the rules of proper behavior. Ramiro never missed an opportunity to instill discipline in the kids. His greatest fear was that, there being so many, he would lose control and they would become vagabonds or worse. Eliza changed the subject by reminding Baldemar that she would pack him a separate lunch of taquitos and hot coffee beginning tomorrow and to be sure and eat everything because they could not afford to waste food.

Baldemar only smiled and replied, "Don't you worry about any waste, Ma. I can't wait to eat that lunch. After my first check, we can buy extra groceries, too." His brothers and sisters looked on in admiration of their big brother with wholesome and hopeful faces. Alicia and Carlos spent the time before falling asleep that night in daydreams about one day getting jobs of their own.

For his part, Ramiro withdrew to his thoughts and aloneness, sitting in the dark in the large, empty living room before retiring to bed. He was unusually at peace that night because Baldemar's new job meant that he could count on a safety net where money was concerned. He thought about Esmeralda's contributions as well, and he calculated that he could very well deplete his savings and buy a car since three incomes would allow for a replenishment of the funds soon enough. His heart then ventured to its somber side, and he began to worry about the overall uncertainty of his little farm back home. Jacobo's image hovered before him, and he sighed deeply as the empty place in his heart reminded him that he would never enjoy his brother's company again.

"Ramiro, are you coming to bed? It's getting late," whispered Eliza from the door to the dining room. He turned around to see her silhouette made from the streetlight that shone through the windows beyond her. She moved out of sight. He followed.

CHAPTER 23: *Ramiro's First Car*

Back home, Ramiro was known for his charisma. He belonged to a family of proud, self-assured siblings. The men had the pride of self-reliance and knowledge of their own worth as men and as human beings. The women had spunk and glamor in the context of their rural society. It was never anything pretentious or ostentatious, but it was undeniable. The family subscribed to a work ethic of old-fashioned hard work and long hours. They didn't go into debt often, but if they did, they were always good for it. They liked nice things, but always in moderation and never more than necessary. Lupita and Timoteo had raised seven children the best they knew how, and by all local standards they had done a superb job. The hardships that Ramiro and his siblings encountered were simply par for the course, so no one thought any less of them for any shortcomings along the way. Struggle was simply the natural order of life. The family figured prominently among their relatives and community. And so it was that, in Houston, Ramiro gravitated toward a social circle that Julieta had developed in the cutout of a neighborhood where they found themselves living. Entry into such a circle required Ramiro to own a car; at least that was his perception.

§

That rough summer of 1957 had transitioned to a tough fall of many firsts for an immigrant family. Ramiro and Baldemar worked long shifts at the smelting plant, and after Baldemar's sixth check, the father had the money for a used car. Ramiro took Iliana's's oldest boy, thirteen-year-old Rafael, with him to help out with the language so Ramiro could negotiate and finalize the transaction. Ramiro, Baldemar, and Rafael arrived that Friday evening at the Bill Davis Chevrolet dealership and headed straight to the used car department. No sooner had the three walked onto the lot than Ramiro set his eyes on a beautiful 1955 Chevy Bel Air. The dealership had placed large numbers on the windshield advertising a price of $1,200. Ramiro had brought exactly $1,000 because he intended to pay cash for the car. "Tell him that I need him to come down on the price a little," he said to Rafael.

Rafael complied and conveyed the message to the salesman. The salesman pursed his lips, twisted his mouth, and shook his head no. He said, "Tell him that I can't do that. The car is loaded. It has a hard top. It comes with a V8 engine. It was $2,200.00 new, plus tax and transportation costs. Those are always extra. Tell him to look at the options in it: Power Glide, over drive, power steering, power brakes. All that stuff costs more. Tell him that no-can-do," the salesman repeated as he guided his brown fedora back onto his head.

Ramiro listened patiently to Rafael's tortured explanations, full of fits and starts. Then he instructed the boy: "Tell him I know the car is nice. Tell him it is also a used car, with who knows what possible hidden problems. When I drove it on the test drive, I heard some funny sounds. I can't pay for this car as if it was new. Tell him I can pay $900.00." Baldemar looked on in anticipation of the salesman relenting and making a quick deal. He couldn't wait to get in the car and be seen by the whole family as he drove up the crushed-shell topped driveway of their home. As Rafael spoke to the salesman, Ramiro reminded Baldemar that there would still be expenses to take care of. "We have to buy seat covers. Those clear plastic protective covers from Sears, with the little bubbled flower designs. It might need new spark plugs. We have to change the oil and buy gas every week."

Rafael again, conveyed the message although he was feeling annoyed that Ramiro was so persistent and, to his young mind, unreasonable. Children are often impatient with the way adults think through things, missing the necessity of a strategy in a bargaining exchange. Again, the salesman shook his head, and said he simply could not go that low, "I'll tell you what I'll do. Tell him I will take $1,100. And we have a deal. He can drive it off the lot tonight."

Ramiro, reading the body language, could tell what the answer was. He pulled out his wallet and opened it for the salesman to see its content. He proceeded to lay out one-hundred dollar bills on the salesman's desk. He looked at the man intently in the face to make sure he had his attention, and he began to count, first in English then in Spanish when he forgot the rest of the numbers. "One, two, three, four, five, six, *siete, ocho, nueve, diez.*" Then he turned to Rafael. "Tell him I will give him one thousand dollars cash right now. If he can't take it, I will have to go home." Then Ramiro, once again, opened his wallet, showed the man it was empty, held it upside down and shook it as if to say, "I haven't a penny more." Ramiro tightened his lips into a half smile, raised his eyebrows, shrugged his shoulders, and held out his hands palms up to indicate that was all he had, so please accept it.

Rafael's eyes were wide staring at the money on the table. He had never seen so many hundred-dollar bills before. "He says he can give you one-thousand dollars right now. If you don't take it, he has to go home."

The salesman let out a laughing sound for a second and continued to shake his head. "He's a tough son of a gun, isn't he?" He smiled. Ramiro followed every move intently. He could see the man's face softening. Finally, the salesman, realizing that indeed that was all the money the immigrant was intending to spend, stretched out his hand and said, "All right. Darn it. We have a deal. Tell him I'll take it, but when you boys go to buy your first car, you better come and buy it from me," he muttered. "Let's start the paperwork."

Ramiro laughed too, thinking, "This guy probably thinks I'm stupid. I'm sure the car is not worth even a thousand." Baldemar smiled widely. Rafael felt great relief that the back and forth was over. He also felt a newfound admiration for Ramiro, now that it was over, as he had never seen his own father negotiate like that. Ramiro was proud to win a small victory. It reminded him of his negotiating days back in Naranjales where he still had his house in the care of the local carpenter. He also still owned a couple of Brahma bulls that he hoped Alberto's eldest would sell off for a good price. The memories of negotiating cattle trading deals and prices for the bulls made his small victory bittersweet. This was a totally different experience, even if he had managed to get what he considered a fair deal.

As the evening had turned into night during the negotiation, it would not be possible to get all the required paperwork done that night, plus the dealer had promised new floor mats and a car wash that would not be ready until the next day. The next morning, bright and early, Ramiro took his usual breakfast and patiently waited for his brother-in-law, Eduardo, and the neighbor boy, Rafael, to pick him up. Baldemar was late getting up, but he didn't need breakfast. He was excited anyway. The four left for the dealership, finished the required legalities, and signed all the various promissory papers. It was Saturday, and the family waited anxiously for their father's arrival with the Chevy, all the kids' faces glued to the windows to be the first to see it. To them, the car represented full arrival into the America.

When the father and son pulled into the driveway, the kids rushed out to surround the beautiful new car. They couldn't wait to get in it. They slid their little hands over the seats, the dash, over practically every inch of the new treasure. Ramiro told everyone to hop into the car, and he took the family for a long drive around the neighborhood and all the way out to Galena Park. On Clinton Drive, he stopped at the Weingarten's and bought every kid a treat as a way of celebrating the special event of owning a car. Finally, on the return drive, he pulled into the gas station with the majorette outlined in neon whose baton pointed toward the gas pumps in flashing lights. The tank was half empty, so he filled it up for 23 cents a gallon. While the attendant filled up the tank and wiped the windshield Ramiro reached in his pocket for a quarter to tip the young man.

The kids were especially excited to have such a luxurious thing in their driveway and they wanted to spend hours just sitting in it, but Ramiro quickly shooed them away. After all, this was a prized possession to him, and he intended to protect it from any and all possible harm, including kid smudges. He did concede to having the boys help him wax the car the next day, since the dealer had only washed it and Ramiro wanted it to shine as brightly as possible. The car was a two-tone maroon and white sedan, and the chrome bumpers and white sidewall tires complemented it perfectly. He told them all that the next vacation they took would be to Mexico and everyone would be riding for hours and hours. He sighed as he thought about showing it off to his parents and the entire Naranjales/Valle Azul crowd.

As he watched from afar the children admiring the car, Ramiro shuddered at the added responsibility of such a possession. He was thrilled to have it, but the car also represented a little more distance between him and his farm. Eliza looked on from the screen door at the kids, then she saw Ramiro's expression and she knew it was all just a superficial thrill. Her own thoughts paralleled her husband's and prayed that he would be alright.

CHAPTER 24: *Tenuous Normality*

The entire year that followed was an intense period of newness and adjustments for every member of the family. Each child and adult went through their own cultural transitions in unique ways, but for the kids the new lessons were as much about discovering their father as about discovering America. There was no habit of close or constant communication in the family, so the kids' biggest disappointment was learning how little they knew their father and how the new man who was emerging before their eyes was controlling and inflexible in ways they hadn't noticed before.

Ramiro was often solemn because of his memories of his dead brother. Something about the manner in which he lost Jacobo continued to haunt him. The feeling that he did not avenge his death, the sadness when he thought of Jacobo's orphaned kids, the emptiness in his heart when he thought of visiting his homeland and finding his beloved brother gone. He sometimes sulked at missing his parents and wondered what might become of them now that he was, in a sense, permanently separated from them. Although he had been absent from their lives for long periods before, this felt different. To be away with his entire family gave him a sense of having severed ties with his beloved parents.

He also bemoaned that he had to give up the new farm that he had sacrificed so much to obtain, wondering if he might return to it soon or never. The children one night observed him weeping silently in the dark, and they were perturbed at the sight of the man they always thought so strong. It could have been the pain of losing a brother or any other number of issues that grownups never discuss with kids. No one would ever know because Ramiro was not prone to sharing such intimacies, much less show any form of weakness.

And it was Ramiro's great pride and fear of ever appearing weak that seemed to get in the way of his own happiness most of the time. He spent too much time giving orders to the point that the kids began to avoid contact with him even as they wished to be closer and enjoy the things they had missed for years. "Esmeralda, take off that paint on your face." "Alicia, don't dance too close with your brother." "Carlos, don't slouch when you sit at the table." "Sylvia, turn down the television." "Antonio, don't talk like you're rushing to finish. It makes you look a simpleton." Only Baldemar seemed to escape such niggling. Ramiro had never indulged them in sentimental musings or self-pity for fear they would become soft and spoiled, but they recalled the father he used to be when he visited from California, and they missed that illusion. Ramiro loved his family very much, yet he had to make it clear that he was the law.

In America, his need to hold on to a semblance of what in his mind was manhood only intensified. His lowly status as a laborer—coupled with resigning himself to having lost his dream of being the overlord of a Mexican country estate—engendered deep feelings of inadequacy in him. The only outlet for the kind of authority that a man of his background requires was to impose his will over his large family of dependent wife and children. But that kind of pride and control extracted a price that Ramiro could not see developing: the distancing of his children and the fear of his wife.

Eliza wasn't much help in leading the family. She followed all of her husband's rules and edicts unquestioningly. Whether she did it subscribing to his philosophy of raising children or out of some sort of fear was a question the kids were beginning to put words to. She often felt just as much the recipient of Ramiro's directives as the kids did, and she dared not contradict or challenge his authority. Eliza took on the role of enforcer of Ramiro's demanding rules, and she became a sort of overseer to the increasingly cowed kids. She found herself overwhelmed at the task of managing so many kids in an environment in which she and her husband had little to no control outside the home. In turn, the kids began to resent her acquiescence and compliance. They could not understand why she didn't assert her rightful authority as the sort of equal partner in marriage they saw on the TV shows they watched. Years later, some of the children would recall her status in the household as resembling that of a nanny more than a mother.

Both parents seemed to be deathly afraid of failing to protect their children should they come into trouble at school or with the law, let alone on the streets. They dreaded the day a situation would arrive that they would not be able to handle. They imagined the kids getting into fights with *pachucos* or involved with other bad elements of the strange society. The girls, especially, were becoming a grave concern to Ramiro, and he felt compelled to enforce his culture's strict code of honor that required adherence to proper behavior and traditional moral codes, especially in public. It was a matter of family honor that they must be virgins on their wedding nights. This was all understood despite the subject of sex being a taboo subject in their household. All the kids ended up learning about the birds and the bees from friends, from school venereal disease films, or from each other's whispered stories.

Seeing their mother helpless, the children soon learned that they had no ally in the house but each other. Each child began to turn to one or another of the siblings until they ended up in pairs, or sets, in which they were able to share intimacies and secrets, but it was all done without adult supervision or guidance. Baldemar was his own set of one, being older and having no brother near his age. Then there were Esmeralda and Alicia, then Carlos and Sylvia despite their gender differences. Finally, there was Antonio, whose partner was yet to be born. Of course, they also interacted as much as possible with all the others outside their pairs, but the alliances stood.

§

When 1958 arrived, the family spent its first Christmas in America. The kids continued to marvel at the abundance of fancy things all around. They wished for all the things they saw advertised on their twelve-inch black-and-white television set with the bad rabbit ear antenna as well as the things they saw at the Gulfgate Mall behind huge plate glass windows and the goodies that seemingly overflowed at the Weingarten's grocery store. But not much of it was to be, because there simply was not enough money for anything beyond the basic necessities. "There is no money," Eliza would say, because it was to her that the children petitioned for all of their longings. To top it off, she was pregnant again. She would be delivering a baby boy sometime in the coming summer.

The kids sometimes felt embarrassed that their school lunches consisted of refried beans slathered onto Sunbeam bread for sandwiches. They yearned for what they saw as fancy cafeteria lunches, with hot biscuits with apple jelly and chocolate cake desserts. Sometimes they took avocado sandwiches, but most often it was a tuna fish sandwich. On the days of tuna sandwiches, they felt almost as normal as anyone. Eliza also liked the convenience of opening a can of tuna and quickly mixing in the Miracle Whip as Julieta had taught her.

The kids never knew whether they should use their daily nickel allowance to buy milk for lunch or save it and buy a piece of candy after school at the ice house and convenience store next door to the school. Some of their classmates teased them about not speaking English, but others were quite helpful and sympathetic. Eliza and Ramiro trusted and depended on the school to do what was right by their kids, as had been the case back home. That meant that Eliza was never at a PTA meeting or any of the normal activities that American parents engaged the schools in. The kids learned that school was another terrain where they would be on their own. This became another factor that contributed to a distancing between the parents and the school-aged kids.

Every Ocañas child failed his first year of school. Alicia repeated fifth grade. Carlos repeated second. Only Sylvia did not repeat kindergarten. They could not speak a word of English when they started school, and although they picked up many words and phrases, they lacked the language for academic competence. Carlos was able to appear to speak English on the surface, but that was only to his parents who spoke no English at all. Indeed, all the children were soaking up the superficial language of social interaction. They pressured themselves to fit in as much as possible, and only English would offer them that privilege.

When September of 1958 arrived, the kids started their second year in school. Alicia was asked to read aloud in class, and she surprised herself and a couple of her classmates, who were also repeating the fifth grade, when she read almost perfectly. In fact, she was speaking the words without really understanding what she was reading, so some might argue as to whether she really was reading. She wondered why her reading was so amazing to her two classmates from the previous year. Alicia had developed the ability to make correlations between the sounds of the language and the written words. The same thing was happening with Carlos and Sylvia. Sometime in the future, Carlos would learn that second language acquisition works in such mysterious ways because it takes a silent period of listening and unconsciously assimilating sounds before the subtleties of correlating sounds with symbols develop. The second language development of the children happened in a structured classroom environment strictly immersed in the English language with an occasional hour set aside for guided vocabulary study.

In the next three years, the kids became proficient in English, only exacerbating the cultural rift that had developed between them and their parents. Ramiro's wishes that the children learn the language were realized beyond his imagination. But with language comes culture. The kids were assimilating and acculturating at a rate that both pleased and scared the parents. Besides the angst and restlessness of the emerging teenagers, there was the increasing loss of Spanish of the younger in the brood. All the kids spoke Spanish to their parents, but the communication between them became greatly curtailed. For their part, Ramiro and Eliza remained in a surreal limbo of living in a foreign world in body while their spirits remained in Naranjales. Not a day went by that the thought of returning home didn't cross Ramiro's mind. The family's visits home became a yearly event, but the older kids were no longer keen in traveling with the family, crammed into a crowded car for hours.

§

The couple welcomed a baby boy in June 1958, almost a year to the day after their arrival in Houston. They named their new American baby Oscar. The child rooted them a little more to the American soil than they had felt before. Ironically, that normally blessed event was as much a thing of pride as it was a lament because it added heft to the idea that there was to be no turning back. The blessed event was a totally new and frightening experience for Eliza.

Because of money shortages and tradition Eliza had received almost no prenatal care during her pregnancy. Her physical strength and previous six births had gotten her through the stressful months of adapting to a new home in a foreign country while growing the new life inside her. She had undergone unusual symptoms of extreme nausea, headaches, even backaches. She seldom complained, choosing instead to save the family the trouble of worrying about her or spending their precious little savings on doctor visits.

One day Esmeralda came home from work to find her mother on the kitchen floor, moaning and dragging herself to the stove for leverage to get on her feet. She was impeded from her reach by the great belly of her eight-month pregnancy. Esmeralda almost screamed in freight, "Mama, what's the matter. Are you all right? What happened?" She rushed to the aid of her mother. The kids were outside playing noisily and Alicia had gone to the store.

"*Hija*, don't worry. I just felt a little faint and I had to sit on the floor for a minute. Don't tell your father what you saw. He has enough on his mind, and he might want to take me to some hospital. I know what to do. I will be all right," she said in her usual no-fuss manner. "Help me to my bed. I just need a few minutes of rest. Look over the rice and brown that chicken for the *arroz con pollo* for dinner."

Esmeralda was beside herself, but she understood there was nothing to do but obey her mother. She helped Eliza to bed and quickly returned to the kitchen. She turned on the stove again, put the chicken in the fryer and checked the griddle to see if it was ready for her to start making tortillas. A half-hour later Ramiro and Baldemar arrived, and Eliza was back in the kitchen stirring the rice again.

When the big day came, it was a lucky thing that the labor pains began just after dinner. Eliza for once dropped everything she was doing, ignoring the pile of dishes that she expected the girls to do anyway. Feeling faint and nauseous, she rushed into the bathroom where she knelt before the toilet expecting to throw up the dinner she had just eaten. The smell of Pine-Sol in the bowl seemed to ease the nausea a little. Ramiro had retired to the backyard with his usual after-dinner cup of coffee.

It was Esmeralda, again, who saw her mother in agony for she was preparing to clean up the kitchen after dinner. The girl heard her mother's retching, and she dashed to her father's side to tell him, "Something is wrong with mama. She is sick. She's in the bathroom. We have to do something."

Ramiro sprang to his feet and handed the coffee cup to his daughter spilling it on her hand on his way into the house. Esmeralda yelped at the hot coffee, but she stifled her protest seeing that her mother's situation was what mattered at that moment.

Ramiro flung open the door to the bathroom,"Mujer, que te pasa? Is the baby here?" He held her arm and guided her out of the room and onto the bed. "Lie down here." Only the three elder kids were aware of what was happening. Ramiro quickly put on a fresh shirt and rifled through his wallet till he found a piece of paper with an address of a hospital that Julieta had given him. He had previously schemed out the area of the hospital's location but had not actually visited it.

The couple had been told by their new friends that in America all births had to be performed in hospitals, so they had been bracing for the experience of dealing with a bunch of strangers invading their most intimate and emotional moments. Eliza was terrified at the thought that a male doctor was going to perform the delivery. The couple, therefore, was only marginally prepared for what was about to come.

Ramiro guided Eliza slowly and tenderly to the car. He instructed Baldemar to run over to Julieta's and tell her what was happening. He instructed Esmeralda to look after the kids, and he set the car in motion. The hospital was about a half hour away, in the North Shore neighborhood.

In their rush to get there, Ramiro had not procured a translator, so he panicked for a minute. He drove directly to a door that said "Emergency" because he understood what it meant and certainly felt he was in an emergency. The hospital was small and simple, but they did have a Spanish-speaking nurse, which greatly alleviated Eliza's anxiety.

As soon as Eliza stepped out of the car, her water broke. The orderlies rushed a gurney to her side and helped her onto it. They rushed her to a semiprivate room and drew the curtains. Eliza was in agony with painful contractions. Ramiro saw her grimacing face as his wife attempted to stifle her screams. "Don't worry about anybody. Go ahead and scream all you have to," he told her. He held her hand tenderly and felt his heart burst in sympathy for her pain. He had never been beside her at the moment of childbirth. It had always been a woman's world until the child was out and crying in the midwife's arms.

The doctors and technicians rushed into the room. They yelled out orders and barked instructions. The nurse, Elena, told Ramiro they would be moving Eliza to the operating room. She told him not to worry and she pointed him to a waiting area where they would come to give him updates as necessary.

Eliza was both wide awake and aware of all movements and deliriously unaware because of the pain and her own fear of all the strangers who were touching her body. She was given a shot to relax, but it wasn't enough to ease the pain. Then before she knew it, she was slid onto another bed and bright lights were turned on. She felt herself being hoisted onto delivery position, some sort of cold apparatus spreading her legs wide and shaming her as never before. She gave up trying to make sense of any of it and fell back. She could hear the male doctor's voice, but she focused on Elena's Spanish voice sweetly telling her to push.

The pushing part was easy for this was her seventh child. In less than five minutes, her new son was out. She heard the crying as she secretly celebrated the easing of the pain. Elena brought the crying baby up to the mother and placed him in her arms. Eliza looked up as she was being wheeled back to her room to see Ramiro rush to her side. The baby was right behind. Both mother and baby were made comfortable. Eliza instinctively reached for her breast to feed her new son as Ramiro held the boy and placed him by his mother's breast. Baby Oscar had arrived.

§

A couple of months later the family celebrated Esmeralda's *quinceañera* with a simple house party. The girl had blossomed into quite a beauty, and there was no place the family went that she didn't attract the attention of boys with raging hormones. Ramiro's job of protecting his daughters from the advances of strange boys and men was becoming more complicated.

The party to celebrate Esmeralda's coming out was a far cry from the fancy *quinceañera* that Ramiro had attended when he worked with Don Paquito. Isabel, his boss's granddaughter, had been given quite a feast. There was too little money in the Ocañas household to splurge on such fancy things, but the truth was this family had never celebrated kids' birthdays other than to acknowledge the day with a simple, "Today is your birthday. One year older. Happy birthday," and that was that.

Ramiro and Eliza became part of the social circle of Julieta and Eduardo's. There were eight other families with whom they now socialized on a regular basis every weekend. All of them hailed from somewhere near Naranjales or the surrounding region, including a family from Monterrey and one from Reynosa. Every family attended the party. The kids had never seen so much festivity or so many gifts in one room for just one person. Esmeralda made her own cake from several boxes of cake mix and frosting, her favorite American discovery at the supermarket in which she spent minutes ogling all the choices of flavors and brands of the magical stuff of cakes every Friday when the family did their weekly grocery shopping.

To any outsider, it might have looked like the simplest of birthday parties, but in fact it was quite a celebration. Eliza's superb home cooking was also a star of the show, and she received accolades on her chicken and rice, homemade corn tortillas, and cilantro beans. Ramiro went all-out in supplying soft drinks for the women and kids and beer for his *paisanos*. Despite the usual budget crunching, Ramiro gave Esmeralda a nice allowance for a beautiful pink chiffon dress she found on a rack at the Sears store on Harrisburg Boulevard. He also bought her a dainty ladies Timex wristwatch, her first.

The young woman looked radiant, her bright green eyes beaming with joy at all the attention she was getting on her special day. The only problem was she had no royal court, no church ceremony, no *padrinos* who would sponsor her for the long list of expenses incurred in a large, elegant affair—and no special boy to escort her. Baldemar would have to do as a substitute. In short, the party was just a simple dinner and dancing in the living room because the Valle Azul crowd never passed up a chance to dance even if in foreign lands.

The day after the party was all work for everyone once again. Ramiro and Baldemar went to work bright and early, at 6:00 a.m., to be sure to arrive in plenty of time for Ramiro's cup of coffee before the 7:00 a.m. punch-in time. Esmeralda went to the bus stop about 7 and headed to her new job as an apprentice in a tailor shop across town.

Alicia, Carlos, and Sylvia finished their usual breakfast of sweet *gorditas* and coffee and milk, grabbed the sack lunches that Eliza had prepared for them, and were out the door at 7:30 to walk to school some seven blocks away and arrive before the eight o'clock bell. Antonio and baby Oscar remained home and waved goodbye to their older siblings while Eliza gathered all the morning dishes to wash. No TV watching was allowed in the mornings because Eliza couldn't stand the noise on top of all the kids' fussing about getting ready for school. After the house was almost empty and quiet, she turned it on for the two little ones to watch cartoons, then her mind turned to the usual list of housekeeping chores for the day.

CHAPTER 25: *Death of a Dream*

I t was the spring of 1960, past midnight, so the couple drove in pitch darkness, as modernization had not yet reached Naranjales, no electric streetlights. Three children slept in the backseat. They were on the single cobbled main road and the headlights of the family's Bel Air parted the blackness in choppy and bouncy motion as they approached their desolate *casa blanca.* "I hope we are not waking people up all over the village," Eliza said. "The car is so noisy, all that rumbling." Few motor vehicles traveled those parts at night not only because few people owned them but also because farm folks went to bed soon after darkness fell.

Eliza rolled down the window as if to prevent suffocation. The cool night air had been refreshing via the vent windows of the car, but the mood of the couple on this trip spawned a feeling of stagnation. The rush of air did the trick for a moment, transporting Eliza to days gone by. She half jutted her head out the window to let the breeze tussle her hair. She looked up at the night sky and loosed her hair. The millions of stars that met her eyes suddenly reminded her of nights spent on the cool elevated cement veranda that stretched the entire front of the house, where she and the children sometimes just lay flat, looking up at the stars and played games of naming or counting them, even making up mythical stories to capture the depths of wonderment that such heavenly bodies inspired in them. She had forgotten such wondrous sights because the Houston night sky was so woefully deprived of such a pristine touch of nature.

"Don't worry, *Mujer*. We are almost there. Besides, I'm driving slowly. Don't want any rocks flying or hitting potholes," said Ramiro.

Their second visit home after settling in Houston was bittersweet for the couple. This was not a pleasure trip. It was all business, and it was heart breaking. They were here to sell their beloved *casa blanca*, as they had grown to call it in the short time they had owned it. Ramiro had spent many a night tossing and turning in bed, unable to sleep, tormented by the decision of whether to hold on to his precious dream farm. Selling it meant cutting off, once and for all, the last thread that connected him to his treasured native land. He had sometimes broached the subject with Eliza hoping she would dissuade him although he tended to ignore her opinion. Besides, she was not nearly as sentimental about it and tended to respond tersely, "Go ahead and sell it. No use holding on to it. Even if we go back some day, that day is too far off. It might never even happen."

"Look at this place, Eliza. It's practically deserted. Where has everyone gone? I know why our people left, but so many houses shuttered," said Ramiro. "This is not the love of my life that it used to be."

The old homestead, where Lupita and Timoteo had lived and prospered, was now boarded up after the old folks moved to Valle Azul to get away from the sad memories. They had opened a little convenience store in the outskirts of town, and it was enough to live on and keep them and Lola occupied. The couple and three kids drove directly to their house knowing that the caretaker had dusted it off for the visit. The next day dawned as bright and sunny as ever, but Ramiro and Eliza awoke to a village in shades of grey, in part because their emotions but also because the number of desertions. There was no longer any doubt that the decision to sell their property was the correct one.

Ramiro spent the day with the buyer and the bankers after dropping off the family at his parents' house. He was glad that his farm would be staying with the faithful neighbor who loved the land and produced the honey for most of the villages. The Lozanos were good people. That was about as much as a man could ask for to insure that his prized possession would be preserved and cared for. Ramiro followed through diligently on the sale of his farm then he paid the requisite visits to relatives and close friends before heading back to Houston.

The long ride home was almost as somber as the visit to his deflated parents, but Ramiro managed to pull out of his funk and allow his ebullient sense of humor to emerge. He began to make small talk with Eliza and then tease her about one thing or another although it should have been her cheering him up. Only the three little ones went on the trip, so Eliza had plenty to keep her busy, and she brushed his joking aside as usual. Ramiro's weakness for babies also helped ease the difficult transition. He played with Oscar, teased Sylvia, and quizzed Antonio ("Tony") on addition problems.

§

The years that followed didn't get any easier for the couple. Ramiro agonized about whether to go into debt to buy a little bungalow in the east end of downtown Houston, in a neighborhood known as Second Ward. Eliza yearned for a little house of her own. Finally, the older kids, who were all employed by then, convinced Ramiro that they would help out with the house notes and the bills. He would not have to go it alone or worry too much about the thirty-year note to the bank. In the summer of 1962, Ramiro swallowed hard and put in a down payment on the little house that would become the family's homestead for the remainder of the kids' development into adulthood.

It was in that little house on Garrow Street, in the shadow of the Blessed Sacrament Catholic Church and the giant neon sign of a Maxwell House Coffee cup with the last drop frozen in free fall off its rim where some of Eliza's and Ramiro's greatest growing pains and heartaches transpired. It was there that he watched his kids, one by one, break away from the family to seek independence, adventure, and romance.

The cultural tradition of marrying young was an inevitability, and Baldemar, Esmeralda, and Alicia began to show signs that they were seeking out partners with whom to make their lives. Ramiro was not equipped to share his kids with strangers who did not fit his criteria for marriage material. He considered most of the prospects too vulgar for his sheltered offspring. He prayed that Baldemar, Esmeralda, and Alicia would look only to the children of people like his friends or families from back home when it came time to start their own families. But he could neither control the hormones of the young people nor impose his will over the hearts of a young Mexican woman in love, as he would learn soon enough. Not even the hearts of his own daughters.

The purchase of the Garrow house also meant the final nail on the coffin of the dream of a young, idealistic Ramiro when he first embarked on his journey out of his comfortable farming community to try his luck in the concrete jungle of Chicago. He began to see himself as a man with only one option—to be proud of having raised a good family. By that standard and his definition of "a good family," he was succeeding. To him, a good family meant that he had raised his seven children, first of all to not get into trouble with the law, then to become decent human beings who honored family above all else, and to respect tradition.

Ramiro expected the girls to marry good, traditional boys who would support them and be a good fathers to their children. He expected that none of his seven kids would become a burden on society or on each other by subscribing to his motto of never borrowing from others except in extreme emergencies and never asking the government for bailouts. He expected that his kids would give him grandkids that would be well behaved and show respect for their elders and good manners toward authority figures and all adults. He once told his kids that when he retired, he would consider his life a success if they all came to visit on Father's Day one day and lined his driveway with nice cars.

The problem Ramiro had with measuring his new life's goal was that it involved too many heads. There is a saying in his home country that goes like this: "*Cada cabeza es un mundo*," or "Every head is one world." In the Garrow house, there were nine worlds, and one man can truly be responsible for only his own world. The world of Eliza had been determined decades before by the poverty and neglect of her upbringing and then by Ramiro's controlling, though loving, ways. The older kids had managed to retain enough tradition to understand Ramiro and try to comply.

But the younger kids were becoming American through and through. They spoke Spanish just enough to appease their parents. They understood some traditions but didn't heed them if they became a nuisance. They wanted to fully immerse themselves in the kaleidoscopic pop culture that America offered them. The little ones had gone so far as to threaten Ramiro's ultimate parental tool for discipline: they promised to call the Harris County Child Protective Services office and report him for spanking them with the belt. Such boldness enraged Ramiro so much that he punished Tony and Sylvia doubly for daring to threaten him that way. Afterward, he worried for days that a government car would pull up to his driveway and take him away.

Inside the Garrow house, it was still all about Ramiro and his rules, rules that had been handed down for many generations. Inside that little house, the father ruled as he pleased, and he knew best. The mother was subservient and the kids obeyed all edicts. The rules were strict and unrelenting. Law and order were the way of the world, and Ramiro had inherited his parents' Spanish traditions of implementing patriarchal authority. What the kids considered harsh was only tough love in his mind because a kid without discipline was bound to become a lost soul. Indeed, decades later, the kids would speak of being grateful that their father had been "so strict."

Inside the Garrow house, there was dysfunction that no one knew what to call until decades later when the younger kids would latch onto the in-vogue word to describe their childhood. Inside, there was turmoil, and struggle, and money worries. Inside there was also immense love, for Ramiro would have given his life for any one of his kids had the situation called for it. Inside, it was quaint 1955 Naranjales, and time was supposed to stand still. Inside, it was like that.

Outside the Garrow house, the country was raging with civil rights battles, hippie rebellions, Viet Nam War protests. Outside, Houston was booming with the "eighth" wonder of the world and downtown skyscrapers. Outside, there was a missile crisis and a murdered president. Outside, there was a moon landing, black-light posters, high school football, Watergate, Woodstock, free love, and marijuana. The outside was a junkyard dog whose leash was just short enough to keep it from tearing off Ramiro's flesh.

The years were passing and America was moving at speeds incomprehensible to the immigrant families like Ramiro's. Yes, outside the Ocañas home, Martin Luther King and Bobby Kennedy were assassinated, and the country was about to explode from dreams deferred. But inside the immigrant's home, such world-shaking events were just a ripple. There was too much work to get done. There were too many mouths to feed, too many kids to keep in line, too many bills to pay, too many heartaches to nurse. It would be decades before some of the younger kids took to the streets themselves in newfound indignation over their country's flaws armed with equally newfound empowerment of American citizenship and its spirit of proactive civic involvement to resolve social or political issues.

CHAPTER 26: *Doña Lupita's Death*

t was a sunny, cool afternoon in October 1965. Eliza was in the backyard hanging laundry out to dry. She could hear the phone ringing from where she stood with her basket of wet sheets, towels, boys' jeans, and girls' blouses, but she chose to finish her task rather than to answer it. The ringing stopped for a minute. As she grabbed another handful of clothespins, the phone rang again. The incessant bell began to worry her. The first call had rung almost ten times before the caller gave up, but here it was again. She quickly dried her hands on her apron and ran into the house, following the sound of the phone into the living room where it sat on a corner table. "I'm coming. I'm coming. I wonder what's all the fuss…"

"Hello," she said.

"Eliza. It's Julieta."

"Julieta?" You're crying. What's the matter?" said Eliza. "Did something happen? Is your brother okay, or is it Eduardo?"

"It's Mama." She paused. "We've lost her, Eliza. Ramiro doesn't know yet." She cried uncontrollably, "My *mother*."

"Oh, my God, Julieta, I'm so sorry. Oh, my God," said Eliza.

After composing herself Julieta said, "What time will Ramiro get home? I already called Eduardo, and he is on his way home now. We want to leave right away, this evening. We want to know if you and Ramiro want to travel with us."

"I don't know what to tell you. Ramiro will be home by 3:30. It's almost 2:00. I think we can; we can go with you all. I'll ask him to call you. Oh, my God. How is he going to take this news? I'm so sorry, Julieta." Eliza was glad that all the kids were still at school. Her head began to spin thinking about how she was going to break the news to them. But she was especially worried about Ramiro. She knew he was going to take it hard and recalled vividly how the death of Jacobo had affected him so much only eight years before.

§

Ramiro had gotten into a rhythm and pace of daily existence in his new home, in his new country. He still had trouble embracing that this was his new country, primarily because all signals he received from the established citizenry told him that he was a mere unwelcomed visitor. But the kids reminded him daily that, indeed, "we are not going anywhere because this is home." They were absorbing the language and culture like sponges. Ramiro had to struggle daily to hold on to his manhood, as he saw it, by keeping control of everything and everyone under his roof, but the kids were living in a parallel universe.

As Ramiro and Eliza's family saw their lives evolving in their adopted land, they faced challenges and obstacles of many sorts, but it was the financial precariousness that most debilitated Ramiro. The good news was that Ramiro now had three children helping out with the expenses. Baldemar continued to work steadily alongside his father at the plant. Esmeralda was now an accomplished seamstress, and Alicia had been working since the tenth grade as a cashier at an Eckerd's drug store. It was a great relief to Ramiro that the older kids turned over half their paychecks to the household, which he controlled carefully. But he was also keenly aware that Baldemar was restless and wanted to move out. The boy had pleaded for a car just a few months after starting work, and after a year at the plant, Ramiro gave him the money for a down payment on a used Ford. The growing boy also needed more spending money for car maintenance and socializing on Saturday nights.

Esmeralda was in her prime for marriage, so she could not be counted on much longer. Ramiro was expecting a visit any day from the family of the boy Esmeralda was dating. Alicia was sure to follow in short order. The thought of losing those supplements to his family budget troubled him deeply. Ramiro never studied anything resembling literature, but he had somehow internalized the edict of Shakespeare's Hamlet, where Polonius gives advice to his son, Laertes: *"Neither a borrower nor a lender be, for loan oft loses both itself and friend, and borrowing dulls the edge of husbandry."* The thought of being under obligation to anyone tended to raise his blood pressure and cause irritability. The kids' incomes, modest as they were, doubled his salary and provided for a comfortable cushion and cash flow that gave him much-needed peace of mind.

Little did Ramiro know how fast his premonitions of losing his older kids' support were to be realized. With the four younger kids not yet able to work for their own spending money, there was always one or another of them asking for things. Eliza's well-practiced response of "There is no money" usually ended most arguments. She had become adapt at denying them treats, new clothes, extra lunch money, even special school expenditures like a white shirt or black skirt to sing in the Christmas pageant. The kids had become accustomed to the phrase, and they knew not to ask for anything that would appear foolish, expensive, ostentatious, or extravagant. Ironically, the children never considered themselves deprived. They stubbornly refused to apply the word "poor" to themselves, even when they saw television ads for toothpaste that was often missing in their bathroom for lack of money or noted the sleek ranch-style homes and fancy furnishings of TV families on *My Three Sons, Leave It to Beaver*, or *Bewitched*.

Carlos was the most assertive about demanding items for school, such as a new lock for gym class. He also asked for new black pants and a white shirt so he could sing with the seventh-grade choir. Somehow Eliza felt compelled to take Carlos' requests directly to Ramiro, and Ramiro usually relented and found the money for such "necessary" expenses. After all, Ramiro was a man of honor, and he had made it clear to the kids that if they were committed to school, he would do the best he could to help them.

That summer, Ramiro surprised the whole family when he allowed a traveling salesman to come into the house and make a pitch to sell the family a set of World Book Encyclopedias. By the time the salesman got through listing the many marvels of having so much information at the fingertips of the young students, Ramiro was so impressed that he not only ordered the set of books but he also added *Childcraft: The How and Why Library* as well as six years' worth of the *Year Book*, plus a special shelf on which to display the collection. The kids jumped for joy, and Carlos in particular was forever grateful that his father made such an investment. It was a good thing that Ramiro had woken up in a particularly good mood that Saturday.

The older kids had gotten jobs and were helping with the family budget, but the younger kids were following a different track and Americanizing at a rapid pace. They had stopped listening to Mexican music altogether and were glued to the TV, trying to imitate the dancers on *American Bandstand* every Saturday. To make matters worse, the family's economic scarcity did not allow for Mexico visits more than once a year, and then for barely a week.

§

The father and son pulled into the driveway of their Second Ward house at close to four o'clock. Both men looked forward to the usual pampering of a great home-cooked meal that typically awaited them at the end of the day. Baldemar noticed it first. His mother was waiting on the front porch. That was not her customary place at this time of the day when she would have been busy in the kitchen, starting dinner for her large family after having set up the bath for her husband to shower after a long day at work.

"Funny. Mama is standing there as if she can't wait for us to be home," Baldemar said.

Ramiro looked up in the direction of the porch. "Yes. She looks troubled. I wonder what the kids got into today?" He waved at her as he pulled slowly past the porch and into the garage.

Eliza stepped back into the house and almost trotted back to the kitchen and out the back door to greet them. "I have bad news."

"I thought so," said Ramiro. Baldemar looked on anxiously.

"It's about your mother," said Eliza with a pained look in her face that he understood immediately.

"About Mama? What about Mama?" he said although he knew what was coming next.

Eliza grabbed his hand. "I got a call from Julieta. You should call her for the details. Your mother's left us. It was a heart attack. I'm so sorry, Ramiro." She hugged him and held on to him for much longer than was normal for her dispassionate personality and despite his not having changed out of his dirty work clothes. "Call Julieta. She has all the information. She needs to talk to you."

He was stunned. His heart sank to his stomach, but he somehow had been expecting such bad news for a while. He allowed Eliza to hold him a few minutes as he exhaled his pain onto her shoulder. She could feel his body shake gently as he allowed himself to shed a few silent tears on her hair.

When Ramiro hung up the receiver after talking to Julieta and listening to the news of his mother's death, he made the decision that he and Eliza would go home for the funeral, "Just the two of us. It could be too much disruption to take the kids out of school. The others can't take off work. We would lose too much income. Mother would understand." Nor would the couple ride with Julieta and Eduardo. He would drive himself. Ramiro seemed to take the bad news better than Eliza expected, but somberness invaded the house.

He loved his mother dearly, so the eight-hour drive home was harried and painful. Ramiro imagined the worst scenarios involving his grieving father and siblings, and his mind and soul became invaded by a loneliness that made him despair. Still, Eliza was surprised that he did not weep openly, not even a tear.

In keeping with Ramiro's delicate constitution, they had decided not to rush onto the freeways that very evening. Rather, they went through all their evening routines. They broke the sad news to the kids and instructed them to be at their best behavior for the next few days. They left the older kids in charge, instilling in them to be kind and protective of the younger ones. By 5:00 the next morning, the couple was on the road to McAllen.

Eliza had a completely different panorama swirling in her memories as they drove through the small Texas towns on the way to the border. She recalled the many instances Doña Lupita had been unkind to her and others and felt a little ashamed that she could not share in her husband's pain at the loss of her mother-in-law.

When they finally arrived in Valle Azul, it was nearly 2:00 in the afternoon. Ramiro was exhausted from all the driving, because Eliza never learned to drive a car. They were not greeted in the usual celebratory manner of former years, of course. There was no one rushing out the door to embrace them. There were just a few village folks milling around with sad faces in the family's living room. They were not customers of the store, but once the couple adjusted their eyes to the dark rooms, they recognized some old friends and neighbors from the old village.

Ramiro's heart was sinking even lower, and he rushed toward the bedroom where he encountered Julieta, tired and puffy-eyed. He held out his arms to her and she extended her hands to hold his. Then she welled up and a long yelp-like cry escaped her lips. He held her close for a minute and held back his own tears. Then he saw Lola slouched down in a chair beside the bed. Dear Lola, who had been inseparable from her mother all these years, sacrificing her youth and marital prospects. His heart ached for this devoted sister to whom everyone owed much. Lola did not cry, for she was cried out already. She merely looked up at her brother, her eyes sunk and vacant, and she allowed him to hold her for a good, long while.

The scene was dark and forbidding. Doña Lupita's body still lay on the bed, but it was covered from head to toe. The sight of his dead mother wrapped in white sheets stabbed his heart, but he remained stoic and robotic as he went through the motions of embracing his other relatives throughout the house. He returned to his mother's body and stood beside the bed in silent prayer. He closed his eyes and struggled with the choking feeling in his throat. How he recalled a million memories of this great woman who had raised him and loved him so much. "I'm going to miss you, mama," he whispered. "I'm going to miss you so much." His brother Alberto put a hand on his shoulder and walked him away.

Ramiro sat beside his brothers and stroked his nephews' heads as they came to their fathers then went on their way. The sporadic wailing of one sister or another as she received a condolence or simply needed to express her grief sent a chill to his heart every time. He wondered for a second whether it would have been better to bring his children, but quickly dismissed the thought with his practical "No sense in everybody missing school or work. There is nothing they could do here but get in the way. I'm sure mother would have agreed that it wasn't necessary."

§

Back home the kids went about their business in a sort of trance of their own. Each was mulling his or her own thoughts regarding the loss of their legendary grandmother. They had heard so many stories about Doña Lupita's strength, courage, boldness, and magnificent skills in every facet of pioneer life. Each child knew that something special was being taken from their lives forever and that they might never really understand how much they were losing. They wondered why things had to be a way that wouldn't allow them to pay their last respects to their esteemed grandmother.

CHAPTER 27: *Depths of Despair*

A week after returning to Houston, Ramiro spent his Saturday with a mechanic friend of his and several other men who dropped by to hang out at the old mechanic's shop, at the back of his house. Ramiro accepted every offer of beer he got, unlike his usual refusal after getting a bit of a buzz. This time he wanted to ease the pain of losing his mother. Her absence made him feel worse than an orphan. He was grown up and middle aged, but losing his mother was like losing his center of gravity. His mind kept painting pictures of his childhood home in Naranjales. He saw himself happily arriving to the comforts of home and his mother's special strength and loving guidance. When he was about to set foot in the door, it was all a mirage, and it was gone.

The void she left in him could only be described as utter hopelessness. He felt hopeless about ever owning his treasured farm. He felt hopeless of ever living free of money woes. He felt hopeless of tearing Mary's memory and the guilt she caused out of his heart. He felt hopeless about stopping his children from leaving soon, or keeping the younger ones from abandoning their Mexican identity. So he drank. "Another Schlitz, Ramiro?" "Sure. I'll take another." He lost count of how much he drank that day.

It was ten o'clock that night when he finally left his friend's shop. He was starving, so he headed straight to the nearest Prince's Drive-In for his preferred meal, the fried shrimp basket. A cheery girl on skates rolled up to his window and took his order. He managed to point to the items he wanted and in his inebriated condition was bold enough to call the items by their English name although the waitress couldn't make out what he was saying. He ate his fill and sobered up a little then pulled out to head home, ignoring the horde of young people out for a good time on a Saturday night.

The first indication of trouble was when he forgot to wait for the waitress to remove the window tray. As he pulled out of his slot the tray caught the pole holding up the canvas roofing and it splattered debris on the parking lot with a bang. A couple of the *pachucos* in the car next door yelled at him with raised arms and slammed their palms on the trunk of Ramiro's car. At that violation of his car, Ramiro immediately lost his temper, slammed on the brakes, and rushed the two youths. When the boys saw the man coming at them, they whistled and an additional three of their buddies appeared.

Ramiro stopped cold in his tracks realizing that he would take a beating if he didn't stop. He turned around to get in his car, but as he opened his door his head was slammed against the roof of the car. He felt a sharp pain and a dizziness came over him, but his instincts told him survival meant get away, so he quickly drove off without even closing his door.

As he sped away on Wayside Drive toward Harrisburg Boulevard, he heard the police siren. He was charged with reckless driving and driving while intoxicated. He would have to spend the night in jail.

Even in his state of drunkenness and misery, Ramiro felt a deep shame for being put in a cell. That was the kind of thing that he would have denounced his sons for doing. He felt he had sunk to the lowest point in his life.

Meanwhile, Eliza was dying of worry. She called Julieta. She sat by the phone. She didn't have Freddy, the mechanic's number. The girls didn't know any way of trying to locate their father. When Baldemar got home form his night out, it was three in the morning. Pulling in the driveway, he noticed every light on in the house and knew something was terribly wrong. He had had his share of drinking that night himself, but when he was told that his father was missing, he sobered up. The strong coffee Eliza gave him also helped him get focused.

Baldemar knew from his own escapades that grown men who went missing were often found in the city jail for any number of reasons, usually drinking. That was the first place he went to look. He picked up Mariana, Baldemar's gal, to assist with the language. When he bailed his father out of jail, Ramiro didn't say a word to him, nor did the son say much to his father except, "I understand, Pa. Let's go home. You will be fine tomorrow." Ramiro made a motion of let's get the hell out of here. He never acknowledged Mariana, and she kept quiet in the back seat on the ride home. Baldemar dropped her off and took his father home.

When he got home, Ramiro, again, didn't say a word to his wife. He simply undressed and went straight to bed. It was nearly 6:00 a.m. Eliza covered the windows so the coming sunrise would not disturb his sleep. She went into the kitchen and began to prepare the morning breakfast although it would be another two hours before anyone in the house would be up to eat.

CHAPTER 28: *Firstborn Son*

Baldemar staggered into the living room on his father's shoulder. Ramiro was half supporting him, half dragging him in. It was about three in the morning. His face was black and blue. Eliza almost fainted from the sight. She let out a barely audible yelp and quickly covered her mouth so as not to call attention to herself or make Ramiro angrier. Eliza was like that in repressing her emotions for fear of appearing self-indulgent. She had been up sick with worry for the last hour, the darkest hour of the night, the devil's hour. It had been thus since the fateful phone call that jolted her and Ramiro out of bed, she fearing the worst from a call at such an hour.

Just as she had guessed upon hearing the tiny bell from the guts of the blue plastic rotary phone, the voice of a frantic unidentified "floozy" had summoned Ramiro to go out and get his son "before they returned and killed him."

"You must come, señor, please! It's Balde. He's been in a brawl. There were seven or eight of 'em, and he was drunk. He couldn't really defend himself. Please come fast!" The unidentified woman begged. "We're on the corner of Main and Pine. It's in the north side, by the Latin Knights ballroom. You know the one, don't you? Will you come, señor?" the girl sobbed hysterically.

Ramiro was beside himself with fear for his errant son. All he could say in his anger at the girl, whom he unfairly judged as all vice personified and thus the culprit of his son's troubles, was a limp, "I'm on my way."

He hung up the phone and looked over at Eliza, her hands steadied on one side of the archway in the living room, staring at him in wide-eyed agony. "The boy's in trouble. Got into a fight," he said shaking his head. He walked back to his room and quickly slipped into his work khakis, which Eliza had lain out beside their bed for him, clean and crisp to don in a mere three hours when he was to leave for work at the galvanizing plant.

"He's okay. I'll bring 'im home. Look for some monkey blood and bandages," he spoke in Spanish and used the old terms of his Mexican ancestors when requesting the mercurochrome, "monkey blood."

It bothered him as much to see Eliza sick with panic as it did to imagine his firstborn lying helpless in some ditch, perhaps mortally wounded, "with only the aid of some stupid *pocha*." Yet Eliza's heart, so clearly visible on her sleeve, was a peculiar comfort to his misery as well. He'd long ago learned that her stoicism was stronger than his, and he was grateful for her self-control and her unquestioning support of his more mercurial emotions despite their repressive effects.

Ramiro prayed an agnostic prayer that the girls, who now slept in what would have been the dining room in a normal household but in his large family's small bungalow had become a bedroom, had not been awakened. He knew they would soon be awake when he dragged their brother past their room into his own. But at least one of the girls was fully aware of the goings on. Esmeralda, the clever nineteen year old, who never could miss a good dramatic moment, had been awakened by the sound of the phone. The girl feigned sleep and froze her slender body in place, not even bothering to brush off her long brunette tresses from her face, as she would have if conscious. She shielded her eyes with a veil of her hair to peek at the developing scene.

The two younger boys, in the second bedroom that they shared with Baldemar, were also quick to perk up their ears sensing the fear that lay heavy in the house. Only sixteen-year-old Alicia could sleep her pretty brown eyes through anything. Sylvia woke up for a minute before quickly falling back asleep.

And so it was that the mother and sisters waited anxiously for an hour that seemed an eternity while the father brought home the fallen son.

It was a clammy, hot summer night in the big city. Outside the bungalow, the coffee factory belched in usual aromatic clamor. A passerby approaching home after a late night party could feel swallowed and lose his footing. Inside, Eliza carefully prepared the first-aid items in silence. She made a pot of coffee instinctively, knowing that Ramiro would like some, and maybe Baldemar, too, would need a cup to sober up.

Eliza was so nervous and tormented with wild imaginings that she absent-mindedly kept herself under control by mixing some flour, water, and eggs and making dough for her special griddle cakes, *gorditas*, for the morning's breakfast. She, too, prayed her functionally illiterate prayer to her runaway saints that her golden boy was intact and that the other kids would not awaken. She knew Ramiro's self-control was as fragile as hers was strong and that his anger, unrestrained by pain, could rain an unpredictable torrent of belt lashings on Baldemar despite the boy being grown, although Ramiro had shown uncommon restraint when it came to inflicting corporal punishment on the kids after they reached puberty.

But the wide-awake children were feeling her emotions and fearing their father's possible wrath at their troubled big brother, who, despite enjoying firstborn favored status, was not beyond the harsh tongue lashing of the disciplinarian Ramiro. They knew even a face slap was possible. They respected their mother's pride too much to interfere with her agony, or to add to it. Instead, they looked on from their cots and sofa bed, keeping mum, hoping in shared familial intensity that Baldemar was all right.

Finally, everyone heard the engine of the newly-purchased Oldsmobile pulling into the driveway and felt a collective sigh of relief, knowing the men were home. No one missed any of the subtle sounds associated with people getting out of an automobile: the one door, then the other slamming in quick succession, the force or less force behind shutting them. They listened for the groaning or for reproachful language, but there was only quiet, except for the soft steps of the father and the scratchy steps of the injured son.

They pictured the distance of the footfalls up the concrete stairs onto the front porch, the screen door slowly opening, the door knob turning, the front door opening with its usual squeak, and the picture of the father holding up his injured son that only Eliza could see because they were all too respectful, or scared, to get up to satisfy their curiosity and quell their worry.

What Eliza saw was her handsome firstborn sluggishly entering the room on his father's shoulder, Ramiro's right arm bracing the boy around the waist. She saw Baldemar's gray-blue eyes bloodshot, one swollen eye almost shut completely. His slender frame of 5'9" and 150 pounds was not destroyed, but his good wool trousers and *guayabera* shirt were a mess of bloodstains, mud, grass, and nondescript debris.

It wasn't the first time Baldemar came home with injuries from some fight, but this was the worst she'd seen. No matter how often she had seen her boy hurt, it always felt to Eliza as if it were the first time.

"Just look at you. How are you, boy?" Eliza whispered in her practiced, feigned gruffness that no longer fooled anyone and that made her pain somehow more poignant to her children. "Where have you been?" she continued after a pause, her voice almost breaking. "*Muchacho*, just look at you," and she could no longer contain herself. She hugged him tenderly then took his arm leading him to the easy chair. Still, she held back her tears.

"Ma, I'm alright. Don't worry yourself. Do you have some coffee?" mumbled Baldemar, as Ramiro stood silently by the door watching the mother nurse her son. Ramiro was furious with his son but managed not to lose control. "I'm all right, Ma," Baldemar repeated, sounding not nearly as ashamed as Ramiro felt he should have been. "I just want to go to bed, Ma."

"We left his car on the side street of that joint," said Ramiro. "We'll pick it up tomorrow."

Apparently, Ramiro had already had his say during the drive home. Baldemar hoped it would all be forgotten as soon as his father scolded him one more time the next evening as he expected. Ramiro would make sure that the lesson was driven home more plainly to a sober Baldemar. He would miss one day of work at the plant tomorrow. That hurt him more than any berating or beating of Ramiro's, hard as they might be. He knew that his allowance would be halved the next payday, but that wasn't as shameful as not bringing home the usual paycheck to the household. How he wished he could do better at picking his friends. He really wanted Ramiro to be proud of him, to know that he could depend on his son to carry his load. His manhood depended on it.

"You boys, just stay in bed. Try to go back to sleep as soon as this is over," Eliza told the boys as she led Baldemar into the room and seeing the younger boys sit up and stare at their big brother.

After nearly crashing into bed from exhaustion, the pain from the beating, and the lingering effects of the liquor, Baldemar lay very still while Eliza applied loving care to his wounds, occasionally jumping at the sting of the medicine.

"Ay aayyyy, ay ay ay…Ma!" he whisper-screamed.

"Be still, boy. Not the big tough man now, huh?" Eliza chided him.

The weary parents managed to get just one more hour of fitful sleep that night before beginning their morning routine to send Ramiro off to work and the younger children to school.

Upon waking, Eliza stealthily rushed to her firstborn's side and held back a great impulse to crash down in tears at the sight of his swollen face. "Oh, my boy, my boy," she prayed, biting her lip. She touched his swollen cheek then quietly started her kitchen duties after an unconscious and fleeting glance at the little ones to reassure herself they had not witnessed her temporary softness. Eliza's very survival, she was convinced, had always depended on that exterior wall of toughness she had carefully built around herself.

Soon Ramiro, too, was up and out of the shower.

"What will become of this boy," he thought as he made his own trembling check of his firstborn, once his greatest pride. He looked around to reassure himself that the others were all asleep. Some paternal impulse compelled him to reach for his son's grass-stained trousers, muddied and scraped, searched the back pocket noticing that the security button had been torn during the scuffle, pulled out the boy's wallet and examined its contents. He furrowed his brow and pursed his lips. His eyes involuntarily glistened as he felt the impotence of a man whose son was beyond his domain. Ramiro knew he could no longer protect his son from the harshness of the world. He lay down the boy's wallet and reached into his back pocket for his own. He opened his wallet and pulled out a five-dollar bill. He placed the bill in his son's empty wallet.

"What will become of this boy?" he said to himself. "He's too impulsive. He doesn't know how to pick his friends."

Baldemar uttered a faint moan as the morning sun began to accost his battered eyes.

CHAPTER 29: *Esmeralda's Perfect Wedding*

Esmeralda fell madly in love with Marcelo the day she first laid eyes on him. She was a romantic, and he fit the bill of a long checklist of qualities she wanted in a man. The couple met on her eighteenth birthday. Ramiro had rewarded her with the treat of an outing to the downtown movie house, El Ritz. Esmeralda and Alicia had been allowed to go to the movies on Sunday afternoons since Esmeralda's sixteenth birthday, when her father thought it fair enough to let the girls venture out into society as long as they were well chaperoned. Carlos being the only son near in age to his sisters, was sent along to chaperone. The girls and Carlos, all wearing their Sunday best, walked the three blocks over to the bus stop on Harrisburg to make the short trip downtown.

Ever since Esmeralda turned fifteen, both girls had been deluged with suitors' offers of all kinds, which they politely declined, waiting for just the right boy. The movie theater was the only place where a decent girl could go to meet boys, and El Ritz was the only movie house showing Spanish language movies from Mexico. The girls found it easy to get around the little brother's chaperoning by giving him a quarter to go sit elsewhere. Carlos appreciated the extra money for candy, but he sometimes simply left the theater and roamed the desolate Sunday streets of downtown Houston to admire the architecture, smoke shops, and display cases for exotic showgirls at various locations near the theaters. He continued to be fascinated by the concrete canyons of the city.

The problem with twelve- or thirteen-year-old boys wandering around in empty downtown streets is that they may end up in mischief, either of their own making or as victims of some sort. The few people around on Sunday afternoons could be found at bus stops and an occasional bar or diner. As Carlos wandered past the Metropolitan Movie Theater—the one with English-language movies—he didn't notice when an older man approached him. He thought it was just a nice guy being friendly when the stranger invited him for a 7 Up and a sandwich. The soda sounded good on that hot August day, so he accepted. The man pointed him toward a small, run-down diner, and they sat down to chat. Carlos began to sense unease with the man asking so many personal questions, so he blurted out that his sisters and boyfriends were expecting him nearby, and he had to go. When the strange man tried to convince him to stay a little longer, Carlos panicked, and pulled away, saying, "I have to run. I'm late. My sisters will tell Papa. Bye. Thanks for the 7 Up!" and ran back to the Ritz, where he waited outside until the girls walked out a half hour later.

That Sunday of Esmeralda's eighteenth birthday, the girls expected to sit together with Carlos and watch the movie. Maybe a boy or two would flirt with them, but there would be no need to send Carlos away. But it was a fateful day for Esmeralda.

"Pardon me. Hello, what's your name?" a voice asked Esmeralda as she stood at the concession stand waiting for her strawberry Nehi.

Esmeralda turned around curious to see who was speaking. Her eyes were met with a handsome and wholesome face, smiling and yet hesitant for fear of scaring her off. "Hello," she said. "And who might want to know my name?"

"I would very much want to know your name. My name is Marcelo. Marcelo Iberia. How do you do?" Marcelo said extending his hand in hopes she would take it.

Esmeralda smiled a beautiful, friendly smile, feeling reassured by his Monterrey accent and sensing the great manners that she admired in a boy. She quickly calculated he was a year or two her senior. Perfect.

She shyly stretched out her hand and met his in almost a shock of electricity at the touch of his manly fingers. "Pleased to meet you, Marcelo. My name is Esmeralda."

"Esmeralda? What a beautiful name. Unusual. I bet you're from around my hometown," he said.

"I am, if your hometown is Valle Azul, Nuevo Leon," she teased.

"Well, as a matter of fact," he laughed. "No, I won't lie to you, but I have been to Valle Azul, so not too far off. I'm from Monterrey." Marcelo said. "So, you're from Valle Azul? Pretty women there, I hear. Now I have proof," he winked.

Esmeralda blushed a little. "I am actually from a village just outside there. Naranjales, it is called. That is why my name is unusual. Lots of old-fashioned people with old-fashioned Spanish names," she smiled.

"Oh, I see. I get it now. Beautiful name, just the same. Great that it is uncommon like the jewel it represents," he said.

"Thank you," she said. She seemed unable to stop smiling. Her body felt warm all over. His big brown eyes drank her up as she got lost in them. His cologne was almost intoxicating. His touch so warm and inviting that she wasn't sure if it was he or she who held the initial handshake much longer than was proper for two strangers meeting for the first time.

"Can I ask you to sit with me for the movie?" he asked.

"Well, I don't want you to think I'm easy or anything, now." Esmeralda said.

"Oh, no, no, no, absolutely not. I can tell just by looking at you that you are not that kind of girl. I promise to be a gentleman, and if I lose control, you have my full permission to slap me or walk away." Marcelo assured her. "But be aware that I have no intention of doing anything to blow it, because you are the most beautiful thing I have ever seen, and all I want to do is impress you," he continued in hopes of convincing her to sit with him for the next two hours.

"Well, if you put it that way, I guess I have to give you the benefit of the doubt," she said, "but no hanky panky, or touchy feely stuff, now."

"Promise," he said crossing his thumb and forefinger and raising them up to his lips and up to heaven. "Here, let me pay for that," he said as he took out a dollar to buy her and Alicia's drinks. Alicia had been standing beside them the entire time, but neither of them acknowledged her until that moment. "Marcelo. Pleased to meet you," he said as he extended his hand to Alicia.

"Nice to meet you, Marcelo. Thanks for the Coke. Don't worry, I will sit nearby but leave you two to get acquainted alone," said Alicia as she looked at Esmeralda with a reassuring look of "Don't worry about a thing," and "Go for it." "Our little brother is around somewhere, so don't be surprised if he shows up anytime," she warned him.

"Thanks for letting me know. No problem. Would love to meet him, too. He has to be a great guy with such lovely sisters in the family," Marcelo put on the charm.

Esmeralda could not believe her eyes or ears. She was swooning already and he had not even tried to kiss her yet. "A family man!" she thought.

And that was the beginning of a romance that was as close to traditional as it could get. Esmeralda and Marcelo continued to rendezvous every Sunday they could, and they managed secret telephone conversations whenever possible. Esmeralda kept her romance a secret from her parents, but both Ramiro and Eliza knew that something was going on. Shortly afterward, Alicia, too, was involved in her own secret romance, only her beau was of a different sort.

The courtship of Esmeralda and Marcelo lasted nearly two years before the couple had the courage to face Ramiro. The old man was completely aware of it, of course, but he chose not to acknowledge it in the hopes it would not last and that things at home would go back to normal. Alas, the course of young people in love cannot be averted by ignoring it or by forbidding it.

At the appointed time of eleven one night, Esmeralda stealthily tiptoed out of bed so as not to awaken Alicia or Sylvia who were sleeping beside her. She carefully picked up the receiver of the telephone in the living room and dialed Marcelo's number, straining her eyes in the dim light. The couple had determined that eleven was the best time to talk because all their relatives in both households would be fast asleep by then. Ramiro had a strict all lights-out-by-nine rule, and he tolerated no activity past that time, because he needed his rest to get up early every morning. Esmeralda depended on the attic fan's noise to muffle the sound of the rotary dial and to hide her whispered conversations, which often were nothing more than just listening to her beloved breathe for stretches at a time.

After the third ring Marcelo picked up on his end. His situation was more flexible than hers. He lived with his married brother, and the apartment complex had a public phone just down the hall. Besides, the rules were always more lax for men in their culture. He simply slid out of bed and waited beside the payphone until it rang, usually between 11:00 and 11:15. If it didn't ring by then, he understood that Esmeralda was not able to get to her phone or that her dialing was impossible somehow.

"Hello, my love. Is it you?" he asked.

"Ha ha, yes, of course, my love. But be careful. What if it was someone else, and you called her 'my love?'" she admonished. They both had learned the hard way that they could be jealous and possessive, but they relished knowing that they each wanted to belong only to the other in every way possible and to no one else.

"It's so wonderful to hear your voice. I have been so anxious all day long for this moment. Eleven o'clock is my favorite time of the day, and it will always be so." Marcelo said, as he had done many times before, but it was true, and she never tired of hearing or pledging just as many love promises to him.

"I know, my life, my heart. I can't wait for Sunday to come around to hold you in my arms again. Every week that goes by without feeling your warm skin and tender kisses is an eternity. Even a single day seems impossible to bear if I can't have at least these few moments of your voice," she cooed.

"My sky, my heart, what would you like to eat this Sunday? We can have hamburgers at the diner near the Ritz before the movie. Can you get there early so we can spend more time together?"

"Oh, my love, yes....." Esmeralda started to say when she felt a cold, rough hand strangle her dainty fingers and snatch the receiver from her. Before she knew it, the receiver had been recradled and her father was clutching her wrist. His grip forced her fingers to throb with fluid, causing her pain. Her surprise and fear allowed her to utter only an inaudible moan.

Ramiro bent down to her ear and hissed, "Aren't you ashamed? Get back in that bed and don't you dare get up again." That night he had been awakened by an urge to go, and that was when he heard his daughter whispering into the phone as he walked in the hall that led to the bathroom.

But Ramiro understood tradition and nature too well, and he knew it was inevitable that his girls should be looking for a mate as they were in their late teens now. When the next day came and Esmeralda asked to speak to him after dinner, he braced himself for an unpleasant conversation. Esmeralda had dug into the deepest recesses of her courage to face her father with the truth about her desire to marry the man of her dreams, Marcelo. She had prayed all day that the scene would not turn ugly, and, to her surprise, Ramiro kept his composure and agreed to receive the Iberia family when they came calling to ask for the young lady's hand in marriage. Esmeralda assured him the visit would be in about a month. Meanwhile, he consented for Esmeralda to go out alone with her soon-to-be fiancé.

It made Ramiro secretly happy that the boy was from the old country, even if he did come from the big city of Monterrey. Ramiro had spied on the two lovers on more than one occasion, so he had a pretty good idea about Marcelo, as Ramiro considered himself a good judge of character. Coincidentally, Marcelo even held most of the same traditional values as Ramiro.

Esmeralda, having been ingrained with her mother's ideas of fe-

male submissiveness in marriage was thrilled to have found a traditional man to marry. The only major hurdle left to pass was to see whether
there would be any chemistry between the two men once they met in
person. Ramiro was too quick to judge other families on any number
of issues that he found distasteful, such as having divorced parents or a
relative of ill repute. He even objected to families in which the females
were outspoken or controlling of the men of the family. The irony that
his own mother was rather powerful in exerting influence over her husband never dawned on him.

Despite her spirited personality and brilliant mind, Esmeralda
fully embraced the prospect of becoming a homemaker to the handsome, conservative Marcelo and mother of the house. It was the kind
of married bliss all the little girls of her time and place envisioned for
themselves one day. She fully shared in the belief that children must
always have the mother around to guide them and look out for their
needs. She had learned from her family and community that women
who stayed home and became the backbone of the family were the major source of family unity and happiness, especially of the children. She
was prepared to take her mother's role and embrace it as an empower-
ing thing, not a burden of submissiveness and subservience to a domineering husband. She had every intention of having a strong say on
every aspect of her children's lives and the management of the house.

When the day came for the visit from the Iberia brothers, Ramiro
was not quite ready, but he instructed Eliza to prepare a *merienda*, or
afternoon coffee social, worthy of any special guest. The Iberia brothers
arrived in the company of Marcelo's sister-in-law and an uncle who was
visiting from Monterrey especially for the occasion. The visit started
out awkwardly, with Ramiro at first refusing to sit comfortably on the
sofa, instead choosing to lean on the armrest.

Esmeralda was instructed to keep out of the room, so it was only
Ramiro and Eliza attending to the guests. Baldemar had been invited,
but he refused to cancel his bowling plans with his buddies. When Esmeralda, who was peeking from around the corner noticed the discom-

fort in the room, she defied her father and entered the room, chatting up a storm and carrying a tray of homemade wedding cookies. Eliza tensed up and looked over at her husband, but Ramiro seemed fine with the intrusion. He took a seat and began to change his stilted tone.

The wedding took place six months later in Valle Azul, as tradition dictated that the ceremony and festivities be held in the bride's hometown. Since most of the groom's large family resided in Monterrey and vicinity, Houston was out of the question. It could not be a real celebration without Marcelo's large clan. Even so, some of Marcelo's snootier relatives were not thrilled about traveling to a small town for such a formal affair, but once they met the fair Esmeralda, her charm and beauty won them over and most criticism vanished.

The Monterrey society to which the former country girl was being inducted understood that beauty always covered the price of admission in their circles. "Marcelo was lucky to have found such a traditional woman for a life mate," they all said. They speculated that the couple's children would surely be attractive, and that mattered plenty. Once the engagement was made formal, Marcelo's five sisters quickly volunteered to assist with any necessary wedding arrangements that Esmeralda could not handle long distance.

In Houston, the family struggled financially to make the trip. All the children would attend as Esmeralda had insisted on a December date so everyone could be out of school during the Christmas holiday. Once Ramiro consented to the wedding and gave away his daughter's hand, he participated as fully as any father of the bride would. Ramiro's frugal practicality even gave way to a little whimsy, and he decided it would not be proper to exclude the children from this affair, expensive as it might be. All the children got new outfits. The boys were taken to Montgomery Ward and Sears for new suits of clothes appropriate for the affair. Carlos and Tony were thrilled to be getting their very first suit and tie. They even got a new pair of shoes. Everyone was feeling beautiful and successful in the store-bought fancy clothes.

On the day of the wedding, Eliza was especially dolled-up by the bride herself. The family invaded Lola's house. Everything in the house was upside down with the excitement of all the preparations and so many guests getting ready that morning. The local beautician was summoned, and she worked on all the women's hair after arranging the bride's long brunette tresses in perfect cascading curls interlaced with baby's breath flowers.

Esmeralda loved makeup, so she did that part herself then she made sure her mother looked just as radiant. Eliza had not looked so elegant in her life. She could have easily been mistaken for a Monterrey society matron. Eliza was not one to fuss over fancy clothes or frivolous girly stuff, so she allowed herself to be guided by her daughters and tried not to look uncomfortable. Alicia was the maid of honor and was herself the very picture of beauty. Even Sylvia, the tomboy, looked smashing. Ramiro, for his part, was all of a peacock, relishing the attention he was receiving from so many guests and relatives as the father of such a beautiful bride and handsome couple. The occasion with so much hustle and bustle almost made him forget that his mother would not be attending the wedding.

The Valle Azul church looked the part, as if straight out of a movie set, for such a wedding. The little town was small and quaint, but its residents aspired to all the traditions of respectable Mexican society. Weddings and funerals were formal occasions, and everyone was expected to dress the part and demonstrate the manners and etiquette that went with it. Ramiro walked the bride down the aisle and later danced the symbolic last dance with her as he handed her over to the groom for the wedding waltz. Despite all the celebration, most of Esmeralda's siblings were experiencing a strange sadness at the thought that their big sister would never again be fully theirs. When the couple finally said their "I do's," many a guest wiped away a tear.

The reception and dance were held at the local Lion's Club. There was plenty of food and beverages to feed all the guests, and seconds for the kids as well. The Lion's Club of Valle Azul was no match for the majestic halls of country-club style in Monterrey, but it held its own for the place and time. Finally, the reception was over and the couple drove off to Monterrey where they hopped on a plane for their honeymoon in Mexico City and Acapulco. Neither bride nor groom had ever been on a plane before, so that experience alone proved to be a highlight of their honeymoon.

And so it was that at the age of twenty, on December 20, 1964, Esmeralda Ocañas, eldest daughter of Don Ramiro Ocañas and Doña Eliza Cervantes de Ocañas became officially a married lady in the eyes of God and of society, assuming the name of Esmeralda Ocañas de Iberia.

CHAPTER 30: *Ramiro's Lament*

A few weeks after Esmeralda's wedding, Ramiro sat on his front porch on a Saturday evening sipping his usual three beers after dinner and watching the neighborhood kids at play— or any passersby—and whatever traffic. He sat all alone. Eliza was in the kitchen doing dishes with Alicia and tidying up. After a half hour, Eliza dried her hands, opened the refrigerator, and grabbed a can of Schlitz. She opened the can and sprinkled salt on the opening then wrapped a napkin around it and took it out to Ramiro.

"Here you go. Have you finished the first one?" she said, even as she knew the timing well.

Ramiro was expecting the fresh beer, and he quickly chugged the last swig of his now-warm beer although it was mid-January and a typically mild Houston winter that nevertheless brought chilly nights. "Here you go," he said, and absentmindedly stretched his arm out with the empty can without looking at her.

Eliza set the fresh beer on the TV tray that stood beside his webbed folding aluminum lawn chair. She took the old one and walked back into the house before getting chilled outside. No other words were spoken.

Ramiro took a swig of his fresh beer and wrapped his corduroy jacket lined in fake wool a little tighter around him, then adjusted his wool Stetson.

He turned toward the door when he heard the squeak of the screen door. It was Baldemar, who had been watching TV in the living room.

where the only TV in the house was located. The other kids were in their room or in the backyard. The two looked at each other as a form of acknowledgment or hello but said nothing. Ramiro had become used to the silence around his children even when they were in the room. Baldemar was already dressed for his Saturday night party scene, but he seemed to have something on his mind as he lingered then went and sat on the porch railing, pretending to look out at the sky and street scene.

"Look at those two over there," said Ramiro. "Just look at them. As if they had no parents." He was pointing to a couple of neighborhood kids, a boy and a girl, the boy about fifteen, the girl about thirteen. The two kids were on the devil strip of the yard across the street, and they were engaging in some kind of wrestling match. "What kind of people let their girls run around with boys like that? I don't want my kids hanging out with those two," he said indignantly. When the kids began to kiss and roll on the grass, Ramiro became enraged.

"Well, Papa, they're from here. They don't follow the rules like we did back home," said Baldemar. When the kids noticed they were being watched, they ran off around the bock.

"Disgraceful and shameless," said Ramiro. "Something on your mind, son?" You look like a man with something to say."

"Well, Pa, since you ask, I do have something to say. I am thinking about m-m-marriage," he said, stammering over the word "marriage."

Ramiro though he'd choke on his beer when he heard it but maintained his composure. "Marriage, huh? With that *prietita*, what's her name, Maritza, Maruca, Marrana? Is it?" he said, his voice betraying his emotions. Mariana had the misfortune of being too dark, too monolingual, and too Chicana for Ramiro's idea of a wife for his firstborn son. He knew about her, but he had hoped it would be a passing fancy that Baldemar would outgrow and move on to dating a respectable, traditional Mexican girl from back home.

When Baldemar heard him call her *marrana* (sow), he knew it was going to be a tough conversation. "Don't call her that, Pa. I'm in love with her."

Ramiro set down his beer. "I suppose you have your mind made up. What do you want me to say? That I approve, that you have my blessings, that I'll throw you a big wedding?" he said, his face becoming increasingly red, his heart pounding in anger and disappointment. Worst of all, Ramiro felt the last semblance of control slipping away. He saw his entire world crashing before him as he recalled images of his second daughter getting off a bus with another character he could not approve of. And now this.

"You know, Baldemar, I wish I had never brought you all to this country. I should have let you all stay put in Naranjales, or valle Azul, or even Monterrey, but not put myself in this inferno you all are giving me," he said.

Baldemar tried to reply but he was silenced by a wave of the hand of his father's. "Let me finish."

"I have slaved in pits of hell for you and your brothers and sisters and look at the thanks I get. As soon as she could, Esmeralda rushed off to marry. Alicia is dating some Indian wetback, and now you telling me you are going to run off with some Chicana whose family can't even speak Spanish and her parents live in separate houses," he went on bitterly as Baldemar just hung his head and listened.

"Look at the others. Carlos, Sylvia, Antonio. They barely speak to me or your mother. All they do is talk English. They demand this and that as if they were gringo brats and I was made of money. They want to wear those ridiculous clothes and hippie hair. Well, I won't have it. They can mope and curse in their dirty English all they want. In this house they will abide by decency and respect. Next thing I know they'll be smoking cigarettes, or marijuana even." Ramiro looked a shrunken replica of his old self as he sunk into the chair the longer he spoke. Then he got up and began to pace the length of the porch.

"They're never satisfied with what I give them or how your mother kills herself to feed them everyday. Have they ever not had a roof over their head, have they ever been hungry, have they ever not had decent clothes to wear? Oh, no. Now they want to be the boss. They want to tell the parents what to do, not like the old ways," he said sarcastically, growing increasingly angry yet somehow limp and defeated.

Baldemar stepped aside and stood on the steps unsure of what to say. He had never seen his father so torn. All he could think of was getting away and joining his Mariana at the Poppa Burger on Main Street and then dancing at the Latin World Nite Club.

"Yes sir, I was so much better off when I was here alone, breaking my back and sweating in the goddam factories alone. My love is not enough to hold this family together. Everyone wants what they want, and runs off. Just look at your fancy pants all ready to run off for the night with your *pocha*. Well, go on. Get out of my face. Go on and do what you have to do." Ramiro's thoughts then shut off the boy. He walked down the porch steps and paced up the driveway, which ran along the length of the house to the garage in the back.

"I'll stay home tonight, Pa, if you want," said Baldemar, but Ramiro heard nothing. Baldemar turned toward the door to see Eliza behind the screen. He thought he saw her wiping a tear from her eye as she slipped out of sight. She apparently had been watching her husband's laments. Suddenly he needed to take refuge in Mariana's arms. He had to get away. He headed to his room to finish dressing.

CHAPTER 31: *Alicia's Wedding Sorrows*

The year following Esmeralda's wedding was a tectonic one for Ramiro and the family. Baldemar moved out of the house and went to live with the Chicana whom Ramiro found completely unacceptable simply because she could not speak Spanish and her parents were divorced. Then, a few months later, Alicia pleaded with Eliza to be an envoy to her father to allow her to date Pablo openly.

Alicia had managed to graduate from high school despite the lack of support from home and the pressures of having to work since the tenth grade. The family attended her graduation ceremony, but Alicia didn't feel her accomplishment was appreciated enough. She found it troublesome that her *quinceañera* had been a bigger event than the milestone of graduating from high school. She blamed it on her parents' country background not allowing them to see the importance of education for women, or even the value of education for obtaining jobs that did not involve physical exertion. Shortly after graduation, she was ready to escape the confines of her father's controlling household.

Eliza agreed to plead Alicia's case to Ramiro. He was not surprised to hear that Alicia, his favorite daughter, was ready to move on. The problem was that Pablo was not acceptable to Ramiro. Pablo was from the southern region of Mexico, and his dark complexion made Ramiro feel as if he was looking at an alien. He was also a "wetback." It was never clear to Alicia which of Pablo's supposed faults were the most objectionable to Ramiro, but none of it mattered to her. She was in love, and that was, simply, that.

When Ramiro saw the girl's persistence, he knew he had no choice other than consenting to the relationship, but he was determined to do whatever it took to break them up before they took it a step further into the realm of marriage, for that would be entering a place of no return.

Indeed, Alicia and Pablo did enter into such a land. After refusing to give her away, Ramiro eventually consented, but he let it be known that he would not be participating in any festivities related to a union that he adamantly opposed.

§

"Dear God, please don't let Papa be there. Please let him be in a good mood today," whispered Alicia as she sat on the bus heading home that Friday in October.

It was 7:30 in the evening, and Alicia was beginning to panic because her curfew was nightfall. As she sat on the eastbound bus to her Canal and Eastwood stop, she prayed silently that Ramiro would not be waiting for her as he sometimes did. She also prayed that her fellow passengers would not notice the tears that were welling up to rain from her round brown eyes, fully capable of producing a torrent, right there in public, "*What a spectacle that would be!*"

Her mind was engaged in a fierce battle with her heart, and her emotions swirled about like zombie children in a surreal black and white landscape, jumping on and off a runaway merry-go-round. One moment she was blissfully happy, the next darkly sad.

"*It's just not fair,*" she kept thinking.

She wanted to shout it out to the whole bus, to the whole barrio even, as if they could intervene in her behalf, "*It's just not fair. My God! Help me! Lord, Jesus!*"

But she preferred happy thoughts. Tomorrow she would be marrying Pablo. They would become Mr. and Mrs. Pablo Mar. Alicia

Ocañas, heretofore petite, lovely, doting child of "Don" Ramiro Ocañas, was about to exchange the sheltered world of favorite daughter, chaperoned and repressed, for the presumably still-sheltered but joyous love nest of a newlywed bride. She couldn't help but linger on the word, "sheltered."

"Sheltered? More like hermetically preserved," she muttered.

"Funny how perspective colors everything," she thought. To an objective observer she might have been merely sheltered. To her father and family, she was protected. To her friends and social contacts, she was repressed or abused. To herself, the kind of monitoring and adherence to rules that she succumbed to on a daily basis were a stifling, suffocating, muzzling prison. Marriage promised to change all that although the role model she apprenticed under could not reassure her of the freedom that she yearned for. For now, love would be enough, she thought.

Suddenly, she noticed the headlights of an on-coming car, and her heart raced. *"It's getting dark so quickly. Please, slow down, Mr. Night! My father will be furious if I get home after dark."* Ramiro had a strict rule that no daughter of his should ever be out in the world after dark. It was his way of protecting them from possible predators as well as ensuring their reputations were never tarnished. He associated unescorted women on night streets with dishonor, as if the woman was worldly or the men of the family neglectful of their duty to provide and protect.

Her brain was right in sync with the evening's perturbations that awaited her at home. Ramiro was already pacing the short length of his humble wood frame house, from the living room that doubled at night as a bedroom for the little ones to the would-be dining room that was then Alicia and Sylvia's improvised bedroom, albeit in completely public space. He paced robotically. He didn't speak a word, but the whole house hung on his every step. He looked into the fragrant kitchen where Eliza was almost done preparing the evening's dinner, barely containing her fear of the tumult that she expected was about to transpire.

"Where the hell is this girl? Where the hell is she?" He half-whispered, half-mumbled, red invading his face and enhancing the existing red put there by the flame of welders' torches with which he had worked all day. He was addressing no one in particular, but it was as if he were speaking to Eliza, for Eliza was always his default sounding board.

Eliza could only muster timidly, "You know those buses."

"I know the god-forsaken buses all right! They run on a schedule. She gets off work at five o'clock. She should have been here no later than seven. Seven, even if she missed two buses!" He was livid. Despite his best efforts to outgrow his possessiveness and pride he could not contain his emotions that evening that in his mind was the last time he would see his daughter. "She still lives under my roof. This is disrespectful. I will not have her disrespect my authority and this house this way! Walking the streets after dark! Engaged or not!"

He repeated the cursed word: "Engaged!! HMMMM!"

Ramiro continued spouting at Eliza and to the house in general, although the younger kids—Carlos, Antonio, Sylvia, and Oscar—were witnessing a scene they dreaded. "To be married! Ha! To that goddam Indian wetback. What have we come to, Eliza, what did we do wrong? You talk to 'em, and tell them. Give'em advice, and you love 'em. You try to protect them from scum like that. This is how they repay you. Marrying a wetback Indian! Marrying against your wishes, betraying their father."

Ramiro's darkest instincts were now in full display. It was a side of him that contrasted with the normally compassionate and accepting man that Alicia had always loved. But when it came to his daughter, he felt justified in making any judgment necessary that might put some sense into her head.

Eliza was trying her best to be a calming voice, carefully trying to avoid any words that might make it worse. "Ramiro, don't agitate yourself. The kids can hear you. Dinner is ready, why don't you come and eat? I'll call the kids," she said. Deep down she knew that what was truly troubling him was the fact that he was losing a daughter. His pride and stubbornness would prevent him from attending his little girl's wedding, and it was killing him.

"Do you think I can swallow a bite with all this? If it weren't for my work schedule, I wouldn't force down food . . . And those god-forsaken kids of yours had better not make a peep after 8:30 tonight or they will see what they get. I have to be up at five, and . . ."

§

Alicia pulled the stop request chord just past the Milby Street intersection. She tottered down the narrow aisle with her packages. She stepped off the bus, almost tripping over the last step when the big white box she was carrying caught the handrail by the bus door. That bulky white box was the most precious cargo she had ever held in her arms. It contained her wedding gown, made of velvet and silk. That beautiful dress would be making her a radiant princess-bride tomorrow. The joy of such thoughts wrestled with her fears. It was that last minute touch-up of sewing onto the dress hundreds of faux pearls that was to blame for her present predicament. When she stopped by her friend's sewing shop to pick up the dress, Perla had not finished attaching all the ornaments. Alicia was compelled to give her a hand and finish the job, but that delay caused her to miss two buses.

"*But, oh, how beautiful it looks,*" she was thinking just before she lost her footing.

The images in her brain registered hundreds in seconds. She was imagining herself an Audrey Hepburn bride. All her friends compared her to one movie star or another. Maybe she was more of an Angelica Maria of the hip, Mexican go-go movies. Her little brothers even let it escape that they thought she could be a Miss America. "*What a compliment. And what a laugh! What do they know, my little brothers?*"

Alicia's brothers and baby sister were almost as sheltered as she because Ramiro had developed a paranoia about their safety. He kept them on a very short leash, and prohibited all manner of social frivolity or permissiveness. They in turn tried to avoid being in his presence, if they could help it, so as not to be sent on an errand of some sort or listen to him complain about the length of their hair or their tight-fitting jeans.

Being middle children, Carlos and Sylvia were often the recipients of most of the critiques. Whenever Carlos or Sylvia happened upon Ramiro around the yard or the house, it seemed to never fail that the father would call to the kid and point to some minor thing like a candy wrapper on the floor or a cup of coffee on the table and ask, "What is this? Didn't you see this? Pick that up and take care of it." There were always more chores to perform, or they might be told to stand up straight, or speak properly, and so on.

Alicia smiled at the thoughts of her beloved siblings, all so supportive and yet, "All chaperones and spies, really; the very long arm of an over-protective authoritarian father," she said to herself.

"Oh," she said as she felt the box bump against the rail.

A middle-aged, stout woman with a round, friendly face, wearing a satin white and flowered headscarf tied under the chin caught Alicia's package and reached out for one of her arms to prevent her fall. Alicia looked into her smiling eyes for an instant and felt enveloped by a feeling of love and protection that she imagined her new mother-in-law, her *suegra*, would have for her. Her new life with her husband's family would probably be a loving one. How, she wondered, could her father not see that these people were good, "Pablo is educated. He has better education and manners than Papa even," she thought.

Indeed, Pablo was an intelligent young man, and had finished secondary school in his hometown of Casillas, Mexico. His family were successful ranchers who hoped Pablo would one day earn a university degree in animal husbandry.

"*And he's so handsome in those long, lush sideburns, like Tom Jones, framing his deep, sleepy brown eyes and tawny, light-cinnamon skin,*" Alicia's thoughts continued.

She had discovered that his five o'clock shadow made her feel "sexy" as did his deep, yet mildly effeminate voice. It could all have been so perfect if only Don Ramiro did not object so vehemently. She couldn't understand why Mexican fathers had to be so protective and possessive.

"*What's wrong with having Indian blood, anyway? We all have it to some degree. Mama is certainly part Indian. Papa even brags sometimes about Mama's grandfather for his longevity. Great grandfather Eugenio lived to the age of a hundred five, supposedly because of his Indian genes,*" her mind went on rambling.

But the first thing Ramiro asked Alicia when he first spotted Pablo escorting her home the three blocks from the bus stop was, "*Quien es ese Indio?*" She knew right then and there it would not be a carefree romance. "Who's that Indian" was the Mexican equivalent of using the "N" word in America, and she had assimilated enough to condemn such nonsense.

Alicia had been surprised and amused when Ramiro had "encouraged" her to go out with Daniel Blanco in an attempt to break up the young couple. Daniel was the eldest son of Ramiro's friend, Miguel, an old buddy from his hometown of Naranjales. The Don's approval of Daniel was revealed to her by her father's not-so-subtle description of the young man as a "*buen muchacho,*" or good young man. Daniel was a handsome young man of twenty-six, some seven years her senior, but the one time she went out with him to a movie she had been underwhelmed by his conversation. All he seemed interested in was bragging about his guitar playing. There simply was no chemistry between them. Ramiro admired that Daniel was "steadily employed and the son of a good, decent family." Alicia was not impressed by Daniel's eligible bachelor status or his guitar-playing fame.

Don Ramiro explained his racial contradictions thus: "Yes, the Blancos have some Indian in them, but just barely, and it only shows in the handsome bronze tone of their skin, never in their manners. They are a hard-working, law-abiding lot."

§

"Oh, Thank you. I'm so sorry. Thank you. So clumsy of me," Alicia said to the woman who prevented her spill. She imagined the lady was her mother-in-law whom Alicia hadn't met but who was arriving that very evening on a trip made especially for the wedding.

"No, no trouble. Be careful, sweetie. It's dark out there. Don't trip on any crooked sidewalks getting home," the woman said.

After composing herself, Alicia suddenly felt a deep anger at her father for a fleeting moment. This surprised her, but it made her feel strong and indignant. *"How dare he hold this power over me, even on the eve of my wedding? Hasn't he tortured me enough? Two years of interfering in my courtship! I will not be afraid. Even he has to understand that a wedding takes a lot of preparation. And, after all, he did consent to my getting married. Isn't it enough that he refuses to attend my wedding? Baldemar is giving me away. A mere older brother?"* Her thoughts gave rein to her emotions, and that gave her resolve to confront whatever might be waiting at home.

Thus, Alicia knew she could face Ramiro and assert herself despite his possible fury. *"Such a proud, stubborn man, this Don Ramiro, my father."*

§

Ramiro had consented to the wedding only after becoming convinced that if he did not give her hand to Pablo, they would elope. He could not bear to think the family name besmirched by the gossip that would be provoked by an Ocañas daughter run away with a "wetback playboy." To him that was tantamount to the shame of having a daughter in prostitution.

Ramiro had managed to settle down enough to sit at the kitchen table with a beer, then another. That was unusual, as he never drank more than one beer before going to bed. The splendor of the cool October evening only intensified his sorrow. His mind raced, *"Can't she see that I love her terribly? That I only want what's best for her?"* A panorama of memories invaded his troubled mind. He saw her being born, his new angel; in her first school uniform, beauty and brains; reciting a poem at school; in the jump-rope competition; learning to make tortillas by Eliza's side; running to him after work with hugs and kisses; dancing at her *quinceañera* in her rose silk dress. How proud he had been of her sassiness before she turned against him. *"Maybe it's this strange country that makes it so hard to protect one's children."*

How he would have given his life for her, to make her happy, protect her from the wretched world of loose American morals, or lackluster, lascivious Indians, or low-life Chicanos, or *pachucos*. How was a father to know a good man for a husband for his daughter except through family connections?

"She should have died at birth," he thought out loud, and his wife shuddered. Eliza gazed at him and hesitated to put her hand on his shoulder, "Ramiro," she said tenderly. She dreaded the next day attending the wedding without him. She wondered whether she should stay home, fearing that he might turn against her and call her a traitor, too. *"No, I can't do that to my daughter. I have no choice. I will go to the wedding. There is no pleasing this man on this matter no matter what."* She drew from her grandfather's legendary stoicism somehow and held her poise so as not to break down in tears.

Alicia's younger siblings all absorbed the tension of that evening. Their kindred souls all ached even as they sided with Alicia. Their thoughts were Anglicized, democratic thoughts, and they labeled Ramiro "cruel." Yet no one dared challenge the patriarch's authority in his house, now in darkness, except for the bright kitchen where the food was served. All other lights remained off to keep the electric bill low. The children lamented silently that there would be no boyish playfulness tonight, again.

§

"There she is!" The whole house jolted when Tony shouted the words upon first spying Alicia walking up the sidewalk. It was 7:45 p.m. They all turned and saw their sister through a parting in the white plastic curtains of the living room. The curtains were never completely drawn because the attic fan needed to circulate air although it wasn't turned on during cooler weather. Still, Eliza was big on plain, old-fashioned ventilation no matter the temperatures. Tony shouted before he could catch himself, for he knew Ramiro wasn't keen on outbursts, "There she is!" He repeated as if by shouting it he was releasing so much built-up tension.

Eliza quietly pinched his arm, as was her habit when signaling a kid to be quiet. The other three refrained from finding humor in the act, as they would normally have done. Then everyone hushed up and continued eating their *picadillo* listlessly. Eliza resumed her graceful ballet of delivering fresh tortillas from the hot griddle to the cloth-lined basket at the center of the red Formica table. Ramiro stopped his solemn pacing in the adjacent dark rooms. He stood like a sentinel by the archway between the living room and Alicia's room.

"THERE SHE IS!" It seemed to echo endlessly though it was just a minute before Alicia entered the house.

Everyone looked at Ramiro and their stomachs contracted at the sight of the pained, red countenance they beheld in the shadows. His legendary pride of legendary Spain, now alive only through blood, gave rise to his Ocañas family temper that could only be soothed via a violent outburst.

Having convinced herself of her righteousness, a smiling Alicia swallowed hard and climbed up the five concrete steps at the front porch where she, again, let one package slip then fumbled to collect it and reposition her load before entering the house. It was a cool evening, sixty-five degrees. She felt the chilly breeze, but the dark house sent a new, deeper chill down to her very bones. Her mind whirled attempting to grab onto one of a thousand rushing excuses to offer her father for her lateness. In her confusion, she rushed into her room feigning happy greetings to the family seated in the lighted kitchen.

"Hello, everyone. I'm home!" she said.

As she reached for the light switch, Ramiro beat her to it, and he turned on the light. She suddenly felt a powerful, cold grip on her wrist. Before she could adjust her eyes to the sudden brightness, she felt a hot, stinging slap to her face. Everyone heard the clap of Ramiro's hand against her cheek.

"Aaaaarggh. Father, why…," she tried to speak but held her hand to her stinging nose where she felt a sticky moisture.

The girl's pained shriek paralyzed the others, and Eliza grimaced as if her own cheek had been struck.

The boys and Sylvia were riveted by the sight of their sister's blood, the bright red spots staining the white box at Alicia's feet. Her delicate wedding gown spilled onto the wooden floor. Even amidst her horror, Eliza couldn't help but notice how beautiful the pearl decorations shone against the white velvet of the dress. They had all rushed into Alicia's room as Ramiro walked out the front door. Alicia ran into the bathroom in tears, with Eliza and Sylvia on her heels.

Outside, Ramiro stood shaken, his silhouette by the brick column of the front porch made visible by the streetlight. Then he stooped, a shrunken shadow of himself onto a folding chair. He was grateful for the darkness and the cold breeze of the October evening. They helped him escape the glare of god knows who or what. He could hide his shame. He had struck his beloved child, and his heart told him it was wrong. Eliza watched him from inside the screen door. She despised her husband for a moment even as she wanted to hold him in her arms and take away his pain and his shame. She thought about tomorrow. She imagined Sunday, and the days after that. She suddenly felt old. She was tired.

CHAPTER 32: *Barrio Blues*

The days and weeks following Alicia's wedding were a difficult transition for everyone in the family. It spread a gloom over the holidays. Carlos was the oldest child now, at sixteen, and Sylvia was fourteen. Antonio was twelve, and Oscar, nine. The four remaining kids went about their daily school routines attempting normality despite their increasingly balkanized lives. They performed their household chores as if in a trance, without much interaction with their father. Ramiro and Eliza seemed almost like strangers to them, especially because Ramiro's usually ebullient manner and argumentative style of TV watching—because even without understanding the language he would spot any semblance of illogic, point to the tube, and tell the kids why such and such could not have happened, or it should have been done in thus and so a manner, thereby annoying them by interrupting their concentration and derailing their enjoyment—all that animation of their father's had disappeared.

At school, it wasn't much better, as their immigrant-child self-consciousness prevented their fully participating in extracurricular activities or sports. The kids carried a sense of shame because their parents never attended school meetings but instead pressured them to hold part-time jobs as soon as they were able. Carlos had been applying for sacker jobs at the Rice Food Market and other stores since he was fifteen, but no manager wanted to take a chance on someone who came across so unassertive and with the face of a twelve year old. Sylvia was simply too young still.

Carlos and his three siblings rolled with the punches because they were accustomed to their meager rations of resources or competing with each other as if it were "every man for himself" for that last piece of fruit in the house, or that Rice Food Market cinnamon roll they loved so much. Groceries were purchased every Friday, and by Monday most of the fun stuff, like cookies, was gone. The kids simply saw the staidness of the house as a new dimension of inattention to their needs as individuals. Their escape was to take refuge in their respective American pop culture pursuits when not attending to their school anxieties.

To say that Carlos and Sylvia suffered inordinately from teen angst in those days would be a misstatement, given that they appeared to the world every bit the happy-go-lucky, All-American kids. It was in their own heads that they were somehow second-class citizens in the public school universe in which they were too often sidelined.

Their father now focused all his attention on their getting jobs as soon as possible, having lost the three elder siblings' financial contributions. Eliza instinctively complied with Ramiro's expectations even before he uttered a word about how tight the money was becoming. She simply adjusted her food expenditures and rationed the meals a little more, with smaller portions of rice or beans, or one piece of chicken instead of two.

Ramiro lived in his own parental angst, trying not to overburden his American kids because they were so different from their older, more Mexican siblings, but his comfortable budget and cash flow had dried up. The kids' seeming happy-go-lucky routines and manners made him resent them all the more, and he, too, withdrew from interacting with them as much. Eliza never gave him much pampering, but it helped him to talk to her rather than to a mirror. He also rarely kept his strong opinions to himself. Every other evening Ramiro made love to his wife, for he was a creature of habit, and it greatly relieved his stress. Afterwards he would eat his dinner and, just before falling asleep, he would ramble on to Eliza about whatever was on his mind that day.

§

That Christmas, just a few weeks after losing Alicia, the kids felt a palpable poverty, almost as if they were back in Port Houston as new immigrants. But none of the family was prepared for the announcement Ramiro made just after the New Year's holiday. "Listen up, everyone," he started, at the dinner table that night. "You all know that money is very tight. I have been thinking about how we can avoid bankruptcy," he continued while everyone stared in silence, waiting for what was to come next. "Well, There is only one place that you, Carlos, and you, Sylvia, and maybe even you, Antonio, can all work." The kids looked at each other, then they looked at their mother. Eliza herself was caught unaware of the topic of this conversation.

Ramiro continued, "I have decided that we will move to California. It won't be for good. Just until we, all of us, working together in the fields, we can build a cash cushion." He had a look of concern that they might fight him on his decision. The kids could not quite assimilate the implications of the idea. On the surface, it sounded like an adventure, like a great road trip where they would see so many exciting new places. They didn't react, they didn't complain, they nodded as they knew they were expected to do, and then each kid retreated into his or her own thoughts to try to make sense of the news.

Carlos, being the oldest, felt the greatest pressure to help out the family, so he simply couldn't object. As he lay in his lumpy twin bed that night, the news began to weigh on him as one more thing that made his holidays miserable. Triggered by his misery, his mind wandered through the past Christmas seasons that had been so disappointing.

The kids had never questioned why they never had birthday parties or Halloween costumes or Christmas trees with shiny wrapped gifts under them. They had long ago accepted that their parents had few resources for such expenses, and they tried not to overburden them with requests for such trivial indulgences. Through the years, their typical Christmas gifts had consisted of a shopping trip to the grocery store's toy section, where they were allowed to pick out one reasonably priced toy. Or, the older kids were allowed to choose one outfit off the rack at a department store like Sears, Weiner's, or Globe. Sure there had been bright and beautiful moments as well, and Carlos recalled a Christmas of a couple of years back.

On a bright, crisp Christmas morning all the neighborhood kids were out celebrating the season by sharing, or showing off, with their peers what Santa Claus had brought them. The Ocañas kids were no exception, only they didn't feel as lucky as their neighbors and friends. The Huertas, who lived next door and spoke no Spanish because they were fifth generation, or something, American, celebrated Christmas just as any middle-class American family did. They had a big, fancy tree in their living room, flashing with sparkly lights, beside their twenty-five-inch color television set. The family consisted of six kids ranging in age pretty much the same as the Ocañas.

The Huerta kids received bikes, electric robots, racing car sets with elaborate tracks and remote controls, Easy Bake ovens, great big dolls and Barbie dolls with extra outfits, roller skates, board games, clothes, and more. Not so the Ocañas kids. The household did celebrate, however, with homemade treats like tamales, buñuelos, and hot chocolate. The other Mexican families in the neighborhood were not big spenders like the Huertas, but their kids also managed to receive a few nice gifts, albeit more practical. Most of them put up a pretty tree with lights that everyone could sit and look at. Many even decorated the exterior of their homes with lights outlining the roofs and gables of each house, but the Huertas led the way. None of those differences went unperceived by the Ocañas children. But they knew somehow that their deprivation was temporary because one day they were going to grow up and their Christmases would be just like the Huertas'.

That year, Carlos received a new set of clothes. That was exciting enough for him. He got up that morning, and after rushing through breakfast, he put on his new outfit and walked outside for a strut around the neighborhood, feeling like the cock of the walk. Whether anyone noticed how cool and handsome he looked, he did not know. He simply felt great in his cool clothes although his father complained they were too loud, with the bell-bottom pants too low on the hip and too tight. The shirt was blue corduroy with vest-like features and watermelon-red sleeves that Ramiro thought too puffy, but Carlos thought made him look like the pop singer Bobby Sherman.

Sylvia opted for a bottle of Heaven Scent perfume, and she, too, wanted to stroll along with Carlos in the hopes that everyone might notice how wonderful she smelled. Antonio and Oscar each picked out a set of pistols and a bow and arrow at Globe Department Store so they could play cowboys and Indians. They ran all over the yard chasing each other, pretending elaborate war schemes in the old Wild West.

§

A couple of years back, the kids thought they had hit the jackpot when they received bags of toys from an organization called The Goodfellows. It was a charity run by the local newspaper, and it donated to needy children who wrote to them as if to Santa Claus, pleading their case for a nice toy. A neighbor down the street had suggested to Sylvia that she write the letter on her mother's behalf asking for toys, "And be sure and tell them how many there are and how old each one of them is."

§

In the boys' room, the door opened. It was Eliza. "Almost time to put lights out. Remember tomorrow is a school day. Get to sleep and don't be making any noises or your father will be in here with the belt."

The Christmas month had been emotionally grueling for everyone because of Ramiro's depression over losing Alicia. The Christmas presents and time off school had made all the kids feel better, but they remained keenly aware of their father's uneasiness and their mother's constantly furrowed brow. Of course, money was at the heart of their troubles, but something much deeper and indefinable was brewing, tearing the family apart.

§

Carlos and Sylvia had friends getting jobs in grocery stores and local restaurants and shops and even in factories, but they never seemed able to project the maturity or can-do spirit to get a job themselves. Carlos blamed it all on Ramiro for sheltering them so much that he had stifled their self-assurance, but Sylvia blamed their mother for not asserting herself to build up the kids instead of passively letting things be. Ramiro would not have disagreed, although he would have argued that the kids simply were not taking advantage of their privileges, like English-speaking abilities. Ramiro never could understand how someone with good command of the English language could not talk his way into a job. Whenever the kids complained about not being able to find their way, Ramiro's response was, "You speak English, don't you?"

What Ramiro failed to understand was that the kids were viewing the world as American teenagers who depended on parental guidance and encouragement when pursuing a project or a goal. Instead, Ramiro and Eliza thought of the kids' development as a kind of survival of the fittest, naturally falling into their niche in the world. It was a philosophy that required that kids be pushed out into the society to get a job even without skills, on the assumption that their instincts would kick in and the kid would figure out how to get it done, sink or swim.

Meanwhile, the parents prayed and agonized. Eliza and Ramiro encouraged them by dangling privileges reserved for the income-producing ones, such as pampering with dinner and lunch preparation, exempting them from house chores, assisting with bus fare or car rides, and, of course, celebrating their contribution with a little bit of bragging to their friends and neighbors. That had been the example of the eldest three children. Carlos and Sylvia seemed to be late bloomers.

CHAPTER 33: *California Redux*

The following day, Ramiro's words echoed in the kids' heads. "We are going to need to move to California. The pruning season starts in March. I have contacts out there. We can all work, the three of us. I don't see any other way out of this situation. I want everyone to be thinking about this and get ready. We should be on the road to Orange Cove by the first week of March." It was an announcement. There was not a "Do you have any questions?" part to it. There was not a session for discussion. There was not a "What do you think?" In the days following, Ramiro seemed transformed by his decision. Suddenly his speech had musicality and promise. His body language became lithe. His eyes sparkled. He was onto a solution, and it made him feel strong again.

But it began to dawn on Carlos that there might be dire consequences to leaving school in the middle of the year, "Oh, my God. It's all over. My world is over. I am going to be a dropout. I have to check myself out of school and go work like the migrants that have no education or desire to study books or have professional careers." He was devastated. Similar thoughts began to cross Sylvia's mind. The little ones didn't take it quite as hard because it sounded like a great adventure to them, but they knew something big was happening. "I'm going to be a dropout. I'm going to be a dropout. I'm going to be a dropout" was all Carlos could think.

Ramiro was always one to worry about the future, and the last thing he wanted was to be old, destitute, and abandoned by his children. He had done everything in his power to garner loyalty and commitment from the children, but the change in cultures and the changes in the kids as they matured terrified him, and he became convinced that they would indeed abandon him in his old age. He had begun to feel the weight of time on his body. Now middle aged, he missed occasional days of work because of undetermined illnesses.

His plan regarding California was not so much about getting past an emergency or avoiding bankruptcy. He knew, without admitting it even to himself that this trip was about trying to secure his nest egg for his eventual retirement. In his usual astute calculations, he figured the children would find their own way when they got older, but he could not be so sure about his and Eliza's old age. He also made all sorts of mathematical calculations and determined just how much the family would be able to earn and save during the next eight months of three full-time workers. He knew Carlos and Sylvia were not tough, strong teens, but he expected they would do well enough in the orchards with his guidance.

After that New Year's night pronouncement, Ramiro hardly spoke to anyone other than Eliza, but his demeanor was that of a man on a mission. Everyone avoided direct contact with him and went about their usual routines without much hope of amicability. Ramiro still barked his orders to the kids, but these were the four Americanized ones, so they tended not to listen. Carlos had developed a rebelliousness, always asking "why" when he considered Ramiro's orders to abide by traditional propriety unfair or nonsensical. That infuriated Ramiro, and he would reply, "Because I say so! That's why." On at least one occasion Ramiro lost control, and slapped Carlos across the face in reply to the boy's "why?" Of course, the physical reactions were expected, as Ramiro had always been a disciplinarian. That was the way he had been raised. Every child of his had experienced a belt whipping or a slap on the face, especially before puberty. But such dynamics have consequences, and the rift between the authoritarian father and his children gradually led to tattered bonds between them. The alienation from his kids hurt Ramiro because, despite everything, they were his pride and joy and he wished for nothing more than to raise persons of good character.

With Alicia's financial contributions gone, Ramiro became the sole provider for the first time since the family's arrival in Houston. In California, Carlos and Sylvia would be able to work full time for the entire season of six to eight months. The kids were now sixteen, fourteen, twelve, and nine, but in the fields, the two older ones would be allowed to work without any hassles. Even the little ones could work on weekends if necessary. The children, for their part, knew that they could not defy their father's orders. When the end of February came around, they went about the business of withdrawing themselves from classes and prepared their foggy minds for whatever might come in the California farms.

Carlos was feeling that the world had crashed in on him. His mind created images of himself as one of the many migrant workers or uneducated laborers that abounded in his family's circle of friends and relatives. They were disdained by the society, he thought, and they lived in parallel universes like his father. To Carlos they became shadows of themselves, and he suffered imagining that he might be condemned to live the rest of his life on the sidelines of the American mainstream. He felt as if no one understood him or was willing to protect him from the tentacles of the subculture his parents embraced even as they preached about leaving it.

When the end of February rolled around, the family had sold their Oldsmobile and bought a shiny new red 1969 Ford F-150. Ramiro took the family to Valle Azul for a farewell visit to the relatives and for their blessings on his new venture. He teamed up with his brother Abel and his family of five. Abel was a younger brother, who had been the black sheep of the family in his youth. The two brothers were never as close as Ramiro had been with Jacobo or Alberto, but blood was always thicker than water in this family, and the two portrayed a picture of loving, caring siblings.

In Valle Azul, Ramiro felt like a big man again, making arrangements, ordering supplies, hiring contractors, and making deals while telling everyone of his daring new plan.

He commissioned the town's carpenter to install custom benching around the bed of the truck to accommodate the women and children on their long drive to Orange Cove, California. He insisted that the carpentry be painted the same candy-apple red as the truck. He had already installed a camper top with ventilated windows and cabinetry before leaving Houston. It dawned on the kids to wonder, "If the family was so broke, where did dad find all the money to buy a new truck and all the customizing he put into it?"

When they confronted Eliza with the questions, she quickly shut them down, and told them Ramiro had used up the last of his savings from the sale of the Naranjales house, which he had kept in a Mexican bank. "And stop asking such questions about your father. He knows what he's doing." They didn't believe her but let it go, knowing it was no use to hassle her with such things. Finally, the vehicle was all set up and ready to go the three-day drive in style and comfort.

To Carlos' horror, he was designated the road map guy, and he would be riding up front in the cab between the two older men. He would not be enjoying the company of his cousins and siblings in the back, which would have made the road trip much more bearable.

They arrived in Orange Cove on March 5, 1968, and it was deja vous for Ramiro as he recalled his first foray into that lifestyle seventeen years prior. Abel's wife, Beatriz, happened to be the sister of Cousin Salomon's wife, so it was only natural that the two families arrive there. Salomon and Elva hosted them until they found a little house of their own. The arrangement was only for a week, but it seemed an eternity to Eliza, who had always hated imposing on "strangers." The family moved into a small stucco house about a half-mile from Salomon. Abel and his family found a nice little apartment much closer to Elva, and the sisters were happy to be in such close proximity.

The work began almost immediately. Carlos and Sylvia each experienced versions of what their father had experienced seventeen years before. Ramiro recalled his days as a single boarder finding his way around. He remembered how much he had missed his young wife and small children back home. He found himself wiping tears from his eyes as he relived the hopefulness of his youth, and compared it to the desperation of his present condition.

"Carlos, Carlos, wake up. You have to go to work. Get up," Eliza spoke as she nudged the boy on the shoulder where he lay on a mattress on the floor of their new California house, cozy under a warm blanket to offset the air conditioner blowing in the window. Carlos, feeling his mother's gentle tough and gruff voice pulled himself away from slumber and a dream about making all A's in school that semester. He could smell the aroma of fresh tortillas, coffee, and pancakes coming from the kitchen where Eliza had been preparing breakfast and lunches for the past hour. "It's five o'clock, Carlos, you have to get up. She repeated the process with Sylvia until both siblings were fully awake and stirring.

The kids found the work demanding and exhausting, but they began to enjoy all of the aspects of it that Ramiro had once enjoyed: the outdoors, the fresh air, the fresh, delicious fruit in endless supply. The family went shopping for groceries, all together, every Saturday, and they stopped to enjoy ice cream treats along the way. The two kids, who now earned pay checks had a nice allowance for the first time in their lives, and they saved up to buy trendy clothes like burgundy corduroy Levi's pants with flared bottoms. Their employed status also meant that they had no chores around the house and that every night Eliza treated them just as much like royalty as she did Ramiro himself.

The time together made them stronger as a family, as they shared every meal of the day, but communication never got intimate. The new diet was almost three times their normal consumption, but hearty, large meals were necessary to get through the long, hard days, especially when the summer sun became intense. The change of lifestyle and diet turned the scrawny kids into healthy, toned specimens. Carlos suddenly became robust and manly in his father's eyes, and Sylvia blossomed beyond recognition though her natural state was of a delicate beauty. Soon, they began to date other migrant worker children, giving them the challenge of communicating with peers in a Spanish they had largely abandoned. They attended carnivals, picnics, and movies.

"I saw how Pepe was looking at you, and you looked back. Is something going on?" Carlos teased Sylvia about one of the boys who picked peaches along side them.

"That's for me to know and for you to find out," said Sylvia, sticking her tongue out at her brother. "What about Gloria Sandoval? What was it she brought you at break? A pack of Twinkies? She laughed and rubbed her pointer fingers in expression of "shame, shame."

"She sure did," he winked. I asked her to the movies this Sunday. Wanna come with us? You can ask Pepe, too," Carlos said. I hope they don't criticize my Spanish. I'm so rusty," he laughed. Sylvia nodded vigorously in agreement and laughed.

But even as they adapted to the Spanish-speaking world of migrant life, attending carnivals, picnics, and movies with their new friends, Carlos and Sylvia listened to Casey Kasum's *American Top 40* countdown and they read song lyrics in teen magazines, so they could sing along with the radio. That connection to American mainstream and the teen peers they had left behind somehow kept them grounded and in the mainstream of pop culture while straddling the chasm of their new social group.

§

When the California summer ended in late October, Ramiro declared that they would be returning to their Houston house, which had been left in the care of Baldemar, as a tenant. By November, the entire California stint was over. Ramiro's crisis had been resolved without his sharing any of the details with the kids. All the kids needed to know was that they would not be returning to the fields, they could return to school and pick up where they had left off.

Carlos set foot on the high school grounds again, and he almost burst into tears. He couldn't explain it. He proceeded to the principal's office where the attendance clerk told him what paperwork to fill out to get reinstated. Then he was told to go around to the teachers for late admittance into their class. He was feeling upbeat and looking forward to catching up on his schoolwork even though he had lost half a year and was enrolling two months into the new semester.

None of it mattered to him or Sylvia except that they were resuming a normal state of teenage life. But then he entered the cafeteria on the third floor of the building to get signed in by the social studies teacher who was doing "study hall" there that period. The woman looked up from her desk past the top of her powder-blue, plastic, horn-rimmed glasses with an annoyed look on her tired hazel eyes under green shadow. She was about sixty, and she wore her reddish gray hair in a disheveled bun. She looked him over. She took his paperwork and looked at it a long time. Then she pursed her thin red lips and without concealing her disdain grumbled, "I don't know why you're even bothering to check into school. It's two months late, you know. Do you know that?"

Suddenly, Carlos' face flushed a bright red. He wondered for a moment if he should just go home. Her words felt like daggers of rejection. Somehow he had expected that everyone would be happy to see him returning to school, for not becoming a statistic.

§

On December 1970, Carlos earned his high school diploma. He was nineteen. It was a milestone, and he was only the second of Ramiro's kids to get that far academically. He had a sweetheart pressuring him to get married, but he told her he wasn't anywhere close to that kind of maturity. The girl moved on, breaking his heart, but after a few months he knew it had been for the best. As he received his diploma, Carlos wondered whether he had what it takes to go to college, maybe become a teacher and help kids like himself, or an architect, or a lawyer. He wondered how in the world he could possibly afford college even if he wanted to study. He couldn't even imagine where to start, how to fill out a college application.

He decided to put such foolish ideas out of his head. After all, he couldn't possibly be ready for the rigors and challenges of a university education. Could he? Not an immigrant kid from a barrio school. Not him.

CHAPTER 34: *Eulogy*

C arlos did make it into college after a couple of years of confusion and dead-end jobs in fast food. In 1977 he earned his bachelor's degree, and by 1985, he had earned a Doctor of Jurisprudence degree, or JD.

Five years later, Ramiro died at the age of sixty-eight.

Carlos gave the eulogy at his funeral speaking directly to him. He wanted Ramiro to know how much his life had meant to him and his brothers and sisters. He wanted him to know they all loved him and that their lives felt incomplete without him.

"You did not live your life in vain, Dad. ...Papa. I miss you, Papa."

You did not live in vain. That's what Carlos told him.

"We had our differences and our struggles, to be sure, but if I had it to do over again, I wouldn't change much," said Ramiro. "I guess everyone says that kind of stuff after someone dies. There is something about our human condition that makes us cling to our individual essence—of bloodlines, traditions, and experiences, despite their lesser or greater value to an outsider looking in. That is why it is possible to be just as happy living and dying poor as rich. Blood bonds. We are loyal to our ancestry and to our immediate blood ties in mysterious ways that we would rather not think about. I mean it, though. In the big scheme of things, I am generally glad that I was raised by this man," Carlos spoke to the mourners gathered at the funeral home. "Some people tell me I inherited his character. I smile proudly, hoping they

only mean it in a good way. For his good qualities were good indeed,"
he continued.

§

Eliza listened to her son's words intently even as she pondered her
own thoughts about her husband. Ramiro's death was as much a release
of Eliza as a person as it was a loss to her, sad as that might sound. Eliza
Cervantes de Ocañas was finally set free when her husband's soul was
freed. Eliza, was reborn on September 15, 1990, for without Ramiro,
it was the first time in her life that she was no one's "possession." Her
life became her own, despite her fear of it, and her pain. At sixty-five
years of age, Eliza was finally truly free, but she knew nothing of that
concept. She spent her time at the funeral wailing and moaning her
pain as vividly as in any setting in Naranjales, choosing to focus on her
loss. Ramiro would have been pleased with his wife's public mourning
of him.

§

It had all happened so suddenly. Carlos was out on the campaign trail,
as he had become involved in city politics and launched a race for city council. He was holding a public forum with a group of community leaders. It
was the week after Labor Day, when campaign season really takes off. He was
almost done with his speech. Carlos noticed Robert, his aide, taking a call.
He saw his face turn solemn, fixing his eyes on Carlos. It made him wonder if
the other side was up to something. Did somebody steal his yard signs? Stuff
like that. Robert was in the back of the room as Carlos faced out into the
audience from the podium. Robert began to make his way up to the front
until he stood just a few feet from Carlos. As soon as Carlos finished his talk,
Robert approached him and grabbed him by the arm before the crowd had a
chance to approach for the usual political schmoozing and such.

"What's the matter?" Carlos said.

"Carlos, we have to leave right away. There's a problem. It's your
father," he said.

"What's happened? An accident?" Carlos interrupted.

"No, not an accident. He's in the hospital. St Luke's."

Carlos knew immediately what that meant. "He's had a heart attack?" he asked, taking hold of Robert's elbow and pivoting towards the car. Robert had already given Violeta, the assistant, instructions to excuse Carlos with the crowd, and they could hear her voice on the microphone explaining to the people.

On the way to the hospital Carlos called several of his siblings to tell them the news and asked them to pass it on so everyone would know. He arrived at the hospital. Eliza was already there along with Sylvia and Esmeralda. It's always the women who come through first when you get sick. He rushed to them. "Why are you out here and not in the room? What room is he in? Don't tell me he hasn't been admitted," He demanded to know.

"Calm down. It's okay. He's in surgery now," said Esmeralda after the obligatory silent greeting of a hug and a peck on the cheek.

Indeed, he was being prepared for the possible placement of a stent. An hour later, the doctor returned to tell the family about his condition. It was getting close to midnight. "We could not place the stents. His arteries are blocked far worse than we thought. I recommend the family have a conference and consider whether to give consent for open-heart surgery. He needs a quadruple bypass. We have stabilized him for now, but we need to act fast, within a day or so," the doctor said.

The family made the decision to operate on the three arteries that were blocked. Before the surgery, complications developed with his blood pressure and blood sugar. He would need to be stabilized before he could withstand the surgery and anesthesia. It could take a day or several. The doctors could not be sure. It depended on how his body responded to the treatment.

Ramiro looked like the luckiest patient on that floor. He had a throng of family visiting at all hours: sons, daughters, grandchildren, sister, cousins, friends. His room was a revolving door of concerned loved ones showing affection and bringing flowers, cards, and lots of prayers and encouragement. Ramiro loved the attention. All the nurses loved him, too, with his quips and flirtatious banter.

On the third day of treatment, he looked like he was ready. Carlos was home that morning. It was about 6:00 a.m. when the phone rang. It was Alicia. "Carlos?" she said. Something seemed off in her voice, but he wanted to be cheerful.

"Good morning, Ali. How are you?" he said.

"Not so good, *Manito*. It's Papa," she said, her voice breaking. "He . . .died this morning, about an hour ago."

Carlos was sitting at the edge of the bed. Candy, his wife of ten years, was in the kitchen making coffee. His reaction surprised him. It was as if he'd been punched in the gut. "Oh, God. I'll be right over to the hospital. Thanks for calling, sis. Love you. Bye." Suddenly Carlos felt a cold grayness envelop the room. He slid off the bed somehow and onto the floor. He huddled into a fetal position. Tears rolled down his cheeks and his lips were trembling. He kept thinking, *"He died. He died. My father's gone."* When Candy walked in the room, Carlos heard a yelp then he felt her hands on his shoulders and her arms wrapped around him. She lay beside him, both weeping silently, then the phone rang again. It was Esmeralda.

"Our father is no longer with us," she said.

"I know," Carlos said. "Ali called. I'm heading out now. See you soon. We have to make arrangements."

"Yes, of course. Where shall we bury him? You know it was his dream to return to his beloved Naranjales one day. Should we take him home for the burial?" Esmeralda asked.

"Home? He is home. The moment his children set foot on Houston soil his home became America. He just took a little long to realize it," Carlos said.

"Yes, you're right. He is home," she said, her voice quivering.

CHAPTER 35: *Mother's Day 1991*

Today is Eliza's day, Mother's Day. It is the first time since the funeral that the family is reuniting just for this Mother's Day celebration. But Ramiro's presence is unavoidable, and so, along with celebrating Eliza, the family will reminisce about their father. The party is being held at Alicia's, as hers is the biggest house and can accommodate the large clan. Ironic because she is the only daughter Ramiro disowned, albeit only temporarily.

It is Sunday, May 12, and Carlos is the first to arrive. With him are his Candace, "Candy," and their two boys, Richard, thirteen, and Karl, eleven. Karl is named after his maternal grandfather. Candy is of German extraction. She is a former ballet dancer who now helps run the city's grants program that assists all the visual and performing arts projects going on throughout the city.

"Carlos! My love! Well, hello, hello. I can't believe you are the first to arrive. Nothing is ready yet, as you probably know," says Alicia as she hugs and kisses each of them and ushers them toward the great room of the house.

She lives in a large, modern McMansion in the outskirts of Houston, in a subdivision called Sugarland, with her third husband, Abner Johnson. Alicia's marriage to Pablo lasted just five years. They had two children, then he cheated on her, and she discovered that life in the real world was much more complex than she had ever imagined growing up in her parents' home. She was lost for a long time. Her second marriage to a bohemian gentleman of English background was even more tumultuous than the first, though it lasted only a year. Their cultural differences had nothing to do with it.

Alicia developed anxiety, bad habits, and she took to fits of rage, sometimes screaming awful things. Finally, she had to seek therapy. Afterwards, about ten years ago, she put herself in a new path and set out to earn a college education while working as a teacher's aid in a public school. Last year, at the age of forty-two, she completed her requirements for a master's degree in psychology. She married Abner the June after her graduation. He is some ten years her senior, an African American, and the principal at the school where she used to work. Yes, Abner is African American. They had just moved into Abner's house when Ramiro died. Alicia kept Abner a secret from her father. That was to be her last secret.

All of the siblings live in Houston. Carlos expects all will show up today. Maybe some of them can get together again next month on Father's Day and visit with their papa at the cemetery.

The doorbell rings, and it is Esmeralda and her family. Esmeralda has never worked outside the home, much like her mother. But Esmeralda has been the primary manager of the household she built with her husband. Marcelo has been a good provider. He works long hours as an expert machinist and earns an excellent salary with good benefits for his family of six. Esmeralda and Marcelo might be the best tethered to the family's Mexican roots. They travel back and forth to Monterrey to visit his folks and many siblings at least three times a year.

"Hello, my sister, how are you?" Carlos says as the two hug and kiss. They all greet each member of each family in a similar fashion of hugs and kisses. They are all glad to see each other because getting together is a rarity, given that everyone lives scattered throughout the vast area that is greater Houston. The siblings hardly get a chance to see each other anymore because everyone has formed his or her own family, and raising kids or managing careers keeps them busy.

They are anxiously awaiting Sylvia's arrival, as she is the chosen one with whom Eliza decided to live after losing Ramiro. The children all understood that although Eliza was freed after their father died, she nevertheless was far from being an independent American woman. She remained much the old Eliza, only not bound to serving a man or living by his rules, so she still needed housing with a relative, and Silvia is whom she chose.

Sylvia is now thirty-seven. She is working on her Ph.D. at the University of Houston. Sylvia tells Carlos often that it was his example that instilled in her the desire for higher education. She had to make a number of sacrifices along the way, but she was bound and determined that she was going to be a professional woman and a success. Indeed, her advanced degree in English literature will be a huge milestone and a great accomplishment for her.

Sylvia lives with her college sweetheart, Jessica Luna, a young Mexican American woman who dropped out of college to open a Tex-Mex restaurant on the north side. It's called Taco Nazo, and it does fairly good business. When their parents became aware, years ago, that Sylvia and Jessica's relationship was more than just two best friends, they surprised everyone with their acceptance. Ramiro became so fond of Jessica that he simply pretended she was a good friend and never threw aspersions their way.

Carlos' cell phone rings. It is Sylvia calling to tell him that they will arrive within the hour. "Mother is excited. She woke up a little melancholy, remembering Papa. She is lamenting that he won't be there. You know," she says. Carlos does know. The hour is now noon, so the party can expect to start eating the brisket in about two hours, based on past experiences with the family.

The others arrive in quick succession.

Baldemar and his Mexican-born wife, Amanda, arrive with his usual honking of the car horn. His children are expected as well, and the five of them show up at once almost as if on cue. Antonio, "Tony," and his wife, Debbie Gonzalez, arrive with their two babies. Oscar and his wife, Brooke Daniels, arrive two hours later. Better late than never.

Everyone is glad to see each other.

Ever since infancy, Tony and Oscar were lumped together in the style of their parents wishing to minimize the effort it takes to give every child individual attention. They also got the least of the Ramiro discipline, according to the older children. They were born at the tail end of the seven. By the time their papa tried to regulate and control their adolescent activities, as he had done with the older kids, he seemed to have lost energy or focus or desire. Of course, the boys will never be convinced.

Maybe it was the lax supervision or the influence of their peers in the barrio neighborhood and schools, but the youngest boys never considered college. Instead, they looked to the curriculum of their vocational high school and got into auto mechanics and welding. They are both hard-working and honorable guys, and they make good money in their vocations. They can support households of a stay-at-home mom and two children.

How did Carlos achieve his dream of going to college? He applied for and received a Pell Grant from the U.S. Department of Education and matriculated himself at the then open-enrollment University of Houston–Downtown. After two years, he transferred to the Central Campus. It took him five years to earn his bachelor's degree. It was a proud moment for Carlos that his father got to attend his graduation. The two had become estranged when Carlos moved out of the house at the age of twenty, and they stayed pretty much that way through those college years, mostly because Carlos was too busy attending classes full time and working to support myself.

In college, Carlos discovered that he was indeed smart enough for university work. No, his high school had not adequately prepared him for the rigors of university study, but it did a good enough job that he was able to get his foot in the door. After his first semester, he got the hang of how to make it work. He also discovered that he was articulate and passionate about politics. He ran for and was elected class senator his junior year. College changed his life completely, which is not to say that any of it was easy. Far from it. Carlos had to work his butt off to keep up, and he multitasked the heck out of life. His degree and major? A bachelor of arts in English with a minor in political science. He taught high school English for a few years then went on to law school at night.

The point of all this is to say that Ramiro's journey didn't end with his life. It continues in his children, as is true of all bloodlines. The feisty, uneducated, semiliterate Mexican immigrant raised an entire family of good, law-abiding Americans. All of Ramiro and Eliza's children are upstanding citizens, and some of them are pretty darned accomplished as well.

"Come with me to the kitchen," Alicia says to Carlos

"Sure. Be right in."

"I'm worried that some of the family is not ready for a black man as my husband. I know that papa would have condemned me for it," she says.

She appears to be having second thoughts about hosting the party. She had hoped that by opening Abner's house to everyone it would also lead to more acceptance of him, as if anyone had shown animosity toward Abner. She had simply assumed that the more conservative siblings like Esmerlda, or the macho Balde were racists. Carlos worries that her anxiety might return if she continues to worry over the racial stuff.

"Listen Sis, I have to tell you, I don't give a damn if anyone objects to Abner. Those days are long gone. I refuse to accept any kind of prejudice in my family. I won't accommodate it," he says.

"I know, Carlos, but you're different. You're a political person. You have to talk like that," she says.

"Oh, no, wait just a minute. I don't have to talk that way. I mean every word of it. Do you think I lied to all the voters when I ran my campaign for city council?" He feigns offense.

"No, *Manito*, Don't take it that way. What I meant was. . ." she says.

Carlos interrupts her, "Never mind. I'm sorry. I'm not offended. Don't worry. All I can say is that if anybody has a problem with racism, it's on them. I will not be sensitive or understanding of it. If that sounds like a politician or politically correct, then so be it. Really, don't worry about it, it'll be ok, Sis." He hugs her.

She smiles, and squeezes his hand.

CHAPTER 36: *Memories*

t is time for the "birthday girl" to open her gifts. The family calls anyone at the center of a celebration the "birthday" girl or boy. On Mother's Day, Eliza is the birthday girl. The children decide to make the gift giving show a bit of a game. "As each person presents Mama a gift, you must tell a story about growing up in that house on Garrow Street, or about Papa since we are all missing him today," says Esmeralda.

At first there are murmurs of approval and some clapping. Then some look around and wonder aloud if it might be too emotional for their mom to hear such stories. "Maybe she can't handle the memories." But Eliza says, "Don't worry about me. I would love to hear stories about your father."

"Yes, that sounds like a great idea," chimes in Esmeralda, who is always game for fun times with family. Baldemar sets his Budweiser down, claps his hands, and says he is all for it. With the two oldest onboard, everyone else agrees to the plan.

"Well, not everyone has to tell a story. Let's make it more a volunteer thing," says Alicia. "I'll start, if it's ok."

Everyone gives her "go ahead" signs, and she begins.

"Well, everyone knows the story of my first wedding and how tough Papa was on Pablo," she starts, a little choked up. "How dumb we were back then. I blamed Papa for all my misery up until the day I married. Then Pablo turned out to be less than the devoted husband I had expected. You know, the cheating. The only man I had known was my father, and he was always a family-first kind of man. So were all our uncles as far as I knew, and even Marcelo. I discovered the hard way that Papa knew what he was talking about. Not about the racist stuff or the superficial stuff, but about the character of a man. Papa knew Pablo was not the man for me, and he was right. I had so much resentment for Father for so long. I denied him my children's company because I feared he might be cruel to them because of their father. It's funny that he came to accept and even respect Pablo after the kids were born.

"Well, my story. I was in the hospital—you all remember Jeff Davis? They tore it down a few years ago. Well I was getting ready to give birth to Michelle when he came to visit me once. I couldn't believe it. We had not spoken since my wedding. It was late in the evening, and I had been dozing on and off. Next thing I know, I opened my eyes and there he was, standing beside the bed holding my hand. I looked across the room, and I saw Pablo sitting on the chair. Pablo smiled at me and nodded as if to say, 'Your father is alright.' I smiled at my father and squeezed his hand. He bent over me and kissed my forehead, gave my hand a gentle squeeze, and left the room. That moment meant the world to me, and I never again doubted that I was in his prayers every day, as he was in mine."

Everyone is glad, if a bit surprised, to hear that story. They wonder why Alicia had never shared it.

"I wanted to keep it to myself. I somehow felt it was good for his pride, and, besides, it was, like, our own little secret. I can't pretend that everything was all right between us after that, but it was alright where it mattered most. Lots of my issues were really of my own making."

Ramiro's life had been a series of disappointments for him. A lot of it was, as Alicia said, stuff that he brought on himself. But it is a truism that a man so often is his own worst enemy. Most people can list so many great qualities of his, but he didn't know he had those assets, or if he did, he didn't know how to use them, or he simply had stronger forces preventing him from acting on them. Pride and fear of taking risks, even a minor risk like taking out a loan, sometimes para-lyzed him. The children know that now. They have all done so much thinking since Ramiro's funeral. Everyone is still processing memories that gives new insights into their father.

§

Esmeralda steps up and gives Eliza a beautifully embroidered tablecloth.

"My story of my father happened just a few years ago. You all may recall that he took early retirement because his health was a concern to him. His entire life was that of hard, physical labor. It was a very hot summer in Monterrey, about four years ago. He had moved back there to be back in is beloved country and close enough to the country of his youth. Unfortunately, it was not to his dream of gentleman farming. Mama, as usual, followed him dutifully, and the two of them made a nice, cozy home near my mother-in-law's.

"As I mentioned, it was a very hot summer. Marcelo and I, the whole family, were visiting as we often do. We invited Mom and Dad to the river near Allende for a picnic and to wade in the rushing wa-ters. Well, the riverbed, as you all know, is all rocks and boulders of all shapes and sizes. The waters are sparkling and run two to three feet deep. Some of the boulders have slippery moss, as do some of the rocks and stones.

"Mama must have been reliving some childhood memories or something because the river is a lot like the one in Valle Azul. She let herself frolic and play in the water almost like a girl. Next thing we know, she slipped and lost her balance, hitting her head on a boulder. We all panicked, and ran to her aid. Papa was at the other side of the river, so I thought we would carry her over to him. Well, before you knew it, there he was. He had run clear across the slippery river so fast, and without falling, to get to his beloved. I had never seen him so pale and protective of her before.

"You guys know that mom and dad were never fond of showing

affection for each other in public, not even in front of us. Imagine my surprise when he held her in his arms so tenderly and then he put a bandage on her bleeding cheek. When he was done, he started to bend his head as if to kiss her before he caught himself and realized we were all staring at them so intently. He stopped and just said, 'Come on out of the water. Let's get you on a comfortable chair. Want a slice of watermelon?' It was such a special moment. I will never forget that tenderness."

§

"Oh, I have one. I have a story." It's Tony.

"Three years ago, Dad and Mom returned to Houston. I guess they realized that the Mexico of their memories and fantasies was not what the real thing had become, especially since it was Monterrey they returned to, not the tranquil Naranjales. I remember helping them move into the house in Magnolia. What a great little bungalow that was. They were so happy there these last years of his life. What an irony that the neighborhood Papa detested as the worst *pachuco* hangout in the sixties became his last home in the eighties. Anyway, I was helping them move stuff in. Suddenly, we heard the sound of a gunshot so loud I thought it was a drive-by or something. I am still not convinced that Magnolia is not a dangerous place, so I was totally freaked. Man, I must have jumped like five feet off the floor.

"Mama was also freaked, and she shouted from the kitchen, *'Dios mio!*, what happened? What was that noise? Ramiro, did you shoot at something?' What? Well, we all know Papa loved his guns. He had a small collection. I am lucky that Mom gave me one of them, my only inheritance. But anyways, it turns out that one of the guns accidentally fell out of one of the boxes I was carrying and it discharged. I was so freaked out, but not Papa. He was Mr. Cool. He calmly picked the gun up off the floor, and told me, 'be careful, Son. You could have killed someone with that gun.'

"Say what? I could have been killed! Man, I can laugh about it now, but what a scare Mama and I had that afternoon, three years ago."

§

They all laugh and nod in agreement as the lot of them recalls his love of guns. They were one of Ramiro's few indulgences. He might not have had much money for any number of "luxuries," but he sure was able to purchase guns, and a new felt hat yearly. Back then no one was obsessing about the Second Amendment as people are today, and certainly he would not have been in tune with the outside world anyway, but he always expressed appreciation that in this country he could own guns, unlike in Mexico.

He loved his Fedoras, too. Carlos was not one of the lucky ones to inherit one of his guns. Carlos figured Eliza knows that he is not a gun enthusiast, so she gave them to the others. He believes there were six of them. Some of the older nephews who had shared Ramiro's love of guns are hoping for the two that Eliza still has.

§

The next one to speak is Baldemar. He hasn't even started speaking when he chokes up. Baldemar was always his papa's favorite, despite his mischievous nature and being a disappointment sometimes. Balde probably has tons of stories to tell since he spent so many years working side by side with his papa in the plants and welding shops. It was a proud day for Ramiro when Balde made it to machinist and was able to double his salary from one day to the next.

Balde's story, like Esmeralda's, is told exclusively in Spanish. The rest of their stories are told in English to respect the family members who don't speak Spanish. There is always someone who can translate to Spanish for those whose English is still a struggle, like Balde and Esmeralda, and, of course, Eliza. So everyone is waiting for Balde's story. Some of the family fidgets as they get ready to code-switch and translate to the monolinguals among them.

§

"The old man was quite the macho man," Baldemar finally starts, having composed himself. "This was about eight, nine years, ago. A couple of years before he decided he couldn't take anymore of being bossed around by nincompoops. There was a chump named Rudy Chavez working as the supervisor of the plant. Pops never cared much for the dude. He was one of those Chicano types that seem to hate Mexicans. He began to pick on Papa almost immediately after being promoted. Well, you all know how meticulous the old man always has been in any job. And you know his temper.

"Well, I certainly can vouch for the fact that nobody had a better work ethic. He always arrived a half hour early. He never punched out before his shift ended. He never asked for special favors unless it was an emergency. He never took breaks longer than required. And so on. He sure as hell was the best worker. Any supervisor should have been happy to have him. But he could never learn to move up the ladder. Beats me why. My old man was always, if not the lowest, then pretty close to the lowest man on the totem pole. I never could understand why, but who am I to ask?

"So this Rudy guy. Man, this dude was a piece of work. He never missed a chance to make some punk joke on Pops, like hiding his favorite broom, knocking over a trash barrel, or smudging his car door. You know how Pops hated for anyone to touch his car. Don't you dare scratch his paint job or smear stuff on it like food or what have you. Well, this was the thing that got him fired from that Tube Turns job. The reason he decided he had had enough and moved to Monterrey.

"It was the end of his shift, and the old man was putting away his stuff, and taking his lunch pail from his locker. It was like fifteen minutes past his shift because he never rushed. I think that was one thing that bugged that Rudy character, that Papa was never a clock-watcher or acted like he hated being there like most of the guys, including Rudy himself. Anyway, on his way out to the parking lot Rudy borrowed the lunch bucket of one of the night-shift guys that was coming in late, and he put it on the hood of pop's car. Pop had gone back to Oldsmobiles a few years after the California thing.

"When Pop got to his car, just about a minute later, he saw the damn thing sitting on the hood. 'What the hell,' he said, and looked around in all directions. Rudy was leaning against his new Ram Charger and smiling from ear to ear. I had been heading to my car, but when I heard the old man speak, I stopped to see if he was okay. Well, when he saw Rudy standing there, grinning and looking like the big jerk that he was, Pops turned red as could be and just rushed the guy. Before I could break them up, Rudy had a bloody nose and a fat lip. I was damn proud of my Pop. I knew he would probably lose his job, but his dignity was that important to him. I'm just glad he wasn't carrying one of his guns that day."

§

The women in the room shudder at the thought of their Papa losing his temper and holding a gun. Throughout the stories, everyone makes quips, comments, and even asks questions. In between the stories, they elaborate on some of the details and add additional related anecdotes. Everyone, including some of the grandkids, is enjoying the stories. The siblings can see folks wipe a tear or two from their eyes from time to time.

Sylvia passes on her story, explaining that it was too soon for her to talk about her Papa. She starts to tear up, and Esmeralda puts her arms around her. "There, it's not necessary. It's ok, *Manita*, it's ok," she tells her baby sister and pecks her on the cheek.

Oscar doesn't want to speak either, but Tony nudges him, so he goes ahead and tells a story about visiting their parents one day when they lived on the second floor of an apartment complex, how he was amused and worried at the same time because Ramiro told off some drunks.

§

"This was just after they returned to Houston, after their failed experiment of living in Monterrey and before they moved to the Magnolia house. Father was always overprotective of the women of the family, and he was, of course, very jealous. He also couldn't stand being disrespected, and if you disrespected his daughter or wife, you disrespected him.

"That Sunday evening, several of the women were visiting their apartment, including Alicia, Sylvia, and a couple of the older nieces. As the ladies were leaving in the evening, they descended the stairs. Across the way was a building of several apartments, and there were several guys standing outside. They were actually older men, in their fifties or so. Well, the guys noticed the women right away, and they immediately began their hooting and hollering. They couldn't keep their eyes off my sisters and nieces. They were so obvious, staring in our direction and practically leering. It was late Sunday evening, so you can imagine. They had been drinking most of the day as they stood around barbequing and what have you.

"Dad was inside the apartment, but he noticed what was going on, and he did not like it one bit. After one of the men called out, *'chulas mamacitas,'* Papa came out onto the balcony and just went off on the guys. 'You so and sos better shut the hell up, you low-lifes. Show some respect. This is a family. You are looking at respectable women here. Which one of you bastards disrespected my daughters? I will kick your ass.' Several times he called them *babosos.* That was his favorite curse word. I mean he was on a roll. Mama was shocked and had a terrified look on her face. She looked at me as if to say, 'Do something. Bring him inside.' The women all told him to ignore the men, 'Don't worry about it,' that it was okay, 'Don't pay attention to them, they're drunk, they're ignorant. We are leaving anyway.'

"I had to literally put my arms around him to get him to stop talking. I slowly pulled him away from the banister and walked him back to the apartment. Needless to say, he had had a few too many himself. It was sad to see him drink so much in his final years. I don't recall him being a drinker before."

§

Of course, they all lament that their father had developed a drinking problem in his later years. It was mostly beer, and he seldom got out of hand, but it put an added strain on their mother. Eliza could always count on the loyalty and protection of her seven offspring in her later years. The kids enjoy seeing her in her glory, like on this Mother's Day. Eliza has opened so many presents. She keeps saying, "I don't need anything. Don't get me anything," and she means it, but everyone wants to spoil her because they know how much she was deprived for so long.

But now they're pressuring Carlos to tell his Ramiro story. They're making fun of "the Councilman." "It's time for the Councilman's story," they chant.

CHAPTER 37: *Carlos's Goodbye*

"Yes, we have stories to tell. So many stories. We were seven children and one widow, and every one of those heads, is indeed a world, as they say. Each of those worlds can be counted on to see the same thing differently but with enough in common for those nods of understanding. There are the stories of the young Ramiro, confident in his quest to conquer life, for earning dollars to build his dream, a farm in Mexico. There are the stories of the family man who never wavered in his responsibility to his family and especially to his kids. There are the stories of the disciplinarian whose tactics we kids so often complained about, but later, in our adulthood and nostalgia, we feel grateful for. There are the stories of his humor, his relatives, his legendary imposition on friends, whom he visited with all seven kids in tow, scaring the heck out of them as they wondered how they were going to feed the little army of unexpected guests on a Sunday afternoon.

"They tell me that my father left the country when I was born. Actually it was a couple of months after. My infancy is mostly a blur of memories that too often seem like just dreams. My early childhood seems to never have been a reality. Sometimes it feels as if my life began when I arrived in Houston and before that nothing was real. What does a toddler know of living without a father? What does a baby know of anything at all except whom to cry to for his needs? I cried to my mother for food, for toys, for love. I have not always understood my father. I didn't really know him for the first seven years of my life. When I began to spend time around him, it was too little time and almost too late. He was a man of many rules and no tolerance for childhood foibles or mistakes.

"He had a hard life, my father. So many dreams repressed, so many thorns in his path. His life was filled with disappointments as well as with many marvelous gifts. Unfortunately, the most elusive of his pursuits was the making of a fortune or a dreamscape of a homestead. He was an ordinary Mexican immigrant like so many others, but he was extraordinary in his exuberance for life and family. My Mexican immigrant father was an imperfect man, but you couldn't ask for a more devoted father. Thorns and all, I embrace him.

"I do want to tell you this story, the one about my regret that my father was not alive to see his son become an elected official in the fourth-largest city in the greatest country in the world. He did see me start my campaign, and he even attended those first few organizing meetings, often standing proudly beside me. The candidate's father. He was even considering becoming a naturalized citizen just so he could vote for me. It would have been the first time he voted in his life. I am grateful we had that time where I did get to see how proud I made him. Not that I hadn't seen glimpses of it before. I think that I was his biggest challenge because no other of his children questioned his authority as much as I did, or defied him so much. Still he was proud of me. I saw that pride clearly when I received my college degree, though I did not always feel it growing up.

"I once overheard him praising me to my mother although he didn't tell it to me directly. We had spent a good two hours or so with me driving; he was teaching me how to drive in the deserted farm roads in California one evening. As expected, he yelled and harangued me for any little mistake I made. I was sure he was going to give up on me, but he didn't. Instead, when we got home, I accidentally overheard him tell Mama when they were alone in the kitchen, 'He's going to be a good driver.' Just hearing those words expressed in a clear tone of admiration put me on cloud nine for the next two weeks, and I never forgot the words or how they made me feel.

"I saw his pride in me again a few more times; when I showed him pictures of me with my students in the school yearbook, he pointed to one of the group pictures and actually said, 'And who's the best looking one there?' I saw him beaming with pride when I got my law degree, and when I showed him my name in the paper after I helped win a case on bilingual education. I can honestly say I am grateful that I was able to make my dad proud.

"One time, in front of my godfather, on a rare occasion that we happened to be visiting in Mexico, he told me to go and bring him a beer. It made him so proud that his *compadre* saw his grown son, a professional man, still devoted and serving his old father. I'm not bragging, now. This is not about me. Well, I guess it is a little about me, but it is really about how much he contributed to each of us. Ironically, his entire life he always believed he had given us too little."

MEET THE AUTHOR

J.C. Salazar grew up in Houston, where he still resides, the child of immigrant parents. He earned degrees in English (BA), linguistics (MS), and literature (MA) from the University of Houston and UH-Clear Lake. He also completed doctoral courses in English at UH. JC is a lifelong educator and community activist, who loves great stories, language, and writing. *Of Dreams & Thorns* is his debut novel, inspired by his immigrant family and community. He hopes you love reading it as much as he loved writing it.

www.ingramcontent.com/pod-product-compliance
Lightning Source LLC
Chambersburg PA
CBHW021209250626

47155CB00008B/2738